THE HUNGER

BOOK ONE IN THE DIARY OF CHARLOTTE

JOSEPH K LITTLE

Editor
LISA GILLIAM

Cover Artist
MELODY KNIGHTON

❀ Created with Vellum

For my family.
By blood or love this is for you.

PREFACE

This is the diary of Charlotte Voclain who would later go by the name Charlotte Villeneuve. She was a homeless Parisian girl of fifteen years at the start of the diary but had turned sixteen and was off the streets when I first met her. She was of average height if a little on the shorter side, and far too skinny. After a while she began to fill out nicely with muscle and flesh in the right places, but she never admitted to such in these pages. With her long black hair and knowing, searching eyes, I was in love with her the moment I first saw her, but I am going beyond my role here. These are her words, and I should let her tell the tale. I can confirm that it is true, all of it, at least in essence.

1

A BAD START

August 1814 AD

The homeless of Paris knew Vincent as a man who found jobs for the hungry. The tall, gaunt man had gray skin and uncomfortable eyes, but despite his severe appearance, many of us waited for him eagerly each day, hoping to be chosen next for employment. Not I at first. I avoided him whenever I could. While he excelled at his job, no one ever returned to the streets after gaining employment through him. Reason told me that someone would have eventually come back to share their bounty with the remaining homeless.

Slowly and skillfully, Hunger began to argue. Who would ever want to return to these dank, dark, and treacherous Parisian streets? No one would. Who would ever want to share their hard-earned food? No one would. Who would risk everything they had found on the off chance of helping a friend from the street? No one would. There were no friends on the streets. Just slaves to circumstance. Slaves to Hunger. She would always end her arguments with a loud growl and a punch to the gut. Every day her arguments became more and more convincing. I was soon ignoring Reason completely. I dreamed of employment, of long hours of work that ended with a roof over my head and food in my stomach. And that was how Hunger eventually drove me to look for the man.

Vincent found me late one night on the Street of Ashes. He had a heel of bread and a minuscule piece of cheese, but it was more food than I had seen in weeks. He offered them if I would meet his masters for an interview. If I did well, the bread and cheese were mine as well as any scraps I could manage from the table. If I did poorly, I would not be able to eat from the table, but the bread and cheese were still mine. He refused to give me anything until after my interview. Hunger was my mistress, and I her slave, so I became bound to Vincent as surely as I was bound to my mistress.

We walked several blocks in the wan moonlight. Vandals had smashed the oil lamps hung over the streets by the police. Darkness clung to everything like a suckling child to a mother's breast.

Reason whispered in my ear, "Run, child. RUN!"

I considered the demand for the briefest of moments before my mistress reminded me of our goal. Employment. Shelter. Food. My mouth watered at the last as I imagined what sorts of food I might find.

Vincent grunted, and I woke from my fantasies. We turned off the street, and Vincent led me down a small alley. Just as we reached a wooden door set in the shadowed alcove of a shadowed alley, someone called out, "Mademoiselle! A word?"

I turned to find the source of the voice as Vincent worked the door. Shadow concealed all, but I thought I heard footsteps approaching. Then Vincent's hands were upon me, and he thrust me through the door. Weakened from a week without food, I fell to the earthen floor beyond. The floor's cool embrace comforted me, while nearby, the feeble light of a single candle died inches from the wick. Vincent closed and barred the door. He picked up the candle before grabbing me by the shoulder and hauling me up.

"Move," he said. His voice was gravelly, and his hand was an enormous gray skeletal vise on my shoulder.

We descended a flight of stairs and soon arrived at another door, this one old stone bound with iron. I heard banging behind us, but when I turned to look, Vincent shook me harshly. I was about to complain, but I met his baleful gaze and my voice fled like a lamb from a wolf.

Vincent pushed me through the stone door, pulled it closed behind us, and snuffed the candle. Water dripped someplace unseen. We were in a long straight corridor of rough stone and mortar. The stones suggested violence if one walked too closely, while the lamplight made mesmerizing patterns of light and dark. Light and dark. Light and dark.

"Who would live here?" I asked aloud.

"Masters," Vincent graveled.

Reason suggested that surely this was a portal to Hell, but my mistress countered that Hell with food was better than an unending purgatory of starvation. My mistress was cunning and knew what I wanted to hear. Vincent's hand pushed, and my real descent began.

Reason seemed absent after that, perhaps having given up hope on my salvation. Perhaps I had become deaf to her voice.

Vincent guided me through the maze of identical narrow corridors. How long we walked I could not tell you, but after what must have been a brief eternity, I heard a sweet female voice.

"Anton," I heard her say. "Anton, you have a bit of something on your sleeve."

The voice was distant but clear. Practiced in the form of the aristocracy and able to carry even in the rough underground tunnels. Anton didn't answer his lady, or perhaps his voice didn't have the same aristocratic weight.

"Really, Anton," she said. "Must you suck the marrow out of the bone like some commoner?"

So, it seemed the pair were common enough, a refined lady and a boorish gentleman. What would drive such people to this extreme though, living underground and supping so late in the night? Mistress suggested they were exiles, living as close to their homes as they dared. They were likely in hiding until their lands and property were restored.

“Yes, I know. ’Tis a sad state we find ourselves. Someone needs to clear away these scraps. I hope your man finds someone soon.”

Yes! Surely Mistress was correct. Somehow, they made the best of a bad thing. The temperature was cool but not cold. The dirt floor had a roof over it. And they were eating, so it seemed they had a steady supply of food.

It seemed we were close to the dining room, and my stomach growled in anticipation of having my pick of someone else’s table scraps. Visions of bread, cheese, fruit, and maybe a pastry or two swirled in front of me. It was foolish, but one does not argue with one’s mistress, especially when one as harsh as mine filled your mind with such pleasant thoughts.

“What, dear? Why yes, I do seem to have a bit of something on my bosom. Of course you would notice, you old flirt. Thankfully it didn’t stain my dress. There isn’t enough time to clean lace these days. Perhaps if I could get my fill or if we had some help. Do we have any more leg of that lamb?”

There was a brief pause in which I assumed Monsieur Anton must have spoken before the lady spoke again, Only bones? Shame. Maybe this once I’ll indulge myself with a little marrow then.”

“Listen,” Vincent said. He spoke in a slow, dry whisper as we walked. Each word ripped the fabric of the air and fell onto my head like dust from a saw. “Be strong. Quiet. Look at toes. Stay out of reach. Do not scream.”

“Do not scream? Why? What have I gotten myself into?”

“Job,” he said. “I bring food. They eat. I eat. You. Understand?”

My mistress hissed, “Yesssss.”

I nodded, content to face my new employers regardless of the situation. My mistress was content for now, but soon she would demand her fill and more.

We arrived at a large wooden door riddled with decay. There was no knob, just a large metal ring on which Vincent heaved. The ring shifted in the rotted wood, threatening to rip free like a bone through putrid flesh, but it held and the door slid ponderously open.

Just beyond lay a large vaulted chamber of earth and stone. It was dry like the tunnels that brought us there but smelled far worse. The far end of the room was shrouded in shadow, but there seemed to be a raised platform with a dining room table on it. Two indistinct figures sat across from each other at the heads of the table, cloaked in darkness. More shadowed forms lay all about the two. My mistress told me the shadows were obviously discarded serving dishes and leftover food. Piles and piles of leftover food much like the old aristocracy were rumored to waste while the commoners they were sworn to protect starved in the streets before the republicans threw them down. It was the sweetest of lies.

Vincent squeezed his vise-like grip once more and shook me. "Look down. No noise."

I looked down as commanded, which was good, since the floor became more and more littered with refuse. Plates, saucers, cups, and all manner of dinnerware lay shattered and discarded amid piles of bones. The bones became larger and more numerous as we progressed toward the raised platform, and the floor became wet with a dark mud that stained my feet a brownish red when I was able to scrape bits of it off. I gagged on the smell.

"Stop," my escort said. His voice carried through the chamber and drew the attention of Madame.

"Ah, Vincent. You've returned," Madame said sweetly. "Anton. Your man has returned with a prospective maid."

"Are you hungry, dear?" she asked me.

"Oui, Madame. Very."

"Good," she said, drawing out the word. Her voice was breathless, almost sensual.

Anton wheezed before mumbling something I could not understand.

"Yes, yes. Excellent idea, Anton. Vincent, show off our little lamb."

Vincent slowly turned me around for the madame and monsieur.

Monsieur Anton coughed and spat before starting to suck on a new bone.

"She's lovely. Isn't she lovely, Anton? She is a bit skinny, but what's the saying? 'The closer to the bone, the sweeter the meat'?"

She was laughing at her odd joke when Vincent spun me a second time. I was ravenous and willing to put up with living underground and playing maid to a pair of disgusting fallen aristocrats just for the food in Vincent's pocket. For their scraps I would suffer their jokes and prying eyes. And I would thank them. Eventually they would come to thank me as well.

"Ah yes, Vincent. Very nice. This lamb will do."

I smiled delightedly and looked up, sealing my fate.

The first thing I noticed was the bones. What I had earlier assumed from a distance were piles of dishes to be cleaned and rubbish to remove were bones and only bones. Hundreds, no, thousands of bones. Some were not human, but most seemed to be. Human skulls lined the wall behind the table from the floor to the ceiling. I could not believe what I was seeing as I turned to look at Monsieur Anton. What remained of my smile slipped from my face.

Monsieur wore ancient black and white dinner finery that was ripped, threadbare, and stained. The stains were all deep reds and browns and concentrated around the forearms, cuffs, and neck. The ancient lace at his neck and cuffs was thick with gore.

Monsieur's frame was skeletal. His gaunt hands had fingers tipped with thick black nails better described as claws. His skin was a sicker, paler gray than Vincent's, but while Vincent's was smooth in tone and texture, Monsieur Anton's was uneven and splotchy with dark stains on his fingers and palms. His eyes were wide, round, lidless portals of nothingness.

He discarded what was obviously a human jaw and spat out a tooth before he picked up another scrap. It looked like a portion of a child's arm. His frail hands snapped the arm like a twig and discarded the smaller end. Monsieur Anton opened his wide lipless mouth exposing multiple rows of knifelike teeth.

I gasped in horror and turned to look at Madame. Where

Monsieur was skeletal, Madame was simply thin with a full bosom. Her deep crimson dinner dress contrasted nicely with her pale gray skin, but her hands, mouth, and chin were utterly black. Her sweet, gentle voice was betrayed by her wide, ravenous red eyes. I met her gaze, and she smiled, causing her face to split horizontally and reveal a cavernous mouth filled with her own ranks of knives.

Madame's hungry eyes devoured me. They stripped me naked to the bone and ate me alive. Those vile eyes begged that I scream, so I obliged. At my scream, Madame's eyes caught flame, and she laughed delightedly.

Monsieur Anton made a horrible rattling shout as he slammed a hand down on the table. The bone he was holding shattered, and he pointed at me with the remnant. His face was filled with contempt.

"Find another," Monsieur rasped.

Madame's laughter intensified, and she clapped her hands excitedly.

Vincent caressed my face. It was the first time his skin touched mine directly, and my screams ended sharply. I still wanted to scream, but I simply couldn't. Before I knew what was happening, I found that I was lying on the stone floor. I couldn't speak. I couldn't feel. I couldn't move.

Vincent stepped over me, lifted my legs up to his chest, and drove massive metal hooks through my legs just above the ankles. I felt nothing. Dragging me after him, he moved over to the table and scraped the center of it clean, pushing bones and scraps onto the floor. He pulled a large bowl out from under the table, and after dumping more bones from within it, he placed the bowl on the table. He lifted me effortlessly, climbed up onto the table, and hung me by the hooks in my legs from some unseen device over the bowl. As my hands dangled, almost touching the rim of the bowl, I realized that he had purposefully turned me so that I could only stare at the wall of skulls. Their empty eyes and eternal grins mocked me.

"Oh, she's a fine-looking lamb indeed, Vincent. You did well this time. I can smell her hunger from here. 'Tis a shame she didn't have the qualifications for a proper maid, but this is perhaps even better than having a maid. What do you think, Anton?"

Monsieur Anton grunted something nonspecific.

"Oh yes. You're right, dear. As always. Vincent, strip her."

Vincent drew a thin blade and began sawing at my clothes. The action spun me slightly. I saw Monsieur Anton gazing at me in lustful gluttony before I rotated enough to see Madame sharply breathing in through my small clothes. Vincent reached up once more with his blade. I didn't feel anything, but soon blood spilled over my eyes and into my nostrils.

"Stupid girl," Vincent mumbled as he stuffed the bread and cheese from his pocket into my mouth.

From somewhere behind me, there was a loud pounding followed by a hollow crash.

"Dear God!" said an unseen voice. It sounded familiar but belonged to none of the others in the room.

Madame screamed, "What manner of intrusion is this?"

Her chair scraped upon the earthen floor.

Monsieur seemed disinterested in leaving his meal of bones. Indeed, between fits of coughing and banging his fists, Monsieur Anton took hasty bites off random items that remained on the table.

"Halt in the name of King Louis the Eighteenth and the people of France!" yelled another.

Madame made a primal scream. There were footsteps followed by a gunshot. I spun slightly enough to see Madame fall back into her chair. A large section of her scalp was missing.

Monsieur Anton beat the table and rasped, "Vincent, clear the room!"

A man screamed in horror.

"Damn that coward Eduoard! Nolan. Armand. Keep that brute off me while I reload," yelled the familiar voice.

I heard the sounds of fighting and a couple of sickening endings, like overripe cabbages being ripped apart. Then there was a loud crash and another gunshot.

Monsieur beat the table even more before trying to stand. He toppled over immediately. His legs, it seemed, had been gnawed upon, leaving almost no meat at all, just bone and sinew. I wondered briefly as everything started to go black if he had done that to himself or if it had been Madame.

I assumed my hunger would disappear once I died, but as I drifted toward oblivion my mistress was there with me, whispering in my ear, "I will never let you go."

And she did not.

2

ESCAPE

August 1814 AD

"She's cold," a familiar voice said. It was the voice of my man who appeared twice at the doors. It was the voice of the one who might have saved me if only he had been there sooner.

"She's lost a lot of blood." The second voice was unfamiliar, slightly deeper, almost a baritone with a slight German accent.

"Give me your coat," said my hero-too-late. They lifted me and wrapped my naked body. I should have been thankful, but the material itched. Neither thought was terribly important enough to focus on for more than a beetle's flight.

"One of us must get help," said the deeper voice.

"I'll stay with her."

"No. More people know about my connections. The fewer people who see you with me the better. If anyone connects you to me, and me to the sergeant... well each of us has a lot to lose."

"But-" my hero protested.

"I know." The almost baritone voice was strained. "It is best though. Don't come back while this place is under investigation. I'll tell the sergeant I told you to follow that gang for a while longer. Find out what you can about them."

A child could have come to term in the pregnant pause that passed between them.

"Go. Use your contacts and get them to return with a stretcher and some water. They can follow the string we used to trace our path. Have them bring some armed men too, gun and blade. That brute may still lurk the tunnels."

"Fine, mon ami." My hero-too-late had to drag the words out of his chest. "Don't fall asleep, and be on guard for that monster."

"I will. I don't think I will ever sleep again."

My hero's footfalls were heavy as he retreated from the room and shut the door.

I don't know how long I lay there before my body began to shake and convulse. Blood and spittle frothed at my mouth, and I moaned. Unseen hands were upon me.

"Calm down. Calm down. Don't move. You'll only make your wounds worse," my guard said. "You are safe. Just lie still."

I continued to convulse.

"Please, demoiselle. The wounds to your legs are quite hideous. Please remain calm."

He began to pray then. I think he was attempting to give me last rights—my Latin was never very good, and it had been years since I'd attended church in any manner beyond begging for food or alms. God had not kept his promises to me, so why should I continue to keep my promises to him? Still, the words calmed me somewhat, or maybe the convulsions were simply passing. I don't know which.

When I calmed sufficiently, and it became apparent that I was no longer dying, the man resorted to talking to me again rather than to God.

"Good. Good. Peace, demoiselle. I am Luc LaCroix, a gendarme for the city of Paris. Well... not officially, so don't go telling people, eh?" He laughed a little. "My friend and I saw you being led away by that brute. We followed. Many people have gone missing in this area as far back as anyone can remember, but no one ever found out why... until now, I think. These creatures... I don't know what they are, but these... monsters may have been the reason. My friend and I killed the two at the table, but the brute was another matter. He was fast and strong like the devil himself. My friend was able to reload his weapon and fire upon it. I would have killed it, but I tripped on a bone. They are everywhere, the bones. The brute fled. I don't expect to see him back, so you can be at peace. Just relax, and we will return you to your family soon."

His voice was soothing despite mentioning my family. I would never reunite with my family. Not now. Not after this.

I was slowly beginning to regain control of my body. I still couldn't feel anything but my hunger, and again I somehow knew that I would always be hungry. It was then that I realized I still had the cheese and bread in my mouth. The food was a dry lump of ash, and I tried to spit it out but was still too weak.

Minutes passed before I could move my arms. I reached up and pulled the food from my mouth. It seemed like a sacrilege, but I could no longer abide the presence in my mouth. I could finally move my tongue and tried to swallow.

"Water," I croaked.

Luc trotted from across the room. I hadn't realized he left my side.

"I'm sorry, demoiselle. I have no water."

"Anything," I begged.

Luc hesitated before he grabbed something from his waist and pressed it into my hands. It was a flask of some sort. Gingerly I felt for the mouth, which was already at my lips. The wetness was a delight, but the liquid burned as it spilled down my throat. I licked my lips and drank more.

"Demoiselle, please. That is too much."

I protested as he pulled the flask out of my hands, but he did not give it back.

I felt my eyes with weak, trembling fingers. There was something thick and wet over my eyes. I tried to wipe it away with my bare hands, but then Luc was wiping my face and eyes with a cloth. When I could finally open my eyes, I could see what covered them: blood. My blood. My hands shook violently.

"H-how am I still alive?" I asked.

"We rescued you, demoiselle."

He did not save you, my mistress interjected. *I did.*

"T-t-the blood. This is m-my blood."

"I don't know, demoiselle," Luc said. "I thought so too at first, but seems quite unlikely since you are still alive and talking to me. I suspect the blood was from some sort of bizarre ritual committed after you passed out. Who knows what those monsters were capable of?"

I knew better. The blood was mine. I remembered Vincent cutting me. I remembered the flow of blood over my body. I remembered the hot, thick liquid coating my face and eyes. I remembered dying, or at least slipping toward Death's Door.

I have chosen you to serve me, my mistress said. *Your hunger is exquisite. Your control even more so. I have given you gifts. Please me, and your gifts will be multiplied. Anger me, and... things will become more complicated between us.*

"Who... who are you?" I asked, not realizing I was speaking out loud.

"I've already told you, demoiselle. I am Luc LaCroix. My friend and I saved you from these monsters."

My mistress was not so understanding. *You know me. Now you must know what you are as well.*

Suddenly I was standing, but not of my own accord. Luc was kneeling beside me, and a lantern rested on Monsieur's chair, which Luc must have moved from the table and positioned between me and the door, angled so that he could see both. The chamber's torches had all burned out, and so the only light was from Luc's lantern.

"Demoiselle..." he started, but his eyes roamed my body now clearly illuminated. He saw the wicked gash in my inner thigh. He saw the metal hooks through my legs. He saw the death in my eyes. His face drew back in horror just before his body started to as well. He knew that I should be dead. That somehow I was dead, yet somehow not.

It was my mistress's will, not my own, when I lunged at him. He tried to flee, but my mistress used my right hand to slash at his face.

Midstroke my hands became tipped with long black claws, and where the claws struck, his flesh peeled open. He instantly went limp and fell backward onto the chair and lantern. He said not a word as the flame smothered and died under his unmoving form.

Plunged into complete darkness, I could somehow still see. I could see as easily if not better than before. My mistress moved me closer to the gendarme's body, Luc's body, and with one hand lifted him and threw him onto Madame and Monsieur's table like so much butchered meat. With a single great leap, I was on the table, straddling his hips. My claws sliced his clothes away from his body like razors through paper. My mistress used a single claw to open the poor man's stomach, and I feasted. Part of me was horrified by my actions, by what I was being forced to do by my mistress. She was violating me every bit as much as I violated the man beneath me. I wanted to be sick, but there was another part of me bubbling up from within. That part said that this was not only natural, but right. It was right for the strong to feed on the weak. Right for the predator to consume the prey.

As I scooped out what must have been my third or fourth handful of entrails, I realized I was no longer being forced to feed. I fed simply because Luc tasted divine. I screamed and ripped myself from the table. Rip was exactly what seemed to happen, because just as I fell to the left, something else fell to the right of the table.

I was myself and in control of my body once more. I lay between the table and the door, and as I stood, it stood from where it lay between the table and the wall of grinning skulls. It was the hideous form of the monster I had just been. My knees quivered and my bladder released. The monster hissed at me and jumped back onto the table with minimal effort. I fell backward onto my posterior. I crawled away, expecting the thing to attack me. Instead it proceeded to rip and tear at Luc's corpse with wild abandon.

I was through the portal and running before I realized it. I fled with as much abandon as the monster had feeding on poor Luc.

"What was that thing?" I panted desperately to no one as I ran.

My mistress answered, *Beautiful.*

3

WANDERINGS

August 1814 AD

When I realized that I was completely lost, I slowed. It was only then that I noticed the giant metal hooks piercing each of my legs about six inches above each ankle. They appeared to be the kind a butcher might use to hang large chunks of meat, but these were bent at the end of the shank so that the eyes would be closer when the victim was hung upside down as I was. Additionally, each had a wicked barb at the end. It was brilliant butchery.

It seemed like my legs were whole, except the flesh around the piercings seemed irritated. I did not think ripping the barbed hooks free of my legs would be wise, as I did not wish to be lamed. Instead, I rotated each hook so that the shanks ran up my legs. The barbs in the hooks sliced crescent-shaped cuts into my flesh. Once the eyes of the hooks were near my knees, the inward bends at the end held the eyes against my legs, wedging the hooks into place. I expected there to be pain, but it was minuscule. I still had to proceed cautiously lest the hooks fall out of place.

The tunnels were maddening, with many branches, rooms, and split slopes up and down to other levels. My typically superior sense of direction was useless to me in the tunnels. The only noise I heard was a distant dripping. It mattered not how far or in which direction I traveled; the dripping remained constant, the same rhythm, the same volume, and same direction, always in front of me regardless of what turn I took.

At one intersection that I had seen three or four times already, I stopped to try to get my bearings. I used the blood coating my body as ink and drew an arrow on one smooth wall. That was when it struck me that the texture of the skin-splitting walls had changed. I wondered when that had happened and how it had happened without my notice. With my back to the wall, I slid down to sit on the floor of the tunnel and pulled my legs to my chest.

Tears tried to pull themselves up from somewhere deep inside of me, but I pressed my anvil heart down on the emotion. I was not one to cry anymore, and I would never again be one to cry. No crying, no family, no friends. There was just me. I had my ~~Reason~~ logic and my determination. That was all I needed.

Despite being underground and completely naked, I wasn't cold. That was almost as convenient as was my ability to see in the dark. I wondered idly if my hearing were somehow changed as well and that was why I continued to hear that insistent dripping. Gooseflesh covered my body then, not due to the temperature of the tunnels, but because I realized that the dripping was gone.

I sat and listened for minutes or maybe hours. When one's heart no longer beats, time becomes somewhat intangible, but I sat there, curled in upon myself for quite a long time. There was something very distant. A scrape or maybe something being dragged in short, labored jerks. The water dripped then, just once. An almost clear tone against the somehow corrupt scraping, dragging sound.

Something hissed. The sound was a proclamation of hatred, and the water quieted once again, chastised.

I bolted upright and once again fled into the embrace of the catacombs for protection. The tunnels twisted and turned, sometimes in upon themselves with no logical system or reasonable symmetry. Soon I entered a section that seemed older than... well, older than old. Everything was completely smooth. The floors had grooves worn in places where feet must have tread over them hundreds of thousands of times.

I stopped and held my breath, a task that should have been difficult after all my running, but my body held no desire for breath. It seemed the only reason I continued to breathe when I did was habit. As I held my breath I listened. There was no evidence of the dragging, hissing hatred. I relaxed a small measure and continued. Every minute or so, I stopped to listen again. No water dripped here, but there was also no hiss whenever I checked.

In this older section, there was a multitude of rooms sized from tiny niches to cavernous spaces large enough to fit a cathedral. I stood in the entrance of what I instantly named the Cathedral of Stone and marveled at the space. It seemed completely natural but was also a work of art. Some sort of worked black stone gave the natural walls a more regular if slightly askew shape. Somehow stalactites and stalagmites were carved or grown in a double row of columns, each stalactite paired with a stalagmite under it. Everything I knew about geology said this formation was an impossibility, yet there it was before me. No pews or benches filled the space, just a large stone altar at the far end of the hall to my right in front of some strange symbol carved into the floor.

I wondered how deep I was. I wondered, "Who built this?" I wondered, "How long ago was it built?" And I wondered, "Why?"

I took a single step into the Cathedral of Stone, intent on examining the seemingly natural columns, but I heard voices, low and vile, the moment I stepped over the threshold.

I froze in place.

The voices spoke in low tones words unintelligible. I moved my left foot back with agonizing caution. My foot landed back across the threshold, and I pulled my body out of the space. Curse my luck, my right foot struck a small stone as I pulled it across the threshold. The voices instantly silenced.

Before I had the chance to turn, the voices returned. Instead of a few individual speakers, now there was a multitude. Instead of quiet whispers, their voices were a riot. And the voices were coming toward me.

Once again I fled from some unseen terror. I turned randomly a few times trying to lose the voices. After blindly darting and turning through several intersections of two or three additional tunnels, I gained a small measure between myself and my pursuers. I crossed another intersection, made two turns, when I found myself facing a door and no other exits. The pursuing voices made it obvious that doubling back was not an option.

The door opened and closed with ease and almost no noise. Once closed, the riot of voices was muted. I would have breathed a sigh of relief had I need to breathe. I almost did anyway but feared what the noise might give away.

Beyond the door was a tomb about ten feet wide and thrice as deep. Rows of niches were carved into the walls one on top of another five high. Desiccated bodies filled the niches in various states of mummification. At the far end of the room was a tunnel leading out, and I took it.

The next room was just like the one before, as was the next. The third room's exit opened into a round, domed room with a plain, dust-encrusted fountain commanding the center. There were three other exits from the room: right, left, and straight ahead. Each seemed just like the others, except in the distance to my left, a faint light glowed. I took half a step toward the light, but the riot of voices was suddenly behind me again. They had found the tomb.

I turned and fled the light. I passed through one more tomb before sliding behind an almost complete mummy on the lowest niche in the wall to my right. I silently excused myself to the niche's eternal resident, pushed myself back as far as I could within, and remained as still and as silent as the dead that I was.

The voices were close enough that I started to hear individual voices within the tumult. I was certain that I was more than happy not knowing the specifics of their malevolence. The riot had calmed to whispers, but the whispers were no better. There was something almost reptilian in the whispers, while the voices were almost human.

I cowered in my borrowed niche, hidden from the entrance, but I was unsure how well I would remain hidden to any creature with a head low to the ground.

The voices stopped entirely then, and I thought the danger had passed, when something black and utterly silent drifted in front of the niche. Tendrils of darkness I could not see through whipped as if from some unseen breeze about eight inches above the ground. The tendrils were about a foot long before they joined into what appeared to be the bottom of a dark flowing robe. My mind frantically searched for the thing's feet, but there was nothing.

The form moved past my niche.

I experienced a particularly odd sensation then. My pulse should have been pounding. My breathing should have been frantic. Instead I was completely still with no effort. Just as I felt somewhat safe, there was a dry crash and thunk followed by some smaller dull rattling sounds.

I almost jumped out of my skin.

There was another crash followed by more thunks and rattles. Then another. And another. I understood what was happening as a dry skull struck the floor before me and shattered. The bones rattled to rest. A desiccated torso followed, crashing with a dull thud behind what was left of the skull. Three more bodies were unceremoniously dumped to the floor, and then the floating form was back in front of my niche again.

Another body crashed to the floor in front of me. Then another. And another. Black tendrils reached into my niche, lengthened, and wrapped around my companion. I held my breath and sucked in my gut as the tendrils came within a finger's width of touching me. The mummy was in the creature's grasp when a shrill shriek sounded in the distance. The creature paused and shrieked in return as did dozens more. My companion fell back into place as the tendrils dissolved into thin air, and then the thing was simply gone.

I lay there and thanked the niche's proper resident for hiding me. His silent grin seemed to say I was welcome.

The voices were back, a riot again, rushing away from my hiding spot. I waited for a very long time. I do not know how long, but twice I thought to leave only to hear movement within the tombs. The sounds were not of the living with their breathing and heavy purpose of life, but the slow silent movement of things found in the darkest recesses of the world. They were the sounds of things such as I was now.

It was then I resolved not to be a monster. I would be human and self-sufficient. I would live life on my own terms—such as my life might be. I would not live in the bowels of the world, in the deepest reaches of creation like a worm, hoping that a spare morsel would come my way. I might be dead, but I would not act the part. I rejected the idea I could not live with humanity because I was no longer a human, and I would not let some monster's destruction of the life I knew to end who I was. I may no longer be alive, but I would live.

I did not hear her voice, had not heard her since just after I fled the monster feeding on poor Luc, but somehow I knew my mistress was pleased, and I became terrified of what that meant.

4

RETURN TO LIGHT

August 13, 1814 AD

During my isolation, I took inventory of my body. I had all my fingers and toes. My teeth were intact. My body was whole and uncut, even where Vincent had stabbed me. My only noticeable wounds were the giant metal hooks piercing my legs and a rash wherever the metal touched or pierced my skin. The irritation slowly became intense.

When I heard the dripping water return, I decided that I was no longer in danger. I slid from the tomb and searched for solutions.

Several corpses littered the floor of the tomb. It felt wrong to leave them, so I lifted them one by one to place them in the niches.

"I'm so sorry, mes amis. I cannot tell which bones belong to whom, but I'll do my best."

Most of the funerary was dry-rotted, but one poor soul was buried under a cheap, rough cloth shroud that seemed to withstand the rigors of time. I collected the poor soul's shroud and placed him once more into his resting place.

"Normally I would not do such a thing, but I'm afraid you gentlemen have me at a disadvantage," I said, holding the corpse's shroud. "I hope you forgive my presumption on taking your shroud.

Even with your clothing such as it is, all of you are more clothed than I am. Gentlemen such as you all are, I'm certain you will give me this small charity."

I ripped up the shroud and wrapped the metal hooks with the cloth. Then I tied the hooks through the eyes at the end of the shanks to my legs, just under the knees. With the rest of the cloth, I made a small bag by folding two-thirds of the cloth, ripping small strips in the edges, and tying them together. To the top ties, I tied a long strip, to make a wide loop. The loop was just wide enough to allow the bag to hang from my waist and leave my hands free.

I took one last moment to thank all the gentlemen, especially my friend who shared his niche with me and the poor soul whose shroud now protected my legs. After I made my goodbyes, I turned, took a single step, and landed on something sharp I could not ignore. I thought maybe I missed a bone of one of my friends, but it was not a bone. The item I stepped on was a gemstone of some sort partially buried in the dirt and detritus on the floor.

Without light, I could not see the color of the stone, but it was as large as the end of my thumb, flat on one side, and came to a point opposite the flat end. I turned to ask my friends if this was one of theirs, but the skulls were all turned away from me. I had not laid them that way. The Charlotte of a month ago would have been terrified by such an experience, but somehow this seemed friendly, as if they were telling me, "We didn't see anything. Take your prize and go on."

So I did.

I wandered the catacombs for days and days. The hooks tied to my legs were much more comfortable with the thick scratchy material insulating my flesh from the irritation. I wandered toward where I thought the dripping must be. Whenever I had a choice, I chose those corridors where the walls were rougher, and moved away from any tunnel or room with very smooth walls.

I found things in the tunnels as I wandered from place to place. A thin, flat piece of rusted metal with two holes on one end, a knife with a curved blade, a comb and mirror set, an intact china bowl filled with pebbles, and a bird-headed pin. A day or two of wandering brought me to a location where the tunnel wall was broken. The sound of dripping was greater through the hole in the wall, so I squatted and squeezed through.

The circular chamber beyond was worked stone, much like the basement of a castle or manor tower. Stone stairs curved upward for twenty feet or more, spiraling above my head and beyond. In front of me, however, was a large wide pool of water, much like a well. A bearded man's face was high upon the opposite wall, carved from stone. From his open mouth, water collected and dripped into the pool below. I set my parcel of treasures on the lip of stone ringing the pool before climbing in and settling in the pool.

There I washed myself clean. I used the comb to straighten out the tangles in my hair. The curved blade allowed me to cut the knots out of my hair, and I scrubbed my body with a semismooth round stone I found in the pool. I drifted in the pool for a while, enjoying the quiet comfort of it.

After bathing, I emerged from the pool. The rough cloth wrapping the hooks in my legs was loose, so I took the time to rewrap them. When everything was secure, I sneaked up the stairs to see where they went. The stairs were open, and the pool of water below was in view the entire way. Perhaps three flights up, the stairs ended at a door in the wall. In the ceiling was an eye hook with an old wooden pulley hanging from it. Near the door was another eye hook, but nothing hung from it.

The door itself was wooden and braced by iron. The wood was swollen into the frame so completely that I could not see through a single crack. I placed my ear to the door, but there was nothing to be heard. I tried the handle, but the door wouldn't budge. I wanted to believe that if I knocked, someone would welcome me with open arms, but I was wet, naked, and in someone's basement. At best I would be arrested, but at worst I would be attacked. I was no stranger to the Parisian Guard, and I was in no shape to fight anyone, especially if my mistress returned with the monster. I turned and left hope to find a more realistic answer.

When I found the area where the walls were made of sharp stones, I knew I had returned close to where I began. I wandered the area, first to the right then to the left, always returning to where I started before exploring some place new. Once I found my path back to Madame and Monsieur Anton's room, I became wary. With one of their own killed, it was equally possible that the place was being watched by Luc's comrades.

My worry was for naught. The room was empty of the living. Even Madame and Monsieur's bodies were gone. I explored the room more thoroughly. The pair had lived—no, that's the wrong word—the pair had *existed* in a sloven fashion. It was a wonder that Madame's dress remained as clean as it was when I was presented. There was dried blood on and around the table where it had spilled. Above the table was the hook from which I had been suspended, fastened into the ceiling. The sight of it made me shiver for the first time since I woke transformed.

Madame's chair lay knocked over where she once dined. Monsieur's chair lay where Luc had placed it. The lantern was still there in the seat. Whoever discovered Luc's body must not have stayed long or given the room much more than a passing glance. Fortune was with me when I found the trunk. It was old but clean and unlocked. Within were blessedly some threadbare clothes, a small wheel of cheese, a large heel of bread, a flask, a stoppered bottle of lamp oil, a small metal tube capped at one end with wax, and a couple gray blankets. Before this had all started, I would have traded anything for the meager contents of this trunk.

When I had everything out of the trunk as I took inventory, I found a ribbon lying in the bottom. I pulled the ribbon, and the bottom of the trunk pulled up to reveal another small cache. Within was a small sheaf of paper, many of which were pre-ruled forms of some sort, a bottle of ink, and a pen with a metal nib and a long wooden handle.

The cheese was passable for food, but it tasted odd. The bread held no taste at all, but I consumed both the bread and cheese, washing it down with half of the flask's contents, which ended up being water. It was more food than I had seen in a month, and I ate it all in a matter of minutes. I might as well have dumped the contents down a well for all the good it did to sate my hunger.

I donned the clothes and stashed the blankets in the trunk. I broke the wax seal on the small metal tube, and the top of the container screwed off with a slight twist. Within the tube was flint and steel for making fire plus a small amount of tinder. I lit some of the tinder with the flint and steel and added a small bit of cloth as fuel. Before the fire could burn out, I and got the forgotten lantern and used a long bit of tinder to light it. It seemed the wick was still serviceable, and soon a warm glow surrounded me. I moved to extinguish the tinder, but the sight of the fire distracted me. I stared into the flames thought I could almost see something there. I was certain if I looked long enough, I would be able to see what it was, but then the flames went out.

In my trance-like state, the small bit of tinder I used to light the lamp had burned down to the tips of my fingers. My skin was black where the skin had burned. I felt nothing of it until I considered the damage. Only then did I feel the burn, feel the effects of the fire upon my body. It was a neat trick if I could learn how to use it. Right now though, I ran back to the trunk to get the flask and pour cool water over my stinging fingers.

It was nice to feel something other than hunger though. I could see the allure of hurting myself in order to be able to just feel, but that was a trap. My father once told me about a group of priests who believed they were unworthy of God's Mercy, so they flogged themselves, to make their lives as painful as possible. They believed through their constant suffering they would one day be granted the Glories of Heaven. I thought that was absurd and vowed then to never hurt myself for any sort of reward. It just did not make sense to me. Now I understood a little better why people might do such things. It still did not completely make sense, but I would no longer condemn people for misguidedly hurting themselves. I would have to find another path to feeling human.

In the low glow of the lantern, I dragged the trunk and all my treasures to the table. I moved Madame's oversized chair to the center of the table so that the grinning skulls would be at my back, and I laid my treasures across the table.

My first treasure ended up being a deep blood-red color. Perhaps it was a ruby, but I hoped that its sale would bring me enough funds to live like a normal person for a few months at least. The comb and mirror set were tarnished black, and rubbing the mirror's handle for a minute showed a lovely silver color beneath the tarnish. The rectangle of rusted metal was just that. I did not know why I loved it so much, but I could never imagine being parted from it. Once I could clean off the dirt and rust, I would hang the metal from a leather cord and wear it as a necklace. The china bowl was in perfect condition. It was brown and green with bone-white accents. The pebbles the bowl held were just that, but I kept them anyway. It felt wrong to part the set.

My clothes were simple and serviceable, not quite a woman's clothes, but I was still in my middle teens, not quite fully a woman yet. The first thing I donned was a pair of white underpants that thankfully covered the giant hooks in my legs. The numerous stains on the garment were unsettling, but I could not complain given my circumstance. There was no underblouse, so I donned the blouse next. It was thin and looked like it might have once been red. Now the only color that showed in the blouse was under the arms and just inside the collar where the faintest pink showed. The skirt was threadbare and black where it had not been patched with random scraps of colored cloth. I guessed it was still technically considered black, but another patch would likely tip the scale.

Everything fit loosely, especially in the bust and hips. The skirt all but dragged the ground, but I was grateful. My father once had a proper dress tailored for me when it became apparent that I would not stand much taller than five feet. The dress cost a small fortune, but nothing ever fit so well. When I eventually found myself living on the streets of Paris, I had only the clothes I was wearing. Thieves and poverty stole everything else of value. I counted my mother as one of the thieves, but at least she was trying to feed us. Well, she tried until

Paul's death. She stopped struggling then and wasted away. Of all the things I lost, that dress was the most painful, however. Well... after my books, that is.

If I could pass well enough as a young lady and not an orphaned street urchin, I might get real employment. That would be superior to becoming the feast of a pair of monsters in tunnels under Paris. A life in the sun, a life in the light to put behind this travesty of darkness, a life to turn aside the monstrosity that my mistress wanted me to become, and a life that I would control, no one else.

Then it struck me that I must not allow myself to become the shadow of my former self like Madame and Monsieur Anton allowed themselves to become. They had no control, no respect of their Hunger. They simply allowed it to delude them. Not I. I would not allow myself to fall victim to such shortsightedness. There was only one way I knew to keep memories after they are long lost. I took the paper, ink, and quill, and I set memory to paper.

5

WATCHING AND WAITING

August 14-17, 1814 AD

I returned to the streets of Paris, my trunk hidden below, behind a wall of bones. I had no family, no friends, and no money. My family was forever lost to me, all dead. There were no friends to be found on the street, only other desperate souls. My only avenue to life then was money. While I had none, I did have treasures to sell. Until I could find a buyer for my treasures and secure some wealth, I decided to operate from the only secure location I had at my disposal. Secure being a relative word.

I needed to sell my treasures. I found a couple of small diamond-studded earrings where Madame's chair had been. These were added to my bounty. I could not tell what the studs were made from, but they appeared to be silver. Unlike the silver comb and mirror set, the studs were untarnished.

The ruby was clear and beautiful.

I was not exactly sure where I might sell such items. I learned during my time on the streets that shops that rarely actually exchanged in commerce yet somehow continued to remain in business were either spies, fronts for illegal activities, or fences. I wanted nothing of spies. I could not trust any shop that was a front for some nefarious illegal activity. I needed a fence, or at least an honest merchant willing to ask few questions. I just needed to find the right shop.

Just don't lose your head in the process, my mistress said to me.

Yes, I had to agree. La Monte-à-regret, that horrid invention of Monsieur Guillotin, had slowed its work of late. She did not run night and day like Papa said it did when I was a babe, but she continued to do her grim work when needed. I did not wish to be among the number to make that final climb into her arms, which is why I always kept my thefts infrequent, petty, and unnoticed.

I wandered the city for three days searching for businesses that seemed to carry on with little to no business. During that time, I made a friend of Monsieur Bordelon. His was one of the first shops that I suspected, but no. His shop was simply a small neighborhood store stuck on a horrible little street, the unfortunately named Rue des Singes. Only a block long, yet the sun's rays never seemed to touch a single brick. The buildings above seemed to lean together conspiratorially, perhaps to judge when the best time to collapse on those below might be. Very few people made their way through the street crowded with trash. Tenants in the dwellings above frequently yelled at passersby and dumped their chamber pots out the windows without regard to those below. Clotheslines stretched between buildings, and I could not fathom how the lower lines were not drenched with human waste. Monsieur Bordelon said his morning, afternoon, and evening was spent cleaning the refuse of others.

The street was truly dreadful, but the shop and its master were not. Once, before the wars, it seemed the street had been clean and bright, the people pleasant. Now he lamented leaving the countryside, but bad luck and worse weather ruined his crops two years in a row. His two choices were to either wager everything on one more year or sell the farm, move to the city, and start anew. His wife had family in Paris then and knew of a small shop for sale, perfect for a grocer. He said that his wife glowed at the mere mention of Paris, and so Monsieur Bordelon felt he had no choice, not really. They had five wonderful years in the city before the revolution began and everything changed.

Each day we talked, he would offer me a scrap of bread, a piece of cheese, or a bruised apple. I refused each offer the first two days, and each time, he made a pained expression that looked quite pitiful if somewhat comical. He was such a nice man. I wondered if his shop was more successful, if he might possess a much larger stomach.

"Please, Charlotte," he said on the third day of our meeting, "you are far too thin. You must eat something. Besides, I need to make room for fresh goods, and these things will only go to waste. So really, you are doing me a favor."

I saw right through his argument, but I was hungry. I also did not wish to pain him more, so I agreed. Then I was struck with an idea that would allow me to refuse charity and instead earn my meal. I stayed for an hour or so until the afternoon rounds of chamber pot rain ended and took up a bucket and broom to clean the street. Monsieur Bordelon fretted while I worked.

"Really, mon chère," he told me as I swept the mud-and-occasional-brick street in front of the shop. "You do not have to do this. My son should be here. He should be doing this work, not a young lady such as yourself."

I laughed at that, *lady* indeed, and then I soured as I thought about what he might call me if he only knew the things I have done to survive. The things that had been done to me in the past few days. "Thief" was probably an appropriate title. I earned that one honestly enough, though only when it was required. "Monster" was my new title, or it would be if I allowed that thing in the catacombs to find me.

She does not need to find you, my mistress said to me then. *You can run far and fast, but it will make no difference. She is always with you. She is you, and you are her.*

Monsieur Bordelon must have noticed my scowl. "Are you all right, demoiselle?"

I shook my head and reached for a plausible reason to be scowling.

"I was only thinking that this would go faster if I had some water," was all I could think to say.

Monsieur Bordelon beamed and darted away. Shortly after, he returned with two full buckets splashing water. I passed him all the solid waste I had collected, and he left with it, disappearing down the street for a few minutes before returning, the bucket empty.

"My son, Henri, should be here doing this," Monsieur Bordelon groused as I poured some water from one of the buckets into the now-empty waste bucket. He swirled the water around the waste bucket. He used the broom to scrub the inside of the bucket, which had the added effect of cleaning it some too. "He's my son, but lazy."

I assumed his son must take after his mother. I never saw her helping out in the store either. He finished cleaning the broom and waste bucket as I was doing my best to splash water in a way that would push mud and waste away from the store entrance. I had just a little left over to rinse the broom and waste bucket one more time before stacking the buckets together.

Monsieur Bordelon wiped his brow with a towel he kept at his waist. "I worry about him. He has made friends with a bad group of boys, staying out all night..." His voice trailed off as if he wanted to say more, but it was a familiar path of pain and regret too often traveled. He shook his head and then smiled at me again. "One child like you, Demoiselle Charlotte, and I could make this shop successful again. Two, and I could turn the entire quarter around."

I smiled like a fool.

"I'm just sorry you felt compelled to help," he said.

"Oh no, monsieur. I did not feel compelled to help. You misunderstand my generosity. I worked for the food."

I stuffed a crusty heel of bread into my mouth and grabbed an apple before waving goodbye. Monsieur Bordelon smiled and waved me away. He would have forced more upon me had I let him, so choosing what to take seemed best. I would neither be in debt to anyone, ever, nor would I take charity. That was my creed now. I was alone. I would remain alone. And I would succeed on my own. I was quite proud of myself as I formed the thoughts. Freedom gives one the power to see clearly.

It is a shame you are not alone. You never will be. I will always be with you, my mistress said to me.

I cursed. I spat out the bread in my mouth, and I cursed again.

My mistress laughed.

Never inspect the teeth of a given horse.

"What?"

It is from one of your saints. It means do not be critical of something of value that is given to you.

"Is that what you have given me, 'something of value'?" I asked.

She did not respond. It felt as if she was both amused and annoyed at me. That was fine. I was annoyed by her as well, though I had to admit that being alive, such as it were, was preferable to being dead. I had a burning inside of me that I was only now starting to become aware of. I had a need other than my hunger that must be filled, but I was not quite yet sure what it was. It was almost as if I could only see the shadows of some familiar form, yet I could not name the form. If I focused on it, this need was deeper than my hunger ever was. If set free, this need would be all consuming. Where would I be then? I shuddered at the thought, so I set it aside. I had more pressing concerns for the moment, or at least I had needs that I could actually identify.

That evening I was eating the apple while walking north and west into Bourse. There I noticed three ruffians cast about hurried glances before sliding into a tailor's shop. My interest piqued, I walked closer and found a place to recline while finishing the apple. The apple was horrid. The taste was far too sweet and the flesh far too soft. But it was food, and while I remained hungry, the simple act of moving my mouth and swallowing was almost a relief.

The shop's window proclaimed it as Giorgio's Fine Tailoring. That was odd. This was a poor district. It was not the poorest, to be sure, and bordered on richer quarters, but few Parisians here would be able to afford new clothes, much less finely tailored clothes. I took smaller nibbles of the apple with each bite and even worked on eating the core. I needed it to last. At least the core was not so horridly sweet. I was well and done eating by the time the three ruffians emerged from the tailor's shop about ten minutes later. I took a few steps down the street and looked into another shop's window. In the reflection, I watched the three split some coins before running off in different directions. I smiled and returned to the catacombs.

Early the next morning I was standing across from Giorgio's Fine Tailoring in a small passageway. Darkness still cloaked the city when I got there, and the passage would provide more darkness in which I could observe the shop without being seen. The only people on the street at this hour were the occasional guard (very occasional in this part of the city), thieves (of which I was not currently one), spies (of which I was currently one), bakers, and dairy men. I made sure to put a stack of crates to my back and ensured that I had a path back, up, and out if needed.

Always plan multiple escape routes when possible. I... I could not remember when or where I learned that lesson. I assumed it was early during my life on the streets.

The sun rose and so did the people. Lights appeared in shops up and down the street. People opened doors and set out displays where they could. Giorgio's store had a large plate glass display window in the front. A small black placard in the window read "Leave Now, Please" written in fine golden script on a square black board. Despite the unusual sign telling people to leave, his was easily the finest shop on the street.

The sun was fully up and lighted the entire street, but there was still no sign of the proprietor of Giorgio's. My stomach growled audibly. The food Monsieur Bordelon had given me was a kindness, but I think it only served in the long run to make me all the more hungry. I considered finding and eating some grass just to fill the void, but something told me that wouldn't work. I needed something different, something... more.

It was the height of summer, and yet a cold wind blew down Rue Saint-Denis. It had been a strange few years. Winter lasted late into spring. Spring lasted well into summer. Summer may have lasted two weeks, maybe three, before autumn returned. Some were calling the prior year "The Year Without Summer," and this year was not much better. Before I could think to hope otherwise, it began to rain, first as a light misting, then a slow but steady shower. In late summer, as it was supposed to be, the rain would have been welcome. But along with the unusually cold weather came more rain than I think Paris had ever seen. At least the cold and wet didn't bother me anymore except for the inconvenience.

Late into the afternoon I began to think this Giorgio was not going to show. No one had come or gone from the shop. This sign in the window still read... When had that happened? The sign in the window read "Enter Now, Please." I was certain the last time I looked it still read "Leave Now, Please."

I cursed myself for missing his entrance. I puzzled over the situation and decided that I would not meet this man today. I would return tomorrow and watch again. So I retreated to the catacombs, disrobed, and dried my clothes over the lit lantern. It cost me more of my tinder, but the light in the otherwise unworldly location was a nice reminder of being human.

The next morning I left even earlier, arriving before even the bakers and milkmen were about. My breath frosted in the chill morning air. I casually strolled by the front of Giorgio's to check within. The store was completely dark, but I could see tables covered with cubic and domed shapes covered by sheets. There were two mannequins, one each male and female. Toward the back was a counter, behind which was a small space and a doorway covered by a curtain. The black placard with the beautiful golden script reading "Leave Now, Please" rested in the window. I gave the door a very slight tug to ensure it was secured and then walked down the street. I found a nice shadow to wait in for several minutes before crossing the street and returning to my original passage hiding spot.

The stars were out, and the moon was new. It was more than enough light for me to see well, yet I knew most ~~other~~ human eyes would be able to see only rough shapes. I was quite proud of my resourcefulness.

By the time the bakers and milkmen were about, I was bored stiff. Since it did not seem likely that my mistress was going to interact with me any time soon, my only companion was the burning ache in my stomach. I had gone longer without eating, but that did not make the experience pleasant.

I made a mental note to buy some knitting needles when I had some proper money, good solid francs, in hand. Knitting would provide me with something to do during the long periods I now had of quiet wakefulness. I did not need to sleep, not anymore. I could... pass time of sorts, by finding a secure location and focusing my attention on one very specific thought or thing I could hear or see until everything else faded away. I first learned the skill on the streets. It was a way to push everything out. The loss. The fear. The pain. Everything. Unless I focused on how hungry I was, the skill was helpful to pass time and forget unpleasant memories. I could not allow myself to be so distracted this morning, however. This morning I was going to see the measure of this man before I entered his lair.

I also made a mental note to learn how to knit.

Paris's morning routine began as the sun rose once again. Smells of fresh bread and wood smoke filled the air. The sunlight was pure and clear. It would not last long, as the sewer smells would rise behind the sun by an hour or so, but for the moment is was delightful.

The sun was not fully risen when the three ruffians from the day before came out of Giorgio's shop. I cursed. When had they gone in? They must have gone in as a horse or carriage passed by, blocking my view. I should have considered that. Tomorrow I would return, but I would find a location high enough to look over the traffic. I was considering different locations to observe from the following morning as the ruffians scattered in different directions. Through the storefront window I saw a large ruddy-complected hand reach down and flip the sign around to "Enter Now, Please."

I was just observing that the man seemed to wear a white shirt, as the cuffs were just visible through the glass, while the rest of his body was obscured by wall and door, when there was a polite but distinct

"Um hmm" to my right that snapped me out of my observation. One of the three ruffians was standing about ten feet away. He wore dark pants and a darker shirt. Both garments were dirty and pulling apart at the seams in places. His hair was cut so short his scalp was easily visible even under his flat cap. His shoes were... well, he didn't wear shoes. His feet were simply so filthy that they seemed to be shoed. If that was The Mud, his feet were going to fall off his body eventually. Paris's concoction of dirt, bodily waste, and poor drainage produced a particularly acidic paste that many simply referred to as The Mud. The Mud could ruin a good pair of leather boots in a few short months if not promptly removed each day.

"Master says to give this to you, mademoiselle," said the ruffian. He had an accent that was off. German maybe? He held a small slip of paper out to me in his left hand. His hands were so dirty that he left smudges of dirt on the paper.

"Thank you," I replied as if I had been expecting him. Or at least that's how I tried to make it sound. Instead it came out more as a question. "Thank you?"

The ruffian smiled. He was missing his front two teeth, and I grimaced.

"Did you lose those teeth in some sort of fight," I asked as I took the folded slip of paper.

A bit of color came to the ruffian's face, what could be seen beneath the dirt. He had bright blue eyes.

"No, Madame, they fell out. Master Giorgio says bigger, stronger teeth will come in pretty soon."

Before I could respond, he gave me a slight bow and ran away as if the Devil were chasing him. How old was he? Six? Eight? Ten? Regardless of his age, he was tall for a mere boy. He looked like a teenager, younger than me, but still... at least thirteen.

I was still shaking my head, pondering the boy's age somewhere in the back of my mind, when I opened the slip of paper and read it.

Instead girl standing alone in alley two days, the note read, *perhaps come inside, like customer or friend maybe.*

I completely forgot about the giant six-year-old and reread the paper several times.

He knew I had been out here yesterday and today? Who was this man?

My only real recourse was to refuse the invitation and leave... or go in. Neither choice seemed rational, but considering this man was likely the type of contact I needed, my choice was made. I brushed off what dirt might be collected on my skirt, straightened my blouse, and proceeded across the street. No one else needed to know this was not entirely my decision, so I would not allow myself to appear otherwise.

6

THE MISER AND THE THIEF

August 17, 1814 AD

I entered the shop and ignored most of the contents. I knew from my earlier reconnaissance there were tables and mannequins wearing clothes, but this visit, I was only interested in the proprietor. He stood at the far end of the room behind the counter, dressed in black pants and belt with a white shirt and apron. The apron was the kind with pockets in the front and ties that wrapped around his body and tied in the front. He was just skinny enough that he was able to tie the apron on properly, but just fat enough not to have any additional slack in those ties. His hair was dark, thin, and lay flat against his head as if he used some sort of oil or grease to hold it in place. His morning shave missed not a single whisker. The only thing disconcerting about the man was his eyes. They seemed to peer through me, or maybe simply into my body to see my soul if there was one anymore.

"Decide inside better than outside, eh?" His diction was clipped and his baritone on the low side. He spoke with a smile and a twinkle in his eye. I could not fathom this man. Part of me wanted to flee him immediately. Circumstances said that was less than pragmatic. Another part of me simply trusted him. That part of me wanted to hug him like a father and fall asleep in the safety of his arms. Then there was a tiny voice deep within that said the man was dangerous. Considering the man's observational skills, as well as his skill at remaining unseen, I was most inclined to listen to the tiny voice.

"Are you Giorgio?" I asked.

His smile broadened, and he spread his arms wide. "In flesh. Girl know Giorgio's name. What is girl named?"

"I want to fence some things."

The smallest, almost imperceptible wave of shock washed over Giorgio's face. I probably would have missed it if I were not looking for it. His smile dropped a fraction, and he squinted his eyes ever so slightly. "Giorgio tailor, not... person who build fence."

"Right," I said, winking in an exaggerated way. I continued my portion of this play with a flat, emotionless voice. "And I am a young lady of the old court that is down on her luck. I need money to eat and find a place to sleep. This is all I have left in the world. Help me. Please."

Giorgio's smile lessened, but there was something a bit more genuine about it. "Maybe Giorgio help bad luck lady... as charity."

"Oh. Thank you, kind sir," I replied.

When I placed the diamond earrings and the ruby on the counter, his eyes bulged.

"Where girl get such?" he asked, waving his hands over the earrings and ruby, never touching them.

"That should not matter to a fence," I said. I realized after I said it that a touch of annoyance slipped itself into my tone. I would have to practice preventing that in the future.

"Bah." Giorgio took a step back away from the counter as if my treasures were dangerous. There was not much space behind the counter, but he used it all. "Giorgio know stolen jewels when see. Giorgio does not... this thing... fence."

I barked out a laugh. "You have a tailor shop in a section of town with a population that cannot possibly afford to shop at it. In two days, the only people I have seen come and go are street urchins and ruffians who leave with more money than when they arrived, and you expect me to believe you are not a fence."

Giorgio's smile faded to a look of concern. "Giorgio... how you say... when finger injured and everyone see?"

"Stick out like a sore thumb? Yes. You are obviously not in the business of sales. Not here. Not in this neighborhood with these goods." I tilted my head back to indicate the room behind me.

Giorgio paused for a bit, resumed the perfectly pleasant smile he had when I first entered, and stepped back to the counter. He lifted the ruby and held it up to the sunlight streaming through the windows at the front of the store.

"Is interesting. Good. Nice color. No scratch. Nice. Very nice." He then set down the ruby and picked up the earrings. "Hmmm... diamonds with silver setting? Strange. Is old. You clean?"

"Yes," I lied. "They were my mother's favorite."

Giorgio barked a hearty laugh. "Giorgio think girl's mother never wear diamond or see even."

I glowered at the man. Who did he think he was talking to? He laughed again after glancing at me. Again I let my feelings show. I had to learn how to keep my expressions from my face.

"I need money for someplace to stay and food. These things are all I have. Help me. Please." I managed not to sound too desperate just then, but I think my eyes gave me away.

"Girl never rich. Giorgio know this. Maybe merchant child, but rich? No. Giorgio think girl 'find' gem and earring. Try to sell them with lies. How Giorgio do?"

Bastard.

"What do you care?"

Giorgio mulled my question over for a moment before dropping all pretense of humor or friendliness. When he spoke again, he was a pragmatic businessman telling the absolute truth.

"Because Giorgio not fence. Giorgio do know fence or two. Also people being interested in Giorgio not good thing, but help out girl seem good thing. Otherwise girl get into trouble, and Giorgio feel bad."

If he was not a fence, who was this man? A spy? With his horrible accent and impossible-to-forget appearance? Not likely. Someone working for the government? That also seemed unlikely. Maybe an informant for one of the factions in the government. That seemed likely. Not exactly a spy. He seemed to know things or be able to figure them out easily enough.

"Fine. You were almost exactly right. The only thing you had incorrect was the sarcasm dripping from your voice when you used the word *find*. I actually did find these things."

Giorgio's eyes narrowed slightly. "Where girl find?"

"That is not important."

"No? Giorgio think is."

"Is it more important than ensuring I end up sleeping down there another night by refusing me? You said you want to help me. The ruby I stepped on after helping out some friends. I would have missed it otherwise. When I went to ask to whom it belonged, they all pretended not to have noticed."

"And earrings?"

"They... they belonged to someone who tried to kill me." Not only tried, but succeeded.

Giorgio took a very small breath as his eyes widened ever so slightly.

"Try?"

"I am here, am I not?"

"Yes. How girl get away?"

"The guard showed up, or maybe whatever that new guard is, the gendarmerie. I ran off as they shot the monsters that were attacking me. Later I went back and searched the area. I found those earrings." I never spoke such truer yet more misleading words in my life. It was a skill I vowed to practice.

Giorgio studied me for long moments. I tried to remain somewhat innocent-looking, but he took too long and I just ended up impatient.

"So are you going to help me out or not?" I asked, probably with more scorn and desperation than I intended.

"Three hundred."

"Three hundred francs?"

"Yes."

"The earrings alone are probably worth five times that. That ruby is almost as big as the end of my thumb."

"So?"

"So?" I returned incredulously.

"Yes. Is what Giorgio said. So? No better price girl get anywhere in city... if not arrested first."

The man was a miser. No, a cheat.

"I need that money for rent and food. How can you justify such a low price? I need a thousand at least."

The man barked out another of those insufferable laughs of his. His eyes twinkled.

"Is easy. One, earrings worth ten times amount alone. Ruby more." My eyes bulged as he continued. "Two, girl between two rocks. No room for wiggle, eh? Three, girl no good at haggle. Probably get maximum two hundred from others. Assuming staying out of jail."

"What makes you think I cannot get more from someone else?" I asked, not wanting to believe him, but maybe if I knew his reasoning, I could use it to my advantage later.

Giorgio smiled as if he had been waiting for this moment. "Girl's appearance. Clothes old and mismatched. Not lady's clothes unless lady pretend being street urchin. Hair. Is long and curly. Black. Very nice, many like. Especially lice. From here Giorgio see bug jumping. Girl lucky not getting thrown out because bugs alone." I put my hands to my hair almost as a defense. Could lice live on undead blood? "Next, girl barefoot. Ugly dirty feet. Steps of dirt from door to counter. I offer one hundred less for this alone. Also, girl stink. Even in stinking city, girl stink. Like rolling in graves and... how do you say... night soil?" He saw the look of understanding on my face and nodded. "Girl maybe not even chance of talk. If girl enter different store and not get right one, owner maybe think girl is thief. Girl lucky Giorgio not like gendarmerie or would be calling. Also, girl is girl. Men maybe see earrings, think girl 'disappear' and earrings free, eh? Giorgio safe, not liking killing girls. But Giorgio take pity on girl. Offer something. Get girl out before stink and bug stay forever."

I said a word then that my mother would have beaten me a week straight for saying. To his credit, Giorgio did not laugh. He just watched me struggle with my inner monologue.

I looked behind me, and indeed there was a trail of dirt that followed me into the shop. My shoulders sagged and tears almost came to my eyes, but I was not going to let that happen, even as Giorgio landed one last hammer blow.

"Giorgio help girl decide. If girl leave, offer half next time girl show up, assuming girl not missing head."

I could only stare for several moments as I chewed on what he said.

"Fine. Give me five hundred, and I will clean up after myself as I leave. Plus the next time you see me, I will be bathed and louse-free."

The man smirked as if the offer was not worth consideration.

"Giorgio give... three hundred seventy-five. Care not if ever see girl again."

Bastard.

"How about this? Four hundred twenty-five francs, when I return I will be clean and louse-free. Plus, I will show you how to blend into the neighborhood a little better. Right now yours is the sorest thumb in the city."

Giorgio cocked his head to one side and smiled.

"Maybe girl not horrible at haggle. Not good, mind, but... not horrible. Is deal."

Giorgio did not have that much coin in his shop at the time, nor did he want me walking around with so much coin on me all at once. I saw the wisdom in his suggestion and agreed to a lesser sum initially to secure a place to stay and a meal or two. He would give me the rest of what I needed when I needed it. It was a gamble, but there was something about the man that made me trust him despite the tiny voice inside me.

When I left Giorgio's, the sun was well on its way toward its zenith and the wide street bustled. Now keenly aware of my filth, I noticed how people tended to give me a wide berth as I moved among them. They likely considered me a cutpurse. Or maybe it was the smell. I could not be sure, and I liked neither idea.

I made my way back toward the Seine. The worst tenements were located there, jammed tightly together just north of the stinking river. I only needed a room to myself to rejoin humanity, a place of solace and security. Giorgio's allowance was miserly, but I could make do.

Between Rue Saint-Denis and Rue Saint-Louis was a swath of the worst kind of dwellings. The streets were cramped and crowded. Horse and human waste piled up in places. Rubbish was everywhere. Very little sunlight penetrated the four- and five-story buildings placed so closely together. The thick, damp air stank of sweat and rot. Wind rarely visited these narrow winding streets. Puddles of standing water were everywhere. Cholera was one of the most common diseases in streets such as these. I was struck then how much the streets reminded me of Monsieur Anton and Madame's dining hall, but in place of bones and discarded dishes there were rats and feces.

7

FINDING A NEW HOME

August 17, 1814 AD

The poorest sections of Paris were populated by largely dilapidated tenements, but the condition of a building did not keep the poorest of poor from filling them to capacity. I knew firsthand almost anything was better than living on the streets. I inquired at several tenements about lodging. All were proclaimed full, but I got the distinct impression many of the landlords were unwilling to rent to me specifically. I avoided some tenements due to the advanced dilapidation evident. The war was still being felt in some portions of the city more than others. Twice I thought I might have found a room, but the way the landlords leered at me made me feel unsafe. Even though my mistress delighted in teaching such men the wisdom absent in their thoughts, I know that a wise woman avoids unwanted attention before it ever has a chance to become more. My mother had few lessons for me, but that one always felt true, and it has served me well.

Off Rue Sainte-Croix-de-la-Bretonnerie was a wide passage that ended in a sunlit cul-de-sac. I passed many such passages earlier in the day without consideration. Such locations were as likely to have a second exit as not. One should always have a way out, lest she find herself mugged or worse, but the sounds of children laughing and playing floated up the passage to my ears. I reasoned that where children lived happily, the place must be safe.

I thought twice about my assumption when I emerged from the passage into the sun. The tenement loomed over the cul-de-sac like Death tending her garden, waiting for a new crop of corpses. I shuddered as I considered how many of the gleeful children playing a game of tag and laughing in the cul-de-sac in front of me would be included in this year's crop? I did not know if I should laugh at the joy of seeing them play or weep at my premonition.

The doors of the tenement were recessed in a shallow alcove. Once painted white, years of collected grime left the doors an ashen gray. Someone had added darker lines that ran from the top to the bottom of the door, making the portal appear to be a set of devouring teeth. I approached, transfixed by the idea that the building might gobble me up.

"Horrendous."

"Excuse me," I said, looking around for the voice. I was so enraptured by the doors that I failed to notice an ancient lady sitting on top of a wooden box, just inside the shadows of the alcove. Her eyes were a piercing blue-gray. Her thick hair was absolutely white and pulled into a tight bun held secure by a bone or ivory comb that seemed more ancient than she. Her skin seemed to be simultaneously as thin as parchment and somehow carved from blotched stone.

"This vandalism," she said, waving a hand absently toward the doors. "Horrendous. Washing it only makes it worse."

She wore a tan wool shawl over a white blouse and had a patchwork quilt of blue and green over a dark wool skirt. Wool and quilt in the summer heat. I did not know what to think of that. She was probably the oldest person I had ever seen. Living, that is.

"Um, yes, mademoiselle," I said. I gave a quick, unpracticed curtsy.

She looked me up and down and seemed entirely unimpressed. "Who are you?"

I gave another quick curtsy, this one slightly less clumsy. "My name is Charlotte, madame. I've come looking for a place to stay."

"This is no orphanage or hostel. We do not take in homeless or strays. Everyone here helps out everyone else. I've got enough children to look after. I don't need one more."

I was more than a little annoyed. I was no longer a child even if I was not married or fully a woman yet. Why did everyone need to test me?

"I am not a child, madame. I am sixteen, I think. I have not been sure of the date for some time, honestly. But my birthday is soon regardless. I have money to pay for a room, and I can help as much as anyone."

The old lady stood and looked me up and down. She was no taller standing than she was sitting, maybe just over four feet tall. "We do not take prostitutes either."

Inwardly I screamed. "I am no prostitute. I am simply a young lady with precious little left in the world. I need a place to live while I look for work."

The old woman snorted and laughed. "If you are not a prostitute now, you will likely be one when the next rent comes around and you foolishly have spent all your money on distractions. Pretty soon you'll be hungry and taking strangers up to your room at all hours of the night being their distraction."

"That will not be happening," I said.

At least not for sex, my mistress said to me.

"Not for any reason!" I insisted.

My mistress laughed in my head while the old lady looked at me as if she were considering an asylum would be a better place for me. Eventually she gave me the rate. I could afford two months' rent up front. I could return to Giorgio's and get more later for some food. Maybe he would be so kind as to provide me some clothes as well, considering how much he stole from me in our transaction.

I started to take out my coins, when the old lady pressed her ice-cold hands against mine. She scanned the cul-de-sac with a frown.

"Not out here, girl. We'll go inside. Never let anyone see where you keep your money."

The little woman shoved against the wooden maw that towered above her. She waved me into the small foyer beyond the doors and turned to the children playing outside.

"Francois, watch the rest of the children until another adult, Theo, or I come back," she yelled out the door. The woman could have easily worked as a barker with that voice.

A boy I could not see gave a curt, "Yes ma'am," as she closed the door. The ancient woman then grabbed my arm as gently as a grandmother might hold a grandchild.

"I am Madame Lacelle, the manager here." She gestured to the hallway to her left as she guided me toward a set of stairs to the right. "Madame Rochelle on the ground floor serves breakfast three times a week plus Sunday. She barely charges anything, so even a poor waif such as yourself should be able to afford her meals—for a while. Just follow your nose and you'll find her. Assuming there isn't a line, that is."

We climbed stairs stained dark with the passage of time. A lighter, almost blond pair of spots adorned each step. Over the ages, the plodding of countless feet wore through to the wood's natural colors. The walls were a uniform shroud of chipped, once-white plaster over barely covered bones. One side of the stairwell had a handrail, the other side only had the metal braces to hold a handrail but nothing else. I came to find that more than one floor was missing one or both handrails. The boxed stair reminded me of a spiral squared. It proceeded straight up to a landing, turned right, and proceeded again straight up to the next floor, where a short hallway led left and right and a long hallway extended ahead.

We did not stop on the second floor and instead turned back around and took another set of stairs next to the ones we just climbed, repeating the process three more times. I was certain had I breath I would be panting, yet Madame Lacelle showed no signs of being winded.

"Bathwater is hauled up to each floor on the first Saturday of each month. Tenants that have been here the longest get their baths before the newer ones, assuming they want one. Almost half do not care for bathing. If you want a bath at any other time, you have to bring the water up yourself from the kitchens. You're in the attic, so you'll bathe with the tenants here on fourth floor."

"The attic?" I asked.

"If you want a place to stay, it's the only room I have. Most tenements are filled to the rafters with people. Attics are the cheapest of rooms. Not everyone has a steady income like Madame Rochelle and her kitchen. Most of our attic is reserved for storage, but we have one available room there. I cannot in good conscience put a family in there. It's too small. The stairs make an awful noise when climbed so a girl can remember to lock her door before someone gets to her room, and I can hear when a girl takes men up to her room for a bit of extra income. Understand?"

"Yes, madame. That will not be happening."

She glanced at me sideways and smirked, but said nothing more on that particular topic.

"There are some children on every floor. Most are on the second and third floors, so they usually gather there if not outside."

Madame Lacelle showed me the small bathing room just down the left hallway.

"Location is the same on every floor," she continued. "Always knock. And lock yourself in once you get inside. Some of the men here wouldn't mind stumbling in on a pretty young lady while she was disrobed. If you don't own any towels, you can rent one from me."

She then led me to a very narrow door at the end of the right hall. Behind the door was a narrow staircase ending in another door. The walls and interior were all painted red, though the paint was old and chipped in places, many places. The stairs were steep and just wide enough for a single person at a time. Madame Lacelle showed no sign of slowing and was halfway up the narrow stairs before I had fully taken in the space. The third step and every other one after made a horrible creaking noise. I imagined in the middle of the night, the entire house would be able to hear the racket.

We emerged into an attic that was bright in the midday light. I was surrounded by unpainted wood from ceiling to floor as flecks of light reflected off dust swirling everywhere in sight.

The left side of the attic was open to the far wall about thirty feet away. Open was a relative word, as the space was filled with all sorts of old furniture, trunks, cases, boxes, sacks of who knows what, and other rubbish accumulated over the course of a lifetime. Well, in this case maybe many ones' lifetimes. I could not imagine how some of the items stored here made it through the tiny stairs behind me, yet here they were.

On my right side was a wall over where I imagined the right hallway wall would be on the floors below. The wall enclosed the entire side from the tiny stairs down to a red brick wall. The wall was the only real color in the space with everything else black, white, or gray. Much of the gray was certainly due to a thick layer of dust over everything, including the air.

"My husband thought we could add more rooms up here and make a little more money back when we and not the Republic owned the property. We managed to section off five rooms on this side of the attic before the revolution threw everything on its ear."

"This side?"

Madame Lacelle flicked a disgusted hand toward the brick wall. "Yes. The wall surrounds the stove pipes from the rooms below. My husband's idea was that it would heat the attic in the winter, and he was right. It helps with the cold up here. The problem is that people cook in the summer too, makes things damned unpleasant at times. The other side has been sealed off for years."

The wall to the right was lined with open doors spaced ten to twenty feet apart. We walked past open doorways toward the red brick wall in the back. Each room had a single dirt-encrusted dormer and was filled with a neater collection of junk and dust than in the open space to my left. Dust motes swirled in these rooms every bit as much as in the open space, and I noticed Madame Lacelle pull her shawl closer to her despite the heat.

"Only the last one has a door. It's also the only one with a stove. You have space for a bed, armoire, and maybe a table and chair."

"So my room is right next to this wall that makes the attic so hot during the summer?"

Madame Lacelle snorted. "You don't have to stay here. But you seem like you would do just fine. You aren't even sweating. Most folk come up here and drip sweat. If it gets too hot, open a couple windows and get a cross draft. Or come downstairs until the sun drops."

I nodded. "Temperatures do not seem to bother me like they do other people, yet you seem to have a chill."

Madame Lacelle fumbled with a massive keyring that she procured from somewhere deep within her skirts. She found a specific key and unlocked the door to my new room.

"I'm old," she said as she opened the door. "I haven't been warm in years. I'll probably be dead within a few more, and I won't have to worry about it."

"I do not like such talk," I said as I followed her into the small space beyond the door.

Madame Lacelle smirked. "That's life, girl. You live. You die. Everything else is chance and what you make of it. So do what you can and make something out if it, eh?"

I smiled wanly but said nothing more on the subject.

The room was small and particularly empty except for a small bedside table, a stove, a small wood slat box next to the stove, and a bed frame with no mattress. Oh, and there was dust. Everywhere. The dormer window had a beautiful view of Paris, or at least that is what I imagined. The glass was too filthy to see through.

"If you want to rent some furniture, that's extra, as is bedding," she said.

I smirked as if I was unsure if I would rent the space or not. "The place is filthy, and why is the mattress extra? Give me a mattress to use and a table and chairs, and I won't complain about the extra heat."

Madame Lacelle gave me a level look and said nothing for several seconds.

"The rent is the rent. I do not haggle, young lady."

I could not help but smile slightly. "Everyone haggles. Maybe you have simply forgotten how."

Madame Lacelle barked a quick laugh that she followed up with a spastic round of rough coughing.

"You've got some tits on you, girl. The rent is the rent, but if you clean up the rest of the attic, get things organized and cleaned up, you can use what you find. At least until someone paying needs it."

I was smiling from ear to ear, or at least it felt like it.

"First," I said, "I am afraid I lack any significant... breasts, not that a lady discusses such things, but I think I know what you mean. Second, may I ask you for the date? I cannot seem to remember."

The old lady gave me a quizzical look and then seemed to brush off the question.

"It is August seventeenth in the old calendar. I haven't learned the new one yet. Don't think I ever will."

"Ah, I am sixteen then, by three days."

"Happy birthday, demoiselle," Madame Lacelle said.

I gave Madame my finest curtsy yet.

"I will take the room," I said, taking out my coins and counting them to pay the two months' rent. This time she accepted the coins, counting them again even though I knew she counted them as I did the first time. "I am also going to need a bath sooner than two weeks."

"I am happy you are aware. Some people refuse to acknowledge that cleanliness is next to Godliness. When you are ready, find me. I'll show you where we keep everything." With that, she handed me the key. Neither of us spoke as I walked her to the attic door. The stairs to the floor below complained intermittently as she descended.

I reentered the room, my room, and placed my satchel made from scavenged cloth on the table. The wood box near the stove still had some wood within it. I set that aside and brought the box over to the small bedside table. I sat on the upside-down box like a chair, much like Madame Lacelle's seat near the door. Knowing the date allowed me to add it to my first diary entry and this one.

I decided to postpone an immediate bath so that I could return to the tunnels to get my trunk. Then I would clean some of the attic to free it of some of the dust. I needed something that resembled furniture, and until I could sort and clean the attic, I had nothing else to add to the room but my trunk. Also the blankets would make something that resembled a bed until I could find a mattress in the mess, if I could find one.

For the first time in close to two years, I no longer lived on the streets—or under them. Granted, the room I was renting was as hot today as it would be cold four months from now, and everything was covered a thick layer of dust. My only real security came from squeaky stairs and a lock on a door that upon closer inspection sat very loosely in its frame. Yet despite it all, it was lovely. As temporary as it might be, I was going to enjoy this time of relative luxury and see where I could go from here.

8

THE STRONGMAN

August 18, 1814 AD

I met Marcel today on the Rue du Roi-de-Sicile as I dragged my trunk from its old hiding spot in the catacombs and toward my new home. I was near Rue des Écouffes when I first noticed him. His approach was timid, with hands together and his body stooped to bring his eyes lower and closer to mine.

"If you would like, demoiselle, I would be honored if you allowed me to carry your trunk for you," he said.

His voice was not quite a whisper but loud enough to be heard over the general hum of the city. It was an odd volume, because he was one of the largest men I had ever seen. He looked like a strong man from the circus my father once took me to. His head was completely bald, and he wore too-short pants with a shirt with wide red-and-white stripes across his broad chest. I doubted he had an ounce of fat on his body.

He would be tough to eat, but you would be stronger for it, my mistress said.

I became aware of the man's scent suddenly. He smelled of musk and oil, and it made my mouth water. I frowned.

"I mean no disrespect, demoiselle, but a young lady such as yourself… in the streets…"

The trunk was not particularly heavy, but it was too large for me to easily wrap my arms around or otherwise get a good grip. I imagined him throwing it up on his shoulder and trotting away with all my worldly possessions before I knew what was happening.

"No thank you, monsieur. I have this well in hand," I said and continued.

The long, continuous scrape of the trunk against the dirt and stone of the street rang in my ears louder than before, until it was altogether absent. I looked behind me to see the large man holding the leather handle on the other end of the trunk.

"Oh my," he said, eyes wide.

"What?"

"A little thing like you dragging this much weight around the city, with no help. I'm impressed."

"I don't know what you mean. It is not that heavy," I retorted as I stopped walking.

The man's eyes widened further. "It's easily forty pounds, if not more."

"Forty pounds is not an extravagant weight," I said. I had assumed the trunk weighed no more than two or three pounds. I remembered being somewhat surprised it had been so light at first but thought nothing of it after. "A mother might carry her child long after that child has gotten to twenty pounds or more. And I am dragging the trunk, not carrying it."

"Well, let me help. I saw you at Lacelle's tenement earlier today. I assume you are a new tenant, no? That's where I am going now. We can share a burden even if it is a light one. If you don't mind the help, that is."

I smiled again and quoted my father, "Daylight burns as surely as candles."

"Indeed it does. Shall we?"

I had to admit the trip went much faster, and my poor trunk avoided more abuse. As we walked, the man introduced himself and explained that he lived on the second floor with his wife and children.

"Occasionally I help out around the tenement in exchange for an extra room. My wife, Nicole, and I have six children."

"Oh my," I said. "Six?"

"Oui. We are unsure, but it may be seven soon."

I could only laugh.

Marcel's voice sounded like he was smiling as he continued. "Our eldest is twelve, and the youngest but two."

I chastised myself for being unable to feed my single mouth when this man must constantly worry on how to feed seven, perhaps soon to be eight, more than his own.

We got to the tenement about a quarter hour later. Four of the dozen or more children playing in the cul-de-sac called out to Marcel. Marcel waved back with one hand.

"Papa," a little girl of maybe six called out. "Papa, come play with us."

"I am helping Demoiselle Charlotte here," he called back. "I will see you inside shortly. It's about time for Mamma to call for dinner."

"Awwww." The little girl pouted and kicked at nothing in particular.

"I'll tell you a story before bed to make it up to you, ma petite chou."

The little girl's face brightened with a smile as only one so young can have.

"Yes, Papa. Thank you, Papa," she said before turning and running away.

"She is adorable," I said as we resumed into the tenement.

"She's smart too. She gets both from her mother. Already she can read better than me. I have to make up new stories every week or two because she's read both of our books several times already."

"Amazing. I was an early reader, but I was nine before I was reading on my own. Of course, by that time I was reading everything I could get my hands on. My father used to say..." I couldn't finish the sentence.

"He used to say?" Marcel asked.

"Nothing. I... I cannot remember."

We climbed four flights of stairs in silence.

"Charlotte, I'm sorry if..." Marcel started to say, but I cut him off.

"It is fine. There are things... things I just do not like to remember these days. Sometimes I cannot, even when I want to."

"Then I shall never again mention it. What room are you in? I thought the fifth floor was full."

It took a moment for me to clear my thoughts well enough to answer the change in topic.

"I am in the attic."

"That dusty hotbox?"

"Yup."

"What did Madame Lacelle offer you to clean the space?"

I stopped and turned to look at Marcel. He had a knowing look that rested somewhere between annoyance and humor.

"I get to use whatever I find and clean that someone else does not need."

Marcel made an *O* of his mouth, and his eyebrows climbed. "She must like you."

I could only shrug. "I do not know. She seems to think I will turn to prostitution before a month or two have passed."

Marcel laughed.

I was impressed the stairs between the fifth floor and the attic actually held Marcel's massive form. He had to shuffle sideways up the steps to keep from being squeezed by the walls. We set the trunk in front of my room as Marcel began to sneeze.

"I have to go," he said between sneezes. "If you need help..." He could not finish. His eyes had begun to flood with tears, and snot was pouring from his nose.

"Yes, yes. Go before you die up here," I told him, and the man was gone.

"Why don't I sneeze?" I asked the air around me.

Because you are not alive, my mistress said.

"What does that have to do with anything?"

The living sneeze because the body thinks something is in your olfactory system that must be expelled, she said.

"And so now that I am... like this, I will not sneeze ever again? Very good."

You are in grave danger if you ever do sneeze, my mistress said.

I tried asking her several times what she meant, but that was all I got from her. So with nothing else to do and no one to talk to, I unlocked my room and pulled my trunk inside.

9

THE NEW WIDOW

August 18, 1814 AD

I wanted to bathe right away but still needed to clean as much of the dust and dirt from the attic as possible first. The windows on the opposite side of the attic were inaccessible until I cleaned a path through the items piled on that side of the space. The remaining windows on my side were all jammed. I was able to open the window in my room and the one in the first room from the stairs. There was a nice breeze blowing across the building, but it did not want to enter the dusty attic. If I leaned out of the window, the wind brought clean smells and relative coolness. I paused a moment to sit in the dormer window in my room, where I leaned out and gazed upon the city.

My view looked to the west. The tenement was one of the tallest in the city, almost scraping the sky at five stories. Most of the surrounding buildings were a story shorter. And the view was as beautiful as I had imagined. Better, for it was real.

After a few minutes of relaxation and quiet contemplation, I got to work. I went downstairs with a bucket I found in the attic. Madame Lacelle had one of the children, Robert, show me to the well. It was inside and was accessed with a pump which, despite being in the basement, was a luxury I did not expect in this section of the city. Most people acquired water from one of the few fountains in the city or, God forbid, the Seine. I filled the bucket and proceeded to leave a thin, spattering trail from pump to attic.

I did not know what to use for rags. My clothes were out of the question. I was loath to shred the blankets, and the burial cloth I was using for my bag I feared would fall apart. I set upon looking through the trunks, baskets, and piles. I found a moth-eaten tablecloth that was more rag than my repurposed burial cloth, but the weave seemed tight enough to keep its many-holed shape when wet. I ripped it into four roughly equal sizes of cloth.

I cleaned my room first, wiping dust off every surface and setting it to the wind. Then I attacked every surface again with a wet cloth. Mother would have been proud. Well... Mother from before would have been proud. I repeated the process for the separate rooms without doors. Once I started to sort and pile things, I would have to do more cleaning. It could not be helped.

I was on my hands and knees scrubbing the floor when the stairs creaked loudly. I stopped mid-scrub, frozen in place, and looked toward the door. My eyes were wide as I considered if I should run and hide. Several creaks later, the knob of the door rattled. The door protested, groaning as it was forced open, and golden light spilled into the room. Light-blinded, I could not see anything but light and dark.

A woman's scream ripped through the attic. The door slammed shut, cutting much of the scream. Heavy footsteps and creaking boards followed. With the light gone, my vision returned and I saw that it had become dark without my realizing. There would be questions, so I wrung out my rags, placed the wet ones on the edge of the bucket, stood, and wiped my hands dry with another rag.

I had tied my hair back with a strip from one of the rags before I started on the floor, and I considered letting my hair down. I decided instead to keep it up. Maintaining the appearance of being hard at work would help ensure whomever had come up into the attic of what I was doing. At least that was my intention.

I followed the screams out of the attic and down the stairs. When I got to the fifth floor, I noticed many doors open. Most people stared through the cracks made between the door and wall. One man clad only in underpants and shirt stood in the hallway with a stout stick in hand.

"Do you know who screamed?" I asked the man with the stick.

"I do not. I came out just a few seconds before you came down. Is there any danger? Are you hurt?"

"No, I am fine. I was cleaning the attic when the door opened. Someone entered with a light, and it blinded me. I did not see who it was, but she screamed and ran away."

Some of the doors opened wider, and a few people entered the hallway. The man in this underclothes lowered the stick slightly, but he did not look like he was ready to let it go entirely yet.

A boy of ten or so ran up the stairs and stopped short as he saw us gathered there. He spoke to me with a questioning tone. "Madame Charlotte?"

"Oui," I said.

The boy's face relaxed. "Madame Lacelle sent me to get you. It seems Madame Rounsaville has had a bit of a fright. She seems really mad."

"Madame Rounsaville?" I asked.

"No, sorry, ma'am. Madame Lacelle. She seems to think you scared Madame Rounsaville on purpose. I think she wants to yell at you. Um. Madame Lacelle, that is, not Madame Rounsaville. I think she's crying."

"You scared Madame Rounsaville?" the man with the stick asked. He grasped the stick a little harder as he spoke and took a half step in my direction.

"No." There must have been something to my conviction, because the man did not move any further. "I would not. I was cleaning when she came up, I swear. I… I will go see Madame Lacelle and Madame Rounsaville."

The man with the stick relaxed a little again. "You do that. And don't start shit in our tenement, or we'll throw you out. Understand?"

I dipped my head to the man in acknowledgment before turning to the boy. "Take me to Madame Lacelle, s'il vous plaît."

The boy simply turned and dashed down the stairs. He was almost to the first turn before I started. I refused to run, though I did walk quickly. The boy bounced on the balls of his feet at each landing as he waited on me. He never waited long for me, but the impatience on his face suggested otherwise.

Madame Lacelle's room was on the first floor, a benefit of being the tenement manager, I guessed. The boy did not knock, he simply opened the door and walked in, leaving it open behind him.

"Grand-mère," I heard him call. "Madame Charlotte is here."

I walked into the apartment and marveled at how full it was. Almost every space held a piece of furniture. Every piece of furniture not made for sitting was covered with some sort of cloth or doily. Every cloth or doily was covered with some small trinket, a stack of books, or a small portrait. The room contained what I thought must be a lifetime of memories.

The boy stood in an open doorway in the wall to my right. I could hear Madame Lacelle speaking.

"Thank you, mon coeur. Now be on your way." Madame Lacelle's voice came from the other room. Just as the boy was about to dash away, she added, "And tell your parents their rent is overdue."

The boy zipped through the room so quickly I was afraid he would crash into something and begin a series of additional crashes that left the entire room in ruins. He seemed blessed with the luck many of his age had, however, and he dodged every potential collision within a fraction of an inch. Having grown beyond the age where such luck was possible, I took my time walking through the room to the door.

The room beyond was nearly as sparse as the room I stood in was filled. There was a small bed, a trunk, a nightstand, a table with a few chairs, a stove, and a cabinet. There was currently a fire in the stove that surely made the room far too warm in the late summer, but it allowed Madame Lacelle to wear only a few layers of clothes. Her shawl hung from a peg on the wall near where I stood, and what

I thought was a larger shawl that she wore under the one currently hanging from the peg was actually a quilt that draped across her bed.

Madame Lacelle sat at the table with another woman. I assumed this was Madame Rounsaville. She was a slight older woman, though next to Madame Lacelle she seemed positively young. Her clothes were rather fine for the neighborhood, and she held herself with a quiet confidence. Both held teacups though no kettle rested on the table. Instead they shared a bottle of brandy.

I curtsied rather clumsily. “You wished to see me, madame?”

“Yes,” Madame Lacelle said as she set down her cup.

Madame Rounsaville’s cup began to clatter against the saucer she held in her other hand. Brandy splashed over the lip of the cup to land in the saucer. She took a long sip of the brandy before setting cup and saucer down on the table.

“Madame Rounsaville says that you scared her,” Madame Lacelle said.

I was just about to object when Madame Rounsaville said, “No, Veronica. I said that I went to the attic to meet our new tenant, and I saw a monster. This girl, she was there too, but she was not what caused me to scream.”

Madame Lacelle turned to look at me again.

“You have someone up in the attic with you already? I told you no prostitution in my tenement.”

“What? No!” I demanded. “I was cleaning, alone. There was no one with me.”

Madame Rounsaville chimed in again. “Yes, she was cleaning, but she was not alone. I saw... something, standing over her like an evil shadow, just waiting.”

Madame Lacelle sighed heavily before turning to speak to me.

“I am sorry, girl. Ysabel, Madame Rounsaville, has a habit of seeing spirts.”

“It is true,” Madame Rounsaville said. “They are everywhere. Many don’t even seem to notice us. A few do, but almost none of them care.”

"So what was so different about this one?" I asked from the doorway.

Madame Rounsaville shuddered. "This was no normal spirit. It was monstrous like some creature intent on devouring the world. And it stood over you waiting, but I did not know for what."

Madame Lacelle shook her head and took a long drink of brandy. When she set the cup down, she frowned at her friend. I thought she was going to speak to her, but instead she turned to me.

"Come in and sit down, girl. It is impolite to stand when others are sitting and drinking tea."

That got me to smile, but I did as told. I was just pulling my chair forward as Madame Rounsaville gasped and cast her eyes down to her cup. She trembled even more than before.

"Madame?" I asked just as Madame Lacelle spoke. Worry and annoyance laced her voice.

"Bel, what is it now?"

Madame Rounsaville took a couple seconds before she pointed an unsteady finger toward the doorway I had vacated. Madame Lacelle and I both turned to look at the doorway, but nothing was there.

"I do not see anything," I said to the frightened woman.

"For God's sake, Ysabel," Madame Lacelle said. "Stop this at once."

But Madame Rounsaville did not stop. Instead, her head snapped up as if to look at something just over my shoulder. Her face drained of all color, and she threw herself backward. Her chair clattered across the floor as Madame Rounsaville fell. When she landed, she continued to push herself further and further back, never taking her eyes off the spot just above my shoulder. When her back struck Madame Lacelle's bed, she pushed herself up and onto the bed to the very corner of the room that the bed sat in. Tears welled up in her eyes, and a low moan pushed its way out of her chest.

Madame Lacelle and I stood, she faster than me I am sorry to admit. I took a step toward Madame Rounsaville to comfort her, but as soon as I did, her eyes grew even wider. Instead I held my spot at the table as Madame Lacelle moved to her friend.

"It embraces her," Madame Rounsaville said. "It claims her for itself. It wants to eat everything. Every… one. It is so hungry. Its mouth is full of so many teeth, too many. But it cannot eat without her."

Madame Rounsaville pointed directly at me and then looked into my eyes. Her eyes then shifted back to the space above my shoulder and then back to me. She did this three more times before she gasped.

"What is it?" Madame Lacelle asked.

"They have the same eyes."

A chill raced up my spine, and the hair on the nape of my neck stood on end. What did she mean we had the same eyes?

"You have invited the devil into your house, Veronica."

It took Madame Lacelle several seconds to respond, but when she did, gone was any look of uncertainty or fear. The stern look behind her eyes belied her tone when she next spoke. Her voice was calm and reassuring.

"Charlotte dear, please wait for me in the other room," she said without taking her eyes from Madame Rounsaville.

I gave a tiny curtsy and returned to the extremely full antechamber. Madame Lacelle spoke to her friend in hushed tones, but I could hear her all the same.

"Has it gone, Bel?"

Nothing.

"Good. I am going to go talk with Charlotte. Then I'll come back and we can talk some more."

Wood creaked followed by a slow shuffle of feet. Madame Lacelle entered the doorway and shooed me out into the hall with one hand. She gave a glance back at her friend before following me. As she closed the door, the sound of sobbing came from the bedroom beyond the antechamber.

Madame Lacelle's face turned very soft then. Tears glistened in her eyes.

"She went up to your room to welcome you. I think she also hoped you might have uncovered an old portrait of hers that she's been swearing was in that attic for a decade now. She was so excited to both meet you and look around for that stupid painting that she refused to wait until daylight like I insisted. Instead, this happened. I'm afraid my dear friend's mind is ruined," she said.

No, my mistress said in response, though only I could hear. *She sees better than anyone else you know.*

I shivered again, and Madame Lacelle only nodded, misunderstanding what I was reacting to.

"She's had spells like this before," Madame Lacelle continued, "but never this bad. I may need to change my bedding she is so scared."

Then her voice hardened as she realized what she just said, "Tell no one about that part or I'll throw you out on your ear and not think twice of it. Understand?"

I nodded, eyes wide.

"Well," Madame Lacelle continued with a softer voice once again, "I'm going to write her nephew. In the past when she's had a bad spell, he would take her to live with him in the country for a few weeks. It calms her down. Until then, do what you can to avoid the second floor. It shouldn't take more than a few days before he comes and gets her."

"Yes, ma'am," was all I could muster. My thoughts swirled as I considered what Madame Rounsaville said she saw in light of my mistress's comment. If what she saw was true, I was not free of the monster at all.

I told you I would always be with you, my mistress said.

"If anyone asks, just say she's had one of her spells. Most people will understand. Those that don't... well, just tell them to come see me about it. That'll shut them up."

I smiled.

"Good girl. Now be off with you. I have a friend to console and a letter to write. I might have to bring out the good brandy now."

I almost laughed but hid my reaction in a clumsy curtsy before turning to go back up to my room. The sobbing was still audible when Madame Lacelle went back into her room. Poor Madame Rounsaville, she did not deserve such fear.

Her fear is natural. Such fear is what keeps lesser beings alive when the courageously blind are devoured.

That is a brutal view of the world, I thought to my mistress.

She laughed then said, *Nature is brutal. Mankind likes to think itself above the natural order of things, but it isn't even your reality's ultimate predator. How can humans be the stewards of this world when they are not even its master? They should all be as scared as that "poor" woman. She is gifted with wisdom and sight. Knowledge is her curse. Fear is the only intelligent response.*

"What is our ultimate predator?" I asked after several seconds of consideration.

Their ultimate predator, not yours, for their ultimate predator is you. You have no predators.

I had more questions, but it seemed my mistress said all that she desired.

When I reached the fifth floor, several people were still milling about, including the man with the stick. All eyes fell upon me expectantly. At first my mind was still cluttered with the things my mistress had said, but then finally, Madame Lacelle's words came back to me.

"Madame Lacelle said that Madame Rounsaville had one of her spells."

Several people, including the man with the stick, nodded their heads or made "oh" shapes with their mouths. Then, one by one, each returned to their rooms. The man with the stick turned before entering his apartment and gestured to the stick.

"Sorry about..." he said before shrugging.

"You look out for your own," I said in return. "I just hope one day if I needed someone to defend me, you might be there with your stick."

The man reddened slightly as he gave me a grateful look. His was the last door to close, or so I thought. I turned toward the attic door, when a teenaged boy came out of his apartment and cleared his throat.

Before he spoke, I said, “Madame Lacelle said that if you have more questions, you can ask her directly.”

The boy blanched slightly as his face soured. I laughed as he turned and all but ran back to his apartment.

“She said you have to go ask Madame...” he said to someone in his apartment as the door closed. I laughed and made my way alone to my room. Well physically alone, that is.

10

A ROGUE IN THE BATH

August 19, 1814 AD

Seventeen. That's how many buckets of water it takes to fill a tub. Five was the number of flights of stairs I carried each one, and then five flights of stairs down to refill. Thirteen was the number of steps per flight. Father trained me at maths at a young age. If I was ever to help with the business. I know my numbers, and I'll often work through number problems when doing monotonous work. So I did the math. I decided not to count the final trip down since I would then be bathed. Therefore, the cost of one bath in the middle of the month was two thousand one hundred forty-five steps up and down.

It was worth every one.

The attic was now spotless. It took four days and several buckets of water before I could declare the space dust- and dirt-free. I still needed to sort through decades of clutter, but I pulled everything away from the walls and cleared an area in the main attic space to sort things out on the floor. The sorting would be a relatively clean job, so I did not fear getting too dirty during that portion of the work.

I expected to be exhausted before I finished filling the tub, but I was not. I did notice that I was hungrier after the exertion, however. Since my emergence from the catacombs, I tried to continue to eat.

Most of my meager meals had very little taste, and nothing since my mistress made me attack poor Luc had done anything at all for the slowly building ache in my stomach. The hunger did not gnaw at me like before I met Vincent. Instead there was simply an absence, a void that needed to be filled in a way that could only be satisfied with one particular thing. What could I eat that would satisfy me?

Flesh!

Was that my mistress's voice in my head or my own? My mistress gave me no clues. How long would it be until I was starving again and she would force herself upon me to force me to feed?

I willed my thoughts from my mistress and the small but growing void in my stomach and surveyed the fruit of my labor. The tub was positioned near the middle of the smallish room, offset slightly so that it was closer to the room's only window. There was a basin, a large white porcelain bowl, chipped and stained with the passage of time, on top of a small dark cabinet close to the door. A small table sat against the wall opposite the basin. Across from the door hung a small soaped-over window that allowed some light in but prevented unwanted eyes from prying. It seemed an unreasonable precaution since those eyes would have to be on the rooftop of the building across the street.

Madame Lacelle told me to dump the bathwater out the window after I was done. The seventeen buckets that traveled up five flights of stairs would become seventeen buckets of dirty water thrown out of the window. I could not wait and wondered if I would splash anyone below when I did.

I disrobed and even untied the bindings around the hooks still lodged in my legs. I wondered if the wounds would bleed. There had been no bleeding since I emerged from the catacombs, so I doubted they would.

"Do I even have liquid blood in my veins anymore?" I wondered.

It was a question that I could not answer, so I put it aside, climbed in the tub, and began to wash.

Before my trek of seventeen buckets, Madame Lacelle gave me a small bit of soap. "This one is free. The next piece of soap costs two sou, but you will get a larger piece, good for three or four months."

The soap was harsh, which was good because I was filthy. I could not really feel any sting it had, and I needed to get as clean as possible. My legs did not bleed at all, which I found somewhat saddening in a way. Dirt and dried blood melted into water from almost every part of my body. I scrubbed everything I could reach. Soon the water was filthy, but after I stood and poured my last bucket of water over my head and into the tub, I was clean.

I tied up my hooks, donned my clothes, and was about to open the window to throw out the dirty water when I noticed that my unwashed clothes were pungent. So I once again disrobed and knelt between the window and the tub to wash my clothes in the bathwater. I was positioned like that and bent over the side of the tub while scrubbing my clothes with the remainder of the soap when he walked in.

He was thin like everyone under the age of twenty that called the tenement home, but he was also tall. His black hair was wild, but his dark eyes were calm. He stood there staring at me. I was frozen as I stared back. I wondered why anyone would wear light-colored pants with a dark brown shirt before I realized that I was naked.

Naked with giant metal hooks piercing my legs.

Blessedly my position concealed my legs, but it did nothing for everything above my navel. I lifted whatever I was currently washing to cover my exposed chest.

"Unusual choice of garments to cover yourself with," he said while leering.

He made no effort to close the door, much less leave.

I looked down, and to my horror I was covering my chest with my small clothes. First Madame and now this rogue. Who else was going to see my undergarments before the year was over?

I wanted to slap the man and push him back out of the room, but to do so would have exposed me fully in more than one way, so instead I concealed myself better behind the tub and put my small clothes back in the water.

"Get out of here! Can you not see I am bathing?"

I was trying to appear angry, authoritarian, ladylike, and not at all smitten. I failed on all accounts. Instead of leaving, he opened the door fully and leaned against the doorjamb. Leaned! As if he had no care in the world.

"You aren't bathing," he replied simply.

He even had the gall to smirk. Well, it was more like a smile. I cursed myself for liking it as much as I cursed him for being technically correct. I hated that I was woefully untrained in dealing with boys. I was baffled by his lazy charm and self-awareness. His calm made me nervous, and when he looked away, a small part of me wished he had not. I was flustered and incapable of a good solid argument, and I hated myself for it.

"Of course I am! I am in the bath room, naked, and wet. What would you consider that I am doing?"

His smile bloomed fully then. Oh how I hated him. Him and that beautiful smile.

"I could think of a thing or two to explain why a girl might be naked and wet in a closed room, but a girl isn't usually alone at such times."

I must admit, I completely missed his meaning until later. I really do not know how I would have reacted. In my naiveté I grasped for reasons why a woman might be randomly wet and naked while in a room with other people. I found none.

"Theo Comte!" Madame Lacelle barked from somewhere in the hallway. "What are you doing spying on young Charlotte?"

The rogue, Theo apparently, jumped and ducked out of the room. He expertly dodged a quick jab from the ancient tenement manager and ran away, giggling.

Giggling!

On his way down the hall, Theo yelled back, "It was nice seeing... I mean meeting you, Demoiselle Charlotte."

Madame Lacelle shook her head toward the retreating Theo and then turned and pointed a sinuous, bony finger in my direction. She was mad, and she was mad at me.

"I told you to lock this door," she said as she closed the door behind her with a modicum more force than was required. "A young lady must always be wary. The likes of him are sometimes all bluster and show. Sometimes they are not. You don't want your first time to be at the point of a knife, do you?"

I shrank down a little with every word she hurled at me.

"No, ma'am," I said.

"Then you lock this damned door and every door between you and them every time you can. You understand?"

"Yes, ma'am."

"Good," Madame Lacelle said softly. "I brought you a towel. When you are done, leave it on the basin. I'll collect it later. This time the towel is free, but in the future it costs one sou to rent a towel on wash day, two any other day."

I laughed and asked, "Why does it cost more on other days?"

"I just don't want to wash them any other day. If you make me work harder, I make you pay extra."

I could not argue that point.

"So does everything cost extra here?"

Madame Lacelle just looked at me as if I were an idiot before saying, "Of course, child, that is life. Everything has a cost. If you don't pay with money, you pay with something more dear."

And with that she put the towel on the basin table and then closed the door behind her as she exited.

"Lock this door," she said from the other side.

Alone at last, I got up and did just that. I could hear her retreating down the stairs after I locked the door. She waited and protected me from Theo and those like him, and from my own innocence, before leaving.

I lifted the towel and smelled it. It was stiff but smelled of lavender, and a bit like lilacs too. The smells were only pleasant because I had good memories tied to them. My new condition seemed to make the fragrance less than pleasant, more neutral. I did not want to smell good for myself but for everyone else. It would be difficult to return to the real world if I constantly smelled of death.

I was dressing into my damp clothes when I heard someone try the door again. I yelled that the room was occupied, and the noise stopped. There was no apology or indication of who it was. I suspected that Theo was back and trying to get another look. Well, that was not going to happen. Probably. Definitely not without my permission.

When I returned to my room, I locked the door behind me. I spent the afternoon in front of my single window lying on the floor drying. As the sun progressed across the sky and the light moved across my floor, I simply rolled with it. I felt more alive than I had in weeks, maybe years.

It was a good day.

11

A GRANTED WISH

August 21, 1814 AD

I walked the northeast side of Paris the entire day yesterday. I stopped at more places than I could count to ask about work. No one was hiring, not even the places advertising help wanted. I knew not if it was due to my clothes, hair, or demeanor, but no one wanted to talk with me for more than a minute or two. Some seemed to physically relax as I left.

Monsieur Bordelon was my first inquiry. While he was more than happy to provide me a bit of aging food for the occasional light help, he could not afford to actually pay anyone. Things were simply too tight. I knew he could not help me, but I felt obligated to ask, as if not asking would be an insult. I felt bad for the man and did not wish to add insult to injury. His wife and son were supposed to be helping him, but I never saw either. If money was no object, I would work for him for free and count myself blessed. I needed a paying job, however, so I continued my search.

The absolute worst response I received was from the maître d' of the café La Plénitude de Vie. He was a thin, stiff man of unreasonable height made taller by his manner of looking down his nose toward me. He stopped me before I could even enter the café. His crisp clean black-and-white suit of razor-sharp lines was somehow every bit as dangerous as his gaze. He told me in low condescension that I could not afford a glass of water at the establishment, much less anything to eat. I brushed off his attitude with a calm grace that surprised me.

"I am aware, monsieur, and that is also why I am here. I see your placard just there..." I pointed toward the window. His contemptuous stare did not waver from me. "... advertising help wanted. If I can read the small writing from here, it even says you need a young lady willing to work any hours. That young lady, monsieur, is me."

"This place and..." he drew out the *and* as if continuing to speak to me was painful. "... any activity herein, be it consumer, server, or scullery, is not for the... likes... of you."

His words, his manner, his contempt struck me dumb. Before I could speak again, he turned and entered the café. The door closed with a significant slap of wood upon wood and the gentle tingle of a bell. He was immediately all smiles as he spoke to a woman. The woman held no better status or bearing than anyone else in the seventh arrondissement. Or was I in the sixth or eighth? It mattered not. The woman was little better off than I, yet he fawned over her. As if reading my mind, he turned to make eye contact with me through the glass. He cast a wicked scowl in my direction and removed the placard with a violent flourish before disappearing into the interior.

I was so furious I was tempted to scream at the man. I wanted to barge into the stupid café and tell everyone how vile he was to me. I wanted to show them all the truth of this wicked man who served them coffee and scones. I wanted him to be scandalized, to feel the embarrassment of the kind of mistreatment that he just inflicted upon me. Then as my rage peaked, I simply wished him dead.

I felt, not heard, a large bell ring in the distance. 'Dooooooooooom,' it chimed.

Done, my mistress said, pleased.

I staggered backward and almost fell. One of my hands massaged my temple as my other held me up and steadied me against the railing outside of the café. Once the bell stopped echoing through my head, I stumbled away and willed my thoughts to clarify.

"What do you mean, 'done'?" I asked as I mindlessly wandered down the street.

Just as I said. I am fulfilling your wish. A good mistress should do that on occasion for her servants.

"I do not really want him dead. Not really," I insisted, apparently out loud because a woman near me gasped.

When I looked up, several people were looking in my direction. One woman held her children close as she made the sign of the cross in my direction before she shuffled away.

I fled the scene.

When I was no longer near any immediate witnesses, I reasserted my desires toward my mistress, but she was no longer listening. Or perhaps she just was not responding. Not only would I need to learn to watch my mouth, I would also have to learn to watch my thoughts as well.

I started to fear for my safety as night approached. My mistress said that I was now the ultimate predator of mankind, but I did not want that. I ran home instead of risking the night, risking my mistress's monster showing up to save me. It took close to an hour to find my way back to the tenement. I actually passed the tenement at least once. I found Bordelon's grocery first and worked my way back to solace.

I wondered why I was not exhausted or even breathing hard when I finally ended my run. Well, I was not breathing at all in fact. I did not breathe unless I actively thought about it.

I climbed the stairs toward my room, when somewhere between the third and fourth floors I realized that I was significantly more hungry. Days passed without my hunger changing regardless of what I did or did not eat. Yet after my run, my hunger was much more pronounced. Finally, I saw the form of my existence.

If I did not exert myself, I could go for days, maybe longer, without needing to eat. A poor living girl on the street might wish for such a blessing. Conversely, exertion increased my hunger. I theorized that if I managed my exertion properly, I would also manage my hunger, and therefore I could manage my discomfort. I planned to avoid eating what my mistress suggested—people—so I knew I would always be hungry. I had a unique advantage, however. My life of starvation and want before my death prepared me for the constant emptiness within.

That is not accurate, though you inadvertently speak at least one truth, my mistress said to me as I wrote these words.

I tried to ask her what the truth was, but she chose to be the enigma again.

Eventually I would have to eat something. What it would be and how I might acquire it disturbed me.

I lay on my cot of blankets on the floor with my eyes closed, when the steps up to the attic screamed in alarm. I wore only my small clothes, so I bolted up and dressed quickly. I just finished pulling my blouse over my head when there was a knock on my door.

"Oui?" I asked.

Madame Lacelle's muted voice answered. "A package came to you this morning. A big man delivered it with a note. Said it was your order for you."

"For me?" I asked as I tucked everything in place. "I did not order anything."

"That's what I said. For you." The door could not mute Madame Lacelle's irritation.

I opened it, not quite properly prepared, to see the little woman holding a large package wrapped in brown paper and string.

"You answer the door looking like that, girl, and you will only draw the wrong type of attention."

"I knew it was you."

"There could have been men with me."

"You would have told me," I said as I took the package and moved past Madame Lacelle.

I set the package down on a round table in the main attic space.

The string holding the package together was tied with a series of slipknots.

"You've done good work in here, girl," Madame Lacelle said as I unwrapped the package. "I think Marcel could come up here now."

I remembered the strongman's sneezing fit when he helped me with my trunk, and smiled. My smile disappeared completely when I finally opened the package.

I almost fainted.

The package contained what must have been thirty pounds of red meat in a variety of odd cuts. My eyes bulged. My mouth watered. My teeth itched to tear into the flesh.

"I told you. I do not house prostitutes," Madame Lacelle said. Her condemnation was as subdued as her eyes were wide.

We were both silent for a moment.

"But," Madame Lacelle continued, "that is more than enough to give everyone in the tenement a taste. If you share, who am I to say where you can or cannot get your food?"

I nodded numbly as my stomach roiled.

"Well, girl? Are you going to share or move out?"

I shook my head and looked at Madame Lacelle for a few long seconds before I recalled and processed everything she had just said.

"I am not..."

"I don't care."

I opened and closed my mouth a couple times. "Of course I will share. I do not know who sent this, but it is too much for me to eat before it would spoil."

Madame Lacelle seemed to glow. "I knew the moment I met you, girl, that you were the best of the wrong type of person."

I got a platter I had found and cleaned on my second day at the tenement. I was smiling as I piled almost a third of the meat onto the platter.

"I've been waiting for a reason to use this."

Madame Lacelle reached out for the platter, but I pulled it away.

"No," I said. "Take that. This will be more than enough for me."

The ancient woman looked at me as if I had given her a pile of gold. She wrapped the remaining meat in the paper it came in and retied some of the strings.

"Bless you, child. I will take this to Madame Rochelle. Everyone will eat well this week."

Madame Lacelle moved toward the exit, and I was turning to bring my portion of the meat to my room when she paused to turn back. "Charlotte dear?"

"Yes, madame?"

"I cannot let you live here for free. The Republic owns my property now. I am just a manager. They set my price, not me. But... well, everything else here is still mine. Whatever you need... let me know." And with that she descended the stairs.

I entered my room, closed and locked the door, and then immediately set upon the raw meat. I took one small bite, reveling in how easily my teeth cut through the flesh. The juices from the meat burst in my mouth as I crewed. It was delicious. No, it was divine. I admit that I only remember taking larger and larger bites and then the meat was simply gone. I smacked my lips. I licked my fingers, and then I licked the plate clean before lying on my pallet of blankets and dozing off, content.

It was just after noon when the stairs up to the attic screamed and groaned again. I got up and straightened my clothes. I had blood all over my blouse. There was nothing I could do about that. I would have to come up with some excuse. I took up my silver mirror and comb to rake out my hair, but my face was covered in blood as well. I grabbed an end of one of my blankets to wipe my face, but it did little to help. I tried using spittle to moisten the cloth, but I could not get my mouth to moisten. Not until I remembered how delicious the meat had been.

There was a knock on the door as I was attempting to wipe the blood off my face.

"Oui?" I stalled.

"Demoiselle Charlotte, I have something for you," came the voice from the other side of the door. It was Marcel, and his voice carried through the wooden door as effortlessly as he carried a child.

"Oh, Marcel. Just a moment."

"Oui, demoiselle."

I managed to make my face presentable, set my things down, and opened the door. Marcel stood on the other side holding a large cloth bundle under one arm and a piece of furniture under the other. He looked at me, and his eyes went wide before his face relaxed and he smiled.

"I see you lack restraint almost as much as I," he said.

I tilted my head in question.

"Could you not wait to cook the meat before you tore into it?" he asked.

I blushed, actually blushed. I could feel the heat in my face when it happened.

"I, um, almost dropped the entire platter and could only save it by grasping it to my chest."

"Oh," Marcel said, nodding as if my explanation was the most reasonable thing. "Well, I come bearing gifts."

That was when I realized that he must have carried the objects he had under each arm up multiple flights of stairs and stood there continuing to hold them while we chatted. I blushed again and waved him into my room.

Marcel had to come through the door sideways. First the cloth bundle, then his torso, and then the piece of furniture that, as he shifted it back and forth to get it through the door, I realized was a small writing desk. I smiled.

Marcel set the desk down first and then the cloth bundle on the slats across the bed frame. He lifted and moved the desk to sit next to the stove before reconsidering and moving it to the outside wall, near the window. He looked around the room again and scratched the stubble on his chin with one hand.

My eyes caressed every contour of the desk. It was small but had a thin drawer under the writing surface. The rich dark wood was well-worn with many years of use. Behind the writing surface were five small drawers on the left side and several square pigeon holes on the right. The whole thing was maybe as tall as Madame Lacelle if not quite.

I popped out of my reverie when Marcel lifted my bed, slats, cloth bundle, and all. He moved the bed across the room to sit near the stove, then put the writing desk in front of the window. Finally, he lifted the bed again and positioned it between the writing desk and the stove. He had to shuffle the small bedside table as well, which he placed first on the side with the stove then back on the side with the desk, finally leaving it there.

The large cloth bundle ended up being a mattress and bed clothes bundled up into a large ball. After he opened the bundle, he began to dress the bed.

"I can do that, monsieur," I protested, but Marcel did not even pause. He simply continued his work with a smile on his face.

"My children have full bellies tonight because of you, demoiselle."

"It was nothing. I do not even..." I was going to finish with "... know who sent me the package," but he cut me off.

"It *was* something, demoiselle. No one would have blamed you for keeping all of that meat for yourself. Everyone is hungry, and everyone wishes they had more. Today you filled many wishes. Please. Let me do this for you."

I did, though I felt very odd standing there watching the man make my bed. When he finished, he stood back and gazed upon his work. Honestly it was a bit of a disaster with wrinkles and untucked sheets hanging free, but he seemed proud of the work.

"Perfect," I said.

He turned and embraced me so quickly that I didn't realize what was happening until I was encased in his giant torso and arms. I relaxed and hugged him back. He broke the hug rather quickly and stood back.

"That was from my wife. She is ready to adopt you. If you ever need anything, just ask."

I blushed again, blushed for real, and looked away. Then, steeling myself, I turned and looked him in the eyes.

"Thank you," I said.

"No, demo..." This time I cut him off.

"Yes! Thank you. This is the most human that I have felt in a long time. It has been easy to forget what not being alone is like."

He smiled and laid a massive hand on my shoulder. We shared a quiet moment before he turned and left. The stairs groaned as he descended. I locked my door. I turned and took another look at the poorly made bed, fixing the image in my memory for all time. Then I took to making the bed properly, adding one of my own blankets as a top cover over the sheets and the other rolled up as a pillow.

I sat on the bed tentatively, unsure how well it would hold my weight, but it held just fine. The mattress wrapped me in a comfort I had not experienced in years. There I allowed my thoughts to wander as I enjoyed the experience.

Eventually my thoughts wandered to the origin of this experience. Who had sent me the meat to begin with, and why?

"Who" was me, said my mistress. *"Why" was because I said I would grant your wish, and one should never waste food.*

"Wish?" I asked, but she did not reply. I did receive an amused feeling from her, however.

What had I just eaten, and worse, what I had given to the residents of the tenement to eat? I did not want to know, but as I searched for work today I happened to pass La Plénitude de Vie. There was a black wreath on the door and city guard everywhere.

A small crowd was gathered on the opposite side of the street. I walked over and asked no one in particular what happened.

A young man turned and looked at me with excited wide eyes.

"Oh, it's you," he said.

I did not know what he meant, until I recognized him as the redheaded ruffian from Giorgio's shop days before. It was difficult to tell it was him at first because his hair was black now, not red, and he had his two front teeth. But once I realized who he was, everything else about him fell into place. He no longer looked like a boy of eight or ten. He looked to be a young teenager, maybe as old as me.

"Oh," I replied, somewhat startled at my revelation. "You are the boy that gave me the message."

He blushed and gave me a queer look before he jerked a thumb toward the cafe. "The maître d' was killed yesterday."

"No," I said, stunned.

"That's not even the best part," he said with a conspiratorial whisper. "When they found him, he was hanging from giant hooks in his legs and bled dry. They say he'd been butchered, with most of the meat from his arms and legs missing."

I staggered away from the boy. He laughed and shook his head.

"Girls. They can't even stand to hear about blood," he said with a smile. Then he turned and watched the crowd and café.

My stomach wanted to revolt, and I meandered down random streets leading away from the café.

As I said. Your wish was granted. And now you—and your entire dwelling, it seems—have a full belly because of your wish and me. You are welcome.

12

ATTIC CLUBHOUSE

August 26, 1814 AD

I spent several days in my room, unable to leave for fear of people seeing me and thanking me. I could not look them in the face knowing now that what they and I ate was human flesh. Madame Lacelle came up to visit me once yesterday. She knocked at my door until I responded. I faked being ill so that I would not need to open the door. She returned later with a bucket of water and a bowl of stew, which she left outside of the door. God save me. They were still eating the maître' d, stretching the meat as much as possible.

My stomach turned at the thought of all those people... No. I could not think of it anymore. What was done was done. Once I made peace with that thought, I ate the stew. No use letting it go to waste.

I washed up with the water and what little soap I had left from my first bath. Tomorrow was bath day, and I would buy another bar from Madame Lacelle. I found a small stack of towels in a forgotten trunk days before and washed those as well as I could to knock the stale smell from them. With nothing more to do, I lay on my bed, guilted by the comfort, yet thankful for it all the same. I stared at the ceiling.

The sun set.

The moon rose.

My contemplation was broken by a huge thump. I bolted upright. Was someone at the door? No. Once I thought about it, the noise came from either the brick wall to my right, or somewhere on the floor below. Unsure if the noise originated from the attic or not, I listened more intently. Several tense minutes passed before there was another thump, louder this time, followed by the sound of something like dirt falling on the floor. The thump came from the brick wall, I was sure of it. Was someone on the other side?

I kneeled on my bed and put my ear to the wall. I heard muted laughter and... singing? It was. Someone, or several someones, was on the other side of the attic having a grand time. To be sure, I went over to the dormer and opened the window. I could hear the singing and laughter better as soon as I felt the night air. I leaned out the window, holding myself in place with one hand while getting as far out as possible. Light danced from a couple of the dormer windows much further away. Someone was in the other half of the attic, near the far end.

I returned to lay in my bed and listened to the voices. All were male except maybe one female. Talking, laughing, and singing continued long into the night. The singing ended first, then the laughing, and finally the talking. Then, just as I started to return to my meditative self-flagellation, another type of thumping came from the other side of the wall. It started off in a slow, steady rhythm and increased in tempo until ending with three hard, sudden slams.

As silence descended, my naiveté finally fled. I was scandalized.

The next morning I ventured out to find Madame Lacelle. She and two other ladies were busy hauling water from the basement to each floor. Madame Lacelle carried two buckets at once.

“Half the trips,” she told me as she caught whatever look must have been on my face.

She would not allow me to take her full burden—it seemed to be a point of pride to her— but she did allow me to take one of the buckets as we climbed side by side to the third-floor bathroom.

Already people were in line for the bath. In fact the rogue, Theo, was the first in line, clad only in a pair of short pants. I pointedly did not look in his direction despite his instant smile and smooth, lean, bare chest.

I thanked Madame Lacelle for the stew and water.

"Think nothing of it, dear," she said. "I always make that stew for people when they are sick. The secret is in the herbs. You use just enough herbs to give it flavor and to feel good on a sore throat but still edible."

"It was very good," I insisted.

She beamed.

Theo tried to get my attention as we left the bathroom to get more water. I pretended not to see him. When we were halfway to the basement, I asked Madame Lacelle who used the attic on the other side of the wall.

"Oh, no one. The stairwell up to that side fell in during the revolution. My husband said he would repair it, but then he was taken by the Republic to serve the Little Emperor and died taking a twenty-square-mile piece of land that was held for all of six months before being lost again." She spat on the floor after mentioning the Emperor. "When the Republic confiscated ownership of the tenement, I felt no need to fix the space. I had Marcel clear out the wood from the stairs up to the attic and nail up the door. We burnt those stairs in our stoves years ago."

"So there is no chance someone could be in the attic over there?" I asked.

"You hearing things, girl?"

"Maybe."

"Well, don't go telling ghost stories," Madame Lacelle said as we reached the basement. "We've already had enough of those. Poor Bel."

"How is she?" I asked.

"Better. She left with her nephew a couple days ago. She seemed better as soon as he appeared."

"Good."

"I hope I get to see her again."

A pretty young woman with long blond hair and carrying a bucket of water overheard Madame Lacelle as she passed us on her way up. She made the sign of the cross and splashed about half of the bucket out at the same time.

"Mathilde," Madame Lacelle chided. "How many buckets have you unloaded?"

"Six, madame," the young blond said. "Counting this one."

"So five," Madame Lacelle said. "And a half. I am climbing two additional flights of steps, and I'm already ahead of you by ten."

"Yes, madame. I'm sorry, madame." The young woman's head was down, and she curtsied with each sentence. I had to admit, her curtsies were much better than my own.

"Do I need to give your job to Demoiselle Charlotte here?"

Mathilde looked up in anguish. "Oh no, please no, Madame Lacelle. We need the work. Please don't."

I put a hand out to calm the young woman.

"Do not worry. I have a job, which prevents me from taking yours," I lied.

Madame Lacelle just shook her head and tsked. The girl rushed up the stars in such a hurry, she splashed much of her bucket onto the steps.

"Mathilde is twenty years old and already the mother of three," Madame Lacelle said as we finished our trip to the basement. "Her husband was a dyer by trade. Seems he made good money when they first married. She never had to lift more than a finger to ring a bell and someone was there to help, but it seems her husband also enjoyed gambling too. He got into a bad spot with some worse folk. Now he's a bricklayer."

"Why a bricklayer?" I asked as I passed my empty bucket to Madame Lacelle.

She hung the bucket under the spout and pumped the well handle. Water gushed into the bucket with each squeaky pump of the handle.

"Because he could do that with only one hand." She paused

pumping to make a chopping motion over one of her wrists with the other hand.

"Oh."

Madame Lacelle switched the now-full bucket with her empty one. "Bricklayers don't make as much money as dyers. Worse, her husband still gambles, and like every man of vice—which is to say all of them—it is his family that suffers. So now they live here, and she works."

I shook my head. I reached for the second bucket as it finished filling, but Madame Lacelle took it instead.

"Best I take the last set up by myself. Theo seemed a bit too interested in you."

"I... I had not noticed."

"I noticed that too. You didn't notice him too much by far to be safe, by my measure."

I blushed.

"Keep away from him, girl. He's a bad seed."

Before she left, I called out, "Madame Lacelle?"

She stopped and turned with an exasperated look. "What, girl?"

"Why did you say that you hoped to see Madame Rounsaville again?"

Madame Lacelle shook her head with a grimace of annoyance. "Because we're old, child."

Madame Lacelle left me alone in the basement to consider her words. I was about to leave when I noticed the bucket I had brought down earlier. I filled the bucket with water. Even if Madame Lacelle would not allow me to help her, I could help someone. I proceeded to find Mathilde.

* * *

That evening I lay in my bed feeling slightly less guilty about my complicity in creating a tenement full of cannibals. Everyone seemed much more lively and happy. I would not allow myself to forget my guilt, but for the time being, I resolved to live with myself and the consequences, good and bad, of my actions.

After several hours, a veil of clouds hid the moon, and everything was silent. It was about the same time as the night before when the noises of merriment came from the other side of the brick wall. Tonight all was silent. I tried to imagine who occupied the other side. I imagined everyone from some of the older children to Marcel on the other side doing the most scandalous things. My most humorous imagining had Madame Lacelle running an illicit gambling house where she bilked high society men in games of Twenty-One. The thought made me laugh aloud.

Soon I could no longer resist the temptation, and I found myself climbing out of my dormer window. I felt the roof with my bare feet. The slate tiles were smooth and slick with evening dew. The wind buffeted me as I stood just outside of my apartment window.

I took a few tentative steps, and my right foot slipped out from under me. For a brief moment I balanced on one foot, five—no, six with the roof—six stories above the Parisian streets while the wind threatened to push me to my oblivion. I gently set my right foot back down and moved more cautiously.

I climbed slowly, so slowly, to the center ten or twelve feet of roof where the slope was relatively flat. The brick wall that contained the stove pipes extended through the roof in front of me. Smoke rose from only one of the pipes. I could only imagine one person who might be cold in the middle of summer, even one as cool as this year's summer: Madame Lacelle.

There were so many of the black clay chimneys poking up through the bricks, crowded so closely together, that I did not trust estimating their number. The image played tricks with the eye. It could have been forty or maybe sixty. Many, I resolved. The number was many, and I left it at that.

The brick wall in front of me and another two split the building in unequal thirds, the center being the largest, and the far third the smallest. At the crest of the roof, each wall rose about three feet, with the chimneys extending another six to eight inches. The top of each chimney wall was level though the chimneys themselves ended in random heights as varied as their number. Combined with the sloping roof, the walls near the edge of the buildings were near three times the height at the center.

From my vantage I could see all of Paris in every direction. Paris is a beautiful city; even in its dirtiest parts such as where I live, this is true. But the view of my beautiful city from the rooftop was amazing. So many gas and oil lamps lit the streets at night it almost seemed to me that the ground mirrored the sky.

My father told me once that years ago, people would likely be robbed if they went outside at night. Merchants and the wealthy would light their shops and homes to keep thieves at bay. The gendarmes noticed that streets that were better lit had less crime. About the time I was born, they started hanging lamps across every street. Gendarmes would light the lamps at night while on patrol. Soon, crime dropped and people started to go outside after dark. Not every street and alley was lit, but I reasoned that one day the city would be so full of light it would be seen from miles away as a glowing beacon on the horizon for all to love. I was never more proud to be Parisian.

After filling my gaze with the grandeur of the city, I returned to task. I hopped the almost four-foot-tall divide in an effortless single bound. When I landed, I was taken by the ease of my jump and the feeling that I was in brand-new territory. I was an unfamiliar person to myself exploring unfamiliar terrain, and I loved every moment.

Despite the light in the streets, the rooftops were cloaked in shadow. Indeed it seemed to me that anyone at street level would find it impossible to see anyone moving along a roof. That would be good for me.

I walked from one side to the other of the flatter section and viewed the dormers on each side. The west was to my right, and several floors below was Rue Bar-du-Bec, which my apartment window overlooked. The street was little more than a crooked alley, but it was open on both ends and every street needed a name.

To my left, the windows looked out over the east side of the city.

There were fewer lights to the east, fewer lights and more poverty, at least out to the Palace Royale. Below the windows was the roof of another building and the cul-de-sac with the tenement entrance.

I strolled along the rooftop to the next brick wall and hopped it as easily as the last. Our tenement joined at a right angle with another building. The south face of that building ran east along Rue de la Verrerie. There were only a handful of dormers on the eastern side of this section of the tenement roof, and then something caught my eye.

A rope hung out of one of the dormers, the one closest to the brick wall of chimneys. I walked to the area just above the dormer. I wanted to look in that dormer. My idea was to descend over the dormer itself. If I slipped, at least I would fall onto the dormer rather than sliding off the roof entirely.

The climb down the roof proved more harrowing than the climb up. There was something unnatural to descending forward on such a steep slope. I considered descending backward, but while it seemed a more natural footing, it was also much more terrifying. After a handful of false starts, I instead hiked my skirt above my knees, knelt, and crawled backward down the roof on my hands and knees.

I was quite the daredevil.

I was relieved when my feet finally touched the dormer roof. It was only about six feet down but seemed much further. I sat on the dormer roof and relaxed. I was tense and strangely out of breath. Why should I be out of breath? I was dead, and I did not breathe. My heart did not pump blood, yet my pulse raced. Or at least I imagined that it did. I wondered if I could simply ignore these impulses, these memories of life.

Doing so is a path more slippery than your current one, my mistress said to me.

I took her at her word.

I slid down the right side of the dormer, intending to stop myself at the bottom with my feet, but I misjudged. Both of my feet slipped out from under me, and I slid the remaining way off the dormer. I hit the roof with the side of my body and continued to slide. I scrambled to get a grip of something, but everything within reach was smooth and slick. I slid toward the end of the roof with increasing speed, when I noticed the rope. It came out of the window and stretched down the side of the roof and presumably beyond. From my perspective as I slid sideways down the roof, the rope was over my head. I grasped in desperation for the literal lifeline, but it was just out of reach. I was about to go over the side of the building. Having no better option, I lunged for the rope.

And missed.

The lunge only seemed to hasten my slide.

I closed my eyes. This was going to hurt.

With an odd transition from hard roof tile to open air, I was free-falling.

Almost immediately I hit another surface.

A new terror gripped me when I opened my eyes during a brief moment of near calm. I lay on the slate-covered roof belonging to the slightly shorter building running along Rue de la Verrerie, but instead of lying across the slope, I was lying with the slope, face down.

With a subtle shift of something within me, I started sliding down the lower roof head first toward oblivion. Unwilling to ignore lessons of the very recent past, I kept my eyes open and searched for answers. The rope was above me now, stretched between some sort of hook on the roof above and the roof edge ahead. I rolled toward the wall where building met building and grabbed for the wall. I rolled onto my side with my right arm pinned below me just as my left hand smacked against the side of my tenement. My palm seemed to find purchase with the texture of the tenement wall, but I did not slow so much as pivot as my legs swung away from the wall.

My hand pulled away from the wall almost as soon as my pivot began, and I squirmed to find something else to grab. All that remained was the roof itself, so I reached out as far as possible with all my limbs in all directions, hoping I would stick to... well, anything. I slid on my stomach spread-eagle for maybe ten feet more, when my toes slipped off the end of the roof. I looked to my right where the rope was. Perhaps if I were to manage another roll, I could grab the dangling rope before falling the remaining four stories.

The toes of my left foot caught on something then. A gutter.

I quickly found the gutter with my other foot and pushed. I could hear the strain of wood and metal bending against an unfamiliar weight, but thankfully, the gutter held and my momentum stopped. I lay there for a few moments panting. I tried to catch a breath I did not have and thanked God I was still alive.

You should thank me too. Otherwise you wouldn't be having this exciting experience to begin with, my mistress said. *Also, you are not alive.*

My mistress chose the strangest times to speak to me and for the oddest of reasons. I should not have been surprised by the conversation, its timing, or its location, but I was.

I laughed.

I was lying spread-eagle on a roof four stories up with my feet in a gutter, and I laughed. It seemed the only rational response.

"I thought you were God. At least my god now," I said out loud.

No, she replied long and breathy. *I would not presume. That one is very jealous.*

"Thank you, Mistress," I said, and immediately I knew she was pleased. "Do you have any advice on how I save myself from this situation?"

Embrace the monster, was all she said.

The ghoul from the catacombs, the one I had been for a moment, feeding off of Luc, the one that Madame Rounsaville could see when no one else could, climbed the ridge of the roof right above me. I screamed and pushed myself back from the creature. My motion, however natural, was unfortunate. Wood and metal screamed again as my own ended. I looked down the slope of the roof to see the gutter separating from the building by two inches or more. The ghoul descended the roof with steady, secure steps. The claws on the creature's feet seemed to dig into the roof. I desperately tried to spread my body weight further across as much of the rooftop as possible, but the majority still remained on the shifting gutter.

The monster stood above me and squatted. It was uncomfortably close, and I could easily see every detail of its naked body. Its skin was leathery, gray, and blotched with dark black, brown, and red stains. It had serrated claws on each foot and a talon-like claw on its heel. Its mouth was full, too full, of teeth. Its eyes were sunken into the skull with completely black orbs in the sockets. Its nose was missing, with only a pair of slits forming an inverted V above full lips that bled from multiple splits. It was completely hairless, and squatting as it was, I could tell it was definitely female. It was not just female, however. It was me... me as the monster.

I considered for the briefest of moments to simply fall backward into oblivion. The action would finish this horrid life, allow me to avoid the monster, and pay for all my sins. I was surely damned. It did not matter if eternity started then or a hundred years later.

Several loud pops accompanied several quick jerks I felt through my feet. My self-pity shattered as the gutter below me pulled further away from the wall. I shifted all at once, and I was six inches further down the roof. The shift ended as quickly as it began, but the metal gutters still groaned. I felt the metal as it strained against moving. Or did it strain to move? I could not tell, and it did not matter. The gutters would move again. It was only a matter of time.

The monster above me reached out a single hand. I thought it was going to push me, then I thought it might rip me apart and consume me. I realized those were the thoughts of a frightened animal, not those of a rational human that needed to survive, but just as my thoughts began to clear, there was another scream of metal and wood. The frightened animal thoughts returned as I realized nothing supported me anymore. I slid toward oblivion for real as a loud crash echoed up from several stories below.

I reached up and grabbed the monster's arm.

Its clawed hand wrapped around my forearm with a steel grip. Then, with an effortless movement, it stood, and I was lifted into the air to come to stand just in front of the monster. It smiled and faded from sight, even as it held on to me. As it faded, my hands and feet tingled. I looked down, and my feet were its feet, my hands were its hands. I wanted to weep. What had I done?

The gutters were still crashing to the ground stories below as the weight of the fallen portions pulled against those still hanging. Glass shattered. I heard screaming metal and the collision of metal and stone as more gutters crashed to the cul-de-sac below.

Lights appeared windows. More than one baby began to scream. People would be out and about soon trying to find the cause of the noise, and while it was dark along the roofline, I did not wish to chance being seen.

My attention again turned to the rope hanging out the open dormer window. It swayed in the breeze, a silent message to seek refuge from the prying eyes of gawkers wondering at the gutters. I tested a few tentative steps, and my footing was as sure or better than if I were walking barefoot on the cobblestone streets below me. I picked up my pace and climbed up to the roof above. Relief washed over me as I ducked through the open dormer window.

The rope was tied off to a brass ring fastened to the inside wall with some sort of brass fitting and screws. A thin green patina covered the brass bits and transferred a blackish-green stain to the rope where hemp touched metal. I pondered the existence of the rope. It likely stretched to the ground below or maybe another tenement window. I worried some gawker would notice it, follow it up here, and discover me before I could get back to my room.

I pulled in the rope and coiled it under the window. Strangely, the vicious claws reverted back to my more dexterous human fingers as I coiled the rope. My feet reverted as well.

Finished with the rope, I looked around the room. This one was about a third of the size of the storage room with all the furniture. This side of the room had two dormers while the other had four. The other windows were boarded up, making the window I entered the only means of accessing the room.

There was a door at the far left end of the room, but it was boarded shut from this side. The wall to my right was brick and likely contained the chimneys for this side of the building. There was also a door-sized rectangle in the wall of newer brick. That was interesting, but it was something I would not be able to investigate tonight. I would have to keep my investigations now to this single room, at least until the commotion outside died.

The room was decorated as a single, large living space. A double bed occupied a space against the brick wall between where I stood and the far window. A table and four chairs sat several feet from the foot of the bed and closer to the opposite side of the room. Across from the table, against the same wall as the dormer I entered, was a writing desk with no chair. Boxes and unused furniture stood piled to the corner along the wall past the writing desk.

Dirty dishes littered the table, the bed was a mess, and the writing table was cluttered with books, paper, and junk of all kinds. Several books and loose sheets of paper were scattered about the area. I picked up some of the books and carried them to a window on the far side of the building to look at the title pages. From the pale light that streamed through one of the larger spaces between boards and my monstrous sight, I could easily read the text. The author of the first was Donatien Alphonse François de Sade. My father told me of the disgusting works by the man. I threw it down, annoyed and disgusted. Most of the remaining books were similar works by other authors. I cast them about the room randomly. It was unlikely the occupants cared a wit about order and so would not even realize the difference.

I checked the books on the desk. One was very small, a novelette perhaps, while the other was larger. The novelette was *René* by François-René de Chateaubriand. I saw no pornography in the pages that I flipped through, and it was small, so I set the book aside. I examined the larger book. Someone had scribbled through the author's name and the title on the title page, but when I flipped the page over I could still read much of the imprint from the original pressing through the paper. It was *The Sorrows of Young Werther*! My father owned a copy of the book, and I read it several times. I would enjoy reading it again, so I stashed it with the other. I moved around the space trying to imagine who would be using it and for what purpose. Near the bed I found a cloth sack, much like those Monsieur Bordelon used to bundle food. I took the sack over to the writing table and put the books I'd set aside in the sack.

A shout from outside drew my attention to the open window. Clinging to the shadows, I peeked around the edge of the window and down the roof. People milled in the cul-de-sac, examining the wreckage. Some men were already at work cleaning the debris. Women and crying children stood together in small groups talking. It seemed no one was going to go back to bed anytime soon. I was stuck here until at least most of the people dispersed. I expected as much but hoped for better.

I looked around the room to see if there was anything else to occupy my time. On a whim, I uncoiled about half the rope. I sat on the floor for the next several minutes trying to get my claws to appear to cut the rope. Just as I gave up trying, the claws appeared, almost as if I had to stop thinking about it for it to happen. Odd. I used one claw to cut the rope in half and let my hands return to normal. I coiled the cut section of rope and put it in the sack.

With nothing else to do, I sat under the window, my back to the small ledge of the dormer, and practiced making my claws appear and disappear. I practiced with one hand, then the other, then both hands, then my feet, then one foot, and then the other. Once I mastered that, I started trying one finger at a time. That was hard, but not as hard as one toe at a time. The first transformation felt strange, almost alien, but as I practiced, the sensation became familiar, almost normal.

Time passed as I practiced. It was near morning when I reached mastery, and the cul-de-sac was quiet once again. I took the remaining rope and dropped it back out the window. Hopefully whoever used the rope to get up here would not think too hard about why it was so much shorter. Maybe they would assume it was cut in the crash of the gutters.

I climbed out of the window, trying to stick to the deepest shadows possible as I scanned for onlookers. Walking on the roof was much simpler and more secure with my feet transformed into those of the monster. I moved over to the edge and looked down. There were stacks of crates piled along the side of the shorter building. Almost the entire gutter system lay twisted and bent across the boxes or in small piles here and there. A portion of the gutter remained attached to the furthest section of the lower building. Either the gutters had worn thin there or the nails held the wood more securely. Where the gutters should have been, wood was splintered irregularly. Large sections of wood were missing, and much of it looked rotted too. I was lucky in a way. The section of gutter that stopped my original fall was anchored in more or less solid wood.

The return to my room was so simple as to be ridiculous. Despite the dampness of the roof tiles or the angle at which I stood, my footing was secure. Once back through my window, I upended the sack. The two books I pilfered as well as the rope spilled out onto my bed, along with a pillow, a small bottle of brown liquid, and a pile of loose gold and silver coins. The extra items must have already been in the bag, yet I did not notice the weight.

The gold coins were mostly twenty-franc coins, but there were a few forty-franc coins as well. The silver coins were mostly five- and two-franc coins. Overall there was over seven hundred francs in the sack. I considered returning the sack immediately, with the coins, but dawn was upon the city. The sun would break before I could return. Not wishing to expose myself to whatever eyes might see me on the roof during the light of day, especially after last night's adventure, I vowed to return the sack the following night and hope that it was not missed.

I considered keeping one or two coins. It would not be unheard of for a coin to fall out of the bottom of a sack, especially if that sack had a previously unnoticed hole in it. One or two gold coins could buy another month of lodging for me. The cost of a year or more of lodging was possible with the coins I found. I rejected the thought outright. I vowed that as soon as I had an opportunity, I would return the sack with the coins, brown liquid, and the pillow. No, not the pillow. I would keep the pillow and count it a reward for being virtuous.

Yes.

I swept up the things that did not belong to me and set them under the bed. Then I realized that if someone entered my room, they might be able to steal the money from me before I was able to return it. Everywhere I considered putting the sack of coins seemed to be exactly where I would look if I were looking for someone's hidden wealth. Finally I settled on storing it in the false bottom of my trunk.

I had to remove everything from the trunk to store the sack with the coins and jar of liquid. I put the pillow on my bed. Luxury was becoming a vice that I could not deny. While I had everything out of the trunk, I took inventory and mentally organized my worldly possessions: one small trunk with false bottom, ninety-seven sheets of paper (seven still blank), less than one-tenth of a bottle of ink, a pen, two books that I counted as liberated from people who did not seem to appreciate them, a small coil of rope of roughly thirty feet, two thin but serviceable blankets, one lantern (with almost no oil), a white china bowl with a brilliant blue pattern inside and out, a steel knife with a curved blade and leather-wrapped wooden handle, a silver mirror and comb set, a lice comb given to me by Giorgio, and a rusty piece of rectangular metal with two holes on one end. I also counted the hooks in my legs.

Considering where I was before Vincent found me, I counted myself burdened with riches. Everything else in my life was borrowed or temporarily in my possession. Of my own money I had less than a dozen sou left, yet it was more than I'd had for years.

I realize as I write this, taking inventory of my worldly goods was the moment that I left my integrity behind. I needed more paper soon. Writing my diary entries was the greatest contributor to maintaining my humanity, and I had to maintain the activity.

I decided to borrow enough money from the sack to buy some more writing supplies. When I next saw Giorgio, I would get more of the money he owed me to pay back what I borrowed. I took a single silver coin of two francs to buy more paper. Then I realized I would need lamp oil and ink as well, so I took another two-franc coin. And a pen. My current pen was worn with all the writing I had done, and it was not exactly new when I had started. That was when my stomach rumbled. I took five more francs to purchase several pounds of meat to tide me over for a week or more. My mistress was amused at the thought, and on reflection I agreed, so I doubled the amount for meat. Then I remembered how excited everyone was when I shared the meat my mistress delivered to me, and how horrible I felt when I realized what the meat actually was. I owed it to them to feed them properly, did I not?

I also needed clothes. I knew I would be climbing out of the roof more and more. The freedom was too exhilarating. I had to find some boy's clothes to fit me. Giorgio could help me, but I did not wish to rely on him, or anyone really. It would be better in the long run to be able to stand on my own, alone and strong. Giorgio could make me soft if I spent too much time with the man. There was something of him that reminded me of my father. Giorgio might have decided to sell to me for less, but my independence was more important to me than a few francs, especially now that I had so much extra.

I left my room later that day with two forty-franc gold coins and a number of silver coins. I was unsure how much I took, so drunk on the thought of all the good I would do, I stopped paying attention to the details. I knew as I left the tenement that day that I was never going to repay the money. It was mine now. I was a thief again. This was my biggest haul, and the thought exhilarated me.

13

A STORY OF LYON

August 27, 1814 AD

After I decided to keep the pilfered coins from the far attic space, which I now call the Clubhouse, I began a modest spending spree. I had grown tired and disgusted in the seventh arrondissement, so I traversed farther west and north, beyond even Giorgio's shop, and into the second and third arrondissements to find some secondhand clothing sellers. I had money now, I could afford to shop in those neighborhoods.

First, I purchased a worn pair of shoes that were falling apart. They would not last a month. The lady selling them knew they would not last the month. I pretended they were worse than my bare feet while she pretended they were freshly cobbled. We settled on what I considered a fair price despite her insulted manner. The shoes fit poorly, but I would not be wearing them for long.

Two shops later, I found a dressmaker who made new creations from multiple sets of clothes so damaged that they could not be repaired. I purchased a dress made of three different materials so well combined that it appeared the original designer intended to create nothing else. The work impressed me, but I pretended it to be complete rubbish. She threatened to throw me out of her stall, but in the end we agreed on a price a five sou more than any secondhand dress should honestly cost. She handed me a mismatched pair of stockings before I left. If held together, the mismatch of colors was obvious. If one viewed the stockings individually, the difference vanished. I thanked her for her generosity, and she thanked me for mine. I would have put on the stockings right then except for the giant metal hooks still piercing my legs under my skirts.

The boys' clothes were easy to find, but I had to pretend to buy something for a younger brother to keep the shop workers from asking too many questions. I said his height and weight to be near my own, and so they used my frame to suggest a few items. After several rounds of haggling, I purchased two pairs of pants and two shirts. The pants were both black, one shirt was an eggshell brown, and the other was a dark gray. I would need to roll up the sleeves until I could alter them properly.

Finally I found a pair of men's leather work gloves dyed black. I purchased these and a small meat pie from the same vendor. The gloves were a trifle too large and the meat pie lacked meat, but I was happy with both. Rather than stop at a butcher's shop, I would buy my groceries from Monsieur Bordelon, the only seventh arrondissement merchant I liked. I'd developed quite a fondness for Monsieur Bordelon. To help him out, I headed east toward his shop and eventually home.

Several hours before dusk, I stopped at Monsieur Bordelon's shop to purchase some groceries for Madame Rochelle. Bordelon's son was there for once. Henri swept the store, or rather it seemed that was what he was supposed to be doing. He stood in one place and idly swung a broom left and right refusing to do anything remotely helpful to his chore, such as move his feet or actually touch the floor with his broom. He eyed me as I walked in carrying the packages I acquired over the course of the day's shopping.

Monsieur Bordelon was bent behind a well-worn, waist-high counter painted white like the rest of the shop's interior. I almost missed him behind a pair of brown metal flour canisters on the counter.

"Monsieur Bordelon?" I asked.

The elder Bordelon snapped his head up and stood. He wiped his face. He frowned before he wiped, but once his hands came away from his face, he was all smiles.

"Ah, Demoiselle Charlotte. How are we today?"

I smiled and tried my best to beam. "I am incredibly well today." I waved my hands over my packages.

Henri's head popped up from his mindless activity as I spoke, but he said nothing.

Monsieur Bordelon seemed to only then notice the packages I carried. "Shopping? I thought you had no money."

I set my packages down on the floor, but when I looked up, Monsieur Bordelon gave me a frown and shake of his head. "Put those things over here," he said as he gestured to space on the counter.

I picked up the packages and put them on the counter instead. "Well, very little, it was true, but I sold the last of my mother's things. I now have enough money to provide for a few more months. I went to the second arrondissement and bought some new clothes."

"Your mother's things? Such a shame, but we all do what we must, eh?" he continued with a touch of sadness. "They must have sold for quite a bit if you were able to shop in the second arrondissement."

My cheeks blushed slightly.

"I am sorry, monsieur, I could not help but live a little fantasy and bend the truth a bit. I did go to the second arrondissement to buy clothes but only to secondhand vendors. There are several used clothes markets off Rue de Richelieu. Many shops only sold overpriced goods, but I had patience and found some nice things. Also, you would not know, but I am quite skilled at haggling. Still, finding good clothes at a value price was easier than finding a pen, paper, and ink at affordable prices."

"I am sad you had to sell your mother's things, but happy that you have enjoyed shopping."

Monsieur Bordelon's manner was deflated, as if something had drained his normal jubilance from him like water from a skin.

"Is something wrong, monsieur?"

Monsieur Bordelon looked at me again and smiled wanly. "We have been robbed."

"Mon Dieu. Is everyone safe?"

"Oui. Well... oui. Ma femme chérie... she is rather upset and will not come out of her room. Her vacation is now in jeopardy. And this one here..." Bordelon's hand waved toward his son. "Henri is despondent that I can no longer fund his gallivanting and carousing. He must stay and help out."

"I am so sorry, monsieur. How much did they steal?"

"Our entire savings, I dare not speak the sum. Plus some scotch, tobacco, and a few other things."

I gasped. "When did this happen?"

"Two nights ago while the wife and I were attending a play. It was the first time we had gone out to enjoy an evening together alone since... well, since Henri was born. It was supposed to be special, but then this happened." We were both silent for a moment before he added, "The thing is, I always hide most of our money in a special place and keep a small amount in the register as a kind of decoy. You know what I mean?"

I nodded. It sounded a wise tactic.

"Despite keeping a little gold and much of the silver in the register, the thief knew to look for our hidden savings too. They must have been watching me when I hid the money. I have been such a fool."

A knot rose up in my throat as Monsieur Bordelon shook his head slowly while he stared at the counter.

"Well, perhaps I can start to repair your loss by making a sizable purchase?"

Bordelon's smile became a little less forced as he asked, "What can I help you with, mon cher?"

"I only have about ten francs left," I lied. "But I would like to get several pounds of vegetables, some flour, and a bit of salt if you have any."

"And how much of your ten francs do you wish to spend?"

I feigned performing math. "Eight, although if you have some good soap, I could spend another."

Monsieur Bordelon smiled genuinely and set about gathering various things around the store.

I was idly thinking how I might further help the grocer when he called out to me.

"Demoiselle Charlotte?" I looked in his direction. He held up two cucumbers that to my eyes looked identical. "Do you prefer the less expensive bruised vegetables or the more expensive and nicer-looking picks?"

He waved one and then the other as he spoke.

"I am going to give the food to Madame Rochelle, who will likely make stews and mash with much of what I bring her. So whatever you think works best."

Monsieur Bordelon nodded. "I know exactly the kind of goods she buys. You will want some sugar too."

His pace hurried as he picked a half dozen various vegetables and started shoving them at Henri, who put his broom to the side to stand vacantly near his father. I blistered at Henri. He was only a couple years older than me, with a lovely family. And he just stood there. He just stood there. I wanted to go over to him. Shake him. Scream at him. I wanted to scream at him, "You have a great life. Your father loves you. Appreciate this, all of it, before..."

I turned my back on the scene. I noticed with pride that no tears spilt this time. I calmed the boiling of my blood with a lesson my father taught me when I once had a horrible toothache. I imagined cool water washing over me in waves. The waves were small at first. Each rolled in larger than the one before. Each crash of the wave upon the shore of my pain caused the pain to swell, but when the wave receded, the water took some of the shore, some of the pain with it. Eventually the waves washed away the shore entirely. The seas stilled, and the pain was gone.

This time the pain was not in my tooth. The pain was in my soul.

"Demoiselle?" Monsieur Bordelon asked.

I opened my eyes and turned to see him packing the goods into a couple of cloth sacks just like the one I had found the money in. Henri stood to the side again, absently not-sweeping.

"Oui?"

Monsieur Bordelon smiled. "This is ten franc, four sou. If it is too much, I can put back some sugar or flour."

"Oh." I opened my purse, rummaged through the remaining coins, and pulled out most of the silver. It was just over eleven francs.

"I have a little more than expected. I will purchase everything," I said. I reached out and felt one of the cloth sacks the grocer placed all my goods into. "I love these sacks. Where do you get them?"

Monsieur Bordelon smiled. "My cousin Claude works at a textile factory in Lyon."

"These are linen though, not silk."

Lyon produced France's best silk textiles and was well known for the fact.

"That is correct, but silk is not the only fabric made in Lyon. Linen is produced there as well. My cousin worked at one of the factories for twenty years. He knew everything about the factory, and when the owner or his family was not around, Claude took charge and ensured everything kept going. Then the revolution happened.

"Very early, the textile factory owners, I forget their names, they were royalists. Claude was not a royalist. He was not a republican. Yes, some people suffered, but the lives of him and his family were good, so he cared not who ruled. The owner became paranoid and sacked everyone he thought might stand against the royalty, including my cousin. When the factory owner would not listen to Claude's appeals... well, in that moment he became the biggest, fiercest republican in the city of Lyon."

I oh'd and smiled. Henri had stopped his not-sweeping and was listening too, though he looked more at me than at his father. Typical.

"Yes. It was a bad time for Claude then," Monsieur Bordelon continued. "Lyon received much trade from the wealthy royalists, and so there was a lot of resistance to the revolution in the beginning. As time wore on, more and more royalists found their peers hanging from the ends of ropes or burned out of house and home. The royalists lost power as the people took back their lives. Claude and several of his fellow former textile workers went to the factory to bring the owner to the citizens' justice, but alas, the entire family fled the night before. The crowd looked to Claude for an answer. 'What do we do next?' Claude scratched his head, looked around, smiled, and said, 'We get back to work.'

"The Republic now owns the textile factory. It makes a fine cloth to this day, and Claude runs the factory. He still harbors a grudge, though, and will only sell the cloth to sack makers. 'A sack for a sack,' he told me. 'I wish I could spit in the former owner's eye every time I says that too.'"

"Oh my. So you buy your sacks from him then?"

"No, Lyon is too far away to purchase sacks. He brings me some a couple times a year whenever he visits. He says he doesn't wish to make money off… well, he says some very nasty things from about that point on. I am likely the only person in the entire city that uses sacks like these. You can tell who shops with me sometimes just from looking at the sacks they carry. Sometimes you can see people wearing clothes made from the sacks. A lot of little boys and girls run around with my sacks on their bodies."

I laughed as Monsieur Bordelon counted out the coins and handed me back a couple sou I had miscounted. I put the remaining coins in my purse and then looked at all my packages and groceries. It was going to be too much for me to carry. I was certain I could bear the weight of it all, but the sheer volume was too much to get my arms around.

"Henri will bring your groceries to your tenement," Monsieur Bordelon said to me. "You know where she lives, right?" he asked Henri.

Henri nodded and then actually spoke. "She lives in the same tenement as Theo."

A jolt struck me when Henri mentioned Theo. I did not know why. I knew Theo lived in the same building I lived in. It stood to reason that others would realize it too. It was not like that fact made people think we lived together. That was preposterous.

I realized that I was just standing there. I curtsied. "He can deliver them to Madame Rochelle. I will let her know to look out for him."

Monsieur Bordelon then rummaged through one of the packs and pulled out a fist-sized, paper-wrapped bundle. "You should take this yourself then."

The bundle smelled of lavender, rose, and lye.

Monsieur Bordelon smiled. I smiled. Henri... scowled.

My smile faltered, but I recovered gracefully enough I thought. I put the soap in one of my packages, gathered everything up, and left the store somewhat delighted. The tenement would eat well again. It was nice to actively do something nice for someone else, but I was now modestly certain whose money I had. I vowed to return it, not to the Clubhouse like I originally thought I would, but to Monsieur Bordelon. How to return it would be an interesting problem. I hoped there was enough left that the Bordelons would see the return as a blessing rather than curse me for what was missing.

14

THE HIDDEN STRENGTH OF MATRIARCHS

August 27, 1814 AD

Monsieur Bordelon gave me far too much soap. I broke the bar in half and rewrapped the larger of the two halves in the paper to bring to Marcel's wife. He had been so kind to me. I wanted to do a kindness for him and his family too. I had to ask Madame Lacelle where Marcel lived. His apartment was on the third floor, last two rooms on the left side.

I knocked on the first of the two doors. A minute later I knocked again, and there was still no reply. I reached up to knock a third time, when a raucous noise erupted from further down the hall. I turned and saw a tired woman in her early forties holding a babe on one hip and leaning out the door.

"What?" she asked.

A chorus of "Who is it, Mama?" and "I wanna see" spilled out from behind her.

"I'm in the middle of..." the woman started to say. She turned and looked behind her and frowned. "I'm in the middle of everything right now. Who are you? What do you want? And make it quick."

I curtsied. I was getting better, but I almost dropped the soap. "I am Charlotte, madame. I moved into the tenement about a month ago. Your husband, Marcel, has helped me out a few times."

The woman smirked. "Yeah, I bet he has. He helps out everyone but me."

"I am sorry, madame. I would offer you some help, but I am afraid I do not know anything about children."

The woman's smirk smirked.

"But," I interjected just as it seemed like she was about to tell me to... do something unladylike. "I do have a gift."

I held out the soap, and the woman just looked down at it.

"It is soap. Lavender and rose. I bought some, but Monsieur Bordelon gave me too much. I thought you..."

And then she was crying, crying great big sopping tears. The woman reached out and grabbed me. She hugged me close and kissed me on the cheek. She set the child down on the floor and took the package in both hands. Immediately the little boy she had been holding tried to climb back into his mother's arms. The other children began to quiet.

"What's wrong, Mama?" One of the older children called, but the woman ignored the child as she unwrapped the package and pressed the lump of soap to her nose.

She pulled me inside, quieted all the children and assured them she was fine. She introduced herself to me as Nicole and then introduced me to each of her children. The woman then began a flurry of activity that was dizzying to watch. She put the soap high on a shelf, rewrapped in the paper so expertly it looked better than when Monsieur Bordelon had given it to me. She then simultaneously prepared a meal, fed two of the smaller children, arbitrated peace accords between various other groups of children, and ironed a skirt.

"My mother could have learned a thing from you, madame," I said.

She only turned and gave me a small tired smile before turning away to drop a dirty bowl in a large bowl of water.

"Is your mother around?" she asked.

When I did not answer her right away, she turned to look at me.

"Oh. She's gone, isn't she?" She said it like a question, but it was not. She knew from the look on my face.

The woman—Nicole, I reminded myself—paused for a moment to come over to me and put her hand on my cheek for the briefest of moments. I looked up at her, and we shared a sad smile. Then she turned and was suddenly doing three things at once again.

"Where did you learn to do so much at one time?"

"I had a great teacher," she said. "Necessity. She's a great teacher and takes payment in tears."

That made me smile, so I got up and finished ironing the skirt. I thought I was lessening the woman's load, but instead she smiled at me and started to wash the dirty bowl and some other dishes in place of ironing.

I stayed for about an hour watching this woman. There were more clothes to iron after the skirt, so I did what I could to help. It was my only real domestic skill other than cleaning, but the place looked near spotless. When I left, Nicole gave me another kiss on the cheek before turning back to work. I do not know if she saw me leave or not.

I was returning to my attic room and approaching the stairs when I heard voices from above in the stairwell.

"I'm telling you, Theo, she had real money."

"You said she sold some of her mother's jewelry, right?" I knew Theo's voice. I hated it.

"Yeah, but if she had gold in her purse, why is she living here? Don't you think she would have moved somewhere else?" That had to be Henri. There was a pause before he spoke again. "It was her. I'm telling you."

"How? You see her, mon ami? She's skin and bones. I doubt she could pull herself up the rope ten feet, much less all the way to the attic."

"I don't know. Maybe she came in from the roof."

Theo laughed. "Her?! A roof runner? No, I don't think so." His voice dripped with condescension, or that was how I imagined it. I wanted to stomp up the steps, grab him by the shirt, pull him up to the attic, and show him what I could do. I blushed as I realized the other implication those thoughts suggested. My stomach gave a little flutter completely unlike my hunger pains.

"Well, I'm going to go up there and find out what she knows."

"No. You're not. It wasn't her. Forget about it."

There was a long silence between the two, broken finally by Theo. In a consoling tone he said, "Come on. We can drink what I have left of the scotch before we go find the Bastard to hit the bars."

"She stole my share of the scotch too," Henri said in a low, muted tone. I imagined him with his lower lip stuck out like a despondent child.

There was a slapping sound as Theo gave a loud short laugh. "Whoever was in our lair may have made off with your share of the scotch, but I know two things. First, it was not my Charlotte. Second, you drank half of my bottle and almost as much of the Bastard's."

Henri let out a quiet chuckle and sigh. "And most of George's too. Well, I might as well help you drink the rest of yours. Then I can imagine that she... or whoever... stole your scotch instead of mine."

"There you go. Now that's thinking like a..."

Their voices dwindled off into the distance, but I stayed there frozen until I heard a door close. I relaxed and leaned against the stairwell wall.

My Charlotte, he had said.

"Do you always block the stairs, Charlotte?" Madame Lacelle's voice made me jump. She stood in the stairwell just below me.

"Oh sorry, madame. No. I... You caught me thinking. Sorry, madame."

"Right. Thinking," the old woman said as if she knew exactly what I was thinking. "Never mind your thinking. Madame Rochelle wanted me to come find you. It seems Henri has delivered some groceries, and Madame Rochelle thinks you had something to do with that."

"Did he, Henri, did he say that?"

"No. She said he seemed quite forlorn when he delivered the

goods. Said nothing more than 'here' and shoved the bags into her arms before trudging off to somewhere."

"He is with Theo. I heard the two of them talking upstairs."

"Ah. Yes. Now I see," the old lady said. This time I knew she knew what I was thinking. I saw it in the sparkle in her eyes. "Well, there's nothing to be done with that now. Go to Madame Rochelle to see what she wants. She probably doesn't have space for everything. Or maybe she has a request. I don't know. I learned a long time ago not to poke my nose in that one's business."

"Really?" I asked, genuinely surprised. "I did not think anyone would challenge you."

Madame Lacelle just laughed. Then she coughed that dry, hacking cough she seemed to always have. "Let's just say that ever since she started serving the tenement, I've kept out of her business. It's purely for selfish reasons, I assure you."

"Madame Lacelle, are you afraid she will refuse to serve you?"

The woman laughed again followed by more coughs, and while she coughed into her handkerchief, she nodded. "Yes... yes. Her food is too good, and she always saves some for me. I know how to keep a good resident happy, and happy residents stay longer."

It turned out that Madame Rochelle wanted to thank me. She hugged me as soon as the door opened, and she talked about all the things she was going to cook. Madame Rochelle informed me that she once cooked in a manor house before some scandal made her unemployable. She did not elaborate. She gave me a couple small parcels wrapped in cloth and tied with string. Then she promised she would teach me how to cook if I wanted to learn. We sat and talked for a short time, then I thanked her and made excuses to return to my room. Again she hugged me as I was leaving. I saw when we parted that the woman had tears in her eyes. Why was everyone crying all the time? Tears were an indication of weakness, yet these were not weak women. I did not understand.

I did not see Theo or Henri when I made my way back to my room. Good. I wondered, though, if I should expect Henri or Theo to sneak into my room tonight. I decided to secure the attic as much as possible. If I got into a physical fight with someone, I was not certain I could keep my claws from coming out. I shuddered to think of the consequences if that happened.

I took a few nails I pulled out of a box I found in the attic rubbish and pushed the nails through the frames and sills of the two windows that would open. Once firmly secured, I bent each nail so I could easily pull them back out. I locked the door to the attic and propped an old bird cage against it. If someone managed to skip all the squeaky stairs and pick the attic door, opening it would cause the cage to fall over. I knew from prior experience moving the cage days before just how loud that noise would be. Finally I succored in my room and waited for thieves in the night.

Nothing happened.

I repeated my new paranoia for several nights. After each passed without event, I got bored. No one threw parties in the Clubhouse. No one tried to sneak into the attic. It should have been a relief. Instead I was bored.

15

STORMS

September 9, 1814 AD

I was in such pain I could not describe, and I hungered more than ever. Between the pain and hunger, I wondered more than once if I would die.

You are already dead, my mistress told me each time.

"But if I am dead, why do I hurt, and why am I so hungry?" I asked in return.

Feed.

Since feeding was not an option, partially because I refused and partially because moving to find something to feed upon was impossible, I write the following account of several days to distract me from the pain in my chest and legs.

September 6, 1814 AD

Boredom and I were old friends, but boredom was the kind of friend that gets you in trouble. It was for me at least. I should have planned ways to return Bordelon's money. Or I should have purchased more books to read. Instead my mind kept returning to the secret entrance to the catacombs Vincent took me through. Surely there were more, but what other hidden or forgotten wonders existed? What other treasures were lost that needed discovering? My questions demanded answers, so I started roaming the streets at night looking for parts of the city that most people never go, like abandoned buildings, hidden parks, and under bridges.

I used the few skills that living on the street taught me to avoid the germane and guards. Anyone who lived on the streets quickly learned to be visible when it was helpful and not visible when it was absolutely necessary. My new boys' clothes helped me blend into the darkness and escape the few times I was noticed. Skirts were not appropriate nor helpful when chased. Well, outside of courting, that is.

Most bridges in Paris crossed the Seine and provided little to no interest to anyone. I crawled around under a few, looking for secret passages or unlocked doors. I found nothing but grime and filthy water.

Private parks were numerous, but all the ones I explored were uninteresting. Some were lovely, but none kept my boredom from returning. The interesting parks were all parts of larger residences with guards. My boredom urged me to explore those, but I finally had some money and a measure of security. I was not going to risk such luxuries fulfilling idle curiosity.

The abandoned buildings were too dangerous to occupy. I entered one beautiful building by climbing a shadowed alley wall and pulling myself through a fourth-floor window to have a look around. Most of the building's interior—walls, floors, furniture, carpet—everything was missing. Well, that was an incorrect statement. It was all there... in a giant pile of junk four floors down. A great ragged hole of emptiness and dust filled most of the building. I stood at the edge of the hole, looking down into the abyss when I felt the floor shift. I hopped backward some five feet to the wall a second before the section of floor I had been standing on fell to join the rest of its body in the pile below. I expected a loud crash, similar to the gutters when they fell, but the noise the floor made as a dull *whomp*. The whole building would follow that bit of floor eventually. I did not wish to be within when it did.

I began looking for partially abandoned buildings. Vagrants and drunks often occupied such buildings. As a girl on the streets, finding such a spot was almost as valuable as hard coin, but it was almost as dangerous too. A wall guarded your back, but it prevented you from fleeing too. I expected that people would want their privacy and would thus scatter between the rooms on all floors as far apart as possible. Instead, they all seemed to cloister together, huddling against the specter of life in groups until the security of death came for them all.

After a week of searching the city for hidden or abandoned locations, I was filthy again. I did not wish to don my new dress while so filthy, and I did not wish for anyone to see me dressed in the boys' clothes I had purchased for my more clandestine activities. So I planned another bath. The thought of lugging seventeen buckets of water up five flights of stairs did not enthuse me, so I counted myself fortunate when it started to rain last night.

Rain washed the world clean, so why not me? I did not want to go down to the ground floor, however. Theo and his friends were there. They spent most evenings now loitering in the alley between tenements, in the cul-de-sac, or roaming the streets. Bordelon's son was one of them, of course, but there were two more young men I did not know. The Bastard and George, I guessed. The four spent their time playing games of dice and harassing women, at least when Madame Lacelle was not around.

Theo's friends harassed me as well. When I did not run to Madame Lacelle after their first advances, they got bolder, as if a girl who did not run to her mommy when annoyed meant she wanted more attention. Their antics were innocent enough at first I suppose, but a person can only take so much before she snaps.

Two days ago on the first floor landing, all four were gathered. As I passed, Theo used a stick to lift my dress a bit, maybe three inches. The boys all laughed. I panicked. What if they saw the hooks in my legs? I whipped around and snatched the stick from Theo's hands, swung it, and smacked the beautiful cretin in the face before breaking it in several pieces. I threw the pieces to the floor at his feet, straightened my skirt to ensure it covered my legs, and stomped up the stairs.

He and his friends stood stunned, but once I was on the floor above, his friends broke out with a louder raucous laughter. They have left me alone since but continue to look at me with increasing lecherousness, except Theo. Theo no longer looked at me at all.

I did not want to be near them. Nor did I want them to see me in boys' clothes or watch me wash in the rain. So I took my other route out of the building. The rain did not slow me down at all. My claws ensured I did not slip. Washing this way also allowed me to practice using my monstrous aspects. I knew it was important, if not why.

More than once my mistress told me, *Embrace the monster. She follows you everywhere. Ready and willing to help you. Remember.*

I did not want to embrace the monster, but the gifts I already had needed to be developed and understood. Both meant I had to practice with them. Practice meant pushing myself to my known limits and occasionally beyond. The thought scared me but thrilled me too.

Maybe I will start with this "roof running" that Theo seems to think I am not capable of doing, I thought to myself. *If nothing else, I can see more of the city.*

Or fall to your death, my mistress put in.

I gave an exasperated sigh and ignored her.

I walked to the far end of the tenement roof, slid down to the next tenement, and crossed its roof. I climbed about half a story to the roof of the next tenement, the three forming the walls to the cut-de-sac below where I first noticed the children and talked to Madame Lacelle about renting a room. My clawed feet and hands made the climbing like child's play. Once I was at the crest of the roof, I turned and faced the wind from the north. Lightning flashed and thunder boomed while the wind pushed at me. The mild drizzle of the past hour became a sudden torrent. It washed over me in fierce waves that threatened but ultimately could not push me off the roof. I was mightier than the wind and rain combined.

I smiled, delighted, as rivers of water washed through my hair and over my clothes. My hands scrubbed through my hair, over my face and neck. Then I sat on the ridge and scrubbed my feet and ankles clean. Paris streets, especially in the section I now called home, were exceedingly filthy. Excrement flowed into the streets from the outhouses or dumped onto it from emptied chamber pots. The inadequate number of drains into the sewers clogged after several days without rain. Excrement from man and horse mixed with dirt, rain, and God knows what else to make a vile concoction that the locals called The Mud. Walking though such filth was a constant concern, as The Mud would eat away a good pair of boots in a year or less, and my feet were not a good pair of boots.

No matter how careful I was, it was impossible to avoid The Mud. While it no longer held the disgusting odor it once held for me, my feet were constantly red and raw from the filth. Clean feet were good feet.

I looked around the rooftops near me for other people. I was not the first roof runner, so others had to exist. But I could not imagine anyone else being outside on a rooftop during a storm such as this. I decided that the new moon and stormy skies would hide me from prying eyes, so I removed my shirt and held it in one hand while I scrubbed my body with the other. I switched the hand holding my shirt and scrubbed with the other hand. I caught as much water as possible from the roof into my shirt and tried to wring the dirt from it. At first I tried rubbing the material against the roof, but the roof itself was filthy. How did a roof six stories up get filthy? I donned my shirt and removed my pants, repeating the process.

It felt brazen to be in such a state of undress while in the open air, and I found that I liked being brazen. I felt alive, so I removed my shirt too and danced naked in the rain.

Once the thrill subsided, I went back to business. I cleaned my legs carefully, especially around the hooks. I still did not know how I would remove them, but I wanted them gone.

I wished I had ripped them out as soon as I was able.

When I finished scrubbing, I made a relatively clean spot on the roof, lay, and enjoyed the simple feeling of the storm against my naked body as I gazed upon Paris at night in a thundershower. What was that word Father used in such situations? Resplendent.

It was resplendent.

An hour later the heavy rains were past and most of the lightning was behind me. A light mist drifted to earth, pushed to and fro by the wind during its descent. Most dwelling lights extinguished during the storm and left the streetlamps in the nicer portions of the city to light my view.

"Someone's up here," a male voice said.

I jumped up and leapt over the ridge of the roof and slid a few feet down. My clawed feet gripped the roof tiles and stopped me before I slid too far. I rushed to don my shirt and pants. There was no time to button my shirt, so I held it closed with one hand as I crept back up the slope until my head was close to the ridge. I peered over and looked toward where the voice came from. It was one of Theo's friends. I did not know if it was the Bastard, George, or someone else. He was the thuggish-looking one with a dirty brown mop for hair and eyes too small. The small-eyed one climbed the rope but stopped on the roof. He held the rope with one hand and gestured to where I was with the other while he looked down.

"I don't know who it is," he said. "All I saw was a shadow. It could be who stole our money."

Their money, hah! I thought just as lightning flashed behind me.

"He's still there on the other side of the roof. Hey you!" the small-eyed thug yelled.

I panicked and ducked. These rogues could not find me on the roof. At a minimum, they would know I took the money. They might even turn me in for the fallen gutter works. I did not want to imagine what else they might consider if they caught me, but I felt Madame Lacelle's warnings bubbling to the surface of my thoughts.

My feet transformed back to their human form, and I slid down the roof several feet. I transformed my feet again and dashed away from my tenement and the young men. Twenty steps was all I managed before I encountered my first hurdle. Rue des Billettes was less than five feet in front of me.

I stopped and surveyed my position. The building in front of me, across the Rue des Billettes, was a story shorter, and the street was narrow, maybe eight feet wide. To my left was the crest of the roof I was on, and to my right was the much wider Rue de la Verrerie. The building across Rue de la Verrerie was half a story or so taller than the one I stood on. Behind me were the boys. If I crested the roof, they would probably see me near enough to tell who I was if they had not already. I had no real choice.

I had to jump across the narrow Rue des Billettes.

With no time for even a quick prayer, I took two large steps toward the side of the building and jumped to the lower roof across the street. Almost by instinct, I rolled as I landed and was on my feet in a flash, running away from the boys. A quick survey of my landing spot showed that I landed on the flatter middle section of the roof. If I had landed another two feet to the right, I could have tumbled off to the street below before I had a chance to catch myself.

A brick wall topped with many chimneys divided this roof too, and I jumped. I looked behind me as I crested the wall of clay pipes. I saw two forms on top of the roof I had just jumped from. Lightning flashed in front of me, illuminating the figures across the narrow street. For the briefest of moments I saw Small Eyes's and Theo's faces. Their mouths were agape.

Shit.

16

ROOF RUNNING

September 6, 1814 AD

I cleared the chimney wall with ease and dropped to the other side. When I landed, I scrambled and pressed my back against the other side of the wall. I held my position for almost a minute before I could hear them again. They were not quiet. I doubt any of them knew the definition of subtle, much less quiet.

"...ing flew over the wall," one said.

"I know. I bet he's a member of the Guild. It looked like he was wearing a cloak," Theo said. I knew his voice. It was the one that made my non-beating heart flutter. My shirt was still open. I hastily fastened two buttons as I listened.

"The two of you are insane," a third said. "People can't fly."

Then Henri chimed in, "Nor is there some grand Thieves' Guild in Paris, and if there was one, it certainly isn't populated by flying men. Besides, I saw nothing."

"What do you know?" asked the first. It had to be Small Eyes. "We saw someone, and when the lightning flashed, we saw their shadow suspended over the wall there like he was flying. By the second flash, he was gone."

"We did," Theo said. "He probably climbed the wall and was

jumping down. We just happened to catch him at just the right moment. But damn, he is fast. We need to jump across the street to the other building and follow him."

They were going to keep following me. I wanted to listen more, but I needed to put distance between us. I dashed away from the wall and up the slope to run along the ridge. The chimney walls were not sloped like the roof, so the wall was much shorter along the ridge and easy to hop. Once on the other side, I peered over the wall toward Theo's group. One was across and helping two more who were hesitant to jump the narrow street. One pointed in my direction excitedly. I ducked and considered my options.

This block was much like the one with my tenement. Several buildings were joined together roof to roof with some variation to the height of the buildings. Some were a story shorter or taller, but no more than that. This block was half the width of the previous block, so I needed to turn to my right soon. I wanted to be on the opposite slope when I turned.

Theo's group was likely to follow me wherever they could. I was still scanning the rooftops ahead when I heard footsteps approaching. I had only an idea of where I would go, but that was all I was going to get.

I ran.

Almost every building had chimney walls. The ones that did not usually had a couple of actual chimneys or pipes protruding in clusters of a half dozen or more around the roof. About one in five buildings had no chimneys at all. I used as many obstacles as possible and made quick progress around them all.

After three buildings, I was almost out of joined rooftops. I stopped and looked back. Theo ran almost as well as I did. His footing was dexterous and his feet almost never slipped. When he did slip, he stopped himself immediately. Then he adjusted and took off again as if nothing happened. I giggled and let Theo have the smallest glance at me before taking off again.

One more building and I found myself without another joined roof. I did not remember the name of the street, but it was more narrow than Rue des Billettes, which was good because the rooftops were the same height.

I forgot to roll, and I landed hard. The hooks in my legs threatened to rip out, but luckily they did not. The roof held as well, but the wood under the tiles gave slightly. I would have to remind myself that many of the buildings around this part of Paris were not in the best shape. I changed my route to avoid buildings with obvious rot or water damage.

It was quite fun running along the roofs of Paris, climbing up or down the sides of buildings, leaping over walls, and letting a boy chase me. I never considered this to be how my first boy would chase me. Then I soured. I was not a girl, not a normal one, and he was not a boy. He was a man, a man with questionable motives and morals. Despite how handsome he looked with his permanently messy hair and causal swagger, he was not someone I should trust.

I did not wish to think sour thoughts, however, not at that moment. It was too fun. So I shut those thoughts away until morning, and I lived in the moment. I was a girl, just a normal girl being chased by a beautiful boy. And if I let him catch me, he would kiss me and we would laugh and fall into each other's arms. And then his friends would try to rape me and beat me and take my things. Why would reality never be pleasant?

I really had to lose them. Theo's skills at running along the rooftops were such that I was not going to lose him for long. I would have to find a way to climb down to the street level and run back to the tenement.

That was when I had a grand idea.

I was still running away from my tenement, but at the next opportunity to run left along another roof, I took it. I realized too late I chose poorly. I looked back. I saw Theo, and he saw me as he climbed a chimney wall. Blessedly there was a new moon and the lightning was even less than before, so I doubt he saw more than a silhouette.

I slowed as I approached the end of the building. The roof hung almost a foot over Rue Sainte-Croix-de-la-Bretonnerie five floors below. The building across the street was the same height. There was no easy way down, but that was not my intention. I ran back about ten feet. I took two deep, if unnecessary, breaths and turned to see Theo about a hundred feet behind me, climbing another wall but still following.

"Mistress guide me," I whispered.

I ran as fast as I could for the end of the building. I was much faster than I anticipated, but I was able to adjust to the faster pace, and at the last minute I launched myself across the street.

Maybe *men* could not fly, but for a brief eternity *I* could.

The wind whistled through my hair and clothes. It was exhilarating. It was glorious. It was over far too soon.

I overshot where I intended to land by a dozen feet or more. When my feet touched the roof, my claws sparked against the slate. I toppled forward as my clawed feet grabbed the surface. Too late to adjust my claws, I fell and started rolling to my right. I used my clawed hands to stop sliding any further down the roof. I rolled over onto my back and smiled at the clouds overhead. I did it. I jumped the distance of the entire street and then some. I lay on the foreign roof and laughed.

"Top that, Theo!" I yelled to the sky and laughed some more.

I rolled back over to see Theo stop at the end of the roof on the other side of the street. He was panting and held one hand to his right side as he looked around. He walked the circumference of the roof line from wall to street, searching over the edge. I crawled to the first chimney wall of my building and hopped over. Once concealed on the other side, I turned and peeked back over the wall.

Small Eyes showed up after a couple minutes. He paused long enough to catch his breath, and then he and Theo talked. Small Eyes held his hand out to his sides while turning to scan the area. Theo shrugged. Small Eyes gestured back the way they came, but Theo just shook his head. Small Eyes puffed and held his arms wide. That I took as, "Well, where is he?" Theo shrugged in defeat.

Henri and the other friend came up after another couple minutes. The other friend was limping slightly, and the two sat on the rooftop while they caught their breath. All four talked, and after a brief conversation, the two sitting boys stood. Everyone turned to leave.

I bit my lip. I knew the game had to end, but I could not help teasing Theo. I whistled as loud as I could, turned, and ran away along the ridge. I jumped over the next chimney wall and looked back. All four stared in astonishment. I continued to run and jump away from them until I knew they could no longer see me. After another block, I began the process of heading home.

On the rooftops, I could run and jump as much as I wanted. I could run faster and jump farther than anything I ever imagined possible. I had no need to hold back. No need to hide who or what I was. I was free.

I was also foolish.

17

FALLING

September 6, 1814 AD

I was two streets away from my tenement when I crossed the street again. While I feared Theo's group might make it back to the tenement before me, I reasoned that they would not. Bordelon's son was limping, and I gave them all a good run. All four were out of breath, and none of them saw me change direction. They likely had no desire or reason to rush back.

Rather than jump across Rue Sainte-Croix-de-la-Bretonnerie onto the roof of my tenement, I jumped to the building across the alley from my window. It was of a height similar to my starting point, whereas my own tenement was a story taller. I continued parallel to the street for one more block and easily jumped Rue Sainte-Avoye. Rue Sainte-Croix-de-la-Bretonnerie turned into Rue Saint-Merri at the intersection there, and I wondered if my jump counted as jumping the same street or not. It was irrelevant. One jump and a little climbing would have me home and secure in no time.

I checked the street in both directions for traffic and then the rooftops in all directions. No one stirred above or below, so I backed up and took another deep, if unnecessary, breath and charged the edge of the building.

It is our small errors, our minor misjudgments, that do us the most harm, I think. Our grand errors hurt others, but our minor errors hurt us. It is a lesson I seem to refuse to learn.

~~The last thing I ever said to my father was in anger. I knew he forgave me as soon as I said it, but that changes nothing. I saw the pain my careless words inflicted, but I also knew from prior arguments that he would be there smiling when I came home. He would chastise me, but we would hug and all would be well again.~~

~~Except it was not well. It would never be all right ever again. And that was my fault. I would never be able to take it back. I would never be able to apologize, to hug him, to feel safe just from his proximity. If God did not damn me that day, I damn myself. He was such a wonderful... NO! I will not do this! I'm writing about falling. Falling alone. Falling is so much easier to do alone.~~

I knew I took one too many steps when I jumped. When I pushed off, a portion of the roof that overhung the street snapped. I lost much of the force required to propel me, and I did not get the height I needed to cross the distance. I knew I was going to strike the side of the other building well before I was even halfway across the street.

Protect your head, my mistress said.

I judged I would collide with the opposite building about two to three stories up. A stone ledge barely a handspan wide ran between floors. The stone was worked into an intricate floral pattern. Some man or men worked long hours pulling beauty from stone, and then someone else stuck that beauty twenty or more feet over everyone's heads, ensuring it would never be seen, except by me in that moment. Though I doubted anyone ever factored flying ghouls into the possible appreciation of their art. I started to wonder if this was the man's finest work, but I hit the wall.

I hit claws-out, very catlike, but my feet did not find purchase, and I bounced. Off the building. I scrambled and grabbed what I could of the ledge, and my hands found purchase. To my horror, the floral stone slid from its place in the wall, and we both drifted into the void above the street. The pain from the fall was such that I allow myself the following: Fuck whomever set the mortar for that stone.

I barely had time to ensure I fell head up when I hit the street feet first. I heard something snap as I fell backward. A blinding flash of pain bolted up my right leg, but before I could scream, I pitched further back.

My right leg was caught in place as I fell back onto a pile of something hard with a low metallic crash. My leg felt like someone was shoveling hot coal into it as I heard a sickening rip and the dull crash of metal. More decorative stones from the ledge followed their brother in my hand. I held my arms over my head as all but one of the falling stones struck the ground all around me. That one struck my outstretched left leg.

Fuck that mortar guy twice.

Finally, I screamed.

Somehow my scream was silent. Silent, long, and complete. I now think my mistress protected me with the silence. Animals bolted out of sundry secret hiding places and ran as directly away from me as possible.

Dogs howled in the distance.

I did not know how much time passed. I simply existed for some matter of time between the blink of an eye or the duration of the creation of the universe. When I was aware once again, I assumed very little time actually passed. It was still dark, and no one had yet come to investigate the noise. I pulled myself to sit upright. Someone stacked the fallen gutters from the alley days before, and I fell into that stack. My legs were buried and twisted in wrong ways among the metal.

I had cuts and scrapes across my arms and hands. My chest was a mass of pain. My ribs were certainly broken, but my legs were worse. I could not pull up my pant legs, so I had to slice them open from hem to knee to get a look. Both were a tangled, ugly mess.

My left leg looked like I had a second knee below my actual knee. Bones ripped from the wrong bend, and the hook dangled from where it pierced my leg. The hole gaped wide from the competing forces of stone, leg, and ground. Meat splayed in all directions from the wounds.

My right leg was worse. It was also broken but in at least two places. The hook had ripped free entirely, forced out by the bend formed by the broken bones below my knee. The bones were not exposed, however. Where the hook pulled free, there was a clean hole inside my leg while the outside was ripped violently with meat flowering around the edges of the wound. A bit of muscle dangled from the hook. Just inside of the wound, my anklebone was visible. Everything was visible. My foot hung from a thin band of muscle, sinew, and skin.

I tried to force the pain aside, but it would not disappear. I was able set aside just enough of the pain to function. Unable to walk, I had to find a way to move before someone found me. So I crawled.

It was almost impossible to ignore the pain at first. It was too fresh, too raw to ignore, but I had to move. People would wake soon. With my grievous wounds and almost no blood to speak of, it would be impossible to hide the fact that I was... different.

Instead of blood, it looked like my veins were filled with a thick black ooze. The lack of blood was unexpected, but the black ooze was strange. I considered my circumstances and admitted to myself that I was hardly surprised.

I crawled into Rue Bar-du-Bec pulling myself forward little by little with my arms. At first I dragged my legs behind me, but eventually I managed to push with my knees if I lay flat enough.

Everything was wet, and the center of the street was flooded. I did not cherish the thought of crossing it, and paused for a moment as I tried to catch my breath. It did not occur to me to wonder why I was short of breath, as I was dead.

I heard whistling as I lay panting for breath I did not need.

Someone was walking down the street and approaching the alley. I was about a third of the way across the alley and into the beginning of the flooded section. I stopped breathing and was dead still. I clearly heard someone's footfalls as well as the padding of smaller, quicker steps.

"Oy there, Reine," the whistler said. "It looks like someone has knocked over Gaut's work."

The voice sounded like it belonged to an older man, maybe not ancient like Madame Lacelle, but certainly older than my father had been.

There was a throaty but hushed *woof*.

"You don't think that someone's still around, do you, girl?" the man asked.

Another hushed *woof* followed. I doubted the man could really talk to his dog, but from the sound of their conversation, and considering the things I have seen and done recently, I was not going to make assumptions.

"Hmmm," the man said. "Fine then. Go see if anyone is around. Be careful. I'll be right behind you."

The dog barked.

Water splashed behind me.

I panicked.

The horrible but familiar form of the monster my mistress wanted me to be stepped up beside me and squatted to look down at me and the damage I had sustained.

You need help, my mistress said. *Embrace the monster. Kill the man and the dog. Feast. And you will be whole again.*

"No," I said as quietly as possible. It came out with a sob. "I will not kill an innocent man and dog."

Then you will be discovered.

"Can I do the scream again?" I asked. The dog seemed to hear me and woofed. Small padded steps splashed in the water around the nearest corner and approached rapidly.

You will need to walk as well.

"Yes," I said. Then there was no more communication. The monster disappeared, and I was the monster once again. My legs were less than whole, but they were straight.

A tall black-and-white hound turned the corner and skidded to a stop when it spotted me lying less than ten feet away. It barked once, the sound bouncing off the buildings along the narrow street. I screamed the silent scream in return. The dog tucked its tail between its legs, turned, and fled in the opposite direction.

"Reine," the old man yelled from somewhere farther down the street.

I pushed myself into the deepest portion of water in the middle of the alley. It was much deeper than I expected. The mud under the water was deeper yet, and it swallowed me almost completely. With my body and most of my head submerged, the cool water and mud soothed the burning of my wounds. I sighed in relief.

That was a bad idea. Sighing moved my chest, which was painful with my broken ribs, even transformed. I grunted from the movement of bones in my chest.

"Who's there? What did you do to Reine?" he yelled as he turned into the alley.

In desperation I submerged myself completely.

"Come out, whoever you are," the man yelled again. The water muffled his voice. "I'll get the police if you do not come out."

I lay completely still.

My mistress spoke to me from the silence. As always, her voice was clear.

Kill him, she said to me. *Feed on him and your problems will disappear*.

Again I refused. Killing him would not solve all my problems, it was simply expeditious. *My Lord*, I thought then. I was thinking about the consequences of killing people. Who has thoughts like these?

I felt vibrations in the water and earth. Footfalls. I heard his feet strike the water in which I lay. He stopped when his boot hit something underwater, my broken foot. I gasped in pain and inhaled filthy water as I clenched my claws into fists. My whole body tensed. I felt on fire despite being submerged in water and mud.

He poked at the water with something, a stick or a cane maybe. He missed my foot several times, but it seemed he was getting the general shape of what his foot struck. He solidly jabbed my leg twice.

I was about to bolt out of the water and end the man. I could see no other way to end my fear or the torture he was inflicting on me.

All I wanted was for him to go. If he would simply go, he could live. I could live.

LEAVE, I shouted in my mind as hard as I could. I pushed the thought, the command, out of my head and toward him. He paused his jabs before taking a hesitant step backward. Something splashed into the water as the man turned and fled in the direction his dog went.

I waited ten heartbeats, or what would have been if my heart beat, before lifting my head out of the water. The street was empty. I was alone. Finally.

I rolled over as best I could and exhaled filthy water. I coughed several times, and each expelled a mix of filthy water and something thicker and darker. Each time, I inhaled as much air as possible. The pain was incredible, but I was never so delighted to cough in my life. I wondered if I would get sick like those who almost drowned often did? A disease might not kill me, but I imagined that it could certainly make death—or rather… "not life" (I have to come up with a better term than that)—miserable.

Once I could move again, I stood hesitantly. The monster's legs were just strong enough to hold me upright, but any significant pressure would snap them completely. I hurried as much as I could toward the nearest portion of my tenement's wall. I wanted to rest, but lights were starting to appear in windows around me. More than rest I wanted not to be found. I had to get to safety. I had to get to my room. I had to get to my window. So I climbed.

The first few feet were the worst. I pulled myself up by gripping the stone in my claws. My legs, even transformed as they were to their monstrous counterparts, were little use. To make matters worse, while neither hook was embedded in my legs anymore, they were still tied to me. Each foot or two of height gained, one hook or the other would tap the stone wall, sending ripples of pain through my legs, up my back, and into my arms. I could not allow myself to slip or slow, so I placed one hand securely in any nook or cranny I could find in the closely fitted stone walls. When in position, I gripped the stone as hard as I dared and pulled myself up a little more. If there was no handhold, I made one.

Two stories up was a ledge maybe a hand's width wide. I took a very short reprieve and scanned what I could see of the street below. Rain started to fall again, washing me to some degree and keeping people in the tenements a little longer than usual. I saw lights in the first-floor windows, particularly toward the front of the tenement where I originally fell. Only two people ventured out into the weather proper. With lanterns in hand, they examined the pile of gutters. After a bit, they split up, one walking down the street away from the tenements and the other into the street. The man in the street walked its length twice. He also held up and shined the lantern as high as he could. The rain camouflaged me. Had the night been clear or had there been a full moon, he would have seen me. If the man's eyesight was as good as mine, he would have easily seen me regardless of weather or moon.

After about ten minutes, the two men met again at the front of the tenements before returning inside. I relaxed, completely unaware of how tense I had just been, and continued to climb.

I was perhaps eighty steps from where I fell. While I dragged myself, it felt like a distance greater than the entirety of my roof running. Each story of my climb up the tenement wall seemed like a week's worth of roof running. Slowly, relentlessly I climbed. My vision swam at times, forcing me to pause. When my vision cleared, I continued.

At the fourth floor, I paused briefly again to look out across the streets. I could just see the section of roof that gave way during my jump. Almost directly across from me, more of the floral frieze wrapped around the building. I heard barking in the distance. It reminded me of the man, his dog, and how I was almost discovered, so I began the remainder of my climb.

When I got to the roof, I pulled myself up to the rather flat crest and lay face first on the clay tiles. I was panting for some reason and forced myself to stop. Moving my chest hurt, and I did not need to breathe. I felt more than heard footsteps through the clay-tiled roof. I barely lifted my head to scan around me. There was no one near. Whoever it was had to be on the opposite side of the divide.

"I don't know who that was, but this was the most fun I've had in ages." The voice was familiar somehow, but not Theo's, Henri's, or Small Eyes's. It must have been their fourth friend, the one I did not know.

"You would think so," said Small Eyes. Condescension dripped off every word. "I had plans for tonight. Those were ruined."

"Your plans almost always end with a woman. You didn't have a woman tonight," Henri said.

"I can find a woman when I need one. Or a girl," Small Eyes said, a leer in his voice somehow.

"Stay away from..." Theo was saying before Small Eyes interrupted.

"Yeah, yeah. I know. Don't touch *that* girl. Good news for you, I have other orders about her."

"Other orders?" the fourth friend asked.

"None of your fucking business orders, yeah," Small Eyes said.

All of them were silent for several seconds.

"Let's get inside and wrap that ankle," Theo said.

"Thanks," Henri said.

"Fuck you guys, I'm going home," said Small Eyes.

"Me too," said the fourth friend. I was just going to start calling him the Stranger since I had no plan on learning his name.

"Don't get queer on me, Edouard," Small Eyes said.

Damn it. I had just given him an interesting name. My hate for Small Eyes heightened ever so slightly.

Edouard only laughed.

I had to wait, motionless, on the rooftop for another twenty minutes. The light of dawn threatened to creep into the sky soon, and the rain became an intermittent drizzle, when I heard Theo and Henri leave the Clubhouse.

"I don't need your help," Henri complained.

"Whatever," Theo retorted.

Another ten minutes passed. The world was silent. While the sun had not yet crested, the sky was getting lighter and lighter. The dormer of my room was not far, so I dragged myself across the roof and inched to the window. It was open a crack, and the floor beyond was drenched, as was much of my desk and several sheets of good paper. The damaged paper made me want to cry more than my pain. I pulled myself through the window, slid over the desk, and dropped into a heap on the floor.

I was home.

18

MAKING THINGS STRAIGHT

September 7, 1814 AD

Pain flared and woke me. Light poured through my open window and lashed my eyes. Reeling from the light, realization dawned on me. I had been asleep. I did not know that I could actually fall asleep. Well, I guess pass out from pain was actually more accurate. I pulled myself to the nearest wall and propped myself to lean against it. I took stock of my body and found I was fully human again. No single portion of my body was without agony. Deep gashes crossed my arms and hands. A good two-inch-wide section of flesh dangled from the side of my left hand. The dangling part hurt every bit as much as the whole portion. My pants were shredded from my claws, and my shirt was ripped in a multitude of places along each arm and under my right breast. Caustic, filthy mud covered me head to toe. What must have been a pound of dried mud was caked in my hair. Once I could get my mirror, I would survey the damage to my face and neck. Despite the monster's legs being straight and sturdy enough to allow me to stand, my human legs were still the horrid mess they were moments after the fall, and my left foot was barely attached.

Just change to your beautiful form, go hunt, and feed. Everything will be fine once again.

My mistress knew that was not an option, yet she offered. She likely thought it fun to pester me so. I was not the monster, and the monster was not me. No amount of pushing me was going to change my resolve. She quieted again after I thought these words to her, but I felt her smugness through our bond. I sighed.

One of the benefits of being the daughter of a merchant was the number of books that passed through his shop. I had looked through all I could get my hands on, and I read the most interesting, often multiple times. Mother hated the books I was always interested in. Biology, botany, and mathematics bored her, but they trilled me. A thin book on midwifery taught me how babies were made and delivered. Mother banned me from reading Father's books after she caught me with that one, but Father always let me anyway. One section of the midwifery book dealt with common ailments. Among the aliments were broken bones.

I had to clean the wounds, realign the bones, and use a splint to keep them from moving while they healed. No help would be at hand, so I had to figure out a way to do everything myself. I needed to somehow pull my leg straight without assistance. Granted I would prefer to be unconscious while someone else set me right, but I would prefer my mother, brother, and father were all still alive too.

I banged my head against the wall as I sat exasperated at myself. The bitter thought did not help anything except perhaps to ensure that there was no part of me—mind, body, or soul—that was without pain. I sat for several minutes pitying myself until a plan unfolded unbidden in my thoughts. I would need some of my precious few supplies, so I dragged myself across the floor to my chest.

I was proud of myself. I let not a single tear fall as I pulled myself along the floor. They were ready for deployment, of course, but I was the master of such weakness now. Once at the trunk, I opened it and pulled everything out. Each item was set wherever it might land until everything was spread out around me. I closed the trunk and turned myself to sit against it. When the worst of a new abundant crop of pain passed minutes later, I found my legs were… splayed? … out in front of me. I straightened them as much as possible. My tattered pants were in the way and already ruined, so I used my claws and shredded them completely off me.

I untied the hooks from each leg and set them aside. I would use them to set my legs. It seemed despite the fact that they no longer pierced my legs, I was still to be bound to them. Unfortunately, I needed more than just the two hooks.

I threaded one of the eyes of a hook with one corner of a thin blanket and tied it. Testing the knot showed that a small amount of stress made it slip. I had to retie and test the knot a couple times to ensure it would not slip. Once I felt confident the knot would hold, I held one end of the blanket and threw the hook at my wood box by the stove.

Blessed angels in Heaven, my aim was true and the hook landed right in the box. Cursed devils in Hell, the blanket was too short to reach the distance. Before I realized what happened, the blanket slipped out of my left hand and followed the hook halfway to the box. Luc's friends provided me with two blankets, however, and Vincent provided me with two hooks. So after a short rest to recover from exhaustion, sweating, and panting that I did not expect while being dead… or dead-ish… I repeated the process.

The second blanket was no larger than the first. It also would not reach the box, but I was not insane or forgetful. I did not aim for the wood box, I aimed for the first blanket. I had to take another short break after throwing and missing twice. My third throw was also a miss, but the barb on the hook snagged the blanked and left it with an upward fold. My fourth throw landed perfectly behind the blanket. I pulled the hook toward me slowly and to my left before it snagged the blanket securely enough I could pull the second blanket to me.

I had the first one almost halfway to me when the hook slowly tore a hole in it. I fought tears once again when it was only an arm's length away. Very little fabric held the hook in place anymore. Tears could not help me, however, so I mastered my weakness. If the blanket was going to rip, it was going to rip. When it did, I would face that challenge.

The chain of hooks and blankets managed to pull the wood box about two feet from the stove before the first blanket finally ripped through. If that was how it was going to be, then so be it. I was tired of the struggle, but instead of becoming defeated, I got mad.

I dragged myself across the floor the remaining few feet and yanked the blanket once, hard. The wood box came skidding and bumping across the floor. Finally.

I kept my anger—my anger at the situation, at that... box—until I was back in position. The anger helped me work up a resistance to the pain. Once I calmed I knew the pain would flood me anew. It felt like a pressure waiting for a hole to push through and destroy me.

Once I was situated to my liking, I pulled the box the rest of the way to me. I also pulled the covers and more importantly my pillow from the bed. The mattress had been just beyond arm's reach, and the stretch had me sweating and panting once again. I took he pillow, hugged it against my chest and face, and let the pain through.

I screamed and screamed and screamed through the pillow. I expected Madame Lacelle and the rest of the tenement to rush to my aid, but it seemed my screams were the silent kind my mistress granted me. The yowls and barks of a multitude of different animals throughout Paris drifted up to my attic window as I almost fainted. Infants began to cry. I heard their voices follow those of the animals through my window, but I also heard them through the floorboards.

I was not crying though. How the pillow got so wet was a puzzle. More of that muddy, fetid street water probably escaped my lungs as I screamed. I pulled the blanket and pillow back to my chest and relaxed. I must have fallen asleep again, because when I finally looked up, prepared for the next step of my self-administered medical aid, the rectangle of sunlight streaming through my window was in a new position. Maybe an hour had passed. I still ached everywhere, but my energy was restored.

I dreaded what must come next.

I used my claws to slash the thicker of my two original blankets into strips. The hole ripping through the thinner blanket proved it was too thin for this task.

Gathering my rope, I divided it into the three smaller strands that were twisted together to comprise it. I pulled one rope strand apart into the individual strands of twine used to make it. I tied the twine into a single piece and wound it into a ball.

I wrapped one end of a rope strand around my lower left leg at the ankle as tightly as I could. I saw stars, and I bit my tongue as I tried not to scream again. I paused until I could see again.

Before continuing, a thought struck me, so I cut a hand's width of rope from the strand and set it aside. I threaded the free end of the strand through one of the hooks and slid the hook to about the midpoint of the rope. About two feet from where it was tied to my ankle, I grabbed the other end and used the rope to swing the hook in an arc the best I could before letting it drop. My perpetually pained grimace briefly turned to a smile as the hook landed to the right of my heavy iron stove and its momentum slid it underneath.

I pulled on the rope to coax the hook to catch one of the stove's legs. Releasing the portion of the rope tied near my ankle I slowly pulled all the slack from the other end, securing the hook to the front right leg of the stove. The rope tied to my ankle, now ran down to the stove where it looped through the eye of the hook and then back to me.

As I gathered the rest of my materials in my lap, I accidentally tugged the rope. Pain jolted from my ankle up to my thigh. My leg twitched uncontrollably for several seconds as I pulled myself up against the trunk again. Once up, I wrapped the loose end of rope around my torso careful not to tug on my leg again and then took a short break. Sweat drenched me, and waves of tremors wracked my body.

Once most of the tremors faded, I wiped my face with a strip of cloth once and stuck the small bit of rope between my teeth. My hands trembled in anticipation of what would come next, but it could not be avoided. I took two deep breaths, grabbed the rope to the stove in both hands, and slowly, firmly pulled. I thought falling off a building and moving with broken legs and ribs hurt. How I longed for such ignorance in that moment. I managed to keep from passing out just long enough to see the bones sticking out of my leg slide back into the flesh. With one final tug and a small twist to get the top and bottom of the leg lined up properly, I allowed oblivion to swallow me whole.

* * *

September 8, 1814 AD

Voices outside my window woke me. I could tell it was morning again, as a sliver of sunlight was high on my wall where it started its path each day. I still had the short length of rope in my mouth, so I spit it out. I lay on the floor and listened to the commotion drifting up to my window from below. I could not hear precisely what was being said, but it seemed someone had been murdered again, a red-haired woman.

It was not my concern.

For once.

I hoped.

I propped myself up on my elbows and looked down at my legs. Both were badly bruised. My left leg, the one I set, had an massive ugly gash where bone and hook had ripped free. Apparently at least two of my toes were broken as well.

My right leg was still an ugly, disorganized mess.

I sat up as well as I could. The plan I devised to splint my left leg required both hooks, and one was under the stove across the room from me. Crawling to the stove was out of the question. The pain alone was unthinkable. Additionally, the required amount of movement would surely pull my bones out of place again. Instead I needed patience.

I untied the rope around my ankle and unwrapped it from around my waist. Then, bracing myself, I whipped the rope up and down against the floor, sending waves through the rope to the oven. Each wave moved the hook around a bit. First an inch one direction, then half an inch in another. When the hook was no longer directly against the stove leg, I started adding side to side whips as well. Working in such a manner took near an hour with breaks, but eventually the hook was free. I pulled it to me, coiled the rope, and proceeded with my next step.

I gathered my cloth strips and pulled them one by one under my leg, leaving several inches on each side. I started just above the ankle and added strips to just below the knee. I wiped cold sweat from my face frequently as I worked. Once the cloth strips were in place, I laid the hooks to the sides of my leg on top of the strips. I first placed them so that the bends were close to my knee before I realized that arrangement would be noticeable under a skirt. I tried different orientations before settling on putting the bends near my ankle.

The skin around my ankle was black and blue, and there were grooves where the ropes were tied. Both the wounds and the first aid were going to leave permanent scars. It could not be helped. Scarred and alive was better than flawless and dead.

If I was ever going to walk again, I would have to set my bones and heal somehow. Toward this goal, I pulled the cloth closest to my ankle up and around the hook and tied it as tightly as possible. I did the same with the one closest to my knee, then the next one closest to my ankle. I alternated back and forth until all of the strips were tied. I desperately wanted to stop after each knot, but if I stopped I might never restart. When the cloth strips were all tied, I cut lengths of rope strand to make three more ties, one at my ankle, one at my knee, and one between. Finally I took a few more strips of cloth and wrapped the ends of the hooks, particularly around the barbs. I would not stand any time soon, but I did not wish to injure myself any more than I already had. The hooks near my ankles looked like some sort of comical fashion statement. Like a demented jester's shoe worn above the ankle.

My right leg was going to be worse. I had to set my foot and my leg. I was never going to be able to tie the rope around my foot for leverage. I considered looping the rope through the hole in my leg but decided I would only attempt that if nothing else worked. Unable to make a decision about my leg, I went to work instead on my foot.

My right foot was a mess. I would have to do whatever I could and hope for the best. I used my hands to position my right leg with my knee bent and my foot just in front of my torso. This arrangement pressed the bulging bones against the floor, and I released a small whimper. I bundled my thin blanket and put it under my knee and leg, leaving a space where the bulge was to keep it off the floor. My bones still burned with a hot, dull ache, but it was better than the searing flames produced with the bulge pressed against the floor.

I took one of the thinner planks from the wood box and measured it against my foot. I used one of my claws to score a deep notch into the wood, and then I snapped the end of the plank off. As delicately as I could, I moved my foot back into place. I could not feel the foot, so it only really hurt when I pressed it back into place against the stump.

When everything seemed lined up, I took a couple of nails and pressed them into the sides of the plank. I used strips of cloth to wrap around the plank and my foot. Anchoring my foot to my leg required several secure anchor points. I wound twine tightly around my lower leg just above the ankle, biting deeply into the flesh and muscle beneath. Every few rotations, I tied a loop in the twine then continued. Once I had a half dozen loops in the twine, I felt I had enough anchor points, and I tied off the twine around my leg with a knot. Then without cutting or breaking the twine, I wound it between the nails in the plank and back up to one of the loops, which more or less held the foot in the proper position. Eventually the twine would slip, and it would all come loose, but for now it held.

My leg required more creativity. After weighing my options, I realized I needed the stove again. That meant I needed to move. The next twenty conscious minutes of dragging myself across fifteen feet of wooden floor may have taken one or two hours. The light through the window appeared to move in fits and starts. When I got to the stove, I realized that blessedly, somewhere in my delirium, I was rational enough to drag my supplies along with me.

There's a reason I chose you.

Quitting was no longer an option. One simply does not practice so much discipline and endure so much pain only to give up before the prize was obtained.

There's another.

I tied one strand of rope around the leg of the stove and the other end around my right thigh. With my upper leg securely in place, I spread my legs as wide apart as possible. I bent my right leg at a right angle and grabbed my lower leg in both hands just above the rope holding my foot in place. I wiped my face, took a deep breath, and pulled my lower leg away from the stove and my bent knee. The bulge diminished and then disappeared. When I released my leg, I felt the broken ends of bones grinding together.

I expected to pass out again or scream, but I did not need to. When I realized that I was getting better at ignoring the pain, my mistress interjected.

I'm helping you directly, she said. *This time.* The first part sounded proud while the second part sounded like a warning.

Claws came out and freed me from the stove. I pulled myself to the wall, then as quickly as I dared, I straightened my right leg. That done, I splinted the leg with planks from the wood box, cloth strips, and rope.

At that point I was finished for the day. Cuts and abrasions still littered my body, but my worst wounds were treated. Drenched in sweat, I was overtaken with shakes. I took my bed clothes and slid along the wall to lie flat on the floor. I pulled my blanket over me, tucked my pillow under my head, and let oblivion consume me.

* * *

September 9, 1814 AD

I woke to find pain returned. My legs ached, and my right ankle felt like it burned in an actual fire. I sat up to get a look at myself and noticed my chest no longer hurt. For the next ten minutes I marveled that I was still functioning. I was unsure, however, if that made me happy or angry. I set that conflict aside to wonder at the changes that happened while I was asleep.

Except for the large flap of skin that dangled from the palm of my hand, the cuts and scrapes on my arms and hands were gone, replaced by ugly bruises. The loose flap of skin had shriveled to a desiccated strip one-eighth its original size. It looked like it would soon fall off. A thick, ugly scab grew where the flesh ripped free.

Each of the braces on my legs were still securely in place. The makeshift bandage for my foot had fallen apart though. I expected a rotten piece of meat dangling at the end of my leg, but to my surprise the foot was attached. Bloody, sticky strands of new meat connected my foot to my leg all around the ankle. I tried wiggling my toes but only managed to get the smallest one to twitch. I flexed the ankle, but the resulting pain caused more spots to form in my vision.

Encouraged by my foot, I removed the splint and bandages from my left leg. Several of the strips of cloth were glued to my leg with dried blood. I used a claw to separate bandage from skin. The wound beneath was covered over with new flesh. I pressed on the broken bones. There was a bit of pain, but the bones did not shift. I wiggled my toes and even flexed my ankle some as well.

You would heal faster if you would feed, my mistress whispered so quietly that I almost missed it. I ignored her.

Time was all I required to heal. With nothing better to do, I grabbed my two books, bed clothes, pillow, and china bowl, and then pulled myself across the floor to my window. Next to my writing desk, I positioned myself such that some portion of my body would remain in the sunlight's path as it traced its way across my room. I propped myself up with my pillow, covered my body with blankets, set my bowl to the side, and began to read about a young Frenchman living among the native Natchez Indians in the New World.

It would be lovely to live in America one day. France had been such a disappointment so far, but it was home. At least for now.

I did not make it through much of the book because it was difficult to ignore the pain in my legs, particularly in my right foot. I kept shifting without realizing it. It was annoying until I realized how alive the pain made me feel. For the past month, the only real discomfort I felt was the constant gnawing hunger. The hunger was quite diminished since the maître d's death, but every day the gnawing increased little by little. Since falling, my hunger had grown such that I could almost use it to block out the pain. Almost.

No, the pain was everything. I wrapped and unwrapped my foot several times to review the progress of my healing. A watched kettle never sings, however, and I never noticed any change. After a couple hours, I tried to sleep again. The effort was futile, as I was constantly waking just as I drifted off. If only I had that midwife book of my father's, then I could find some plants to chew to dull the pain or help me sleep. I considered pulling myself up into the bed. Maybe the increased comfort would help lull me to sleep and pass the hours, but I did not wish to ruin my mattress with sticky half-dead fluids. I worried about sleeping on a giving surface, as it could be bad for my set bones. Plus I wanted to stay in the sunlight.

To occupy my time, I cleaned what I could in the area around the window. I slid my desk to rest against the wall beside the window instead of being under it. Sliding the desk was awkward from my position, but I was just strong enough to accomplish the task. Several pages of paper fell from the desk in the process, and considering what happened as I slid into the room from the window, I gathered the papers and set them as far from the window as I could.

Every action and every movement hurt. When a task distracted me momentarily from my pain, I would find that immediately after I finished, I was in greater pain than before I started. I tried to find ways to lessen the pain, including raising one or both legs over my head, rolling onto different sides, wrapping both legs together tightly within my blanket, and more... so many more that I lost count. To pass the time, I started making notches in the floor every time something failed. At my fifth notch, I dragged myself back over to the desk to get my ink and pen.

I wrote on the floor each thing I tried, and what type and level of success it brought me. To my delight, the act of writing actually allowed me to focus on something other than my pain. That was when I realized that my need to write was what led me to my plight. I was not trying to remain human when I started these pages, I was just trying to ease the pain. So far it had worked, but even with a nearly full jar, I feared writing to distract myself from this pain would cause me to run out of ink.

19

TATTERS

September 15, 1814 AD

Four days ago, Madame Lacelle knocked on my door. I spoke to her from where I still lay on the floor and informed her I was sick but improving. I worried she was about to let herself in, but she did not. She eventually would, however. I checked to ensure the bones in my legs were set, which they seemed to be, so I removed my splints and stowed the materials in my trunk. I passed out from the exertion.

When I awoke, I had a worm's-eye view of the floor. It was filthy and would raise questions. I crawled on my hands and knees and cleaned the floor as best I could, wiping up bits of dried blood and mud with a handful of rags. I wanted to throw the debris out of my window, but the act was beyond me. Cursing myself for my weakness, I swept the pile under my desk. Darkness intruded to the edges of my vision, but I should not be found sleeping on the floor only a few feet away from a bed. I forced the darkness away until I crawled into my bed. I was asleep in seconds.

Madame Lacelle returned the next day, and for three more days, to make her inquiry, leaving only after I assured her I was fine. Today she threatened to unlock the door to see if I had men in my room. I knew she was just making an excuse to see how I was in person, so despite the heat I felt over my entire body, I sat up and wrapped myself in my blankets. Sure enough, Madame Lacelle used her own key and opened the door. She took one look at me before leaving in a hurry. She returned with a large bowl of soup, some bread, and a tankard of water on a wooden tray. I tried begging her off, but she had no part in my desires at all.

"Eat some bread and soup," she said. "I know you say you are not hungry, but I know what's best. I have seen at least five of your entire lifetimes. I know what I'm talking about. So eat."

I meekly broke the bread and chewed on the ashen lump. The bread was probably quite tasty to normal humans, but for me, if it was not meat, the taste of most things no longer held any appeal. Dunking it in the soup helped. Madame Lacelle smiled.

"Good. You keep on until I get back." Then she left, closing the door behind her.

I took a couple more tired spoonfuls of soup, and when I looked up again, Madame Lacelle returned with a basin full of water.

"You need to bathe. Get the dirt and sweat off you. Can you handle that, or do you need help?"

"No," I said. "I can handle that. I just need a nap. But I will wash up first."

She stared at me with an intensity that seemed to bore into the granite around my soul. She finally seemed content, but frowned. I would have to distract her train of thought before she decided to hold me down and clean me herself.

"Could I have more bread?" I asked. I did not want more bread, but I certainly did not want her seeing my legs.

The look on Madame Lacelle's face changed from insistent disciplinarian to helpful grandmother. "Of course, girl. Rest. Nap. I'll bring you some bread and leave it on your nightstand."

"Thank you. I should be fine in a day or two," I lied. In reality I had no idea how much longer healing might take. I conceded to myself I might never heal beyond this point. The rate and degree to which I had already healed was quite miraculous, but I could only hope I could soon stand and walk without collapsing.

My nearly severed foot had healed well enough to function. I could flex it and even wiggle most of my toes, but the look of it was ghastly. The flesh at the tear was a hot, sticky mess of new pink flesh, red sticky strands of meat, and thick crusted ichor. I summoned my claws on the foot, and though the transformation hurt, my ankle was stronger while it was in effect.

The once-gaping holes in my legs were reduced to shallow, skinless, weeping pits. Bandaging them did not seem to help. The wounds wept through the cloth bandages, which in turn stuck to the newly forming tissue. I kept them loosely wrapped now to keep things tidy. There was little actual blood to any of my wounds. Much like my ankle, the blood-like stuff in my veins formed a crust-covered syrupy layer over the wound. It was so much like thick syrup that I considered taking a taste. It smelled sweet, marvelous in fact, but my mistress stopped me.

That way is monstrosity. If you want to be like Anton, continue. Else you must find your sustenance elsewhere.

The advice stopped me immediately. I did not wish to start down the road to become something like Monsieur Anton, and I was grateful.

"Thank you, mistress," I said.

I felt her satisfaction.

I'd planned on catching rainwater with my china bowl to wash myself, but the basin of water that Madame Lacelle delivered worked nicely. I waited to wash my wounds until it rained again, however. It would be hard to explain so much bloody water if Madame Lacelle were to return before I could dispose of it.

Standing did not immediately equate to walking. I tried a couple tentative steps but could not put much pressure on my broken foot. Examining the wounds and my legs, I realized that my left leg, the one with the compound fracture, was just a little shorter than the other. I could only stand on it for a couple seconds before I was breaking out in sweats again and having to sit. I lasted almost a minute on my right leg.

Great.

I did not take that realization well. After stifling back tears, I grabbed a piece of the former wood box and snapped it in half. I then snapped the halves in half again and continued until there was little more than kindling left. I reduced two more boards to kindling in a similar fashion. It was a dreadful waste of resources, but I felt marginally better after. I scraped up the kindling and bound it in a strip of cloth in case I ever needed an easy fire. After setting the bundle beside the stove, I lay on the bed with my defeat and disappointment as my only company, my only solace.

I woke in the middle of the night to lightning and thunder.

My legs were still not strong enough for walking, so I crawled to the basin Madame Lacelle had left me. Sometime while I slept, it seemed she had replaced the water, so I used the clean water to first wash my face and hands, then more of my body, eventually stripping my blouse in the process to make my job easier.

I bathed to the flashes of lightning, and lamented that if only I had thought about finding a basin before I went out that night to wash in the rain, maybe I could have avoided all the rest.

My mistress interrupted my lamentations, *Then you wouldn't be as beautiful as you are now.*

I could not contain the thought that sometimes she could be a real bitch. She was not pleased with me for such thoughts, but I did not care. Grudgingly I had to admit I enjoyed the entire night until my fall. Those experiences would not have been possible without the gifts she gave me.

Experiences are rarely all good or all bad. One must consider possible consequences of her actions and be prepared to deal with the repercussions when the unexpected happens.

That was not my mistress. When I asked who spoke, neither my mistress nor this new entity answered.

"How many otherworldly beings will meddle in my life?" I asked the air.

No one answered.

I paused writing these accounts and asked the question again. I waited several minutes for a response, or at least a feeling of amusement or disdain. Anything. Of course no one responded. That would have been helpful or at least informative. Instead of waiting for the fickle nature of the unfathomable to reply, I continued writing my account of washing.

I used my ruined pants and shirt to soak up most of the water spilled while I washed. When I finished, I wrung the soaked clothes out the window before I laid everything out on the floor. If nothing else, I could use the cloth to make more bandages.

Thinking about the clothes brought the realization that I was stuck wearing the threadbare used skirt and blouse from the gendarmes. I could not wear the dress I purchased with my boys' clothes. It would scream to Henri that I had his father's money, and I did not wish to travel that road. I would be unable to wear the remaining boys' clothes until my legs healed properly which might never happen. I could only wear those clothes out on my excursions at night, not where anyone could see. It would be a scandal within the tenement alone, much less in public. The realization brought its own kind of pain.

I shook my head, realizing the kind of person I was becoming.

A survivor.

I was honestly unsure whose voice that was. It might have been my own for all I knew at that moment. The answer was pragmatic and logical, but I did not like it any better.

Once I finished cleaning myself, I dressed in my small clothes and considered the state of my old clothes. Both the blouse and skirt were starting to fall apart. Both appeared to have been dragged across stones. The skirt had holes large enough for me to slide two fingers through, while there were large patches of my blouse rubbed so thin that I could easily see through the material. One wrong move would rip large sections of material away, effectively leaving me nude from the waist up. I would have to buy more clothes, something more like my old clothes, before I could repay Monsieur Bordelon. At that thought, I realized that I might not hold back the tears if they came, but I disappointed myself once again, because they did not come.

20

LIVING AGAIN

September 16, 1814 AD

Hunger's call woke me midmorning the next day. The smell of the city was light and clean in the manner only possible after a heavy rain. Light streamed through my window to shine on my writing desk's temporary new location. Previously I thought hunger and my mistress were one and the same. Oh, how I wished that were true. My mistress was intelligent, mysterious, and occasionally kind... in a way. My hunger was stupid, simple, and violently cruel. The subtle void I felt in modestly increasing increments for near a month was now a many-toothed worm writhing within my stomach, eating me hollow.

I moaned in discomfort and rolled around in my bed for a solid five minutes before finally pushing myself to sit. I was unlikely to resolve my hunger lying in bed. I had to get up and do something. Anything. The damage to my legs and the subsequent pain may have forced me down to rest, but the pain in my stomach forced me up to act. I had to get something to eat, or I might lose myself to the hunger. My first attempt to stand ended shortly after, as my head swam and I was suddenly sitting on the bed again. I took my time standing once the world stopped spinning around the edges of my vision. The difference in my legs caused me to stand slightly lopsided. I tried to keep my right knee slightly bent, but when I walked around the room, I limped and wobbled, which made me dizzy once again.

I sighed heavily. There was no use in trying to do anything else about it. Like my monstrous condition, I had to learn how to make the best of things. Crying and lamenting my fate would only hold me back. I considered finding a good sailor to teach me some appropriate salty phrases to use when my frustration became too great.

I used the comb and mirror to untangle my lengthening hair. My mother's hair. It refused to grow properly straight once the length reached my shoulders. It refused to curl properly too. Instead, I was left with a purgatory of black, twisted, limp straw. At least there was one positive consequence to my fall. Once properly washed out, the Mud left my hair shiny and soft.

I pulled the comb through it more and more harshly as it got stuck in more and more tangles. Two massive and unrelenting tangles required I use my claws to slice through them. My hair annoyed me to the point I no longer cared how much was lost when I sliced through the first knot. When I saw the shockingly large lock of hair fall to the floor shortly after, I corrected my attitude and was much more careful with the second knot.

My mother gave me very little other than life and grief. One other thing she gave me was a spirit to never give up. Ironic, considering how she... Never mind that. I did not give up, and I thanked Mother for that spirit.

My appearance still needed work, so I used what materials I had and applied my imagination. I took the nails from the wood box out of my trunk and bent each one in the middle. Then, using my claws, I took one of the smaller wood pieces I had not turned into kindling and carved it into a pair of rough two-prong hairpins.

I pulled my hair back from my face. Using the bent nails to hold it, I stuck several small curled strands above my ears. Then I braided and wrapped most of what remained and used my wood hairpins to secure the small bun to the back of my head.

No one would confuse me for a lady of the court, but for a girl not quite a woman whose mother was... well... mine, it was a fair performance. I was proud of myself.

Self-reliance. If I could be proud of myself for one thing, that thing was my self-reliance.

My old clothes had become improper, and I could not be seen in any of my new clothes, so I rummaged the attic. I was in my small clothes only, but the attic was mine, and I would hear anyone coming up the steps long before they could get to the door. Since I had cleaned and rearranged everything when I was doing nothing else—which, for someone who did not normally need to sleep, was a significant amount of time—I knew there were several trunks with older clothes. Nothing was in particularly good shape. Most of it was likely stored with the intention to give it to the ragamuffins or perhaps saved for whatever ragamuffins did with unusable cloth. There was a blouse and skirt similar to my own or close enough to pass. Moths, time, and prior use had left many rips and holes, however.

I used two remaining nails on the most aggressive gaps. I had to pinch the nails closed once they were in place. Still, anyone viewing me might see through my blouse in very inappropriate spots, so I wrapped a blanket around my shoulders like a shawl. An ugly, thick, oversized shawl.

I was the height of fashion.

I took several deep breaths. If I blended in and kept my human contact to a minimum, I should do well enough.

I took a handful of francs from Monsieur Bordelon's money and placed them in a small purse I had purchased while shopping. It was likely the only thing I purchased that would not draw attention, other than my terrible shoes, which would not fit my still-swollen feet.

Just in case, I cleaned my room as best I could. I put my hooks, ruined clothes, shredded blanket, bandages, and diary in the false bottom of my trunk. The remaining money I stored in the stove.

I limped to the door and locked it behind me. The attic stairs were so steep I went down them seated. When I made it to the bottom, I brushed myself off, opened the door to the fourth floor, and continued to the stairwell.

The stairs were rather difficult to navigate with my limp. I could not go down these as I did the attic stairs. Too many people would see and ask all the wrong questions. I had to traverse them as normally as possible.

The first step down I made with my right foot. Pain shot up through my leg and into my waist. I almost fell but grabbed the wall just in time. I realized too late that I had grabbed the wall with a clawed hand. I quickly looked around to see if anyone noticed, but the hall and stairs were blessedly empty. I changed my hand back to normal and continued down. I leaned against the wall to take some weight off my right foot. It helped.

Two floors below mine, several children were playing in the hall. One saw me and called out my name. Seconds later they all waved or ran toward me.

"Bonjour, mademoiselle," said Francois. He was a boy of ten and a delight.

"Bonjour," said Marie, Francois's seven-year-old sister. She followed her older brother everywhere.

The other children ranged in age from nine to four. They all played together under one watchful parent's eyes or another. As such, they could be found playing on almost any floor. Their number was once larger, but all the older children were now working as chimney sweeps or in the textile factories. It bothered me that children this young could be put to work, but no one would give me a second glance.

"Bonjour," I replied. "Who is watching you today?"

"I am."

My heart jumped at his voice.

He stepped out into the hall and dragged a lazy hand through his tumble of hair. He smiled and rubbed his face where I had slapped him weeks before. The youngest child, Paulette, ran barefoot to him and grabbed at his pants leg. He bent and reached out with a bright and pure smile.

"Tio," the little one exclaimed as Theo lifted her.

She smiled lovingly at him, and for once I saw—damn him—the

mask of the rogue disappear. His smile matched her own, and then to her delight he began to cover her in kisses. Paulette squealed and tried pushing Theo's face away from hers, but he deftly avoided each of her protesting hands. The other children pointed and laughed at the two.

There were too many people, so while they were all watching Theo and Paulette, I tried to slip away. I made it three steps down when Francois called out.

"Mademoiselle Charlotte," he said sweetly, "you're limping. Are you hurt?"

"No, no," I said without turning as I tried to hasten my descent, but I stepped poorly and bent my right ankle sideways. I balled up my fist and hit the wall twice.

"Are you sure, my mouse?" Theo asked as he approached from behind.

He gently lifted my left arm and draped it over his shoulder. Then he wrapped his right arm around me and supported most of my weight. The help scared me a little, being so close to another person, but it also thrilled me to feel his arm around me, helping me. His hand was incredibly close to my breast, and despite my nature, I found myself blushing and taking quick, shallow breaths. Those breaths brought his scent, which was musky, almost spicy. My stomach tried to pull me through the floor as I salivated. To my horror I could feel row upon row of teeth pressing themselves through my gums, around my tongue, and down through the roof of my mouth.

I forced myself to stop breathing and shook my head. Control, I needed control. I held up my right hand to stop Theo for a moment and concentrated on the pain in my legs. The pain could distract me from thinking about just how good he smelled. I told myself repeatedly that I was not going to eat him.

Are you sure? my mistress asked.

Yes, I thought.

Good, she replied.

Just when I started to think I had some idea who my mistress was, I realized I had no idea.

"Are you well?" Theo asked, his mask still gone.

"Yes," I replied after a moment, after the teeth were gone. "I simply had a dizzy spell. I have been sick. I will be fine though."

He considered my words for a moment before continuing down the stairs. Halfway down the landing as we turned the corner, he called back up to the children.

"Francois, you are in charge until I get back. Keep the little ones away from the stoves and stairs."

"Oui!" Francois replied.

After we turned the corner, I had to ask, "Your mouse?"

"Heh," he laughed. The roguish mask was back. "It fits. You are small, cute, and unassuming, but you're also quick and have teeth that bite."

Cute? I wanted to ask, but the rest of what he said soured my delight at the compliment. I did have teeth, and I could indeed bite.

"Do not forget," I warned.

The full weight of my statement was lost on him, because after we descended a few more steps, he replied with a lazy smile and a sideways glance, "Maybe I like to be bit."

At the next landing, Theo let me rest a second as he spoke. "Only one flight left. If we see Madame Lacelle, you must vouch for me. I have been good. I have not even caressed your breast despite it being so close at hand."

"Such a gentleman," I replied, blushing.

"Well," he said, "it is not sporting to chase a wounded doe. Heal up. Maybe in a few days, we'll see?"

With my left arm wrapped around him, my hand rested on his lean-muscled shoulder. I used that hand to grab his ear and give it a pull. He yelped then laughed.

"You surprise me, little mouse. I like that."

I smiled at him. I felt coy. Experienced.

"You really do not want to find out what I am capable of," I said.

"Oh I'm not so sure. In my experience, most girls surprise themselves more than they surprise me," he said.

I sighed. "That is what I am afraid of."

When we reached the ground floor, I thanked Theo for his assistance. He gave me a squeeze, almost like a hug, before letting me go.

"Are you sure you want to do this alone?" he asked. He almost seemed genuinely concerned.

"Yes. I can make it from here," I said.

Theo looked me up and down once more before frowning. Then his eyes lit up, and he dazzled me with a breathtaking smile.

"I know," he said as he snapped a finger. "Wait here just a minute," he finished before charging up the stairs. Shortly after, I heard muffled voices. Theo's was one of them. He raised his voice to the kids it seemed, something about Paulette and the stove. The others responded, and then more thumping on the stairs as he ran up more flights.

I reclined against the wall and waited. Madame Lacelle hobbled in, looking ancient and wise. She had a cross-stitched canvas bag that hung at her ample waist today. I was convinced the woman wasn't fat so much as she wore twenty skirts and ten blouses in an attempt to stay warm. Her bony hands and sunken face supported my theory. She looked me up and down as she frowned.

"Your clothes are a mess, girl," she said. "But I have to admit, you seem more alive than you were days ago."

"T-thank you," I said, unsure if I was just paid a compliment or not.

"You better?" she asked.

"Oui, but my leg hurts. A sprain from trying to get up and move around too soon," I said, lifting my right leg slightly.

"It is going to be hard finding work with a sprained ankle. Do you have rent money?" she asked, and I immediately cringed.

"No," I admitted. "Well, yes... but I have to go get it today, n-now actually. I need a new skirt and blouse and your rent money. I could probably sleep another three or four days, but not until I ensure I have a place to sleep."

"Good," Madame Lacelle said with a sharp nod and a stern look. "You understand priorities. Most your age struggle with such things. Many older do as well."

I felt a modicum of pride at her declaration. I first met this woman less than two months ago, but her respect had since become fiercely important to me. I gave her a little curtsy, but the movement hurt, and I grimaced. Her face softened as she looked at me.

"Oh girl, I saw the state you were in. I wouldn't force you or anyone else out on the street for being honestly sick."

With that, Madame Lacelle came near me and opened my blanket shawl. Instinctively I tried to be modest and cover the worst parts of my blouse, but she slapped my hands and pulled my arms wide. She tsked before turning her attention to the skirt. There she noticed the large holes pinned shut with the bent nails.

"What happened to you, girl?" she asked as she released my arms, allowing me to close my shawl.

"My clothes are falling apart. I rummaged through the attic to find something I could go out in. I found this. I will get something new and replace these where I found them when I get back," I said, hoping she would drop the matter.

"You look like you were attacked by a lynx." She studied me some more and had me do a little turn. It reminded me of my interview with Anton and Madame, though I trusted Madame Lacelle infinitely more.

"I do not know how you bent the nails to make those pins. They'll work well enough for now, but eventually the small holes you made putting them in will become larger," she said.

Motioning with her hands, she had me bend at the waist so that she could look at my hair.

"They work better in your hair," she said, "though you would be better served closing the pins even more. Your lice are gone. That is good. How did that happen?"

"The man with whom I traded my mother's jewels gave me a comb for free," I said.

"When are you going to learn there is no such thing as free?" she said.

"Yes, I know. I think the reality is that he felt bad for taking advantage of me and threw the comb in to ease his guilt."

Her hand felt through my hair. She adjusted the braids and metal pins here and there.

"Or more likely he wanted you to think he was giving you something out of the kindness of his own heart. Men give nothing for free."

"Who does?" I asked, laughing. In this woman's world, the real world, everything had a cost.

"Stupid girls who've fallen in love," she said dourly. When she continued, her voice was more curious. "Where did you get the wooden hairpins? They aren't much to look at, but they are functional."

She let me go, and I stood straight again. I touched my hair to ensure the hairpins were still in place and feel what she changed. My hair was tighter, more secure. A few of the metal hairpins had been adjusted to hold the tighter shape and hidden even better than I had done myself.

"I made them myself," I said. I could not help smiling just a little.

"You made them?" she asked. "With what? Your fingernails and spit?"

Basically.

"I have a knife," I said. "And a lot of free time."

Madame Lacelle smirked and was quiet for a bit. I thought she was going to reprimand me for not spending more time looking for work.

"Think you can make more?" she asked.

"Oui. I made these quickly. With a little time, I can make them even nicer."

"A little nicer would be good, but some just like these would be good enough. At some point you learn good enough is better than better. If you will make me ten of your hairpins, I will give you an old sewing box of mine with some needles and thread. It will help you maintain your clothes," she said.

"What are you going to do with ten hairpins?" I asked.

Madame Lacelle looked at me like I was thick. "I've got an idea to add some of my embroidery to the ends and sell them. Do good work and I will give you money next time. Money you can use to help pay your rent that is due soon. What you have in your hair will sell for a few centimes, more with my embroidery. Maybe we can get a franc per hairpin from a merchant if you can make them nicer. I'll give you a quarter of what I make."

"A quarter? Surely I should have half," I replied.

"Ha!" Madame Lacelle barked. "Do you know who to sell to? Do you know how much to sell them for? My embroidery will sell your hairpins, not the other way around. Do not be so quick to assume you are my equal in this just because I've asked you to participate. Do you sew? Embroider? Knit?"

I shrunk back against the wall slightly and shook my head to each question.

"My mother never taught..." was all I could get out.

"I can find someone else to carve some hairpins," she continued. "Or I can sell my embroidery some other way. I don't need you, but you need me. I am offering you a way to earn a little more money, maybe enough to allow you to eat more than once a day. Maybe enough to pay rent? Who knows until you try? Maybe if you are nice, I'll teach you how to embroider, so when I'm gone you can have a real craft."

I could not argue against anything she said. She also had an intensity to her eyes when she spoke, a surety of being right that made me feel wrong or at the very least unsure of myself. There was much I could learn from this woman.

I nodded quickly, unable to find my voice, and Madame Lacelle smiled.

"I'm happy you are feeling better, girl," she said.

Madame Lacelle's smile slid from her face as a series of great thumps grew in intensity and frequency from the stairwell.

"You." Madame Lacelle stabbed a bony finger toward Theo as he came down the last few stairs. "What are you doing making such noise? Shouldn't you be minding the young ones?"

Theo blushed. Blushed!

"Charlotte has a hurt ankle. I thought I would let her use my father's cane," Theo said, holding out the scarred dark-enameled wood cane to Madame Lacelle.

Madame Lacelle flinched ever so slightly and stared at Theo for a couple seconds. She measured him in that stare, perhaps for the hundredth time. Well, maybe more like the thousandth time. Finally she nodded and glanced down at the cane before looking at Theo again.

"Well," she barked. "I don't need it. Give it to the girl."

Theo jerked his hand back before walking to me.

"Here," he said, handing me the cane. "Use this while you heal. You can keep some weight off your ankle. It should help, but please return it when you no longer need it."

"Thank you," I said.

I do not know how much time passed, but Madame Lacelle interrupted our eye contact by demanding our attention with a rather loud cough. Theo and I still held the cane. He let go. I swore I felt my heart beating.

"Let Charlotte be on her way, Theo," Madame Lacelle said. "You need to tend to those children."

Theo moved to the stairs and stole one more glance in my direction before running back up the steps.

"That one," Madame Lacelle said quietly. "I don't know if that one is sinner or saint. Don't go falling in love with him. You don't want either a sinner or a saint for a husband."

"Why is that?" I asked softly, still gazing up the stairs. I could still smell him as if he were standing right next to me.

"The sinners will do you wrong, and the saints are just boring," Madame Lacelle said with a little chuckle.

It took me a couple seconds before I realized what she said.

"Then what kind of person should I marry?" I asked.

"A man," she replied before heading up the stairs. "They're usually a little bit of both."

21

A VISIT WITH GIORGIO

September 16, 1814 AD

The cane was a bit too tall for me, but it helped immensely. Giorgio's shop was almost a mile away. I thought the pain in my ankle would be so severe that I would not be able to walk the entire distance without needing to stop. I admit that my pace was quite slow. It took close to an hour before I reached his shop.

The walk took almost all I had in reserves of energy. I felt depleted by the time I got to Giorgio's shop, and so I stopped in an alley across the street. There I rested as people passed. Very few looked at me, and I was all the more comfortable for it. Here, the lamps hanging above the street were intact. The streets were cobblestone, and the sidewalks rose above the Mud, unlike the area surrounding the tenement.

A slow tide of hunger washed out from my stomach, filling me with need. I held my abdomen while I mastered the sensation. When I regained a measure of control, I found myself almost doubled over. I was propped against one wall of the alley. My face was wet, so I wiped it with my blanket shawl. As I looked up, I was startled to see Theo's accomplice, Small Eyes, exiting Giorgio's. He was with a tall, lean gentleman, one I knew from somewhere I could not place. His poise, the manner of his walk, and something about his face taunted my mind, a memory too distant to be distinct but too true for doubt.

The gentleman wore a black suit with tails. His shirt was a dark, almost black shade of blue with a white collar. His face was clean-shaven, and he had a bit of a hook nose that I distinctly remember, but from where, I could not say. His top hat was banded with dark blue satin that I could only just make out against the black beaver pelt. I found it odd that one such as he carried a whip at his belt. His hand seemed to seek the thing. When he touched the whip, he stroked it absently, tenderly. But then he would pull his hand away, only to have it return on its own accord. It was as if the hand and whip were lovers struggling to unite, with some outside force always ripping them apart.

I decided then that I did not like the man.

After the shop door closed, Small Eyes asked the man something. The man glanced toward the door before saying something in return. A carriage pulled forward and stopped in front of the two. The man boarded it. He spoke to Small Eyes the entire time. Small Eyes simply nodded once, twice, and a third time before the carriage pulled away. Small Eyes cast a final look a Giorgio's shop before pulling a flat cap out from behind his back and donning it.

I was able to master my hunger in the time it took Small Eyes to disappear from sight. He walked in the same direction as the gentleman's carriage for several blocks before turning into an alley much like the one in which I rested. The thought made me shiver, and I found myself looking around the alley as if there were more cretins like Small Eyes hidden behind me. I was alone, but I shivered regardless.

I leaned heavily on the cane as I made my way across the street. An oncoming carriage took no care watching out for me, and I had to throw myself out of the way. I shot the driver my best seething look, but he had no idea or care that I had been there, much less my thoughts on the matter. Bastard.

Kill or be killed, my mistress said. *It is time you fed. That carriage driver would be a fine meal, and he deserves it too. How many other people's lives has he endangered? How many has he taken? I can bring you to where he lives. You could feed and sate all of your appetites at once.*

There was something in what she said that rang true, not that I should murder that driver for almost hitting me, but something nonetheless. Maybe feeding on the guilty was less horrific than feasting on the innocent? I was still chewing on the thought when I entered Giorgio's. The sounds of people walking and conversing, the rumbling of carriages pulled by horses with rattling bridles, hawkers doing their best to vie for attention over the general clamor, and more were all suddenly muted as the door banged shut. It is funny to me that often we do not even notice such things until they are gone, and then we ask ourselves how we ever failed to notice them in the first place.

The sudden relative quiet of the shop pulled me from my thoughts into the present. Sunlight poured in through the four front windows, three left and one right of the door. A handful of mannequins scattered about the space displayed his wares. I could only imagine that these must be his finest pieces. All of the pieces on the left were ladies' dresses while gentlemen's pieces were on the right. Two rows of tables split the remaining space. Low stacks of neatly folded breeches, blouses, and vests were arranged on the tables. The walls were lined with what looked like bookshelves but were not filled with books but more folded garments. Pity that, but I conceded a clothier should sell clothes, not books. At least this way I wouldn't be tempted to spend all of my ill-gotten money and trade my minor possessions for things I didn't absolutely need.

I had missed the details on my first visit to Giorgio's, but now I realized that the clothes on display were worth a small fortune. Most ladies spent their free time spinning thread, thread to make cloth. Cloth itself was therefore a laborious task to create, and then to turn around and create clothes from that took additional time and more thread. Where did he get all this wealth?

"Ah, lice-ridden girl. You return. Please tell me you use comb, and not bringing lice in store."

The door had just closed, and already I was reconsidering my entire morning. I shook off the effect of his words, marched forward, and stood before him defiantly.

"Bonjour, Monsieur Giorgio," I said. I was trying to be polite, but my tone might have cracked with a touch of annoyance. "I need more of my money, s'il vous plaît."

I rested my hands upon the counter and gazed up into the man's face. The action seemed to only draw the man's eyes. His hands twitched, and his fingers curled back, making fists of his hands. He quickly flexed them open again and wiped his hands slowly, methodically against his apron.

"Have you kept from stealing more things?" he said.

"I told you the truth. I found those items," I replied. "I need more of my money today, but eventually I would very much like it if you gave me an opportunity in the future to buy them back."

"Giorgio is no… how you say? Lombardy?" he asked.

"Lombardy?" I did not understand what he meant.

The shop bell rang again, and Giorgio's eyes, just his eyes, moved to see who was at the door. His mouth tightened just a bit before he smiled. It was an odd smile. It started with his mouth but took a couple seconds to reach his eyes as he forced it from birth to maturity.

"Ah, Jean would know," he said to me quietly, and then louder he asked, "Jean, what is word meaning person buys things without question and resells to same person, charging extra? You know. Lombardy."

"I do believe you mean a 'pawnbroker,'" a voice said.

I turned to look, and it was a young man, heroic in bearing every bit as much as Theo was a rogue. He moved with a quiet confidence that did not suggest stealth as much as it conveyed a sense of being exactly where he was supposed to be at all times. He was tall with a head of short, dirty-blond hair. He stood straight, not overly rigid, but comfortably formal, and he wore informal clothes of creams and browns that seemed to flow together. His pants were a moderate cream with a touch of brown, while his shirt was light brown and his waistcoat was slightly darker. His shoes were so light a cream as to almost be white. White shoes on Parisian streets, but they were clean. I could barely hear his footfalls as he approached.

Giorgio watched me covertly as I watched Jean. Jean slowly strolled toward the counter and stopped next to me. He smelled of cinnamon and coffee and something else I couldn't place but knew. Frustrated, I wondered why so much of the world consisted of things that give me half-remembered sensations?

My mistress said, *Because half of your brain is dead and you refuse to feed.*

"Yes. Giorgio no pawnbroker. No Lombardy banker."

I was not seriously interested in buying the ruby or earrings back, but if I were to later need more money, say to repay Monsieur Bordelon, then I might need to sell more of my discoveries, many of which I did not relish the thought of parting with.

Jean addressed Giorgio, but his eyes were upon me. "Where did you get this treasure?"

Inadvertently I made a little gasp at the unexpected compliment. Jean's smile didn't exactly change, but it deepened some way I could not put my finger on. It was as if he almost radiated confidence and pride.

"This," Giorgio said, "is Charlotte Villeneuve."

I gasped again, louder. What was happening to me that I could not control my own unneeded breath? My surprise was genuine, however, because while Giorgio did not have my correct surname, he knew my first name. I had very carefully ensured that I never told him my name.

Jean turned to him. "I am not familiar with this name. It sounds new." Then he turned to me and asked, "What did your family do, Mademoiselle Villeneuve?"

I was still chewing on my lip, trying to puzzle how Giorgio might know my name, and was startled to be addressed directly again. I could not answer. I could only stare at the man behind the counter. Giorgio noticed and nodded ever so slightly as he glanced at me, and then suddenly his eyes were steel. In the moment it took Jean to turn back to Giorgio, I was shamefully unable to control my mouth as it hung agape. My mind was awhirl with half-formed questions but no answers. That's when Giorgio surprised me again.

"Is Paul Villeneuve daughter. Father was merchant and collector of rare things Giorgio sometimes buy."

Again the surname was wrong, but my father's Christian name was correct. Who was this man?

"Oh?" Jean asked. His features seemed to brighten. "What kind of rare items?"

"Books," I spurted out, delighted I could finally find the mental stability to form a single word.

Jean turned again to look at me, half of a smile making the second best use of those lips that a girl could imagine.

Giorgio also looked at me, but the steel was back, not only in his eyes but around his mouth as well. "Shut up," he demanded without saying a word. Immediately his appearance was again amiable in the blink of an eye.

"Yes. Once or twice Monsieur had book, but Giorgio buy, how you say? Painting? Drawing? Carved thing? Maybe pretty wall clothes," he finished while mimicking something large and flat hanging down from a flat top.

"Tapestry," Jean said with a chuckle. "'Wall clothes' would be tapestry. The rest together would be 'art,'" Jean said, never taking his eyes and smile from me.

Giorgio looked grateful for the language lesson. "Yes. Paul sell Giorgio tapestry in back room. Make ugly wood wall seem happy. Once or twice sell me book too."

I remained silent through the exchange in part because I was so confused. My father never sold any of those things, certainly not tapestries. He only ever sold books, paper, and writing implements. I wanted to say such once or twice, but Giorgio's look kept me silent.

"And where is Monsieur Paul Villeneuve now?" Jean asked.

My dreamy smile shattered. I was immediately cloaked in grief, and I bowed my head to hide my weakness.

"He died more than a..." I started, but Giorgio piped in and cut me off.

"Was soldier to Napoleon. Died. Horrible. Was good man."

My father was too old to serve under Napoleon, I thought. I had to work to keep a frown from my face, but somehow understood that was exactly what I needed to do.

"Well," Jean said, "if this young lady is in need of a fence, she's come to the wrong location. Monsieur Nikolaev here buys and sells things, this is true, but his clientele tends to be a bit more... royal, am I right, Giorgio?"

Giorgio's reaction was imperceptible, but something changed in his demeanor, a tension that lasted a breath and simply vanished as he spoke solemnly. "Giorgio sell anyone with money. Is true, royal have less. Giorgio prices good. Two combine, make many sale. Giorgio make money. Giorgio also sell republicans. Is good selling everyone. Giorgio find republican fashion too... how you say... no flavor?"

"Bland?" I suggested.

"Yes. Republican too bland. No flavor. So Giorgio sell much royal, less republican. Is not plan, is how is."

Jean simply smiled. "It's fun to watch you squirm, Giorgio. You do it so well that most people probably don't even notice, do they?"

Squirm? I thought. *Giorgio?* I saw no squirming.

Giorgio gave Jean a level look before taking a more relaxed stance and placing his hands flat on the counter. "Giorgio is Giorgio. Young Jean too clever, Giorgio think. Read too much into subtle clue."

Jean simply smiled and shrugged. "Perhaps."

"So what can Giorgio do for Jean?"

Jean glanced at me and, with a tilt of his head in my direction, said, "The young lady was here first. You should see to her before me. I can look at some of your examples as you speak."

Giorgio and I watched as Jean simply walked off and began looking at random items in the store, starting with the tables closest to the counter and making his way back toward the front of the store. I looked to Giorgio, and he simply shrugged.

"I need money," I said.

There was a bang behind me, so I turned to see Jean pulling his foot away from a table leg and sliding the now-askew table back into place. Items neatly folded and stacked on the table's surface shifted. Though nothing spilled, Giorgio's eyes narrowed ever so slightly. Either he was planning Jean's demise, or he was calculating the time required to place everything back on the table just so. Considering the state of the shop and the lack of malicious nature exuding from the man, I assumed the latter.

Giorgio turned back to me and was suddenly talking to me like... well, I don't know... familiar, maybe. He spoke what seemed like gibberish at first.

"Yes. As discuss before. Girl need job. Giorgio has position, but before, girl too proud. Cannot admit girl cannot sew, but Giorgio teach."

"What..." I began, but Giorgio's eyes narrowed, and he flicked his eyes at Jean for an instant before he bore his gaze into my soul. Then the look was gone, as quickly as it came. "... are you offering for pay?" I finished.

I could see Jean just out of the corner of my eye, and I wanted to test a theory. So before Giorgio could formulate a cogent response, I continued in a slightly lower tone, "I hope it is more than that pitiful franc a day that you offered last time."

Giorgio's mouth twitched, but at the same time, Jean looked up toward us and then back down at whatever might be in front of him. If I remembered the store's layout correctly, he was in the ladies' small clothes section.

Giorgio smiled slightly, and his eyes twinkled a kind of pride toward me, or at least that's how I read it.

"Girl unfair. Know Giorgio also offer room and food. Also teaching. Learn skill more valuable than money."

"I have never seen myself as a seamstress," I said. "Which is why I never learned in the first place. I wanted to be a midwife before, well, everything that has happened."

Jean was suddenly next to me again. He had to have moved

quickly to traverse the distance in such a short time, but I didn't notice his footfalls at all. "Sorry, but I could not help but overhear. Monsieur Nikolaev is offering you an apprenticeship? That is quite the valuable offer."

I looked up into his eyes, and while I swam in them, his words sounded as true as anything I had ever heard. Then he said something completely unfair.

"And if you are working here, I'll know where you are. I can come visit anytime I want." With that he lifted my hand and held it between his.

I was swallowing the rather large lump in my throat when Giorgio chimed in gruffly. "Girl have no time for young man. Will sew till fingers bleed and then more. She learn avoiding eyes of charming man. Instead she learn how charm man. Get good price for work."

Jean looked away, and I was myself once more, as if a spell had just been broken.

"Charming you say?" Jean asked Giorgio. "I don't know." He turned back to me, and I could feel his gaze. My reaction was to look back into his eyes, once more enraptured. "What do you think, mademoiselle? Am I some charming man come to get his way with some young woman?"

Yes, my mistress shouted.

The spell was once more broken despite still looking directly into his eyes. I pulled my hand away and put on my most insulted face.

"Monsieur should not be so forward with a young lady," was all I could say. I was tempted to slap him, but I was hoping deep down that he would still come to the shop to see me.

What was I thinking? I was already putting myself in the shop as an employee. I had not come for that and I had not agreed to it. This was spinning out of control too quickly, and I had to right things.

"Five francs a day, plus all the rest... and some new clothes," I said, expecting Giorgio to haggle for a while. Haggling would give me time to reorient myself.

"Is deal," Giorgio said.

I whipped my face around to look at him. He was all smiles.

"What?" Jean and I asked simultaneously.

The smile dropped from Giorgio's face, replaced by confusion. "Is deal. Girl very smart. Will learn quick. Maybe bring young men to shop. Sell more clothes. Is good decision."

Jean watched the flash of emotions on my face as I stared at Giorgio. Then he did something cruel. Jean stepped up to the counter and spoke to Giorgio in a hushed tone. I could still easily hear him. In retrospect I imagine he intended just that.

"You should reconsider, Giorgio. The girl... well, she's dirty, and look at those clothes. I was putting on before because I didn't think you were being serious. This girl... she'll drive away the last of your customers."

At first I thought Giorgio was going to ball up a fist and punch Jean, but instead he seemed to be mulling over the advice. I was livid someone would say such a thing about me, especially out of the blue, and Giorgio only made my emotions more out of control by seeming to actually consider the beautiful ass's words.

My mistress was saying something, but I did not hear her. Whatever advice she might have had was lost in the whirlwind of my thoughts and emotions.

"And her hair," Jean continued. "My grandfather has wigs from when he was a boy with style more modern than her bun. What is that going to say to your clientele? Her place is not here but as a scullery maid or perhaps a ragamuffin. She obviously does not contain the skills needed to be a tailor, as she is not a man and therefore ill-equipped for the task at hand."

I must have been as red as blood.

Hands behind your back, my mistress demanded.

Thankfully I heard her this time, because my claws were out. Luckily my hands were under my blanket shawl. I was slightly crouched too, so I slowly stood up straight, put on airs, and put my hands behind my back until I calmed down. If either of these men discovered my secret, I would likely have to kill them both and flee the city. I didn't want to do either. So I stood there impotent in my fury and embarrassment.

Giorgio's eyes squinted slightly before turning to Jean. "First, Giorgio hoping Jean step back from counter. Is too close. Giorgio like space, not smelling mouth. Second, maybe Jean apologize to girl. Girl is girl. Has worth as creature of God. Plus hair not so bad. Giorgio cut hair. Make even. Also, girl good haggler. Final, Giorgio has clothes girl can wear until girl learn how to make better. Is part of deal." At least that's what I thought Giorgio said. He told me something like that later. I could only hear the sound of my heart beating in my ears.

It was quiet for too long before Giorgio openly frowned at Jean and lifted a hand toward me.

Jean sighed. "I'm sorry, mademoiselle," Jean said, stepping away from the counter and turning to me. "I was perhaps a bit harsh." Then he turned back to Giorgio. "But I do think she would make a better scullery maid."

"I'll take it," I croaked.

Giorgio turned to me and smiled. "Good. Girl need job. Giorgio need help." Then to Jean he said, "Jean is... word for being sneaky?"

Jean smiled. His teeth were perfect. "Sneaky."

"Is same?"

Jean nodded.

"Ah. Jean sneaky. Thank you. Girl agree working for Giorgio, and only three franc each day. Is good."

The men laughed. I saw red.

Giorgio lifted a wrapped package from behind the counter and slid it to Jean. "Is all there. Four shirts. Two pant. Four stocking."

"And the..." Jean asked as he tapped the top of the package.

"Is there. Is good."

Jean smiled and pulled the package to him. As he turned, he looked at me and smiled. "I'm sorry about all of that. I have sisters. I usually have to say things that are not exactly true to get them to see the right course of action. I could see you were about to refuse Monsieur Nikolaev, and that seemed unwise. Because I have found that most women do not like to be talked about in such a fashion, I thought such talk would work. It usually does the job, and it was for the best. I hope you can forgive me. I will delight in seeing you whenever Monsieur allows you out of the back to great customers." Then he smiled and departed.

I vowed to hate the man, Jean, possessor of luscious lips that must taste of the finest wine and eyes a girl could swim in for days without coming up for air. I *would* hate him. One day. I vowed it. I would.

22

TRAPPED

September 16, 1814 AD

I may have watched Jean until he could no longer be seen through the shop's windows, after which I spun to face Giorgio.

"Three francs? The agreement was five."

Giorgio wore a wolf's grin with a sheep's eyes as he bellowed with laughter. I did not know if I was more surprised by my tacit agreement to our bargain or Giorgio's sudden and outrageous laughter. Tears poured from Giorgio's eyes as he laughed, and his nose started to run. He produced a handkerchief from somewhere. I did not know where, as it appeared suddenly from nowhere, and he wiped his eyes and blew his nose as required. This went on for what felt like several minutes.

"Oh, ho ho ho ho," Giorgio said in great trumpeting bellows. "Girl exactly like Charlotte's mother."

The proclamation was like a slap to the face. All I could think was, *He did not just... the bastard.*

"You... very strong like her," he said through laughs and tears. "Mother never take help, even when knowing best."

I was unprepared to hear that. My mother was strong? She did not seem that way. In fact, she seemed quite the opposite. After my brother Paul died, she became comatose. She died broken and weak. Not I. I loved… no, I love my brother even now. He died in that wretched textile factory trying to provide for our weak mother and me, and she… she did nothing. I am nothing like her!

Giorgio regained his composure with a final wipe of his eyes and a blow of his nose.

"Giorgio sorry, mademoiselle," he said, using the honorific with me for the first time. "Not considering girl's wanting. Only saw chance and grab. Please work with Giorgio. Is good way making money."

He still wore a bit of the wolf's grin, but it was mostly gone. His eyes seemed true, at least as far as I could tell. I did not know what to say. I was still reeling at his comparison of me and my mother. It did not help that I needed money and this was the only person in all of Paris that seemed willing to consider giving me employment.

I pouted internally. I wanted to show it on my face and stomp my heels, but that would hurt my pride and my literal heels, considering the state of my legs. Still, I looked for work for almost two months and made no progress. This man had my money, so working for him seemed like a good way to remain close to the money he owed me. Finally, free clothes and the ability to make my own seemed too good to be true. I needed to keep some distance, however, so I could not live with him. The rest seemed ideal.

"The agreement was for five."

He shrugged. "So it was. Girl agrees then?"

"Not entirely. I cannot, will not, live here. I have my own room at the tenement, and I plan to continue to live there."

Giorgio smirked and thought before continuing. "Is long hours learning. Sometime late night. Early morning. Girl get little sleep if walking."

"I know, and that is fine. I do not sleep well anyway and always keep late hours. I live in the attic, so getting to my room late at night will not bother others."

Giorgio was nodding. "Perhaps compromise. Girl live here at first.

If keeping up, can stay at tenement. If falling behind, take room above shop. Agree?"

I thought about that for a while, longer than I probably should have. The offer was sound. I would not have to buy food, and if times got tight off my five francs per day, I could move in here and save money. It seemed too good to be true. Pride refused to let me agree to his terms, so I modified them slightly one more time.

"I will stay at the tenement, but if the hour gets too late or if I need to be back too early in the morning, then I will sleep here. As long as you do not play some game and arrange it so I am always here working late and waking early, I will not argue when you tell me I need to sleep here to get an early start the next day."

"And if becomes problem and girl keeping job, shop become full-time home."

"Assuming I am the reason for the problem and not you, sure. I will agree."

"Good. Is good deal. Giorgio agree."

"So, what is the catch? Five francs a day is a lot of money, and you agreed too easily." I expected many potential answers, but never the one I got.

Giorgio chuckled and nodded. His eyes shone with confidence, the smug bastard.

"Girl train as tailor. Is good craft. Make much money if having skill. Girl also train as thief."

"What? Train as a thief? Were you not the one complaining I had stolen the items I sold to you?"

"So girl agrees. Gem and earring stolen."

"No. I stick to my story. I found those items. I am pointing out your hypocrisy in treating me poorly when you thought I was a thief and now you demand that I train as one."

"Ah. Yes. Seeing problem now. Giorgio not wanting girl be thief. Not like thief, but thief have skills Giorgio need. Is fine. Giorgio teach girl only good skills, no bad."

"Good and bad thief skills? They are not all bad?"

"Oh no. Some skill very good."

"Such as?"

"Ability being quiet." He gave me a look I ignored. "Also escaping, very good skill. Physical mastery," he said, flexing his arms in a manner I would have expected of Marcel, but not Giorgio, not this well-dressed, large if modestly plump man with kind but hard eyes. On Giorgio the pose was comical.

"I am plenty strong," I said, but Giorgio continued to pose.

"Strength important, yes. But mastery more. Too strong and crush baby without knowing. Too fast and hitting things unseen."

There may have been a few things there that would be worthy of learning. My mistress seemed to agree, though she did not speak.

"Also, learning art, very important. Giorgio teach girl masters and how spotting fake. Teach girl gems and jewelry. All important skills. Girl learn biology. Know organ locations. Know blood vessels. Know nerves. Good skills. Giorgio teach healing, herbalism. Learn good from bad poison."

"Good and bad poisons now too?" I asked.

"Oh, yes. Giorgio teach. Some poison help healing if right amount given. Too much? Dead. Too little? Just wishing dead. Good skills knowing."

I did not wish to give the man any credit, but I saw the value in what he was saying. If I knew more anatomy and biology, I might be able to help people, maybe even save lives to help make up for the one I took and the ones I may take. Still the sheer number of "good" skills seemed disproportionate to what I assumed the number of bad skills would be.

"So, those are the good skills. What might be some bad skills then?" I asked.

"Same."

"Same? What do you mean?"

"Giorgio mean same. All good skills also bad skills."

I stared at him for a moment. He just smiled and waited for me to continue. I rubbed my face and pinched the bridge of my nose.

"Fine. I will give in. How are all the good skills also bad skills?"

Giorgio's smile broadened. "Is good girl ask. Very important. Answer is application."

"Application?" I asked. "Whatever do you mean?"

"Application. How girl use skill, important to determine good or bad."

"So you mean to say, knowing poisons can help me save someone's life, either by giving the person just the right amount to overcome something like a fever, or if I know the poison, I might know how to counter the poison and save a life that way—a good use of the skill. But I could use that same poison to kill a perfectly healthy person, which would be a bad use."

"Exactly."

"So what about physical mastery? How does that have a good and bad side?"

"Physical mastery excellent example. Girl climb wall, enter room. What girl does inside make skill good or bad. Save person trapped in fire? Good. Kill sleeping person? Bad."

I was growing tired of this exchange. The man had an answer for everything. So I changed the subject.

"I still need money."

Giorgio smiled and pulled a small red purse from somewhere under his apron. How long had that been there? Surely he had not known I was coming today. "Is balance."

"It must be mostly gold," I said almost reverently.

Giorgio sniffed. "Five franc gold, five franc silver is same. Five franc."

"Giorgio, you must understand. I have never held gold before this month. Now this is the third time I will hold it since."

"Yes. Metal pretty, but girl learn not caring. Coin is metal. Only value what man give it. Why gold more valuable than silver? Rarer? Maybe. Real reason, someone say it. People agree. Everyone believe. Still is metal lump someone hammer flat. Now purse. Is unique. Giorgio take special cloth few have. Much rarer than gold, yet gold buy. Imagine. Giorgio think very strange. Then Giorgio have idea. Cut cloth. Pull thread from cloth. Destroy one thing, make another. New thing unique. Can never be purse like again. But gold impress girl, not unique purse."

I barely heard him as I opened the purse and riffled through the coins. There were so many gold coins I wondered if I knew enough places to spend them all.

"Be careful," Giorgio and my mistress said simultaneously, but only Giorgio dared explain himself. "Money draw attention. Make someone think using bad skill."

He is right.

"Yes. Understood," I said, breathless.

The amount of money was significant, more than I had ever held in my hands at one time, but it was not so much more than the amount I found in the boys' clubhouse. It was the sheer amount of gold coins, most of which were the same five-franc denomination, the same printing, and all sparkling as if freshly minted, that amazed me. I held pieces of artwork, no matter what Giorgio said, every one of them the same, and every one of them beautiful in a way I had never before noticed. I decided to start collecting coins for the beauty of them. I would keep one of these perfect golden disks for display—no, two, so I could display both sides simultaneously. In an instant my new hobby was costing me twice as much. I giggled slightly.

"Girl happy... or insane?" Giorgio asked. I guess he was unable to read the giggle.

I smiled and beamed up at him as I closed the purse and secured it inside my blouse under the shawl. "Happy," I said. "Quite, actually. It seems I have a new hobby. I need something to pass my time, so why not coin collecting?"

Giorgio gave a little harrumph. "Because girl poor?"

That was honestly a good point. "I will... start small."

Giorgio nodded his head to the side slightly and gave a contemplative frown. "And if girl need money, collection of coin buy more food than collection of bug."

I laughed. "Yes, I suppose it does, though my first coin will come out of this purse, and I am never going to spend it. I will starve first."

Giorgio frowned deeply then. “Is probably too much. Girl able getting new coin. Is only one Charlotte.”

I kept my smile. He meant well, but he did not know how wrong he was. There were two Charlottes, the one before I died and the one after. I guess I was not entirely able to keep my emotions from my face.

“Something wrong?” Giorgio asked, suddenly sober.

I cursed myself. He would not believe me if I did not say something, so I grasped at straw thoughts, most of which pulled through my mental fingers, but one remained. I bowed my head slightly and paced the length of the counter. I hesitated, trying to figure out the correct words.

“Recently I… found some money,” I began.

Giorgio’s eyebrows slammed against his hairline then pulled together in a tight knot between his eyes. “Found like earrings?”

“In a manner,” I said, using the smallest voice I could.

“Explain.”

So I did. I explained how I explored the attic clubhouse by crossing the roof to the other side. I explained the condition I found the room in and the discarded books, and I admitted to taking those. Giorgio seemed disappointed in me. I thought about explaining how those books were treated like junk, but I knew things would get worse, so I did not want to use whatever forgiveness he might give on a couple books. I explained then about grabbing the flour sack and stuffing my pilfered goods within, then taking everything back over the roof to my room.

When I explained finding the money, he seemed shocked. “Hundred coins and girl not notice weight?” His eyebrows seemed to be crushing rocks between his eyes.

“I swear, Giorgio. I thought the weight belonged to the books. I… was excited. I did not notice. Plus, there were other things in the flour sack. I thought it was all trash. I mean, who keeps anything of value in an old flour sack?”

Giorgio seemed to chew on my question.

“I know who now, but I did not then,” I said. Giorgio’s eyes relaxed from anger to annoyed but curious. I continued before he could ask what was so plainly on his face. “Yes, I will explain. Just give me a moment to get there.”

He did not relax exactly, but his eyebrows stopped crushing rocks for the moment. So I continued and explained how I expected that the money was stolen, how I would borrow some money to buy clothes and things I needed, and my plan to repay the money when I received the rest of my funds from Giorgio. Then I swore I would return the money back where I found it. I left out the part where I decided I would never actually pay back the borrowed money. I doubted he would forgive me.

“Borrowing is slippery slope,” Giorgio said, and I agreed. “Soon borrow become just having.”

“Yes, yes. Just let me finish,” I demanded, and he relented.

I explained the rest, the shopping and how I found out about Monsieur Bordelon being robbed, the cotton sacks and the story of Leon. How I later heard Theo and Henri talking in the stairwell and my determination to sneak the money back into Monsieur Bordelon’s shop. I told him that I hurt my leg, leaving out the unbelievable details, which was to say most of them, and then I lied and added a story about how I got sick and was bedridden for near a week.

“And that brings me to now,” I said somewhat triumphantly. “My leg still hurts, and I still have a bit of a chill. But I can walk, so I came for my money so I can replace what I have spent and return the money to its rightful owner. Plus, I need rent money and new clothes.”

“Is interesting story,” Giorgio said. “Now... repeat.” He made me repeat the entire story, three times. The fourth time, instead of making me repeat the entire story, he asked specific questions. An hour later, I was ready to rip out his throat and told him as much.

He just laughed.

I... used the Lord’s name in vain, then I cursed him using a similar profanity. I instantly regretted it, but he was just so infuriating. When he finally wiped tears from his eyes, tears from laughing at me, he held up one hand and pressed the other just under his heart.

"Giorgio believe girl. Girl already better thief than Giorgio think. Is good. Girl need less training." He chuckled a bit more before relaxing. "Plan returning money is good. Bordelon need knowing son is thief. Bad thief stealing from father. Multiple sin. Very bad."

Again I shook my head. Who was this man? He kept confusing me with what he did and did not find important. "So... how do you think I should progress?"

Giorgio thought about it for a moment. "Is good question. Let Giorgio sleep. Good answers come with waking."

"Um, fine," I said. "Can I go now? My leg is throbbing horribly. I would like to get back to the tenement and pay Madame Lacelle for the next month before lying down for a day or three."

"Yes and no. Girl free leaving, but come tomorrow. Training begin."

"Already?"

"Yes."

"Tomorrow?"

"Also yes."

"But my leg..."

"Girl walk here. Stand hours. Now walk back. Girl repeat tomorrow. Is good."

I stared at him.

He shrugged.

I stared harder.

"Use cane. Maybe Giorgio teach other uses."

"What if I do not show?"

"Girl will show. Or Giorgio know truth. Girl dishonest bad thief."

So now it was a matter of honor. The bastard.

"I need to replace my clothes."

"Yes," he said as he reached below the counter again to reappear with another package, which he set on the counter before me. "Is work clothes. Giorgio guess size. Tomorrow Giorgio measure girl, get good fit."

I eyed the package suspiciously. "You knew I would be back."

Giorgio gave the smallest shrug. "Giorgio like being prepared."

I lifted the small, dense package and placed it sideways under one arm. I walked along the counter with the package to ensure I could keep it in place, but it kept sliding. Giorgio disappeared for a moment before returning with a narrow canvas bag. The opening was along one of the longest sides instead of at the narrow top as I expected. A flap of the same material hung from the opening, as did a strap. Giorgio set the strange sack upon the counter and unfolded it. He waved me over.

He took the package from me and slid it into the mouth of the sack. It fit rather well with room to spare. He pulled the flap over the mouth and used a pair of canvas cords sewn to the bottom of the flap to secure it to a pair of brass rings sewn into the bottom of the sack.

"Put bag under one arm," he said, mimicking how I had been trying to carry the package. "Strap go over head."

He mimicked pulling the strap over his head to his other shoulder. I did as he suggested and the bag hung easily, but the strap was too long and the bag dangled close to my knees. Giorgio chuckled and motioned for me to hand the bag back.

I laid it on the counter as Giorgio produced an awl, a knife, and a small box from under the counter. In short order he measured the strap to a length more suitable for my use, cut it, and resewed the strap together near the ring that connected it to the bag. Before he cut the extra strap from the bag, he had me try holding it again. The bag now hung high on my hip instead of near my knees.

"Giorgio confident strap right size," he said as he took the bag back and removed the extra bit of strap with a single slice. The knife had to be razor-sharp to cut through the strap so easily. "But taking action before knowing, always bad."

He handed me the bag once more, and I slid it over my shoulder, now confident I would not lose my new clothes.

"Always?" I asked.

He shrugged. "When can be helped, is best. Girl's first lesson. See? Giorgio already teach."

I said my farewells and left the shop. I revised my original assessment of the man. I was growing fond of him. He was still insufferable, but he seemed to be a good person.

I expected the walk back to the tenement to be twice as long and painful as the trip to Giorgio's, but my thoughts regarding the day and what my future might entail kept my mind occupied. Before I knew it, the tenement was only a block away. If only I could set aside my pain and hunger on command as easily.

But you do, my mistress said. *I often try to reach you through your hunger, but you have learned to ignore us both completely. I have had to find other means to speak to you on occasion.*

I thought you were hunger, I thought in reply, but she was silent.

Why must everyone insist on only ever giving me a part of what I want? I could almost imagine Madame Lacelle's voice telling me, "That's life, girl. Get used to it."

23

SHIT ON A SHINGLE

September 17, 1814 AD

I did not sleep last night. My mind raced as I considered all the possibilities the coming days might hold. I never imagined for a moment how the day would end. If I had known, I would never have left for Giorgio's, and in the end, two people would still be alive and several hearts would not be broken. But I get ahead of myself.

I left for Giorgio's well before dawn dressed in the work clothes he had given me. I had a proper dress now, in the fashion that many shopkeepers' wives wore. He said that as long as I worked in the store I should wear the dress. He also sold me a modest spinster's dress on credit, and this I carried in a tight bundle with me so that Giorgio could alter the dress over the course of the day. Half of all my wages would be applied toward that dress, and it would take weeks to pay for it. He had me change into both sets of clothes before leaving, and he made some measurements, which he wrote into a small notebook. I had to beg for him to leave my legs alone, saying I was too tender and shy to have someone touch my legs. Instead he measured the lengths of each dress by eye.

Just before dawn I reached the same alley I had taken refuge in the day before. The long walk exhausted me, which made the gnawing worm in my belly larger and more painful. I walked the length of the alley ensuring it was empty before I settled in. It was a dead end with only a few doors leading into it, all of which had a thick coating of grime sealing them shut. If anyone came out of any of the buildings, I was certain I would hear them well before they could see me, so knowing I was alone and secure, I allowed myself to react to hunger. I doubled over and let the pain flood over me. The feeling was so intense that I felt it in every part of my body. I languished in the pain for a moment or two, learning what it was and accepting it as a part of myself, as my reality. It dwarfed me. The pain in my legs was no less acute, but in comparison trivial. Once I thought I understood the pain of my hunger, I started regaining control.

First I imagined a force squeezing the tips of my fingers and pushing out the pain. Where I pressed out the hunger, it did not return. I methodically pushed the pain up and out of my hands in the same manner, first the left and then the right. Once my hands were free of the hunger pains, I continued up each arm. I did the same with my legs, starting with the toes and gradually working the pain up and out of each limb. When I finished with my legs, much of the soreness was gone as well, not all of it, but a significant amount. Then I focused on my head and torso each in turn. I willed the pain toward my stomach, shrinking it little by little until it was a hot white mass at the core of my being. Finally I imagined cool water pouring over the pain, dulling it, cooling it, and washing it away. I breathed out and imagined the steam from the cooling pain being released out of me and into the air.

When I recovered, the morning sun was just breaking over the city's skyline, bathing the roads with its golden warmth. I took a moment to feel the chill around me so that I could also experience the sensation of the warm glow of the sun passing over me. As it did, it filled me with tranquility.

It was short lasting.

"How long girl waiting?" a voice asked from the alley behind me, Giorgio's voice.

I jumped. How? I turned and stared, but he just stood a handful of feet away from me. He wore a black overcoat looking like a solid slab of granite and shadow. His hands were in his pockets. He was calm, as if his question, his very presence, did not beg several questions in return. His eyes smiled though his mouth betrayed him not. After the slightest hesitation, I put a hand against my chest as if below it a heart hammered against its confines.

"That was not funny," I said.

That was when he allowed his smile to blossom. Despite my startled anger, I had to admit he was handsome when he smiled. Not classically handsome like my brother had been, or beautiful like Jean, or even roguish like Theo, but Giorgio had the kind of handsome that comes to hard men when they allow their edges to soften and some of their light to spill out. The realization made me relax and smile in return.

"Look on face. Ha! Charlotte should have seen," Giorgio said as he grabbed the small bundle that was my everyday clothes. He walked past me toward the shop. His footfalls were heavy and distinct. How had I not heard him? Was I so caught up in my sunbath that I lost track of the world around me? That hardly seemed possible, but it also seemed the only logical explanation.

I followed, still using Theo's cane.

"Girl must be aware all times," Giorgio said over his shoulder. There was something of a smile in his voice, but it was edged with sincerity too. "Woman, all woman, need be especially aware. Much bad in world, people and not people. Woman easy... what the word? Thing hit with bow?"

"Target," I replied.

He noticed that I was falling behind and turned to look at me. His smile disappeared as he saw me hobbling.

"No," I said the moment I saw his smile fade and his body shift ever so slightly to come toward me. "I will do this on my own."

My command seemed to do the trick, but as fate would have it, the tip of the cane slipped on a particularly large and smooth cobblestone. Suddenly I was falling to my right as pain burst from my ankle. I never hit the ground, however. Before I knew it, Giorgio was kneeling and held me in his arms like I was a rag doll fallen from a shelf. First he was quiet as a mouse—no, quieter, I can hear mice—and now he crossed the distance of half the road's width to catch me before I hit the ground. His arms were strong but gentle.

Who was this man?

Giorgio lifted me as gently as a babe and carried me in his arms. I stupidly thrashed at first.

"Set me down," I demanded. "I can make my own way."

"Yes. Giorgio know this," he said as he bent over. Instead of setting me down, he gathered ~~my~~ Theo's walking stick. "Giorgio also know, sometimes girl need relax. Do not be too strong. Diamonds very strong, but strike with hammer and crush into million tiny pieces. Strong but brittle."

He carried me toward the door of the shop.

"Willow very soft wood. Pretty. Delicate. Like girl should be."

I scoffed at that. I was no pretty, soft thing.

Not anymore, my mistress said, and indeed she was right.

"But willow also very strong in own way," he said. "Wind blow hard, tall strong trees split, fall. Willow bend, does not break. Willow survive when oak destroyed."

We reached the door. He held me with one arm while he unlocked and opened it. He was not out of breath, and not a drop of sweat appeared on his brow. He did not even struggle to hold me in only one arm. I considered asking the man if his father was a bear, but bears smelled bad. Giorgio… Giorgio smelled like pine and wood smoke with a hint of cherry? It was the oddest combination of scents I had ever noticed, but somehow for him it was right.

Once inside the shop, Giorgio relocked the door behind us. I started to suggest I could manage, but I was sure he would not hear me in that regard. He was making me angry, however, and I wanted a fight.

"So are you saying I should be a willow? Maybe I should just find a young man, throw myself at him, let him have his way with me, and then once I was with child, I could force him to marry me," I said with no small amount of derision and scorn lacing my words. Instead of feeling the sting of my lash of words, he smiled and chuckled softly as he paused just inside the doorway.

"If Charlotte is this person," he said, "perhaps."

I opened my mouth to lash at him again, but he continued before I could, still carrying me through the quiet shop of fabrics, mannequins, and clothes.

"Is not Charlotte though, Giorgio think," he said. The bear of a man stole my chance at a retort and kept talking before I could come up with something new. "No. Giorgio suggest girl not be someone Charlotte is not. Giorgio suggest Charlotte know own strength. What is type? Use that how best used. Be strong, girl, but be smart. If needing change, change."

"So what does this have to do with diamonds and willows, exactly?" I asked, not seeing the point of his seemingly wise-sounding gibberish.

He held me in his bearlike grip as he took me behind the counter and through a doorway into a back room. The space was divided into two parts, one a small kitchen and the other a bit of a living space with a couch and a chair so deeply upholstered, I feared I might be swallowed whole if he set me in it. Between the couch and chair was a small, low table. He laid me on the couch, to my relief. ~~My~~ Theo's cane and my bundle he set on the table.

"How better say?" Giorgio asked no one in particular. "Ah, maybe this. Diamond is diamond. Willow is willow. Right?"

"I suppose," I said as I shifted on the couch in a manner that relaxed and concealed my legs.

"Right," he said. "What does willow know of being diamond? What does diamond know of being willow? Nothing. Charlotte is not diamond. Maybe not willow either." He laughed before continuing. "No. Not willow. Charlotte's strength different than both. Find what strength is. Use strength best way. Charlotte be much happier person."

Once my things and I were settled, Giorgio looked me over, smiling happily.

"Gloating, Giorgio?" I asked, trying to make the sound of my disdain a physical thing that he could see. Giorgio's smile faded slightly, so I pressed my point. "You and Jean wrapped me up nicely yesterday. Did you have this planned ahead of time?"

It was a ridiculous question. Jean had no idea who I was, and Giorgio had no idea if he would ever see me again after our first encounter. Yet there I was, and in that moment, it seemed like the truest thing to believe.

"Somehow you saw this girl who was just starting to become self-sufficient and you, the two of you, determined that she, that I, needed a man's guidance, a man's wisdom to be able to properly live my life. So you conspired to trap me into some agreement that leaves me indebted to you."

"No," he said, shaking his head. "Giorgio just wanting help."

"Help me? You swindled me the first time I came here. If you really wanted to help me, you could have done it then. You should have done it then! But no. Apparently you knew my father, knew who I was, and I assume you know what happened to us... yet... yet..." I couldn't continue.

The memories of the past few years came flooding back. My father's smile, his blood in the streets, my brother going to work, word of his death, my mother paying his debts with her body, her finally giving up and wasting away... all of it came back all at the same time. Giorgio sat beside me and wrapped an arm around me. I wanted to lean over and cry into his shirt, but that was a weakness I would not allow myself. No more crying. No more depending on others. I was my own person now. I would not rely on others in any way, shape, or form. I scowled and pushed him away. Or tried to. He moved like a mountain.

There was a knock at the shop door, which Giorgio ignored. It came again a moment later. After the third knock, he patted me on the back, stood, and walked to the front of the store. A thin beam of light lanced into the shop, some of it making its way into the living space behind the counter. Giorgio spoke quietly with someone outside before closing the door and extinguishing the light.

He came back and walked into the small kitchen, where he

busied himself. When he returned, he had a simple metal tray. On it was a small white plate with two croissants, two empty cups, and a tall glass-and-metal contraption that held a dark liquid. While I did not know what the contraption was, the smell emanating from it was both recognizable and delicious. Coffee.

Giorgio saw me looking at the contraption holding the coffee. "Device is thing Giorgio make from tale Charlotte's father once told."

I looked up at him in surprise.

"Yes. Is true. Giorgio know him. Good man. Loved family. Is bad what happened." He waved a hand back toward the contraption. "Charlotte's father exchange letters with gentleman... name Benjamin Thompson. No. Was Sir Benjamin Thompson. English insulted when leaving off titles. Such proper people."

Giorgio paused for a moment as he rolled his eyes in an exaggerated manner. He returned to his story as he poured coffee from the device into two cups. As an afterthought he stuck out his little finger.

"Thompson want..."

"Sir Benjamin," I corrected while shifting slightly in preparation for coffee.

Giorgio flushed slightly at the correction. "Ahem, yes. Sir Benjamin want rare books. Learned girl's father had one, not others. Lucky, your father knew someone with one or two more," he said as he pointed to himself with a smile, "and perhaps same man know getting others."

He finished pouring the cups and handed one to me. The bitter aroma made me smile.

"Sugar? Giorgio not bring but can get. Giorgio drink coffee black and bitter like good lover, but not everyone same."

"No thank you. This is perfect."

He smiled, sat, and continued.

"Giorgio having two books, and knew ways getting others. But were... complications. Books very expensive. Girl's father not poor, but not so rich. Also, Giorgio did not want losing one book."

"Why?"

It was strange talking about my father, whom I'd tried my best to forget lest I lose myself like my mother did, but there at that time with that man, it felt right remembering him. Thinking of him was comforting for the first time in years.

"It was... special. Yes, special. Bizarre, written in way that was... what is word... un-de-ci-pher-able. Giorgio tried. Giorgio good at sort of thing, but impossible. Also, book was made by scribe, all written by hand, with odd images Giorgio cannot describe, paintings and drawings throughout. Some page much larger, folded to fit book. Even now, years later Giorgio close eyes and see some drawings. Strange yet amazing."

He paused in a sort of dream state. I sipped my coffee. The taste was bold, sharp, and bitter. Delicious. The coffee really did need sugar, but sugar would only make the taste worse for me. Sweet was no longer part of my palate.

Unless the sweetness comes from rotting flesh, my mistress said.

I shuddered, but I was unsure if it was from disgust or elation.

"So," he continued, "make agreement. Giorgio lending father coin needed. Then he pay back with interest after sale. Good arrangement, but Giorgio requiring secret as well."

I looked at him, confused.

"Yes, yes. Giorgio knowing look. Giorgio love secrets. Secrets move world. Secrets join people and break apart people. Secrets form nation, build fortune, give power, and loosing secret can tear all apart. Secrets having power, shake foundation of world."

He paused momentarily. I was certain he was basking in his own romantic inclinations about secrets. He seemed to really like dramatic pauses, so I sipped the coffee and quietly wished I was gnawing on his leg, sucking the blood out of his veins. I had to shake myself from the vision surely sent by my mistress. I attempted satisfaction by sipping the coffee. Only the coffee.

"Giorgio think asking for single secret bargain. Book having maybe hundred secrets. Maybe more. But truth?" He paused as he took a sip. "Giorgio hoping Sir Benjamin cipher strange book, give Giorgio taste. Instead, girl's father tell Giorgio device Sir Benjamin invent for... what is word... something like cooking liquids? Ah, brew.

Brew coffee. Charlotte's father explain device brew strong coffee. Best part? Almost no grounds.

"Well," he continued after a long sip and a bark of a laugh, "Giorgio loving coffee, accept secret. Father let Giorgio copy letter Sir Thomson send. Letter contained crude drawing. With small corrections, good blacksmith, and excellent glassblower, Giorgio have very own percolator. Maybe first in all France. Since getting rid of bizarre book, Giorgio having more free time, sleep better, and enjoy finest coffee in city. Giorgio think making good deal that day."

He smiled and sipped more of his coffee. I set mine down and waited patiently for him to continue. He reached for a croissant and offered the other to me. I gave him a thin, closed-mouth smile and waved him off.

"What? Girl must be hungry."

"No," I said. "I am quite fine, thank you." I was starting to get quite good at lying.

He gave me another long look before shrugging and taking a croissant for himself. He took a slow, sensual bite of the pastry and savored the moment. I wished I could get such pleasure from something so normal as a croissant. The spell was broken when, like some country barbarian, he dipped the remainder of the croissant in his coffee several times. He looked like he was shoving a washcloth in a bucket to generate suds.

"So," he said before taking a bite of coffee-laden barbarism, "Charlotte must let Giorgio look at leg. Giorgio good tending wounds."

Damn the man. His gentle kindness mixed with his knowledge of my father disarmed me. I vowed to not make that mistake again.

"I cannot," I said.

"Is Giorgio's turn asking single-word question. Why?"

Stupid single-word questions. "I said I am quite fine. Besides, since... since my... well, since I started living on the streets, I promised myself that I would be strong and not depend on anyone else. I will tend to my legs. I will take care of Charlotte. Giorgio should take care of himself and leave me alone."

Giorgio set his cup and plate down and wiped his hands on a cloth that he took from somewhere unseen. He was frowning slightly as he looked at me sideways, then after dabbing his mouth and stashing the cloth... somewhere... he affected his best priestly facade. "Everyone, even strongest girl, need someone. If like oak, need someone. If like willow, need someone."

"If like Charlotte," I said, interrupting him, "need no one."

Giorgio made a dismissive blow through his lips that demonstrated his thoughts of my statement. Had he long mustaches I imagined they would have fluttered in his exasperation. I thought he was going to argue his point more staunchly, but instead he sat back into the chair and crossed his arms as he just stared at me. After a moment he spoke.

"Girl believes this thing? Needing no one?"

I crossed my own arms and tried to stare him down. For some reason, I could not and ended up looking away. I stared at the contraption that my father helped bring to Giorgio and France as I replied.

"It does not matter what I believe. It has to be true."

"Oh? Man once tell Giorgio, truth is as unknowable as weather. Usually is as expected. See sun, is sunny. See clouds, is rainy. Is summer, is hot. Is winter, is cold. But this year, last year, summer never come. Rain all time. Is bad. Winter will be worse. Or will winter be hot? Not knowing. Impossible to know until happens. Sometimes weather change during day. Day start hot. Clear. Then clouds and cold air. Before night is snowing. Truth same way. So when girl say, 'has to be true,' girl remember truth change. Girl change, girl's truth change. Is how it is."

I was not certain that I completely understood him, but I just nodded as if his explanation was completely reasonable, though that would be predicated on if I understood him or not, which I did not always.

"Well, let me say that it might be dangerous knowing me, and I do not want anyone to get hurt. So just stay back and let me run my life as I wish. I can take care of myself. I do not need anyone else."

"What? Charlotte think girl is first risk Giorgio ever take? Ha! No. Giorgio dance with death number time. Giorgio pluck jewels from bosom of ladies while dancing. Lordly husbands watching from side, never know. Once in Romania, Giorgio hunt dead with wild Englishman. Englishman always understating things. We get into big trouble. Giorgio survive. Once Giorgio almost burned at stake in Rome. Giorgio speak to crowd, convince people riot. Giorgio make escape. Giorgio live. No. Small, scared, weak girl is not really risk."

"God damn it, Giorgio, I said no!" I all but screamed.

Giorgio was set aback. "Thou shalt not take my name in vain, saith the Lord. Is third commandment. Remember for confession," Giorgio said, making the sign of the cross.

I pulled my arms to me tighter and scowled at Giorgio. "Bah. My life has already been a living Hell. God has already cursed me and turned His gaze from me. I cannot do worse now."

I silently mulled over my ill fortune and circumstances. I must have been lost in thought, because when I looked up, Giorgio was moving around in the kitchen chopping, crushing, and mixing something. I assumed they were herbs of some sort. He worked quickly and deftly. When he finished, he poured the contents of his pestle into a tea diffuser and dropped it into a small teapot. He lifted the pot by a dainty handle and swirled it in small, gentle circles. He returned with a fresh cup, the same design and size as my coffee cup—all three matched the teapot and plates in fact—and poured the liquid into the new cup.

"If girl refuse letting anyone, even God, getting close, then let Giorgio make tea. Good for pain. Help small way."

"I can function without..."

"Yes, yes. Giorgio know. Is favor for Giorgio. Makes Giorgio think girl not suffer so much. Giorgio feel better."

It sounded like some sort of sideways excuse to get me to drink the tea, but I had to admit, a little relief from the throbbing ache of my ankle and shins would be welcome, so I took the cup with my most sincere sulk and blew on the steaming liquid.

"Is better drinking hot. Taste is... how you say... terrible but worse?"

I grimaced trying to think of a word, but I just shook my head. "I do not know what word you are thinking about, but I think I understand."

I waited for the liquid to cool just a little more before taking a sip. I was unsure if Giorgio was making a joke on my behalf or if my sense of taste was different than his regarding this tea, but it was delightful. I decided to make a face and pretend the taste was horrible.

"Echk..." I sputtered through pursed lips as I squinted my eyes. When I opened them, Giorgio was watching me and nodding.

"See? Giorgio tell girl. Very bad-tasting. Drink quick, all at once."

I complied and quaffed the entire cupful in one long series of sips. I felt hundreds of teeth emerging from every part of my mouth and throat simultaneously and flexing in delight as the liquid spilled down my throat into the gulf of my stomach. I shuddered with delight, but hid it under the guise of horrible-tasting medicine. It occurred to me then that if the medicine was supposed to be horrible-tasting but instead tasted wonderful, it would only increase my pain when it was intended to reduce it. Well, there was no turning back. I had already consumed it.

Once Giorgio saw that I had consumed the entire cup, he set about picking up the cups, saucers, pot, and plates. He took everything to the little kitchen area and began sorting and washing the pieces. Seconds later I was sleeping.

I woke up to an empty room and a weight across my legs. I bolted up from my reclining position and looked down at them. A heavy quilt lay across my legs. I pushed it aside and pulled up my skirts. My bandages were all my own and looked just like they had when I wrapped them this morning, plus a little extra seepage from the wounds. So I pushed my skirts back down and re-covered my legs. I just lay there then and relaxed. Instead of taking advantage of a circumstance, it seemed Giorgio simply provided a small boon and moved along, respecting my desires.

One more time I was left wondering, who was this man?

It was midafternoon when I finally came back around. Two mannequins stood in the living area where I reclined. Both wore slight dresses. One of the dresses was causal while the other was more formal. In fact the second dress looked much like Giorgio's own uniform.

Giorgio then moved into the room from a hidden doorway I had not seen before. He was carrying a third mannequin, which he set down beside the others. Instead of wearing a dress, the third mannequin wore leather breeches, a dark silk shirt, and a leather vest. The leathers were all stained a very dark brown. The shirt was all but black. Thin straps crisscrossed the vest and pants in various locations, for what reason I could not fathom.

"Ah, girl is awake. Good timing," Giorgio said. "Sometime tea make person sleepy. Usually when hurt very bad. But sleeping last long time. Days maybe. Is good to see girl awake. How feeling?"

I had not thought about it, but I felt... good. I did not feel delighted or energized or even without pain, but there was no portion of my body that was screaming for attention for the first time in weeks.

"Better," I said, smiling.

Giorgio smiled in return.

"Giorgio arrange new clothes for Charlotte," he said. His hands indicated the mannequins while his eyes never left my own.

"What are these for?" I asked. He had already given me some clothes.

"Ah," he said and indicated the casual dress. "Is for shopping and not wanting be noticed. Is very plain, but not too plain. See color on sleeve? Is very popular. Person seeing girl in dress remember maybe height, was wearing dress, what hair looking like, and extra color on sleeve. Could be Charlotte. Could be hundred or thousand other girl too. Is easy to blend."

He moved slightly to display and discuss the second dress, the one that looked much like his own. "Is formal in shop. Girl wearing if working there." He pointed out into the shop proper. "Girl wearing today clothes when not working shop."

Finally he moved over to the most interesting outfit. "Is for girl working night."

"Giorgio!" I yelled in surprise.

Giorgio turned and searched my eyes for the mirth, then finally realizing what I meant, he blushed. "No, no, no, no, no. Is outfit for being thief."

I tilted my head wondering how this outfit would help me be a thief, not that I was entirely sure I wanted to be one, mind you. Giorgio must have seen the look on my face. He held up one finger and positioned himself behind the mannequin.

"Fits tight. No catching corners like dress," he said as he moved his hands over the form of the suit. Even the straps were arranged such that they did not stick out from the suit so much as blended in as a part of it. "Material under strong, flexible. Leather thin where bend. Thick were body need protecting." He emphasized the protection by producing a dagger from somewhere and stabbing the suit in the stomach. The blow glanced off the body, turned aside.

"That was not just leather that turned the dagger," I said.

Giorgio simply smiled. "Yes. Very good. Small metal plate over vital organs. Protect heart, lungs, neck." He indicated each location as he mentioned them. "Must tailor special for lung. Bone protect much. Giorgio adjust metal straps, sit where bone not. Give flexibility but provide defense where most needed. Collar also reinforced. Chainmail inside collar protecting from knife, garrote. Maybe sword, but better not risking."

"It looks like it is hot and heavy."

"Yes. Girl train during day when hottest. Train with weights. When wearing at night on roof, no weights, will feel light and cool. Girl see."

I looked at him dubiously.

He chuckled quietly and spun the mannequin. He ran his hands along the lower back and buttocks. "Each side, here," he said, pointing to a completely innocuous portion of the armor, "here, here, and here. Pockets holding small things." Then he indicated several spots along the waist, ribs, and back where there were small slits in the leather. "Buckles hidden but accessible. Girl attach things. Belt. Harness. Whatever." He shrugged.

"I wish my legs were better. I... I want to try it on," I said, and it was true.

I wanted to wear the bizarre leather suit. Never in my lifetime had I imagined that I would want such a thing. It was sleek and secret. Even though I did not wish to admit it, the suit was also sexy. Just the thought made me blush inwardly.

Giorgio smiled showing teeth. His eyes sparked. "Giorgio thought girl like. But know this. Suit made for boy. Taller. Heavier. Needing adjustments. Must fit against skin, so girl must lose modesty before wearing."

"I... I do not know if I can do that, Giorgio," I said.

Many people were accustomed to being naked, even in this day and age. It was not uncommon to see bathers in the Seine without clothes, or poor people on the streets robbed of the very last of their possessions and dignity wandering nude. For years before and during the Revolution, women would wear clothes baring their breasts as a fashion symbol of some sort or other. Some still did. I had always avoided anyone outside of my family seeing me nude since I could remember.

Giorgio nodded. "Is what Giorgio thought. Why telling now. Giorgio have idea. Girl very slight of build. Is good for thief work. Bad for social work, but have ideas. Giorgio will make girl special underclothes. Keep modesty. Mostly."

I wondered what he meant, but wearing underclothes in front of a man was better than wearing nothing. Well, maybe there were a couple of men I would...

No, I told myself. *Stop thinking like that. Romance is no longer an option in your life for more than one reason.*

You make such odd declarations, my mistress said to me.

I scowled.

Giorgio must have mistaken my scowl to be intended for him. "Girl see. Will be very nice. If girl like, Giorgio make more than one set."

I recovered as simply as possible by shaking my head. "We will see, Giorgio. I remain skeptical, but I will not disagree until I know for certain."

He nodded, which I took as him thinking he had won. He had, mind you, but only because I had fallen in love with the bodysuit. I would have stood in front of the man naked for hours on end to eventually be able to wear it. I imagined myself running from rooftop to rooftop wearing that instead of boys' pants. Sliding down rough surfaces and crashing against brick walls would scrape the leather but leave my flesh intact much better than my normal clothes. Yes, for the first time in my life I was in love, and it was with a suit of leather and silk. I was a wicked, wicked girl.

* * *

I spent half an hour looking at the clothes on the mannequins while Giorgio helped customers. When he returned, he ensured I could stand. I could, so we spent another hour or more with him measuring different parts of me before moving over to one of his projects and making marks on the cloth with a piece of chalk. Sometimes he would take a single measurement and mark all three creations. Sometimes he took the same measurement three times, once for each outfit. Often he would produce his little notebook and write something in it.

I tried to sit while he worked on the clothes, but that rarely lasted long. He would return, stand me in some odd pose, and take a measurement, often one he had taken several times before in other poses. Then he would go back to the mannequins or his notebook. I was up and down a dozen times or more. Finally, he moved the mannequins to what I assumed was a closet before closing and locking the door. When he was finished, he went to the kitchen and returned with a bottle and two small glasses. He unstoppered the bottle and poured a dark red liquid into each glass. I hesitated to take the one he handed me, but he insisted. It smelled sweet and alcoholic.

"Brandy. Is good," he said as he took from his glass the smallest sip I had ever seen a man take.

I had never had more than a glass of watered wine before, so I was curious and excited when I took my first large sip. I instantly understood why Giorgio took such a small sip, and for once I wished I'd followed his lead. The liquid fire burned its way down my throat. My eyes watered and my lungs wanted to breathe but could not. My entire throat constricted, and tears streamed down my face. I was *not* crying. It was a reaction to the alcohol, not the pain. I felt the glass pulled from my grasp, and a wet cloth wiped my face. Several long seconds later, my body started to come back under my control. I was able to relax my throat just enough to gasp and then moan.

"Is girl fine?" Giorgio asked. I could barely hear him even though I could feel him sitting on the edge of the couch next to me.

All I could do was nod.

"Is sure?"

I nodded again. He remained in place until I managed to croak out, "Yes. I am fine."

I took the wet handkerchief from the man and began wiping my face.

Giorgio laughed as he got up and moved away.

"Is first time girl has brandy?"

"Yes," I tried to say, but my throat still burned and threatened to seize shut again. I simply nodded when the word would not come out fully formed.

"Is worst first taste Giorgio ever see," he continued when he could force actual words out between laughs.

"That was a vile thing to do," I said once I could.

"Giorgio not knowing would happen," Giorgio said. "Otherwise would have poured less. Promise, one day, girl will enjoy. Until then, is Giorgio-only treat."

I was not going to argue.

Giorgio had consumed almost a third of his once almost full glass of brandy by the time I fully recovered and was amiable to conversing once more.

"Now. As said, Giorgio love secrets. Secrets have power..."

"Yes, yes," I said. "Form nations, build fortunes, tear it all down. I remember."

"Right," Giorgio said. "This Giorgio steal: secrets. This what girl learn. Steal secrets and sell when needed."

"Steal secrets? You mean become a spy?" I asked.

"No. Spies work for someone. Giorgio work for Giorgio. If girl smart, do same. No. Giorgio is Thief of Secrets." He said the last part like it was a title bestowed upon him from on high. Well, considering what he must think of himself, maybe he considers that to be the case.

After a moment I asked, "I am going to learn how to sew, right?"

At first it seemed as if he had not heard me, but then Giorgio threw his head back and thundered with laughter.

"Yes, yes. Charlotte learn sew, cut, and measure, but only to hide being thief. Good skills."

I did not know what to say. So I went to take a drink of my coffee, only to find my cup was empty. True to Giorgio's statement earlier, there were no grounds in my cup. A glass of water was on the table near my empty coffee cup. I assumed it was to help me recover from the burning brandy. I took a few sips. Giorgio must have seen my disappointment, because he stood and moved to the kitchen area to begin the process of heating more water.

"So, why?" I asked as he worked.

"What girl mean?" he asked in return.

"Why trust me with this job? With this secret of yours? Why do you think I can learn this? Why do you think I even would want to? Why, all of it. Why?"

"Ah," he said as he walked back and leaned against the back of his chair, addressing me from over it. He rubbed the chair as he thought and looked at me from above the overstuffed monstrosity. "Girl smart. Capable. And need job."

"That is not enough. There must be thousands of girls in the city that match that description."

Giorgio flushed slightly and scratched idly at his chin with one hand.

"Well, Giorgio know special secret. Is unimportant thing. Or was until Giorgio find out another unimportant thing. And another. Then several unimportant thing make one big important thing. Maybe."

"I guess I follow you so far, but what does that have to do with me?"

"Yes. Giorgio recently lose two... um... employees."

"The ruffians I saw coming and going from here?"

Giorgio gave a little annoyed frown at that.

"Yes. And thank you. Giorgio not realize getting sloppy until girl find shop so easy."

I simply shrugged. "It really is not that hard if one knows what to look for. I did scout several other locations incorrectly before I found yours. If you want to be more discreet, you really do need more customers and less... finery."

Giorgio nodded at the customers part but seemed offended at my suggestion of limiting his finery.

"Giorgio, taste, refinement is all same. Maybe Giorgio stop sweeping outside."

I never saw the man outside of the building. When did he do this supposed sweeping?

"So you lost two employees. Did they quit?"

Giorgio was quiet for some time. "No. Both dead."

I gasped. "How?"

"Accidents. One fall from roof, break neck. Other drown after falling into canal."

"Are you sure those were accidents?"

Giorgio smirked again. "No other explanation."

"And you want to hire me to replace them? Again I have to ask, why me?"

Giorgio wringed his hands.

"Secret Giorgio find involve Charlotte. Not directly. But Charlotte will need knowing. One day. Giorgio need telling girl, but girl need learning not dying first. Then girl learn secret. Decide what next."

The pot started whistling, so Giorgio walked back to the kitchen and completed a new pot of coffee.

I sat confused while he worked. What was so terrible he thought I would run off and get myself killed? It seemed an entirely ridiculous proposal, but the work came with free clothes. It sounded interesting and potentially exciting. I did not need any more secrets in my life, but maybe this training could help me determine new truths from the assembled secrets of others like a web of secrets crisscrossing over the city of Paris and beyond. Which would I be, the spider or the fly? If I did not learn how the game was played, I could only ever be a fly.

You are so much more than an insect, my mistress said. I frowned. I did not feel like more than a fly in her presence. *You were a fly, but now you are so much more than a spider. Play these games if you wish, but remember what you are.*

I imagined being a spider in the web, and then I imagined being more. If I was outside of the web, above it, could I control the actions of both the spider and the fly?

The sound of cups clattering on saucers drew me from my contemplation. Giorgio was back in the little living area with a new pot of coffee. He poured a cup for me but not one for himself. Instead he continued to work on the now mostly empty glass of brandy.

The man's throat must be clad in metal.

"So," I said and took a sip of coffee. On reflection, I think I must have been smiling as I toyed with the idea. "What would I be doing? Climbing castle walls to listen in to private conversations? Skulking through hidden tunnels to find secret documents and return unseen? Maybe perform the occasional assassination when required?" It was a joke of course, and I laughed as I took a deeper drink.

"All that and more," Giorgio responded.

I almost choked.

No. I could not be an assassin. How would that separate me from the creature my mistress wanted me to be? For all his talk of good skills and bad skills, here was the same man casually telling me I would be stealing and murdering. What separated the good people to kill from the bad people? Just because someone stood on the wrong side of some argument did not make them evil. How many royals did the republicans kill before and during the Revolution? Hundreds? Thousands? And not just the men and rare women who held power, but their powerless spouses and children too.

My father told me that before the Revolution, times were difficult for the people while those in power lived easy, carefree lives. Well the Revolution had come and gone. The Emperor rose from the ranks of the people, waged war, and nearly conquered Europe before being defeated and removed from power. For the poorest of the poor, life just continued being harder and harder. Father suggested that yes, the people were not as quick to anger, but that was not so much because things were better as they thought they were better. Plus, with so many dying in the war, there were fewer to complain.

New people came to power and left, but largely the lives of the people were the same. Thousands upon thousands of men died so that the people in power could change, but the lives of their subjects barely saw any change. That was a game I did not wish to play.

Sneaking into someone's home and snooping around for secrets? That sounded exciting, just a little dangerous and romantic too. But the very thought of sneaking into someone's home to kill them? All I could see was Luc's poor defenseless form when I considered it.

I was still sputtering and coughing when Giorgio handed me a fresh handkerchief. Where did he keep them? I found that I had coffee on my face and blouse. Giorgio tsked as he looked at the spots.

"Coffee stain difficult removing. Use little soap and vinegar. First thin vinegar, using more water. Dab mixture, little at time. With patience, spots come out," he said, completely ignoring what we had been talking about.

I sat up and set my cup and saucer down. Fresh pain raced up and down my leg as I adjusted myself to sit upright, both feet on the floor, and back rigid straight. My mother would be proud I was finally not lazing in the presence of a man. It mattered not that I was injured. Proper manners always required attending. The distraction of my mother's disappointment helped me to clear my head, but one question lingered: Do I take this man seriously?

I shook my head. "Assassinations? That is too much, Giorgio. I do not know if I can do this thing you ask of me."

He looked like he was about to speak. Probably to tell me that some people just needed to be killed. Maybe that was true, but who was I to make such decisions? No. I could not allow myself to be persuaded with words to kill other people. It was... beyond me. So I pushed on, not letting him speak.

"I need simple work. Something with my hands maybe. Madame Lacelle has an idea for selling my hairpins that I created out of wood. She is going to teach me to sew too."

Giorgio looked as if I hit him.

"Bah! What you do with hairpin? Sell for franc, two each? Sell how many in week? Ten? Twenty?" He spat. "Make maybe thirty franc a week before 'Madame' Lacelle take cut. She take half or more, Giorgio sure. Leave girl with what? Five franc per week? Bah!"

I offended him. I wanted to kick myself for it, and I was just about to respond when he spat again in the same spot. I got distracted momentarily as I wondered how wet that one spot would get before we were through. This time he continued before I could speak.

"Madame Lacelle sew like blind left-handed seamstress missing three finger. Worse. Lacelle teach not good. Giorgio teach right way sewing. Teach girl spinning finest thread. Make beautiful loom work. Cut perfect pattern. Make new pattern too. Lacelle teaching girl that? No. Lacelle tired old woman. Need distraction passing time. Eat girl's youth like vampire. Bah."

"So how is your plan any better, monsieur?" I asked. I desperately wanted to defend Madame Lacelle, but in reality I barely knew her. I had not even seen any of her work. Giorgio's work was all around me and was quite good.

"Ah! See being thief allow girl to make more money than need. Madame Lacelle ensure girl having enough paying rent, maybe eat. No more. Woman is tired old... what is word for old witch eating small children?" When I did not respond immediately, he continued, "Is insult intended for old, ugly woman."

"Hag?" I asked.

"Yes, yes, hag. Is tired old hag."

"I am sorry, Monsieur Giorgio," I said as I rose to my feet. I staggered a little at first, and to my surprise Giorgio moved with such alacrity that he was standing over me before I was fully risen. I half expected him to push me back down and force me to listen to him, but he did not. Instead he helped me to my feet with strong but tender hands.

"I am sorry," I began again. "I just do not see myself as a killer. I barely see myself as an accomplished thief or spy. The killing is just too much."

Once I was standing, he stepped back to regard me. He looked disappointed, almost sad, but eventually he just nodded and took a step back from me. Then he held up one finger. "Before going, wait moment. Giorgio give gift. Help thankless girl refusing good job."

The last part he said with a wink and a smile.

I stood there for the next five minutes. I refused to sit. It was a type of declaration of strength, and once I had made up my mind to remain standing, I refused to change it. So I stood. When sharp needle pains raced up and down my right leg, I continued to stand. ~~My~~ Theo's cane helped on occasion to lessen the pain as I shifted some weight to it. At one point, I worried that living with pain was my new reality just as I lived with hunger.

You need not live with either if you just feed.

My mistress was of a singularly devoted mind. She reminded me of myself then, but that made me uncertain if having a singularly devoted mind was a good thing or not.

When he returned, Giorgio carried a small parcel similar in size to the one I used to carry my work clothes.

"Giorgio give Charlotte fresh clothes," he said as he untied the bundle. The everyday clothes from the mannequin consisted of a charcoal-gray wool skirt, a soft blue blouse, a matching blue scarf, white undergarments, and a set of black silk undergarments that looked like they would fit snuggly to my body. On top of that was a book.

"Giorgio guess pretty good measurement. Probably fit very good.

If problem, easy fix. Giorgio think Charlotte need blue. Color is hope, like good sky after rain," he said, indicating the blouse.

Next he pointed at the black silk. "Already make silk undergarments. Giorgio guess girl modest, so prepared. Again, Giorgio guess measurement pretty good. Should fit very snug, like wearing nothing." He moved his eyebrows up and down several times, and I had to grin like a fool.

"Book is for borrowing. Girl take. Read. Bring back, Giorgio give another. Drink coffee, talk about book. Is way staying in touch when girl making much money sewing like old woman. Maybe Giorgio meddle girl's life, little bit."

I wanted to be weak then, to cry into this man's chest. Why was I constantly tested like this? Keeping my strength apparent, I did something like nod and smile as I clutched the parcel to my chest. Giorgio patted my shoulder. I was certain that if I so desired, he would have wrapped me in a giant bear hug. I did not think my strength would remain if that happened, so I added the parcel to the canvas bag he gave me the day before and moved toward the door. The distance between us grew greater with every step. I managed a weak thank-you as I opened the door.

"Charlotte visit sometimes," Giorgio said, his accent, whatever it was, thick. "Shop get lonely. We talk. Remember days we not spend together."

"Yes, I would like that," I said.

Giorgio smiled sadly.

"And maybe Giorgio convince girl taking good-paying job adventuring. Maybe learn many secrets. Together," he said.

The door closed behind me.

Maybe.

24

THE BUTCHER …

September 17, 1814 AD

The walk back to the tenement was worse than the walk to Giorgio's, and I had to stop several times. Thrice I was almost trampled by a horse or team of horses pulling a cab. I was passing a butcher shop on Rue Juiverie when my stomach pinched into a small rock that pulled me so violently I was down on my knees before I was aware of it. Having some money, I decided to test a theory. I would purchase some raw beef and eat that. Then maybe I could regain some measure of control.

The relief will be fleeting at best, my mistress whispered. *You know what you need to feed upon. Find a suitable meal and FEED.*

I ignored her. Besides, fleeting relief was better than no relief.

The entrance of the shop was flanked by a pair of fat geese, feathers and all, hanging from hooks through the meat of their legs. I shuddered at the sight of it. Of the memories.

The shop interior was regimental. A low counter faced the entrance, and behind the counter were shelves with all manner of dried meats, spices, and other goods in tight neat rows. The counter stretched to the right. An open case displayed a limited variety of meats in the middle of the counter. A bloodstained chart on the rear wall of the case outlined several types of cuts. The customers' space between the wall and the counter was close, maybe wide enough for two or three people to stand deep, but the counter ran another eight feet or so where a register sat. A heavyset man on the opposite side of the counter wrapped a package for a tall, arrow-straight woman. She nattered about something while the butcher worked with bloodied hands, paper, and string. He wore a red-and-brown-stained apron, a wrinkled blue-and-white pinstriped shirt with great sweat stains under his arms. I could not see his pants, but I imagined them in no better condition. Giorgio would be appalled at the man's lack of professionalism.

I was drawn, by my stomach, to stand in front of the case. Quantities seemed limited. The war was over, but food was still scarce. Rain was frequent and cold. Crops were sparse, and the animals that lived on them were thin and often sickly.

My last visit to a butcher shop was years ago. Father brought me. Mother thought it unseemly that a young girl should enter such a place of blood and flesh. Father thought the exposure was good for me. It was the year before we visited his parents in the country for the first and last time of my life. I was eight, and being a child of the city, I had never really considered where meat came from. The trip to the butcher shop was to show me how the meat looked before we brought it home. Later, during the visit to my grandparents' farm, I would find out what the meat looked like before it made it to the butcher. After the holiday at the farm, I gave up eating meat. That lasted almost a month, before my mother made my favorite stew for the fourth time. For all her myriad faults, my mother was an excellent cook. The tactic was unfair of her, but eventually I gave up my abstinence and devoured the food with relish. How stupid was I then to have given up meat? It was so expensive. So delicious. Some things, at least, never change.

Note: As I wrote that sentence, my mistress said, *Your mother knew best. Just as I do. If you wish, you may call me Mother.* I will NOT be calling her Mother. Now she seems both insulted and humored. How annoying! Well, at least she has that in common with my mother.

"Thirty franc for a leg of lamb?" said the woman, handing over several coins to the butcher.

His hands were clean, almost too clean. He just smiled as he received the money and slid the small paper-wrapped leg across the counter to the woman. "I do not make the prices out of the air, Madame Pelletier. Demand and scarcity makes the prices higher. It costs me more to buy the whole lamb, so I must charge more for the leg. I cannot change how things are. I'm sure you understand."

The woman gave a little frown and turned up her nose as she accepted the leg and walked out, muttering something about the city allowing thieves to set up shops now.

"Thank you, Madame Pelletier. Please come again," the butcher said, smiling.

It was a full smile that even touched his eyes. For three breaths the butcher stood smiling as he watched the woman leave. In the span it took me to blink, his face went from smiling to acrid.

"Whore. I hope you choke on a bone," he swore, and I laughed.

I tried to hold it back so instead of a dainty, ladylike laugh, it came out an abbreviated snort. The butcher jumped with a start. His face blushing, he rushed over to stand behind the glass case.

"I'm sorry, mademoiselle. I should not say such things, especially in the presence of someone so young and innocent."

I laughed again, this time out loud. My mistress echoed me in my head. I tried to appear to blush, but the blood in my body was thick and pooled in my legs, especially around my healing bones.

"I take no offense, monsieur," I said. "I have heard my own mother say worse. And in this case, I side with you."

The butcher smiled again, but I could not trust his smile now. It had fooled me once.

"What can I do for you, mademoiselle?"

"Well," I said, trying to feign patience, "I have scraped together and saved my spare change for a year now. It is my mother's birthday, and I wish to buy her something special. Alas I only have a few francs, and I must buy some wine as well."

The butcher's smile deepened somehow. It became... *predatory* was the best word I could manage.

"Mademoiselle," the butcher said. "For three francs I can provide for you a thick cut of goat and a bottle of swill." He did not actually say "swill," but he might as well have.

I grimaced.

"I am sorry, monsieur. My mother will not touch goat. One bit her when she was young, and she vowed to never touch another in any form whatsoever."

The butcher's smile disappeared, replaced with a frown. "It is my turn to be sorry, mademoiselle. To imagine. Instead of goat, maybe two cuts of beef a finger's width thick?"

I came for beef, but suddenly I did not want it. My eye had caught sight of a pale, tender roast of pork and suddenly that was all I wanted.

I know why, my mistress said almost playfully, which confused me.

Irritated, I shushed her mentally. She did not like that and hit me with a wave of hunger that crashed into me so violently I reeled. My knees buckled, and my next conscious thought was to wonder why I was staring at the ceiling.

You seemed to need a reminder, my mistress told me.

I tried to ignore her.

He has spiders, I said to myself. *The rest of the place is spotless, but the rafters have spiders.*

Suddenly the butcher's form was over me, obscuring the vermin above.

"Are you well, mademoiselle?" he asked.

"I am," I said as he helped me stand. My legs shook. "I have a condition..." What was that word? I only read it a couple times. "It is like a palsy, but on occasion it causes me to fall for no reason. My legs shake even now."

The butcher looked at me as if he expected me to fall over again.

"I am fine, I assure you," I said. The genuine concern in his eyes made me think that maybe I could turn my mistress's reminder into an advantage.

"Perhaps I could sit?"

The butcher nodded and disappeared through a door behind the counter. When he returned, he carried a narrow high-backed chair. It had no cushion, and in fact it barely had any wood to it. My guess was that the thing was held together by string, glue, and determination. I thanked the man and sat. Once he was assured I would not fall again, he returned to his position behind the counter.

"How much pork might four francs purchase?" I asked.

"I thought you wanted something special, mademoiselle. Pork is a poor substitute for beef."

It was true. Royalty and rich merchants ate beef. The poor ate brains and entrails. Pork was little better.

"Yes, this is true," I said. "But I would prefer to sacrifice some quality for quantity. It would be nice to remember my mother's birthday for more than a single meal."

The butcher nodded as if I were the wisest woman in Paris.

"Three franc will not buy much more than a pound," the butcher said remorsefully.

I saw something of a twinkle in his eyes that suggested he and the truth were uncommon mates.

"That is a shame. This tenderloin looks marvelous. My mother would love it, I think."

The butcher grimaced. "That would cost eight franc I am afraid, and I fear I cannot cut it in half. I know of a chef that will pay almost ten franc for it whole."

I shrugged. "I see no chef here now, and I must say that while the tenderloin looks lovely, it seems that one would not pay quality prices for a piece that is maybe three days old?"

Something I could not quantify passed across the butcher's face.

That is what I thought, I said to myself.

"Tell me, madame, is your father a butcher?"

I smiled. "No, but he was a merchant. My mother remarried after the war to an older man who had been a butcher in another life. He taught me what to look for on a good piece of flesh and what might indicate something past its prime. I think this tenderloin is a day away from being almost unsellable, well at least for any real profit."

The butcher frowned. I pressed my point.

"I will pay four francs for the whole tenderloin and a bottle of your house white to go with it."

"You insult me, madame," the butcher said. We both knew the deal was a good one, but he was trying to squeeze me for more money.

"Considering how my mother no longer shops here because she once overheard the manner in which you sometimes refer to your customers, and considering what I witnessed myself today, I do not believe that I am the one with the inclination to insult others. I must admit, however, that I enjoy your shop and you as well. The manner in which you handled that previous customer was entertaining, and I applaud you. Because I like you, might I suggest the following?"

In the end, he drove a hard bargain, but despite my disdain for my mother, not all of her lessons went unlearned. I drove a harder bargain. I left the shop with the whole tenderloin, a modest-sized collection of stewing bones, and about two pounds of beef fat trimmings. I settled for a bottle of slightly inferior white wine as well, all for four and a half francs.

When I handed the butcher a gold five-franc coin from a purse that jingled with more coin, he looked crestfallen. I smiled brightly at him as he made my change. He wished me a good day, but I did not believe his sincerity at all.

Every step I took home seemed both lighter and heavier. I would eat soon, and for that I was delighted. To have fresh meat so close to me was a punishment. Holding the package was awkward as I handled it and Theo's cane. I should have placed it in my canvas bag, but I feared getting blood on the clothes. Plus the smell of the meat was so delicious, I wanted it close under my nose.

In Quartier de Bonne-Nouvelle, I slipped and scattered the contents of my paper package across the sidewalk and road. A carriage passed, running over the tenderloin, leaving a thick, bloodied depression in the middle of it.

Nobody helped me. Why was it that people acted like this around me now? It was as if instinct told them to ignore me. I scrambled on my hands and knees to gather my parcels as best I could.

I stood and began a slower hobble home, but a few streets later I could not withstand the call to feed any longer. A tangle of dark passages surrounded me. I chose the darkest, narrowest alley I could find and slid in. There I opened the package of fat trimmings and tentatively took a bite.

I cannot say the experience was pleasurable, but it was food. The experience was almost like eating gruel. Something about the consistency or the texture was not quite right. While the trimmings tasted like what I remembered beef tasting like, it was unsatisfying in a way I could not pinpoint. My stomach demanded more even if my tongue was hesitant. Before long I had ravenously devoured the entire package of fat trimmings.

The next package was the pork tenderloin, which I tore open. I originally wanted to save it, to eat it a little at a time over the course of days, but then I was devouring it. The pork was nothing like the fat trimmings. It was savory and tore apart between my teeth in a pleasant manner. It was not as good as the maître d' had been, but at least this was an animal instead of a person.

One of my teeth cracked on something hard. The pain was intense, but I did not stop. Instead, my tongue found the hard bit, and I spat it out. It was a pebble. Disgusting.

I stripped the tenderloin of its wrapping and brushed it clean as much as possible. I wondered briefly if I could simply swallow the whole thing without chewing, and in the next instance I was doing just that. My mouth opened wider than I knew possible. Innumerable teeth unfolded into my mouth, stretching toward the meat, yearning for it. My throat opened, and teeth unfolded down the length of my throat, stretching upward to accept the tenderloin. I lowered the meat to my mouth and every tooth sunk into the meat, shredding the flesh and pulling it down, down, down into the abyss of my soul.

I do not remember much else after, except waking as if from a stupor. Filth covered my hands and clothes. Discarded packaging lay all around me. No meat remained, and even the bones were missing.

I was ashamed. The meat was supposed to be several days' worth of food, and I ate it all before I could make it home. To add insult to injury, my hunger remained. The void abated somewhat and was more manageable, but it was still present, still alive, still demanding.

What would it take to finally feel full?

I picked up the empty packages and placed the paper in a pile of trash heaped in one corner. My clothes and hands were my next concern, and I tried to clean them as best I could. It was an impossibility without soap and water.

"Hey Henri, look what we have here," someone said behind me.

25

... AND THE BUTCHERED

September 17, 1814 AD

I whipped around. At the entrance of the alley were Henri Bordelon and Small Eyes.

"Theo's little mouse," Henri said with an ugly smile on his plain face.

For a moment, all I could think was, *Theo speaks of me?*

"It looks like she's lost her way," Small Eyes said, laughing. "Have you lost your way, little girl?"

Something in his tone snapped me back to reality. It might be a sin to hate, but God as my witness, I hated Small Eyes.

"No," I said. "I simply made a wrong turn. I thought something was here, a shop—for soap, but it is not. I will be going if you do not mind."

I gathered up my things and began to walk around the duo. Small Eyes moved forward, and Henri glanced quickly at him before following. They stood side by side and blocked my passage.

"This little mouse is caught in a trap," Small Eyes said.

I was caught, I realized. In my hunger I forgot the one rule I told myself over and over again, 'always have a way out.'

He looked at me as if looking through my clothes. I tried to push past them, but there were two of them, and they were taller and had more leverage. I was not about to use my unnatural strength and start rumors. Not if I did not need to.

Small Eyes shoved me hard, and I fell to the ground. He began to loosen his pants.

"I'm pretty sure no one's going to come in here, Henri, but I do like to work undisturbed. Be a friend and watch the entrance. You can have a go with her when I'm done."

Wide-eyed, Henri looked at me, then Small Eyes, and then back at me.

"What?" Small Eyes asked him, never turning around. "You are going to do this with me. We're going to enjoy it. And then we are going to go back to the club, get drunk, and not say a word to Theo. Understand?"

I was pulling myself back, away from the two boys—no, boys do not play these kinds of games, but neither do men. These two were monsters, monsters no different really from Monsieur and Madame, but were they monsters different from me?

All humankind are monsters, my mistress chimed in. *There are none among you that are sinless, and there is no sin in killing monsters.*

Again, I tried to ignore her, but Reason left me long ago. There was no counter voice to lend me aid against my mistress. I grimaced and began to shake.

"Oh ho ho," Small Eyes said. "She's old enough to know what's coming. That's good."

I scrambled away like a crab as far and as fast as I could. My elbow landed on something hard, Theo's cane.

"Look at the little mouse try to flee." Small Eyes seemed to come alive then, as if he had never actually been alive until that very moment. His pants pitched from his excitement, and his hands worked more hurriedly to release his desire. Henri looked back at me with pained eyes and then left.

Bastard.

With Small Eyes's pants loosened, he held them at the waist with one hand as he walked to stand over me. I lifted Theo's cane and swung it at Small Eyes, intending to stun him long enough get up and run.

He caught the cane with his free hand. The smack of wood on flesh was almost sickening, but he did not seem to even feel the pain. His eyes were aflame.

His pants dropped as he took the cane in both hands and snapped it in two. All I could see then were the splintered pieces falling to the ground around him in a rain of wood, black enamel, and hope.

He was on top of me, lifting my skirts and pushing himself closer to his goal. His hands brushed over my half-healed scars, and Small Eyes looked down.

"Fuck, girl, what happened to you?" Small Eyes asked. "Henri, look at this bitch's legs when it is your turn," he called over his shoulder.

"Don't do this," I begged him. "Please."

He leered down at me. "I always love it when they beg. About half do. They are my favorites."

I was pushing him back as best I could. I wanted nothing more than to throw him off at that moment, damn who knew how strong I was now, but my strength fled me.

Why should you have access to my gifts, when you continue to refuse me? The voice was my mistress's, but it was no longer within my head. It came from the shadows behind Small Eyes, who seemed oblivious to the voice.

I pushed against him with my feet and knees, but he slowly advanced, avoiding my kicks as if he knew how I would react before I did. His knees were between my legs, pushing my skirts higher and higher up my thighs. I beat and slapped at him, then finally I did everything I could to hold him back with my hands on his shoulders. That was when I finally understood what he meant when he said, "I always love it when they beg. About half do. They are my favorites."

"No," I said. "You sick bastard. You have done this before?"

"It is my favorite sport," he said, smiling from ear to ear.

He was taking his time with me at that point. For some reason he wanted to draw this out as long as possible. I slapped him. I raked my nails across his face. I battered his chest with my fists. He only smiled and licked at the blood that blossomed on his lips.

"Henri, please. Help me," I yelled toward the alleyway entrance.

That gave Small Eyes a pause. A tense fist of seconds passed as neither Small Eyes nor I was certain if Henri would come to my aid or not. We only heard the general uncaring clamor of the city. When it became apparent that Henri was not coming, that nobody was coming, Small Eyes just laughed, reared back, and punched me in the face. My head whipped to the side, and stars exploded into my field of vision.

My vision swam, and Small Eyes pressed further, laughing all the while. I felt his desire on my thighs, hot, wet, and sticky.

Mistress spoke again. This time her voice came from a dark form that stood behind Small Eyes. *You have denied me for too long, girl. This will be the price you pay.*

"No," I cried. "No please."

Small Eyes cackled, and in his distraction I was able to get my hands back into place, holding him just far enough away to keep my chastity, if barely. My defense would not last long.

I saw my mistress then. She was beautiful in her horror, a machine with a single purpose, to kill and devour.

This, she said, gesturing to her own horrible beauty behind a man I considered the greater monster. *This is who you really are. It is power. It is your reward, but you must finally embrace all the gifts I have given. No more will you be the victim to your family, the victim to your country, the victim to your situation.*

"No, no, no, no," I repeated over and over again to both Small Eyes and my mistress. I shook my head as I pushed physically against Small Eyes. His desire brushed against my underclothes, and tears stung my eyes.

There is no sin killing the monster on top of you. He deserves punishment for what he has done to a dozen others and will do to dozens and dozens more if you do not stop him. You would do your fellow man a service. Accept this and learn what true control, what true independence is.

Accept my gifts and be free. That is what you have always wanted, isn't it? Freedom?

"Please, please don't," I begged. "I do not want to do what you will make me do."

Small Eyes paused for the smallest of moments before he said almost kindly, "Oh, little mouse. You don't get to choose anything right now, and when I'm done with you, you will be done good. I don't care what the boss says, you are mine. I'm going to use you and then dispose of you like the trash you are."

I knew he was telling the truth. No one cared what I wanted. No one cared that I lived or what happened to me. Only I cared. Well only I and my mistress, but even she was holding my fate ransom.

All of humanity sins, but some are worse than others. Some need to be removed from the rest, culled for the good of the whole. Accept. Be free to move and act how you wish. If you wish to be the hand of Judgment herself, you may. You will feed frequently and always have more to judge.

I wept openly. My prior objections to be an assassin hit me then. Who was I to judge people? Then I realized that while I might be incapable of judging people, I knew firsthand that I was perfectly capable of judging monsters.

My mistress was nowhere to be seen as I extended my claws and buried them into Small Eyes's shoulders. His tiny, close-spaced eyes went wide, and he grunted with the pain. He began to pull back, but I pulled him forward. His face was directly in front of mine. In the reflection of his pupils, I saw my monstrous smile as my teeth emerged.

My mouth was impossibly wide and so full of row upon row of long needlelike teeth, I could not fathom their number. My lips disappeared, making my mouth a violent gash in dead gray flesh. The flesh spread across, up, and down my face and neck just as I was sure it was spreading up from my hands and feet.

My nose disappeared into two gray slits. I could smell him then. Really smell him. He smelled like the pork I just ate minutes before. He smelled better though. Better because he also smelled of excrement and sweat and blood and musk. He smelled delicious.

I could see that he wanted to but could not look away. He was as transfixed as I at the sight of my deathly transformation.

My eyelids vanished as dead gray skin spread across my eyes. The whites of my eyes turned blood-red, and my pupils became horizontal slits. I could see him then. Really see him. I saw into him. His blood coursed through his body in myriad pathways converging into larger and larger paths that eventually joined the heart and lungs. A pale blue glow of panic blossomed in the core of his brain. It radiated outward, down the back of his neck, and across his body in a flash. I could drink that panic, consume it if I so chose, but it seemed wrong somehow, so I did not.

He almost screamed. I know because I saw his lungs begin to fill with air a frantic heartbeat later, but I jerked him toward me and kissed his cheek. Immediately he lost all control of himself, a limp rag doll in my arms.

I rolled us over so that I lay on top. I caressed his face with the back of my hand, my fingers bloody. He had tears in his eyes.

"You thought I was begging for my life?" I asked. "No, you repugnant misery of a man. I was begging for yours."

I stood and disrobed. My clothes were largely shreds as protrusions of bone sliced through the material across my arms, legs, and back. The exposed bone shredded my clothing at the slightest movement. A wealth of clothing ruined in a handful of seconds.

You will not care for money one day, my mistress said. This time she was neither within me nor without, but rather everywhere all at once.

When I was naked, I showed my completely transformed body to Small Eyes. I had to stand over him a bit, as he was flat on his back. He was the first man I ever wanted to see me so completely, and he could not take his eyes off of me.

"I hate rapists," I said, squatting beside him. My voice was dark and thick. "After my brother died, my mother tried to pay his debts, our debts, to his foreman. The man took all of her money, most of our remaining things, and then he took her honor. He said that she was not any good and so she still owed him. He told her that he would send others to visit her, and they did. They raped her, sometimes two or more at a time. Each paid my brother's foreman for the act."

I thought the memories forgotten, too painful to remember, but they came to my lips all the same. Anxious to be said. Anxious to be heard.

I slashed my claws across his chest, just high enough to cut only his clothes. Well, maybe I cut him too, a little. I pushed the cloth away from the two parallel cuts on his chest. They were not deep, but tiny roses appeared along the edges. I leaned down and licked the blood from his chest.

Good? my mistress asked.

"Mmmmm, delicious," I said out loud.

I sat back up and continued. "The only time my mother ever fought back, much less complained, was when some of the men wanted to take me too. She screamed and clawed at them long enough for me to flee. *She* never ran, however. She just took it. She lost everything else, so why not this too? She did not want that for me. That was the last time I ever saw her alive."

I played at slicing more and more of his shirt away from his body. Soon his chest and arms were laid bare. I touched his chest lightly, drawing imaginary shapes on his smooth skin. I considered a simple stab of one clawed finger through the bone covering his heart. Death would come instantly, or at least as fast as a pale horse can fly.

But he had admitted—no, bragged—to me that he had done this before. Several times it sounded like. This was the kind of man that toyed with his victims before raping and killing them. He deserved no less. Maybe when I killed Henri, he would go quickly, but not this one.

His pants were around his ankles. His knees were filthy. All rigidity was gone from his manhood. I knew what I wanted, what I needed, and it was not that flaccid thing. So I finished stripping him, brushed the larger bits of dirt and debris from his feet and legs, and began my work.

You can make him feel it, my mistress told me. *If you will it, you can make him aware of every touch, every stab, every bite, every rend, and you can make it so that he can do no more than just lie there and feel it all.*

I hate to admit it, but I considered what she said. But such an act would only prove that I was the greater monster. As I wanted to be somewhat human, I resolved to do no such thing.

Heaven was no longer a possibility for my future, but for the next few moments I felt I was there. Every hunger pain I had accumulated in the past month evaporated all at once. The void filled, and instead of hunger, all I felt was bliss. My toes curled, my nipples became stiff, my skin became flushed, and a warm glow filled my stomach and groin.

When I was sated, I transformed back into my human self and crawled up to lie beside him. I gave him another kiss, this time on the lips. The kiss was long, deep, and covered his mouth in thick gore when I pulled away.

"Do you want to live?" I asked, my voice a gentle purr.

He could not move, but I saw it in his eyes.

"Then when I release your voice, you will call Henri for his turn," I whispered as one lover might to another. "Then we shall see who is the better man."

Tears poured from his eyes as I kissed him hard again on his lips. I used my tongue to lick the gore from his mouth as I willed him to regain the use of his tongue, his lips, and his jaw. His tongue came alive in his mouth as it pulled back away from mine.

I released him.

I pulled Small Eyes back to prop him against the wall of the alley in the kind of shadows that only suggested shapes and forms. Then I slipped through the shadows to stand near the entrance.

"Call him, my sweet," I said.

"H... Hen... Henri?" Small Eyes cried.

Henri did not show.

"Again," I told Small Eyes. "Louder."

"Henri!" Small Eyes tried again. His voice was rough under his blubbering cries. "It is your turn, mon ami."

Still Henri did not appear.

I slipped closer to the entrance of the alley, but Henri was nowhere to be found. I returned to Small Eyes.

"He has abandoned you," I told Small Eyes. I wiped tears from his eyes and tasted them. "He abandoned us."

"That filthy shit. I'll fucking kill him," Small Eyes said. Spittle and blood flew from his mouth as he did.

"No," I said. "I do not think you will have the chance."

Small Eyes stared at me, his face blank, his eyes full of tears.

"But you must not worry," I said. "I will exact revenge upon him." And I knew then that I would, though unlike Small Eyes's death, Henri's would be fast.

I cradled Small Eyes's face to my chest and stroked his hair.

"I really enjoyed what we did just now. Did you?" I asked.

"I don't know. I... I can't feel anything. I saw... I saw you t-t-turn into a m-monster," he said.

"No," I told him. "I'm not the monster here, you are. Aren't you?"

He did not answer.

"Well," I said, "I want more of what I just had, and deep down I bet you do as well."

"Um... yes," he said. "I want more. I would like to feel it though."

I purred with the thought, but still I did not want to go down that path to become that kind of monster.

You can make him feel as you do, my mistress said. *Will it, and he will feel everything you feel as you feed.*

"Maybe," I said to both my mistress and him. "I might be convinced. You mentioned your boss. Who is he, and what does he want of me?"

As I asked my question, I took one of Small Eyes's hands in mine and showed him that I held it. Then I stuck one of his fingers in my mouth and let him feel it. His eyes brightened.

"Yeah. Oh yeah, I like that," he said.

I rolled his head to look straight up, transformed into the monster once again, and began to eat his finger as I sucked on it. A nibble at first, and I willed him to feel how it made me feel.

He moaned and smiled. He closed his eyes. "Whatever you are doing, do more of it."

I obliged.

After finishing one finger, his erection was full and twitched violently. I resumed my human form and placed my face near his.

"You mentioned your boss," I said. "You said that you did not care what he said, that I was yours. What did you mean by that?"

Small Eyes blinked several times. Then, as if from a dream, he started to speak.

"I cannot," Small Eyes said. "He would be very upset if I said anything."

"Oh," I said. "I guess the good feelings end now."

"No. Please no," he begged. "That felt so good. Please. I want more."

"I am more than happy to give you more, but you must give me all you know."

When he seemed to resist, I nibbled a little more on another finger. His penis twitched again.

"And that's the end of that," I said.

"Paillard. Monsieur Paillard," Small Eyes said.

"I need more than a surname, silly."

"Albert Paillard. He lives in the first arrondissement in Château de l'Epée."

"Oh," I said. Then, using my teeth, I stripped the flesh from his finger from the knuckle to the tip. He ejaculated and his eyes rolled back into his head.

"What does he want of me?" I asked when I could see his pupils once again.

When Small Eyes did not respond, I took another nibble.

"Please tell me," I purred. "I can make you feel even better."

Small Eyes was panting and sweat blossomed over his body. Impossibly he smelled better than before. I wanted to devour him completely right then and there.

"Please?"

"He... he... he wants to know all about you," Small Eyes said.

"Where you are. Who you talk to. Says you are important to him. Something about knowing your mother. That's all I know. Really."

"My mother?" I asked. "Just my mother?"

"Yes."

"How long?" I asked.

There was a pause.

"How long what?" Small Eyes asked.

"How long have you been keeping tabs on me for him?" I asked.

When he did not immediately answer, I took a large bite out of his hand. His body spasmed as his flaccid penis renewed to life.

"Four years," Small Eyes said.

I was stunned. Four years ago, my father was still alive. Why was this person having Small Eyes follow me all this time?

"What else do you know?" I demanded.

There was another pause before he spoke again.

"N… nothing else," Small Eyes said. "I promise."

"He knows where I live?" I asked.

"Yes," Small Eyes said. "Now do me some more. I have to feel that again."

"What else does he know about me?" I asked.

"Everything," Small Eyes said. "He knows you don't have a job. He knows you were sick recently. He knows that your leg is hurt. He knows that fat sack of shit, Giorgio, has been helping you. Everything."

"What else?" I asked. "What else is there?"

"He… he's," Small Eyes said. "You have to fuck me if I tell you."

"If the information is worth it, then maybe I will," I said.

"He wants you to need him. So once he comes to you, you'll want him and love him and he can be your knight in shining armor. He's the reason you cannot find work. He's the reason your mother could never find work. He's the reason your bother had the accident at the mill. He's the reason your father…"

"My father what?" I asked. My voice was dark and throaty. I was fully transformed into the monster.

"I… I cannot. Fuck me. Fuck me and I will tell you," he said.

My hands were on his throat, though he could not tell. My claws were inches from the thick lines of blood coursing through his flesh. One more cut and he would be done.

But that would be too fast.

Instead I transformed back into my human self. It was difficult, but I managed it. The monster in me wanted me to finish this. The only reason my human self was able to assert control was the promise that we were not finished feeding.

"My father... what?" I asked one last time. The tone of my voice was hard as I fought every desire to kill this beast of a man and finally rid the world of him.

"Your father's death. It wasn't completely an accident. Paillard hired some thugs to beat him up. I showed them where you live. He... Paillard, wanted something from him or owed him money. I forget. But then your father fought back, said he didn't have time for this. The thugs chased him down as he ran around the quartier randomly. They fought and your father staggered into the street. That's when the carriage struck him."

"So, you were there? When my father died? You were part of the reason?"

He did not respond immediately. When he did, he seemed to have reached the conclusion that maybe he said too much for his own good. His fate was sealed from the moment I fully accepted my gifts.

"I told you what you wanted. You... you're going to fuck me now, right?"

In answer, I propped Small Eyes up against the wall and gave him control of his body over the shoulders. He spat as he tasted the blood in his mouth and as he licked his lips. His eyes widened as he felt the gore still crusted on his face.

Small Eyes's gaze flicked madly around the alley before landing on the space right in front of him. All that was left of his legs was a bloody trail from where I ate them to where I propped his body.

"Where... where are... are my legs?" he asked.

I stood and walked into a shaft of light in front of him. The process of consuming his legs healed my own completely. I could even feel blood flowing through them once again.

"They are here, on me now. See how good they look?" I asked.

Small Eyes's tears came out with great blubbering cries.

"D... did... you..." he tried to say.

"Did I what?" I asked, moving to lie next to him once again.

"Did you... eat them?" he asked. "There's blood all over you, all over your face."

Stroking his face with the back of my hand, I said, "I begged you not to try raping me."

"I... I am going to die. A man cannot lose so much blood," Small Eyes said. His voice was a plea as much as a statement of fact.

"Normally that is true, but I stopped the flow of blood to your legs. Otherwise we could not have had our conversation," I said. "No, my sweet. You will live on."

He relaxed slightly as I moved close and gently kissed him once more, willing him to be fully paralyzed once again.

"You will live on as a part of me," I finished, smiling.

I consumed the rest of his flesh, leaving only the bones, some of his internal organs that did not seem particularly appetizing, and his flaccid penis. No part of that retched appendage would ever find itself in me.

26

CONSEQUENCES

September 17, 1814 AD

By the end of things, I was covered in blood and gore. I reasoned this was why monsters moved in the dark. At least the alley was secure. There were no ground-floor windows opening out into the alley, only a single boarded-up door at the end. Above it was a battered awning, and above that was three floors of blank wall and... and a window that I had not seen.

It was open.

Panic tried to rush through me, but oddly, in the monstrous state such as I was, the panic became curiosity, as if I was incapable of panic. I instantly understood the potential for such a life, a life with phenomenal power and no fear. It thrilled and terrified me.

If someone saw you, well... you would have to eliminate them too. It is only sensible. And if you are going to eliminate them, then you get to feed again. Win-win, said a monstrous voice to me, but this time it was not the voice of my mistress. The monstrous voice was my own.

I understood with stark horror where such monstrousness could lead. To retain anything of myself, I had to fight that voice from the monstrous side of myself. I was still considering my plight when I realized that the monster was climbing the alley wall hoping to find someone to kill.

The monster wanted to jump right into the room as soon as I reached it, but I screamed with all my will that we should tread lightly. First we should investigate with caution, otherwise we might find ourselves surrounded by men with cold iron. How or why I knew to say "cold iron" escaped me, but it worked. The monster reacted immediately and became more cautious. I forced the monster aside and took control. We—no, *I*—crawled above the window and hung upside down to peer into the room beyond.

There was no glass in the window. Only a pair of ruined shutters existed to protect the interior from the elements, but they hung loosely on rusted hinges. Sun-bleached gauzy tatters were all that remained of the curtains protecting the interior from the sun. I tentatively stuck my head through the window and peered around.

The room itself was small and sparse. A small table and chair, a couple cabinets, an armoire, an ice box, and a bed were all that populated the room. It looked empty, but I felt a presence, as if the memory of a person remained. I climbed in.

I expected the floor to be riddled with rot from rain coming through the open window, but the floor was strong and, like everything else in the room, covered in a thin, perfectly uniform layer of dust. The monster in me lost all interest at that point and once again I, the real me, was in complete control. With a small effort of will, I reverted to my normal self. On the off chance someone caught me here, it would be easier to explain the presence of a young naked woman than the presence of a monster. That was when I realized that my canvas bag with my clothes was still in the alley below.

I told myself, *As long as no one comes along and discovers the body, I should be able to retrieve my things once I manage to clean myself.*

No sooner than I thought that, I could hear shouting coming from the alley. A woman screamed and voices were raised as a crowd gathered to inspect my artistry. Moments later I heard the whistles of the gendarmes and a growing tumult of the crowd.

Panic surged within my human form. The monster wanted to

return, and a part of me wanted the monster to return, too, so that I would not have to deal with the fear. If I allowed the monster too much control, my only path was toward ruin. Instead I searched the room for anything I could use.

One cabinet held some cast-off rags, barely fit for cleaning. I used them to wipe the excess gore from my body, but there was too much and the rags were soon soaked. In my frustration I noticed my own bloody footprints leading back toward the window where there was blood on the windowsill, the curtains, and I assumed the wall outside as well.

I had to get out.

I grabbed the blanket off the bed. Dust scattered into a roiling cloud above it, causing light streaming in from the window to glint in a million beautiful, sparkling motes. I wished for the briefest of seconds that I could stay there and simply watch the dust play in the air all day and forget what I had become. Reality was a harsh mistress, however. I had to go.

I wiped my feet on the floor until I no longer left bloody footprints. I wrapped the blanket around me and checked the door. It opened into an empty hallway. Just to my right was a stairwell leading down. Further down were two more doors, one across the hall and one at the end. To my left was a trio of doors with one on each wall.

Raised voices and heavy footsteps ascended the stairwell. The twists and turns of the stairs muted the voices, but they were becoming louder with every heartbeat. I realized my heart was beating because at that moment it thundered.

Terror pushed me away from the stairs, so I checked each of the doors to my left. Every one of them was locked.

"... butchered like some animal..." came a random handful of words up the stairwell. The voice was gruff and angry, and I imagined the words were spoken from under a great bushy mustache.

As quickly as I dared, I moved back down the hallway and past the stairs to check the remaining two doors. Again both were locked. Those ascending were close and I had nowhere to run, so I made a path. I transformed my arms and legs and shoved on the nearest door, the one at the end of the hall to the right. Wood snapped and the door opened.

There was an undignified explicative shouted from the stairwell as the tempo of the footfalls quickened. I put myself on the other side of the door and looked around. This room was much like the previous one. The single window was directly across from the door and shuttered tightly.

I reached for the first piece of furniture I could find, an armoire, and dragged the heavy oak piece across the floor to rest in front of the door. The large piece of furniture rocked as the door slammed against its side. Desperate, I pushed the armoire back against the door even harder, moving it a few inches. There was an audible snap and a man screamed. I pulled back slightly on the armoire. The door slammed against the side again, then all resistance disappeared. I shoved the armoire back into place and paused to catch my breath.

Yes. I had breath to catch, and it was marvelous.

The shutters on the window began to rattle and the latch began to jitter loose. The men on the other side of the door gave a renewed shove. I shoved back against the armoire, but they must have been shoving something through the door. Each time they pushed, it opened a little further. Try as I might, I could not force the armoire or door back.

The monster told me that she could take care of everything if I just let go. I refused. I was not going to let the monster have its way and kill most if not all of these men. It would likely rationalize the killing of everyone in the building once that was accomplished. I would allow none of that.

There were only two potential exits, and there was someone at each. I ran to hold the shutter latch shut when the door slammed against the armoire again, shoving it an inch or two. I tore a long double-hand-wide strip from the blanket I had, and I wrapped the strip around my head and face, leaving only my eyes exposed. The armoire was pushed further and further, and the shutter rattled. I wanted to wrap strips around my body as well, but there was no time.

When my face was concealed, I darted to the shutters, lifted the latch, and shoved them open.

Whoever was on the other side fell with a short scream that ended with a wet thud on the street three floors below.

Through the walls I heard someone in the building yell, "Mon Dieu. Luc has fallen. He... he's dead."

Another man named 'Luc' dead because of me, I thought.

Putting my thoughts of unfortunately named me aside, I jumped into the window, naked save for a strip of blanket wrapped around my face, just as the armoire crashed to the floor behind me. To my right was another building, and I leapt. I easily reached the overhanging roof, and I began pulling myself up. There was a loud crack, and a piece of clay tile exploded close to my face.

I screamed and climbed faster. When I got to the crest of the roof, I turned to look at my attacker. There were two men in the window I had just jumped out of and another in the window of the room next to mine. The lone man was the one with the gun. I knew him.

Jean.

I stood there and displayed myself to him. Here and now he could see me in all my glory, all shame lost... or maybe overcome. Would he know me? He did not seem to as he lowered his weapon and began to squeeze the trigger. I did not know if I could flee from him then. Maybe I should have died months ago. At the very least I should have starved to death several times over, and since then I had killed two men and been used to kill a third. Not only that, but if Jean did not kill me then and there, I knew I would kill again. Henri did not deserve a place in this world, not when my own brother was dead. Not when my own father was killed in the streets. Not when my mother sacrificed herself to save me from a fate that Henri had left me to. Maybe I should let Jean kill me, and I could be done with it all.

Instead he released the trigger and looked up at me, his head tilted slightly. He lowered his weapon, and for the briefest moment I was both overjoyed and disappointed at the same time. I do not remember hearing the crack of the gun blast, nor do I remember feeling any pain in my shoulder where I was struck. Instead, the next thing I knew, I was rolling and sliding down the opposite side of the roof.

I fully transformed and clawed at the slate of the roof. Tiles broke and slid out from under me as I scrambled. There were screams below me as tiles rained onto passersby below, and I dangled from the roof from one fully functioning arm.

Within seconds, my arm was already healing. Less than a minute later and, while it was still sore, I could reach the roof and pull myself up. I heard the men attempting to get onto the roof. They cursed and yelled back and forth as they tried to follow. I did not give them a chance.

I loped on all fours from rooftop to rooftop.At first I felt like an animal fleeing the hunters' hounds, but I quickly put enough distance between myself and my pursuers that the panic dwindled and evaporated. My shoulder hurt, but the pain was bearable and quickly lessened even with the exertion.

I found an abandoned building in which to sequester. It must have been a church or cathedral at some point because it had a steeple. A large round window decorated each side of the steeple. One window was open, the top tilted inward and the bottom out. I climbed up the side and ducked quickly inside. Pigeons burst into life around me, and I almost lost my grip on the window frame. The floor had long rotted away and crashed down three floors below me. While I was certain the fall would not kill me, I still did not wish to have the experience of landing on another pile of debris.

Several beams and supports crisscrossed the arch of the roof. Each was still solid enough to hold me. I grabbed onto one and pulled myself up to sit atop it. Sunlight beamed through holes in the roof and walls, illuminating the space below. I wedged myself in the crevice formed where two beams joined nearest my entrance. Once I felt secure, I examined my shoulder.

The bullet had passed through my left arm just below the shoulder, taking a sizable amount of flesh and muscle with it. Dried blood streaked from the wound down to my hand. I unwrapped the cloth from my head and used it to wipe the blood away from the wound to clean it, but it was already closed. Pale pink flesh stretched over the missing muscle underneath.

I told you I have given you many gifts.

"Yes," I replied. "The gift of getting shot at."

I expected my mistress to be angry at my retort. Instead she said, *You have always wanted a more exciting existence.*

I lay back in the rays of sunlight and let them warm my cold body. A light breeze passed through the space.

I soon found myself dreaming. I dreamed of beautiful boys, their sweet kisses, and then I ate them alive.

* * *

At first the voices were indistinct, almost whispers.

"Where?" asked a rough voice.

"There. See?" said a second, younger voice.

"I do not see, Brother Bernard," said the rough voice. "Remember Ephesians 5:18."

"I have not been drinking," Brother Bernard said. "The sun is setting now, so the spot is in shadow. Cover your eyes to shut out the sunlight and look into the darkest spot."

I heard them clearly now, especially since Brother Bernard raised his voice. They were not whispering so much as they were distant and speaking in low tones.

I jerked up at the realization that there were others in the interior of the abandoned building with me. The strip of cloth I had used for a mask was caught by a breeze and drifted down almost ten feet before getting caught on something jutting from the wall.

"There," exclaimed Brother Bernard.

"Judas Priest," said the older voice.

I scrambled to the window and pulled myself through. The pigeons startled into flight once again and flapped wildly as I escaped.

"Sorry," I told the birds as I bounded away.

Had they seen me? Rather, would they be able to recognize me? I had no way of knowing. All I knew to do was flee, and for the second time in a day, that was exactly what I did.

* * *

I found myself in a section of the city that I was unfamiliar with. I could see the Bastille from the tallest rooftops, so I knew I was not too far from home. I climbed down to the edge of the roof and scanned the area below for hints of my location. The setting sun left the narrow street below me in shadow. I was lucky. Laundry hung from more than one line crossing the street. There were several open windows, but I saw no people.

I climbed down a drainage pipe to a small ledge below one line. The line was stretched between two pulleys. A dress that looked like it might fit me hung in the middle of it, but when I pulled on the line, it was locked in place. Trusting in my mistress's "gifts," I stepped out to stand on the bottom clothes line.

The line on which I stood bowed significantly, and the top line snapped taut. I slid down toward the center, knocking clothes off to drift to the street below. Within seconds I was balanced perfectly on a thin rope two stories over the middle of the street. There I bent and unclipped the dress in question, white with small blue flowers. Giorgio would approve of the color I thought. I stretched it over my head.

"Mamma!" a small voice cried from one of the windows.

"What is it, Pierre?" A woman's voice came from further within the tenement apartment.

"There's a lady, Mamma."

I whipped my head around to find the source of the small voice, a little boy no older than six.

"Yes, Pierre," his mother called back. "I'm sure there is."

The boy turned to look at his mother, but she was uninterested. When he turned back, I waved. He returned it, his mouth slack and eyes wide. I gave the little boy a smile and a curtsy. Why did I have to curtsy? He smiled instantly, but just as quickly, the line rolled from under my foot and I fell.

The line on which I once stood shot upward with an audible twang. It took all of my heightened reflexes and more luck to reach out with one hand to catch it. I continued to fall, but this time more slowly as the line stretched tight again.

A little less than two stories of empty air existed beneath my dangling toes. I looked up to see the boy. His eyes and mouth were even wider, but now he was leaning out of the window, both hands braced against the sill.

"Pierre, come away from the window at once. You'll fall out," the mother shouted.

Heavy footsteps thundered closer to the window now above me. I blew little Pierre a kiss and used a single claw to cut the rope. The shorter side of the line snapped back toward the pulley opposite Pierre's window. I held the other end with both hands as it pulled me toward the opposite wall as I fell. The wall and I met about eight feet above the street just as the locking mechanism gave out. I fell the remaining eight feet, tumbled, and stood unharmed.

I ran and tried to blend in with the few remaining people on the street. Less than four blocks later, I heard police whistles behind me. I jumped and began to run, but stopped myself after only a few steps. I was just a girl walking home. There was no reason to run.

I heard several people running in my direction from little Pierre's tenement. My heart thundered in my chest to match the smacking sounds of hard heals on cobblestones. Thump thump thump thump thump thump thump thump.

At a four-way intersection, I turned right and ran for half a block. I crossed the street and ducked into what I thought was an alley or narrow passage. Instead it was the entrance to a small garden.

The garden was built in what looked like the void left by a building that had burned or collapsed. The side walls were perfectly smooth and showed lines in the brickwork that suggested a shared surface in ages past. There was no roof, but there was a bit of a canopy formed by trellises overgrown with flowering vines, many of which dangled at head level. A pair of whitewashed wooden benches rested to the sides, and further back from the entrance was a shallow but running fountain. Lilies covered the bottom pool's surface. Few insects buzzed in the air around the plant life at this hour, but I imagined I could hear the echoes of their droning from earlier in the day. Their song was slowly being replaced by that of the night crawlers as they woke from their daytime slumber.

Outside the little Eden, the footfalls made it to the intersection. There they paused as I ducked into some of the overgrown, dangling vines. I ensured my position had a clear view of the entrance. The feeling of vines as they seemed to grab my hair was odd. It almost felt as if a lover were caressing my hair. When inevitably I thought about what kind of bugs must live in those vines, my scalp instantly began to itch.

The heavy footfalls did not return, but I did not know if that meant the people chasing me had slowed to a walk or were standing still. I held breath I did not need and suddenly had to pee. At what point would I forget the annoying parts of being human?

Relish in those. They are the last to go.

A new set of footfalls made me forget about my bladder. I tensed and shifted to get a better view around the vines. My movement must have pushed something, because a small clay pot shattered. The footfalls turned out to belong to a man and his daughter of ten or twelve. They passed the garden, walking toward the intersection. The girl turned and looked in. Of all the things to look at or to see in the garden, her eyes locked on mine. She made no outward reaction. She simply turned away and continued with her father.

I dragged myself out of my hiding spot and moved closer to the entrance as quietly as possible. A deep shadow formed along the far wall. I hid within it and leaned toward the street in an attempt to hear as much as possible.

"No, monsieur," a deep feminine voice said somewhere closer to the intersection. "I have not seen a girl like that."

A male voice replied, but I could not hear what he said. It was almost as if the man were mumbling with a mouth full of stones.

"Of course, monsieur," said the woman.

I heard the stony, mumbling male voice again. Another voice, also male, clearly said, "No, I haven't seen anyone like that."

I began to relax.

"In the garden," a sweet small voice said. "I saw a girl in the garden. She was wearing a white dress with blue flowers."

I had no recourse but to flee.

Again.

There was not a clear exit, only the one out to the street. I cursed myself for not having ensured I had a second exit and dashed toward the back of the garden, hoping beyond hope to find a door.

There behind a trellis was a void, a space. I pulled the trellis, and it slid forward several inches until the tangle of life pulled back. On the verge of panic, I used a claw to slice through the vines, and the trellis swung outward. I stepped behind it and pulled it back into place. The space beyond was about five feet square. Based on the mixture of soft and solid textures beneath my feet, it seemed that the ground was dirt and stone, or maybe stone with a layer of dirt. The shadows were deeper here, but I panicked when I looked through the vines covering the trellis and saw dark forms moving into the garden.

I was stuck.

Unable to decide how to progress, I was startled when a section of the wall behind me swung open. I kept a scream unvoiced as I crouched and extended my claws. I stared into the space beyond but saw nothing but more walls. I considered my options. Should I take my chances and fight my way through those searching for me, perhaps killing several innocent men in the process? Or should I embrace more shadow and unknown. Either way could spell my doom. There was really no option for me.

I slipped in the open door as quickly and quietly as possible. I cursed my theft of a white dress and longed for the dark leather bodysuit Giorgio was tailoring for me. The door slid shut. I whirled around, prepared to pounce, but there was Vincent, as alive as I had ever beheld him, with his back against the marble-and-stone slab of a wall.

"You!" I shouted.

He turned and looked at me. The flesh on half of his face was missing, exposing the muscle and bone underneath.

"Flee," he said.

I wanted nothing more than to tear into the man, if that was what he was.

You know better, my mistress said. *It was he who turned you, after all.*

Indeed it was true. Neither Anton or Madame had laid a hand on me before my death, only Vincent.

"Why would I listen to you?" I demanded of the ghoul.

Vincent shuffled in place while motioning with one hand toward an irregular broken section of wall.

"Must... go," was all he said as he gestured.

"Look at me," I said. "Look at me when you talk to me."

So far he had not. He seemed reluctant. Slowly his gaze drifted from the opening in the wall, to air between us, and finally to my face.

Once our eyes met, he collapsed in front of me.

"S... s... sorry," he said in a halting manner. "Old m... m... masters... commanded."

I stood confused. Was he crying? His voice remained like gravel regardless. My anger at the man melted. I was not sure why, but I pitied him. I sighed.

"Get up. Lead me," I commanded.

He did. We climbed over a small pile of rubble and ducked into a hole. The entrance descended steeply into a space beyond. It looked like the area was supposed to be filled with dirt or stone, but it all spilled into a greater void further in. I descended the slope into the unknown. As unknown as it was, the known was likely worse. I hastened my crawl and descended with less fear than I would have expected otherwise.

27

IN THE CATACOMBS AGAIN

September 17, 1814 AD

As we entered a corridor in the catacombs that was unfamiliar to me, Vincent placed his hand on my shoulder to lead me as before. Things were different now, however. Now I held the same power he held. More, since I also held the favor of my mistress, something I assumed he did not. I grabbed his hand with my own, ripped it off my shoulder, twisted as I moved behind him, and pushed him against the wall, his arm between us.

"Where do you think you are taking me?" I demanded.

He tried to resist, but for every ounce of energy he exerted against me, I applied two toward holding him in check. I wondered if I would be able to match him two for one as he struggled against me, but before I reached my limit, long before in fact, he surrendered. It happened so quickly, so totally that I almost ripped his arm from his shoulder. Instead I only ripped a few tendons and maybe a muscle or two before I stopped. He grunted but exhibited no other sign of distress.

"Answer me, ghoul," I said. I was far shorter than he was, but I managed to pull him down so that I could whisper directly into his ear. "Where are you taking me?"

Vincent merely grunted, so I reversed my hold on his arm, twisted his body, and slammed him against the opposite wall.

"The mistress favors me, is it not apparent?" I asked him.

He grunted once again.

"I take that as a yes. So you understand who is in charge here?"

His grunt was the same as the first.

"Who is in charge then?" I asked.

He took his time responding, but when he did, I was surprised.

"Mistress. The mistress is in charge," he said.

I released him suddenly. While I had assumed that my mistress was his, I had not considered that she spoke to anyone but me. Such was my arrogance. How else had she killed the maître d'? Had he been the one to deliver the meet to the tenement? Not with his face like that, I guessed.

"Fine," I said. I almost wanted to apologize to him, but if it were not for him, I would not be like I am.

You would likely be just dead, my mistress said. Then, after a slight pause she added, *Or worse.*

I had to admit, my encounter with Small Eyes counted as worse, and I was likely very lucky to have avoided encounters such as those until then. A girl living alone on the streets of Paris was not the safest of scenarios.

"Fine," I repeated. "Take me where our mistress commands."

So once again I descended into the depths of the catacombs of Paris with a dead man as my guide.

We walked for an hour or two. The tunnels twisted and turned, branched and merged, rose and fell. I found it impossible to keep oriented, but it seemed here I was safe from being chased, at least for now. We could have been anywhere under the city. I stopped trying to predict where Vincent was taking me, and he ignored all my questions.

I considered my situation. I lost my bundle with Giorgio's donation of clothes and his book. And my money. It only occurred to me then what I had lost. I wanted to weep, but I would remain strong. I could tell Giorgio that thieves stole my bag. It was a common enough occurrence. Now was not the time to consider such things, for they were future concerns. I needed to think on my current concerns.

I had one major need, well two. I needed new clothes and a bath. Those who were looking for me would surely see the dress or maybe the blood and immediately know me. Depending on how complete a description that the girl who saw me in the garden might give the police, my face may be plastered in wanted posters over half of the city before the next morning.

"Vincent," I said, trying not to feel helpless. "Take me to a cistern or some other safe place where I can bathe. Please."

Vincent's head turned a fraction in my direction, nodded almost imperceptibly, and turned back. I was not certain if he would acquiesce to my demand until ten minutes later, when we stopped in front of a large iron door with an iron wheel in the center just above waist height.

The brute of a man took a wide stance, lowered his center of gravity, grabbed the wheel with both hands, and strained to turn it for near a minute. He shifted his stance slightly and then strained against the wheel once again. The wheel gave a slow metallic groan as it turned counterclockwise maybe five degrees before it stopped again. Vincent's arms seemed to swell in his shirt and jacket as the cloth strained against his flesh. Stitches in the man's jacket began to snap, and then the wheel was turning once more. He turned it almost a quarter rotation, and then he stopped. He turned while keeping his hands on the wheel and his body pressed against the door.

"Grab," he said, nodding toward an empty iron torch sconce on the wall. "Hold... tight."

It was an odd request, but I did as directed. He nodded once more, turned his attention back to the door, and pulled on the wheel to swing the door toward him. The metal gave another groan. It wanted nothing more than to rest but was being roused from slumber. Then suddenly the door was thrown wide and Vincent with it. He and the door slammed against the wall as a torrent of water escaped confinement and spilled headlong into the corridor.

The room beyond had been filled to chest height with water, all of which tried to escape its prior confinement at once. The water swept my feet out from under me. Had I not been holding on to something, I would have been swept away to God knows where.

The water spilled out of the room for minutes. The torrent became a river. The river became stream. The stream slowed and died to become a massive puddle of water standing two or three inches deep. On closer inspection, the flow still remained, but it was slow and lazy. Vincent lay pinned between the wall and the much larger metal door. He slumped over where his body was not pinned upright. I ignored him at first to look into the room beyond.

The room was circular, maybe twenty or more feet in diameter. The ceiling was several floors up, and sunlight streamed in through a storm grate. A stone stairway about three feet wide spiraled upward from stones that seemed to jut straight out of the wall. There was no railing, just blind empty space and God-given fear to keep one from standing too close to the edge. The floor of the room was water. No, that was not correct. It seemed the stairs continued to spiral downward from the landing. The floor was likely one or more floors down, and the space filled with more water over the years than could escape. It reminded me of my bath in the catacombs.

Was that where we were now? I saw no bones during our trip so far, but the randomness of the tunnels was similar to those from before. Maybe these tunnels existed separate but connected to those of the catacombs? I decided to ask Vincent after my bath.

I climbed the stairs until the stones were dry and removed the pilfered dress before diving headfirst into the water. In hindsight, diving headfirst was probably foolish, but it was done before the foolishness of the action struck me. Luckily that was the only thing that stuck me. The pool was deep, clear, cold, and empty. I swam in circles, turned flips, and dived down to the bottom of the pool. Even with my enhanced sight, vision was limited there. Every movement set small clouds of debris into the water. The bottom seemed to be all stones and sediment. Without the need to breathe, I could remain underwater by blowing out all the air in my lungs and then swallowing enough water to equalize my buoyancy. My hunger seemed almost contented at first with the influx of water, but within minutes my stomach began to rebel, angry at being fooled.

The swim to the surface was harder than I would have imagined, but I had never had so little air and so much water in my body before. Instead of struggling to swim up, I swam to the side of the tower, found the stairs, and simply climbed out on my hands and knees. When I reached the surface, I knelt at the doorway and vomited all the water in my stomach. The water might have been clean, but my stomach was anything but. Along with copious amounts of water, some ugly red, white, and purple bits of meat, gristle, and slime that might have once been Small Eyes or might have once been part of me came up as well. Once the offending water was out of my stomach, my hunger returned to the familiar state of quiet anger it usually was.

I moved back to the stairs where they descended into the pool and searched for a hand-sized stone. Small pieces of debris and broken stone lay everywhere, and within a few moments I found what I was looking for. I returned to my spot on the stairs and sat on the first step down from the landing. I was rather clean after the swim, but I used my fingernails to scrub my hair, cleaning both. Then I scrubbed the rest of my body with the rock. It was not soap, but it helped to get the most stubborn bits of dirt and blood off my skin. When I finished, I dived back into the center of the pool, did a couple flips, and exited.

On the platform, I wiped what water I could off my body and wrung out my hair. I put the dress back on and returned to the corridor to check on Vincent. He remained pinned behind the door. I gave it a tug and swung it partially closed. Vincent's body slipped down to the floor with a dull splash.

"Are you dead?" I asked, feeling foolish instantly. Of course he was dead. That wasn't the right thing to ask. "I mean, are you dead-dead?"

I almost jumped when his eyes opened, but kept control of myself. Vincent seemed almost more like an obedient dog than he did a thinking being.

"No," his graveled voice announced.

When he stood, I could hear bones grinding within his chest. I cringed and almost felt sorry for the thing. Almost.

"Where to next?" I asked.

Vincent looked to the door and then looked up.

"Did you bring me here so I could wash, or was this simply on the way?" I asked, somewhat annoyed.

Vincent opened the door and held a hand out to indicate I should proceed. After staring at the man for a couple moments, I decided that getting wherever he was taking me would happen faster than I could bleed answers from this stone of a once-man.

We took the stairs to the top level, which seemed to be maybe eight or ten feet below street level based on the domed slope of the walls and the grate in the ceiling. I heard what sounded like normal life through that grate, and I longed to return to the surface.

The next hour or so we spent wandering unknown tunnel after unknown tunnel. Some of them were obviously part of the catacombs, while others were not so obvious. My original wanderings must have taken me further away or further below the city than I had once thought. Maybe both. Finally we came to the end of a corridor. There were no visible doors, but the stones in the wall at the end were different than those of the side walls. The wall in front of us looked more... decorative. No, regular. The bricks were more regular, like those of a building above ground.

Vincent turned to me and put a single finger to his lips before turning back around and sliding his hand into the wall where a single brick was missing. There was a click, and a portion of the wall slid toward us while a smaller portion slid out, the whole pivoting on some unseen hinge.

28

DEATH TAKER

September 17, 1814 AD

The door opened into a wide courtyard filled with junk pressed against the walls. Twilight's soft blanket covered the sky. One wall of the courtyard was enclosed with a brick wall two stories tall. The stonework was obviously newer with less accumulated grime than the other walls. Remembering my previous alley encounter, I checked for windows. There were several, but they too were all bricked over, creating a very private space in the middle of Paris.

The only visible exit was a door opposite where we entered the alley.

"Go... door. Help... there," Vincent said.

I started for the door, but stopped mid-stride after taking three steps. Vincent was retreating back through the secret door behind us. From this side, the opening looked nothing like a door. Instead it appeared to be a section of wall with haphazardly stacked wooden planks piled in front of it.

"You are going?" I asked.

Vincent just growled low and nodded once. I was just about to ask why when light spilled over us, and my shadow stretched away from me toward Vincent and up the wall.

Someone behind me shouted something I did not understand. The voice was male, surprised but deep. Vincent's face blanched. I turned to face this man, curious to know exactly who would strike fear in Vincent, but before I could turn enough to see, Vincent landed between me and the newcomer. He apparently leaped over me from a standing position.

Vincent growled and pushed me back with his right hand without turning to look at me. The push was with such force that I slid back a foot or more. I heard the clicking of boot heels on the cobblestones. They were fast and suddenly very close. The man charging Vincent was growling as well, the two sounding like bears challenging each other for territory.

I wondered what was happening, but before I could react, several inches of steel burst from Vincent's back. The point of a sword glowed red, as if just pulled from a fire, and slid away from me and back out the front of his body. Vincent gave a grunt as I gasped and hopped back without thinking. I transformed almost instantly into my monstrous form and screamed.

Vincent staggered. I stepped forward, grabbed Vincent's arm, and threw him through the secret door, back into the tunnels.

That voice again called out in its strange language. I turned, expecting another sword strike, and I was right. All I could see was the blade of the sword as three slashes in rapid succession had me stumbling backward. Strangely the blade was no longer red hot. My right arm felt the door, and I slammed it shut as I pushed off it and rolled to my right. I bounced up just in time to see the point of the sword strike where my head had been.

"God damned ghouls," the voice said in French. "I should have hunted and destroyed you all years ago."

Startled, I looked up. I knew that voice.

"Gior...?" I started to ask, but finished with a scream as his sword slashed across my body from right shoulder to left breast. The tip of the sword where it cut my flesh glowed red hot once again but quickly cooled after.

That is Death Taker, my mistress said to me. Awe laced her words.

It has not been seen in three hundred years. Do not let it touch you again, girl. It is a ghoul's doom.

Giorgio wasted no time recovering from his attack and reversed the strike masterfully into a lunge. I hopped to the side, but his sword was a viper chasing me with a multitude of quick attacks that relentlessly followed my every movement.

"Giorgio, it's me, Charlotte," I tried to say, but it was hard to push air from my lungs. The only noises I ended up making sounded more like hisses.

The sword continues to cut you. Your lungs are pierced, my mistress said to me. *It is beautiful in its purpose. You must kill him and destroy it.*

Beautiful? I thought. What my mistress thinks is beautiful I may never understand. Then I told her, *I will transform back into my normal self and make him see.*

Immediately I sensed that that would be the worst thing to do.

If you do, my mistress said, *you will perish. Even with my gifts, your normal body does not have the strength to fight the sword's magic. You will become so weak as to be unable to transform back. Even transformed you do not have enough strength to survive long, but you have more. If you do not feed soon, you will end.*

I leapt backward from another barrage of attacks. All the while Giorgio cursed in fluent French. In the briefest of seconds I had between attacks, I scanned the area trying to find someplace out of the sword's range.

Flee, my mistress demanded.

I am trying, I mentally shouted back.

Despite Giorgio's apparent age and thick-framed body, he moved like a dancer in a ballet. The sword was more a part of him than his own hand.

Who was this man?

I sprinted away from Giorgio, jumped over the piles of accumulated junk, and climbed a side wall, hoping to reach the roof. I was almost two stories up when I hit something solid, something I could not see at first, but there was a blue flash when I hit it, and another when I crashed to the ground among the rubbish.

"Ah ha ha, little ghoul. You will not be fleeing Giragos Shamshian today. I knew a few of you still remained," he said as he advanced, slashing the sword in front of him. "I know of six, maybe seven including you. I will destroy you all and finally leave this shit-stinking city."

I retreated along the wall of debris, but each foot I retreated toward the bricked-up alcove behind me was another foot into what I expected was a trap. Giorgio feinted toward me, and I retreated several more feet. When I realized that I had given up even more distance, I cursed myself. He was pressing me into the alcove.

"The little ghoul has restraint," he said, jabbing at the air between us. "It is impressive." Jab. "But you are a ghoul." Jab. Jab. "So you must die." Jab. "Again." Lunge.

I pivoted to the outside of his lunge. The blade only bit the air between my pilfered dress and my flesh, but it came so close to me that the blade began to glow hot once again. The dress caught flame. I panicked and punched Giorgio across the jaw. His head snapped to the side, and he staggered backward half a step. He pulled the sword upward in front of his body. The gesture, I think, was purely defensive. It seemed he did not expect me to do that. I took the moment to rip the dress off me.

With the sword held vertical and close to his body, Giorgio rubbed his jaw with his free hand.

"You are quick, even for a ghoul, and unpredictable," he said. I could not tell if his tone was admiration or disdain. "It really is a shame to destroy you, but the police are chasing a girl wearing a dress like that. Maybe you are the one who killed my friend's daughter."

"What?" I tried to ask, staggered by the statement. Why he did not strike at me in that moment, I did not understand. He likely would have ended me. He was panting ever so slightly, so maybe he was stalling. I stole a quick glance around the alcove and caught sight of what was the hint of a blue tinge to the air. It was only about a story up. I spun and looked behind me. There was more blue here and there, like a web, and the further into the alcove I retreated, the closer that web was to the ground.

"You see my web? Very impressive. Yes, little ghoul, you are trapped," he said.

Then Giorgio tensed. His face became a mask of resolve as his stance shifted. One hand held the sword low toward me. The other was held up behind him, a counterbalance to the sword.

Two quick shuffles with his feet, and Giorgio was within range of striking me. I had almost lost all hope of escape, when I realized how to get out. I had one chance, and if I failed... well, it did not matter what happened if I failed, not for long. I would be ended.

Giorgio shifted his weight onto his right hip by the smallest degree. I saw him do this earlier, so I knew this would be a midbody slash, maybe followed by a couple quick jabs to push me back.

I feigned left as Giorgio pulled his arm back to begin the strike, then I feigned right. Giorgio adjusted and readjusted his swing with such speed and finesse that would be impossible for most people to appreciate. In truth I was going neither direction. Even as I feinted left and right, I bowed my legs. Giorgio struck, his arm bringing the slash right where my belly button would have been, except with my legs bent as they were, the strike was aligned with my shoulders and neck. I had no time for panic or even to think. Instead I jumped. Toward him and over him.

The hot air of the sword passed within a hairsbreadth of my toes as I pushed my hands against his shoulders to aid in my launch over him. My feet came to his shoulders next. As soon as my feet had purchase on his shoulders, I pushed off. He was still in mid-swing, and so I did not register how he shifted. Just as my feet left his shoulders, I felt his free hand around my right ankle.

Giorgio's grip was that of an iron statue, heavy and unrelenting around my ankle. My momentum was such that it jerked the rock-steady Giorgio from his feet. My jump was halted just as my fall started. That was to say, immediately.

Giorgio crashed to the ground.

I crashed to the ground.

Less than a breath later, Death Taker, apparently thrown from Giorgio's grasp, slammed point first between the cobblestones directly in front of my face. The glowing red blade buried itself several inches into the stone. I pulled my head away and the blade immediately cooled, yet I was still close enough to see my own monstrous eyes reflected in the blade.

Cursed sword, my mistress screamed. *Destroy it!*

I did not know what she thought I might try, nor did I attempt to puzzle it out. Touching the thing seemed like a horrible idea all around. So instead I kicked Giorgio's fist with my free foot, claws and all. Giorgio struggled to maintain his hold or to stand, I was unsure. On the third kick, the claws on my free foot sank into flesh, and Giorgio yelped.

I was free.

"Damn it," Giorgio exclaimed, but I did not turn to look.

I pulled my feet up under my prone form, pushed up with my arms, and launched myself toward the secret door. The moment the door cracked open, I forgave Vincent of all his trespasses against me.

The alley was a blur for a brief few seconds as I raced forward, and then it came back in focus as I slid to a stop before the door. I reached an arm into the gap between the door and the wall to push it open further, but the door slammed shut. Hard. The bones in my forearm snapped. I tried to yelp in pain but made no noise due to the slash from Death Taker across my chest.

I turned to look back at Giorgio. His left hand was extended upward toward me. His first two fingers were bent down toward the palm leaving his ring and pinky extended upward, the thumb out. In the same hand, he held a rosary. I noticed distinctly that the stones were a soft white marble with blue veins. Blue veins that glowed with a faint blue luminescence. Giorgio's free hand tugged at the sword stuck point first in the cobblestones.

Who was this man?!

Before I could collect myself, the sword was free, and Giorgio advanced. His left hand with the rosary was still held in front of him.

Pressure remained on the door. I heaved. The door shifted slightly, just enough for me to reposition my trapped, broken arm. I slid more of my body through the gap and looked back at Giorgio. He was walking a little more slowly, as if he were walking against a stiff wind. He held Death Taker back and away with his right hand. Sweat dripped off his face. With what looked like a pure force of will, he thrust his left hand toward me again, and the door slammed even harder.

I struggled.

I heaved.

I thrashed.

The door refused to move.

Beads of blood replaced the sweat on Giorgio's forehead. His pace was almost a crawl, but he advanced. As he closed in on me, Death Taker began to glow with a deep violent heat. Not just the tip, or the edge, but the entire blade.

I would have collapsed then, but I was held upright by the door.

So this is the end of me, I thought. At least I did not display any weakness in the face of oblivion. How many times now had I faced my own doom? Perhaps it was becoming rote.

Now! my mistress commanded, and suddenly the door opened just enough that I fell through into the tunnel beyond.

"Feet," Vincent growled.

My feet were still between the door and the wall, so I pulled them in. As soon as they were clear, Vincent released the door, which crashed into place. He reached in the single brick-sized hole and twisted something before scuttling backward several paces. I crawled on my knees and one good arm further back into the tunnel and collapsed on my back near him.

We both rested for several seconds before Vincent helped me stand. I was still stunned and reacted slowly.

"Why did you bring me here?" I asked, or tried to ask. Somehow he understood.

Vincent shrugged and looked slightly abashed, if that was possible.

He thought the priest would help you since you seemed to be friends. I told him not to, but somehow he did not listen. I will punish him in time.

No, please do not, I said.

She did not respond.

My mind reeled with questions about what just happened. Giorgio was a priest? He wielded a sword, a magic sword, as deftly and expertly as any I had ever seen. Who was that man? I sighed.

Clarity returned to me when I noticed the hole through Vincent. The spot where he was stabbed by the sword was now large enough for me to see through, about as wide as my little finger.

I checked the wound on my own body. It looked like a simple slash across my chest from the right shoulder to below my breast on the left. But when I gingerly touched the wound, the skin peeled back. The wound was through the skin, muscles, and even the bones. Every time I tried to inhale, a thin wheezing sounded from my chest. When I tried to speak, the air escaped half a dozen spots, none of which were my throat.

You have to feed soon. Both of you, my mistress said once again. *The wounds will worsen until you do.*

Vincent grunted in agreement.

I noticed I was mouthing the words "You must feed soon."

I clamped my mouth shut and willed my tongue to remain still. I would have control over my own body if I could control nothing else in this world. So I drew myself up to my full height.

I will feed, I said to my mistress in my thoughts. *But not because you force me, Mistress. I will feed because I must heal. I have no intention on surrendering myself to Hell or oblivion or whatever lay across the veil for me. Or even to you, Mistress. I am my own. I thank you for your gifts, but if they are indeed gifts, then they are mine. Mine to do as I say, not you. For if they are mine, they are mine alone. Otherwise they were never gifts to begin with, but a curse.*

You recalcitrant child, my mistress said, her voice low with anger. *You stretch the boundaries of our relationship.*

I refused to respond. Her words were harsh, but I was not certain if what I felt from her was anger or admiration.

If I must feed, I would feed on the guilty. Henri left me with Small Eyes. He left me to be raped and murdered. I would feed on him because he was weak. He was too weak to save a young woman from horror, and too weak to take part in the horror himself. If someone had to die, he was the one person I knew deserved the fate more than anyone else in the world, other than myself.

29

SIN...

September 18, 1814 AD

Time passed in unmeasured heaps. Part of me longed for this timeless darkness underground, but I needed the sun of man to retain a shred of my humanity. Life underground would be a comfortable but ultimately empty existence.

My chest hurt. The wound continued to deepen. I felt it advance. Every few steps, I felt the sword slash across my chest in the exact same spot again. Each slash was exactly the same but a hairsbreadth deeper.

Time passed as did the miles of tunnels under our feet. When we stopped, Vincent doubled over. With one hand he clutched his stomach while the other was bent around his body to try to rub his back, both hands reaching for his own sword wound.

I stumbled forward and pulled the hand away from his back. The hole was almost large enough for me to put two fingers through side by side.

Do not worry about him. You need to feed, my mistress told me yet again.

Yes, I know, 'or I will perish.' What about him? I asked.

He must feed as well, but unlike you, he cannot gain nourishment from the living.

How...? I started to ask, but my mistress interrupted my question.

He does not possess the same gifts as you. Vincent is cursed.

I barked a laugh by reflex, but no sound escaped my throat.

One can be more cursed than becoming a ghoul? I asked, amused. *What happened to him?*

My mistress was not pleased with me, and she took her time replying. When she did reply, her voice in my head was tight and tinged with red. I shook from the alien emotion.

You should not dismiss my gifts so casually, she said.

It was my turn to be quiet for a bit.

Vincent unbent slowly like a massive wooden machine pulled upright by cables, strong men, and will. He turned around slightly and looked at me with one eye before turning back. A few steps brought him to a small door with a massive beam for a bar. Vincent lifted the beam with such ease, I imagined it must be hollow or perhaps cork, but its mass became apparent when it made a great *thunk* sound and stirred up a cloud of dust as one end struck the floor.

"Rue de Venise," he said.

So close? I asked with my thoughts. Rue de Venise was a short, narrow dead-end street in the sixth arrondissement only seven or eight blocks from the tenement.

Vincent simply nodded. Pain and stoicism painted his face like a child's clumsy dirt painting made with thumbs and mud. I gave the lumbering corpse a quick hug before sliding by him, opening the door, and sliding out. It was a stupid gesture, but it felt right. The door sealed shut behind me, and I heard the prodigious sound of the bar as it dropped back into place on the other side of the door.

I needed not worry about being seen. The door was nestled in a shallow alcove, which saw the sun less than a handful of hours each day. I wagered only cats and I could see anything with the depth of night and overcast skies.

I slipped out of the alcove, crossed the few feet to the wall across from me, and used my claws to climb it as quickly as possible. I was only halfway to the roof when I heard a horse whinny and stomp once. It must have been standing where the street opened into the only marginally larger Rue Quincampoix.

I moved again, as slowly as possible, to a small ridge in the wall. It was perhaps a chimney, or maybe just some sort of architectural element added by a designer averse to perfectly flat walls.

“Hey there, my sweet,” an older male voice said. “What are you doing there?”

I froze and pressed myself against the wall as flat as possible. There was another noise, like something heavy being set into place, and then a scraping noise.

The horse’s bridle jingled.

“Getting anxious?” he asked.

The horse made a blow and low grunt, and the bridle jingled again.

“It is a little unlike you to act like this,” the man said. “But I know how you feel. I never like this part of the city either. Only a few more stops and we get to go back to the mill.”

There was the creak of wood and metal.

“All right, my sweet, let’s get these last deliveries made before the sun comes up,” the man said.

There was a jangle and then clomps as hooves beat upon cobblestones. Then came more creaking of wood and metal. I scrambled up the side of the building, taking no further precautions.

Once on the roof, I was awash with the faintest moonlight through clouds. If anyone happened to be watching the exact spot I pulled myself to the roof, most would be unable to see anything more than a shadow. A trained eye might see me a bit more clearly, so I ducked into the shadow of what was a chimney after all. There I scanned the rooftops of Paris, looking south and east for the tenement I called home. I found it and could clearly see the rooftop and the dormer windows of the attic. There was a light in the Clubhouse, obvious to my eyesight even with the windows boarded up on this side. Someone from Theo’s gang was there.

I stood straighter and ran across the rooftops. The next building was two stories taller and butted up against the first. There was a small shed next to a pigeon loft attached to the second building. The roof of the shed looked sturdy, so I jumped on top of it and climbed the wall. For the next couple blocks, the buildings were all a uniform height with only a handful of feet difference in each, so it was simple to jump easily across the gaps between buildings. I always jumped before I reached any eaves and aimed my landings well beyond them.

A single street separated me and the tenement. The easiest and most concealed location to jump was the same location as my fall. I stopped well before the edge of the building and examined the eave. At the edge was a significant portion of the roof, maybe two feet wide and almost as deep, that caved inward. The smallest pressure would send the section crashing to the street below.

Across the street, I could see where I hit the building, almost a story below the roof line. Several stones were missing from the decorative frieze. The jump was a powerful lesson I would never forget. I shivered involuntarily, not due to the light, cold wind that drifted lazily over the city, but some new hidden fear. The only thing I knew to do was to tense all of my muscles and then relax. I performed this exercise three times before taking a moment to shake the anxiety from my arms and legs. It was time.

I charged the street, and just as I jumped, I heard a nicker and the stomping of hooves. I peered down to see a horse and small cart trundling down the street. A man sat in the cart, holding the reins and looking up at me. His head turned as his eyes tracked me, tracked me as I sailed across the street.

We will have to kill him, my monstrous self said. It sounded wise.

No, my rational self said. *I am only killing one person tonight. If I can help it.*

He saw me.

No, I told myself. *He saw a shadow, nothing more than that.*

I landed on the opposite roof several feet from the edge of the building and rolled with the impact. Before I knew what was happening, I turned back toward the street and had taken two steps before I realized my monstrous self was moving to kill the driver. I slammed my will against my monstrous intentions and forced my body to stop.

I stood like a statue.

We must kill him, my monstrous self repeated several times.

No, I told myself. *I am in control here. You do what I say. I will kill only who I choose to kill, only those that I must kill, and no one else.*

My monstrous self threw itself against my will like a rabid animal in a cage too small to contain it. Until I reestablished proper mental control, I forced myself to be completely rigid. Like a petulant, spoiled child my monstrous self flailed and cried before slowly calming. Once I was sure it was finished, I relaxed, proud of myself for winning this battle.

I turned and ran along the rooftop past the Clubhouse and to the adjoining building on Rue de la Verrerie. There I jumped the narrow Rue Bar-du-Bec and landed on the slope of the adjoining building that faced away from the Clubhouse. I peeked over the ridge of the roof. A wan light emitted from the open Clubhouse window, and shadows stirred within.

I edged along the roofline where I once showered in a thunderstorm and began a merry chase with Theo and his gang. I remembered how easily it had been for one of them to see me, or my shadow, so I kept my pace slow and deliberate as I slinked nearer.

"None of this makes sense," a voice said. I was pretty sure it was Theo, but his voice sounded strained.

"I... I know, but I am telling you the truth," said another, Henri.

"Tell me one more time," Theo said. I knew it was him when he moved in front of the window.

"Why? I told you three times already," Henri said. "Besides, why are you so interested?"

"I am interested because it seems like Charlotte is out there somewhere. Whatever killed the Bastard may have taken her... or worse," Theo said. His voice was pained. "Sometimes when someone repeats a story, they leave things out that they might remember the next time."

Or they forget what they left out the previous telling, I thought.

Or exactly how they lied before, my mistress said.

"Theo, I tell you. It was exactly as I said. We were heading to Bourse ," Henri said.

"You and the Bastard," Theo said.

"Yes.

"Why were you going there again?" Theo asked.

"The Bastard had to pick something up from a mademoiselle in one of the tenements off Rue du Croissant."

"Who was this?" Theo asked.

"I don't know," Henri said. "But the Bastard kept complaining about her cats. He hates... hated cats."

"Did he say anything about her other than she lived with cats?" Theo asked.

"Only that whatever she had, his boss needed," Henri said.

"Did he give any clue as to what that was?"

"No..."

"Anything at all? Any hunches?" Theo asked.

"Well..." Henri started. I half expected Theo to interrupt again, but he did not. "I cannot say why, but I think whatever it was, it had to deal with Charlotte."

I gasped. I might have given myself away had it not been for the slash through my lungs.

Theo stopped pacing, and neither spoke for several seconds.

"What makes you think that?" Theo finally asked.

"Well..." Henri said, "we were talking about all this when the Bastard stopped in the middle of the street and said, 'Speak of the devil and the bitch appears.' I'd forgotten that last little bit. That was when I looked where he was looking, and there was Charlotte ducking into an alley."

"So you went to her right away then?" Theo asked.

"No. She was several blocks in the wrong direction from Rue du Croissant. It was lucky that the Bastard even saw her the first time, she was so far away, but traffic had opened up enough to give us a glimpse of her."

"And then what?" Theo asked.

"The Bastard told me to get a little closer and follow her if she came out of the alley. He said he would return as fast as he could, but he needed to go see that cat-woman first."

"He left you there?" Theo asked.

"Yes."

"How long did it take for him to return?"

"Five minutes, maybe ten. When he got back, he was panting hard. Then he says to me, 'Did she leave?' and I told him no."

"Then what happened?" Theo asked.

Henri was quiet for a couple breaths before replying. "The Bastard gets really excited. He paced back and forth while staring at the alley. He asked me if I was sure she was still in there, and I said yes. We both knew that the alley was a dead end. After the murders and robberies that happened there several years ago, people just stopped using it and boarded up all the windows and doors out into it."

"Go on," Theo said. "What happened next. Do not hold anything back or exclude anything. I need to know everything."

"Yes, yes," Henri said. "I know." Then he sighed. "The Bastard grabbed his crotch and looked at me with a gleam in his eyes like he just decided to be bad. 'Let us go to her and turn her into a woman,' he said to me."

"And what did you do?" Theo asked.

"God help me, it sounded like a good idea," Henri said.

It was a full minute before anyone said anything else. No one moved. When Theo next spoke, his voice was strained again.

"You resolved to corner my mouse like two feral cats, and 'turn her into a woman'?" Theo asked.

"Y... Yes," Henri said. His voice was small.

"That means you resolved to rape her," Theo said.

Henri's voice became hopeful. "Well not if she agreed."

"Did she?" Theo asked. His voice was as deep and dark as the bottom of a well.

When Henri did not answer, Theo asked again. "Did she?" And again. "Did she?" And then he screamed once more, "DID SHE?"

Henri was weeping. "No."

"I should fucking kill you where you stand, but your father would never forgive me," Theo said. "You will need to stand for your crimes, and I hope they chop your fucking head off."

"But..." Henri started.

"You helped him," Theo yelled, his voice a storm. "You are every bit as guilty as he is. Every bit. Your only moral recourse once you knew his plan was to oppose him. And you failed. You failed yourself. You failed Charlotte. You failed me, and you failed God Almighty. Now you will have to pay for your crimes."

My Theo.

Henri blubbered, "Where... where are you going?"

"I'm going to look for her. And in the morning I'm going to find you and drag you to the police unless you go turn yourself in first. I suggest you go and kiss your mother and father goodbye. You will likely never see them again, unless you happen to catch their eyes as the executioner pulls the rope on the guillotine."

Theo exited the room through the window while Henri continued to sob out of sight. I moved when I saw Theo on the street below turn the corner and pass out of sight. I kept to every shadow and double-checked my footing with every step. I wanted to charge into the room, crash through the window, and rip Henri to shreds. But I did not want to be seen. I did not want to be heard. So I had to move as stealthily as possible. I had to be silence. I had to be shadow.

I made it to the window and pressed my back against the wall to peek into the room. Henri wiped tears from his face with the back of one hand and held a mug in the other. He dipped the mug into something and brought it back to his lips. I could smell the beer from here. I adjusted my stance to get a better look. I knew the cask. It was one Monsieur Bordelon ordered at great cost but the interested buyer never showed. Monsieur Bordelon feared being unable to sell the cask. The loss of funds would hurt the year's profits substantially.

The top of the cask was crushed inward. It was in that hole Henri dipped his mug.

I tried to imagine how Henri managed to bash open the cask.

There had to be an ax or some other device lying around somewhere. Then the piece of wood I was perched on gave way. I slipped ever so slightly and threw myself against the roof to keep from exposing myself.

"Eh? Theo?" Henri said. "Is that you?"

I pulled myself up and on top of the dormer window. My arms burned from the effort, not due to my weight but to the slow constant effort it took to pull myself up without making a sound. I broke into a sweat as I kept every muscle taut and not drag any portion of my body against the wall or dormer. When Henri leaned out the window and looked left and right, I was perched atop the dormer by only my hands.

"Theo?" he asked the air again. "Edouard?"

A cat screeched nearby, and there was a crashing sound in the distance. Henri looked in that direction, shook his head, and pulled himself back inside.

"Fucking cats," he said. "Someone should round them all up and drown them in the Seine."

Had I been wavering on whether or not I was going to kill him before, my mind would now be resolved. I gave the man a minute to settle himself and then peeked over the edge of the dormer to peer in again.

Henri sat on the bed, sniveling and drinking his ill-gotten beer. Minutes passed as he drank alone. When he got up to get a refill, he shuffled to the far corner of the room to relieve himself. With one hand he held his beer and with the other he attempted to undo the fly of his pants. I held tightly to the overhang of the dormer and lowered myself inch by inch to the window. When my feet touched the sill, I grasped it with my foot-claws and let go of the overhang. I folded myself into a tight ball in the open window and unfolded into the room. I took six quick steps toward Henri. He seemed to notice my second step, but he did not bother to turn and look as he concentrated on urinating in a bucket.

"Back to beat me up, Theo?" Henri asked the corner.

I pressed myself against his back and reached around to grasp his manhood. Immediately Henri froze as I paralyzed him. I held his manhood as his bladder finished emptying. I tucked him back into his pants, and as I did, droplets of urine got on my fingers, which I wiped on his shirt. Gently, I laid him down on the floor. His eyes were wide as tears streamed unabated.

I wanted to talk to him as I began to slice his clothes from his body, but I could not. Not yet.

With my claws, I sliced the skin from his chest and stomach in one large sheet. I had to slice underneath to disconnect the thick skin from the tissues below, and the experience left me bloody. Always so bloody. I showed Henri his flesh as I sat on his chest and consumed the beginning of my meal in three great bites. Blood, his blood, dripped from my mouth onto his face. I touched the wound in my chest. New skin was stitched over the wound, but the tissues and bones beneath were still divided.

I tried to speak, and while I was able to push some air over my vocal cords, the sound was wet and inconsistent. Speaking sounded more like a series of phlegmy coughs than speech.

"You have been bad, Henri," I said. "What you and Small Eyes tried to take... got me... hurt. I... least you could do... is heal me. You... agree?"

I could see the confused flashes crisscross his brain, and then a flash of awareness, of realization, and the pupils of his eyes expanded.

"Yes... Charlotte," I said as I stood and put my hand to my chest and curtsied in a mocked formal introduction. Then I sat back down on his chest and looked him in the eyes. "I killed... ate... the one you... called Bastard. You heard?"

Henri let loose a fresh flow of tears.

"Yes... you know," I said. "Out of... love... for father," I said, tapping his forehead with one claw, "I... leave... your face."

Something inside of Henri released.

He is broken child. His spirit is fleeing, my mistress said to me. *Feed quickly.*

And so I did. I opened Henri's chest and consumed the contents.

When I was finished, dawn was nearing, and I was covered with gore. I might have time to reach the Seine to wash, but the water was filled with sewage. I would emerge as filthy as I entered, if only with a different kind of filth. Instead, I would retreat back to the catacombs to find another source of water there. With luck I could find a fountain or spring to wash in.

I slipped out of the dormer window, whole once again, and crawled along edge of the roof. I stopped about halfway, and peeked over the edge into Madame Legrand's room. She was a widow prone to bouts of intermittent crying followed by longer periods of melancholy. Madame Legrand snored from somewhere inside. Across the room I saw a pile of laundry including a couple blouses and skirts. I was getting a little too familiar with thievery, the real kind, not Giorgio's Thief of Secrets nonsense. As quickly and quietly as I could, I slipped in and moved to the basket, where I grabbed the first skirt and blouse I saw.

I turned back toward the window, and there was Madame Legrand standing between me and the window. My first thought was how impressed I was with how silently and quickly she moved. This was quickly followed by how very disappointed I was with my own sense of awareness.

"Just who the..." she started to say, and then as saw me for what I actually was she began to scream.

I was swinging for her face, claws out, before I realized what I was doing. She did not deserve to die because I was a poor thief, but I could not stop the swing. The best I could manage was to make a fist. I struck her rather than slice her open with my claws. Her head snapped to the side, and she spun before landing in a heap on the floor. Silence followed, and I was thankful. Someone would come to investigate, however, so taking my filthy gains, I crawled out of the window onto the ledge and retreated the way I had come, rooftop to rooftop.

Once I was a few buildings and pair of streets away, I looked back toward the tenement. Lights were on in most of the upper landing rooms. Someone was leaned out of Madame Legrand's window and stared at the blood around the room. Someone would eventually realize the trail of blood came from the roof. Once they followed it, Henri would be found.

I found a quiet spot out of sight and wept. I am so sorry, Monsieur Bordelon. Your son was not horrible so much as weak, yet he deserved his fate. God help me if he did not.

30

... AND PENANCE

September 18, 1814 AD

I searched for an hour or more for an open passage into the catacombs, but could find none. Despite the late hour, I distrusted washing in any of the public fountains where I would be exposed. And the public baths were not even a consideration. I would be spotted in a heartbeat. So I broke down and decided to wash in the Seine . The very idea was loathsome. The river was filthy, and if I had any other concealed location in which to wash, I would. I had to wash the blood off of me. There were ways down to the river that were obscured by ruined buildings and steep embankments. I would not smell like a pampered aristocrat, but I would smell like a Parisian all the same. When I finished, I dressed in my stolen clothes and returned to the rooftops.

The sun threatened the horizon when I reached Giorgio's shop. From the roof, I could see that there were lights on somewhere within. And now that I knew where to look, I could see a section of wall newer than the rest, though cleverly disguised with layers of paint and posted bills several layers deep, all of which were the same half dozen advertisements. No light came from the space beyond the wall.

I found a navigable path to the ground using balconies, pipes, a railing, and some stacked boxes. Once on the ground, I brushed myself off and settled my full but anxious stomach as I transformed back to my human self. What was likely to come next would be either a bad end or a questionable beginning. So feeling as well as I could, I darted across the street and rapped on Giorgio's shop door.

The shop was silent as a grave as nothing stirred within, so I rapped on the door again. I considered climbing the wall into the space to the side and behind the shop, but then I remembered the glowing web of blue light. I was not going to put myself in that trap again. Yet here I was knocking on the front door of a man who only hours before tried to kill me. And try very expertly, I might add.

After my fourth series of raps on the door, the light escaping from within wavered. A shadow temporarily blocked the light filtering out between the sides of the window and the shade, and then there were the sounds of footfalls just on the other side. The door rattled slightly and opened a crack.

"Um, bonjour," I said.

The door flew open, and suddenly I was engulfed in flesh and muscle. It took me a moment before I realized that I was being hugged as completely as I believed I ever had been. Then with gentle movements, like one might take with a priceless china doll, the arms around me unfolded, and I was placed back on the floor. I was now in the shop proper rather than at the threshold.

Giorgio beamed as he looked at me. He made the sign of the cross and then kissed the hand making it when finished. I swear I saw tears in his eyes. He seemed choked up and strangely at a loss for words.

"That was... quite the greeting," I said.

Giorgio suddenly frowned and pushed me behind him as he placed his body between me and the door. He glared around at the empty streets before closing and locking it.

"Charlotte," Giorgio said. "Bad times come. Very dangerous. Must not wander street alone, especially at night."

He placed a hand at the small of my back and gestured to the back room. Before I could speak, he continued.

"Giorgio must tell something. Is very... unbelievable."

"Oh?" I said. "I think you might find my ability to believe things somewhat expanded of late."

He chuckled. "Giorgio think Charlotte not understanding."

"I guess we shall see," I said, slightly amused.

He pushed aside the curtain separating the back room from the shop. In a small corner were several votive candles burning on a low table with a small rug in front. I was certain I did not see the candles, or for that matter the rug or table, the day before.

"Please. Sit," he said as he moved over to the candles and blew them out. "Is much to tell."

As I sat, I looked to Giorgio and smiled. "I have reconsidered your offer, Giorgio. I think... I would like you to train me. No, I am sure of it."

He stood gazing at the ceiling for a moment before responding. "Giorgio thinking, maybe bad time training Charlotte. Also maybe best time. Still unsure." Then he shrugged and placed a kettle on the stove to boil. From the cabinet he produced several eggs and a loaf of bread. He cracked the eggs into a small pan and started slicing the bread.

"Charlotte eating eggs how?" he asked.

Without thinking, I said, "Fried with a runny yolk."

Giorgio smiled. "Girl after own heart."

"But umm... I am not hungry," I said. I always loved eggs and lost myself in the luxurious idea of having them again. Giorgio looked like I had slapped him.

"Nonsense," he said. "Is first of morning. Sun not even up. Girl must be hungry. Time break fast. Is God's will."

"Well, I ate before I came over," I said sheepishly yet truthfully. I had in fact gorged myself, but I was trying not to think about it at that moment.

"Girl never eat Giorgio's food. Insulting in homeland. Very insulting," he said. Then he nodded and cracked open two more eggs into the pan. He was slicing more bread when I protested.

"But I am not hungry," I said. "That food is just going to go to waste."

"Is not," he said. "Charlotte not insulting girl, so Charlotte eat. End of story."

"It is not the end of the story," I said.

"No. Is end," Giorgio said as he waved the bread knife in my direction. Then I remembered the sword, Death Taker, and how masterfully Giorgio wielded it. I swallowed and nodded.

"Fine. Maybe… just a little," I said.

Giorgio smiled again, and there was that handsome man I met on the street in front of the shop the day before. He turned back around and produced his coffee contraption from one of the cabinets. There he poured hot water into the device, added some metal bits that were separate, and then poured coffee grounds into a metal basket. Soon the bitter aroma of coffee joined the chorus of smells in the kitchen. It was like I was almost home again in better days just a handful of years ago.

"Um… Giorgio," I said.

"Yes, girl?" he said without turning his back.

"When you are done, before we eat, there is… there is something I need to tell you. I do not think you will like it."

With that he turned his head to me slightly, just enough to see the sincerity in my eyes, before nodding and turning back to his task.

"Girl's leg better now?" Giorgio asked after a moment.

I was lost in thought, but something in the back of my mind told me he said something. After a few seconds I recalled it.

"Oh, yes. Much better now, thank you. I just needed to spend the evening off my feet."

He nodded once without turning around, and then we were quiet while he worked. Within a few minutes the coffee was ready and he poured me a cup, dark and bitter, like a good lover. He set the cup on the table in front of me, and as he was straightening, he looked me in the eyes, saw something there and paused, then resumed standing straight so as to almost make the pause imperceptible.

I sipped the coffee while he began plating toasted bread and laying the eggs on the toast. He took a pinch of salt and another of pepper from a small pair of jars and sprinkled each on the eggs in turn.

As he handed me my plate, Giorgio smiled and said, "Shit on Shingle."

"What?" I asked, laughing as I took the plate.

"Is what egg on toast is called in homeland, Shit on Shingle," he said.

"Thank you?" I said with a question in my tone. We both laughed.

Before he sat, Giorgio stood for a second as I set my plate on the table in front of the couch. Then he said, "Giorgio know Charlotte wish to speak before eat, but think is better to eat first. While Charlotte eat, Giorgio have story that Charlotte maybe find interesting."

"All right," I said, willing to put off the task of telling Giorgio my darkest secrets. Tasting the kiss of Death Taker a second time in one night was enough to give me pause. No, ever. I did not ever wish to see the vile weapon again, yet when I told Giorgio my secret, I suspected that I would be reintroduced to both the sword and the mysterious man that wielded it.

Giorgio gave me a thin smile and sat in his overly padded chair. Sitting straight-backed in the chair, Giorgio lifted the egg and toast daintily, with his little finger extended as if he were sipping tea in court. He brought his shingle to his face and took a long manly inhalation, absorbing the spirit of food. I could see the depth of his pleasure wash across his face in a small, simple smile that stretched from his mouth to his temples. He took an almost dainty bite, and another wave of pleasure crossed his face as he took his time to relish the simple fare. Once he consumed his first taste, however, the barbarian emerged as he took a single bite that consumed half of the egg and toast that remained.

I could not help but giggle, and I never giggle. Who was this man who was part connoisseur and part barbarian, part spy and part merchant, part warrior and part priest?

Giorgio's jaws worked like a giant machine chewing huge plots of land grinding them down into so much soil and sand. The great machine of his mouth paused to allow a look of pure bliss on his face before he swallowed it all in one giant gulp. He exhaled, eyes closed as he savored the afterglow of his almost sexual experience.

Giorgio opened one eye and peered at me for a second before his face fell.

"What?" he asked.

"What do you mean?" I asked back.

"Charlotte smiling like child."

"I am? I had not realized."

"So, why smiling?"

"I do not know. I guess if I had to pick a reason, I would say that I enjoy watching people do what they love," I said. "And you obviously love to eat."

Then Giorgio did something very unexpected. He blushed. To recover, he smiled and waved his hand in front of his face. Within seconds he was the Giorgio I knew once again and polished off his meal with a few more luxurious bites.

"So, when Charlotte begin meal," he said, casting a telling eye toward my untouched 'shingle,' "Giorgio start story."

I eyed the egg and toast like a child might look at a spoonful of medicine. This was not going to go down easily, and I feared it might not stay down. But it had to be done, so I picked up the small plate with one hand and the toast with the other. I held the plate close under my chin to ensure that if I spit out the food, I would not make a mess. Tentatively I raised the toast to my mouth and took a long and languid time to open my mouth, slide the toast in, and take my first bite.

It was delicious. Just as I remembered as a child. My eyes went wide as I chewed and swallowed. I looked at Giorgio as I gave a little sneeze. His face was alight at my delight, but at the same time his eyes held a sort of sadness too.

"Is good?" he asked somewhat rhetorically, and all I could do was nod enthusiastically as I took bite after bite and chewed and chewed, savoring the flavor of every piece.

Giorgio put on his somber teacher's face and began to tell me his tale.

"Is story about greed and want. In France, four hundred years ago, lived count and countess. From good family, long royal line. But grandfather make blunder in court. Lose favor with prince at time. King live in Tours. So count and countess flee to Paris where still having measure of influence. Count and countess both greedy and wanting many things, especially favor of king, but king very angry about insult given to prince and never forgive. So count and countess do very bad things. Send spies to court. Make rumors about prince thinking prince fall out of favor with king, king forgive count.

"Well," Giorgio continued, "King very skilled at court. Prince not so much. King know prince, think rumors untrue, send spies to Paris. Same time arrange kidnapping spy of count. Count and countess thinking spy maybe robbed and killed. Look for replacement. Make mistake and hire spy secretly working for king.

"As Giorgio say. King very skilled at court.

I had just finished Giorgio's "Shit on a Shingle" at this point, and I was licking the crumbs off my fingers. I would have to find out his secret. Would all eggs taste so good? Was it because I had just fed? My mistress was strangely quiet.

"King spy pretending work for count," he continued, looking proud that I enjoyed my meal so thoroughly. "Spy tell king everything. King outraged and send knights removing count and countess from world. Kidnapped spy escape, however, and arrive hours before knights. Count and countess start packing. Spy say no time, must go. Count and countess very angry. Very angry. Countess especially angry, tell spy kill self. Spy plead with count to spare life. Count ignore, because busy putting food in bags and crates, eating whole time. Countess laugh at spy. Spy beg countess, say spy family always work for family of count. Say spy only wanting serve count. Countess curses man. Curses man always serve. Says man will die day man stops serving loyally.

"All three want. Want. Want. Want. Count and countess want everything. Spy only want to keep count and countess safe. To serve.

When time for fleeing, servants tell count and countess knights at every gate. Count and countess trapped. Spy says knowing place where count and countess hide. Catacombs."

At this point, I was starting to get an uneasy feeling regarding this story, but I pushed my fear down. Giorgio probably was trying to warn me of the dangers of the catacombs, but I knew them well. In fact I was starting to see the catacombs as my eyelids became heavier and heavier. Dreams began to wash over me, and I struggled to remain awake.

"When the king's knights reached the Château d'Envie, all they found of the count and countess were many, many boxes stuffed with food, expensive clothes, golden plates and cutlery, bolts of silk, piles of money, and more. So much did the count and countess want for riches, that they could not leave anything behind until they were forced to. Then they ended up leaving everything."

I saw them now in ancient clothes. His suit was black, gray, and sharp. Her dress was a blood-red material that dropped scandalously in the front, exposing an excessive amount of cleavage. I did not recognize them at first, but the spy, the spy I would know anywhere. Vincent.

"The three descended into catacombs, never to be seen again. Well, not for a hundred years at least," he said, but that was the last I heard because everything had gone quiet and dark.

* * *

When I awoke, the first thing I noticed was that all was dark. Then I realized I was restrained as I attempted to move my arm to put my hand to my face. I was reclining slightly back in some sort of chair, and when I flexed I could tell that the chair was solid, likely reinforced with metal because it did not move at all, nor could I hear the creak and groan one would expect of a simple wooden chair. The restraints themselves were comfortable, such as they were. Leather bound each arm at the wrist and each leg at the ankles. It seemed my torso was also strapped around the waist. My head was cradled in some sort of device that was either attached to the chair or a part of it, and a leather hood covered my head. That was when I realized that other than the hood, I was completely nude.

Why am I always naked?

After one or two attempts against my restraints, I realized I was not going to escape. I could attempt to transform and use the additional strength and rending capability of my teeth and claws to escape, but if anyone saw me, I would then have to kill them. Whoever they were.

Giorgio! I thought in alarm. *They must have Giorgio too.*

I was confused. I was filled with alarm and concern, not for me but for Giorgio. Who were "they"? Who could have done this? Who would know to secure me so well? There were too many questions assailing me all at once. I shook my head, or rather imagined shaking my head, because it was strapped securely in place like every other extremity. I needed to try to remember as much as possible.

Why can I not remember anything? I wondered. But that was not right. I could remember some things. I remembered going to Giorgio's. Then him giving me a huge hug. Then I was sitting with him in his back room. I was going to tell him about being a ghoul. My mistress did not like the idea, but I had no one else to go to. No one I could trust, but I trusted Giorgio. And Giorgio proved that he could defend himself even if he did not know who he was showing off to.

And then I remembered... nothing.

"Hello," I called out. "Hello. Is someone there?"

No reply came.

"My friend Giorgio. Leave him alone. It is me you want. I am sure of that. He is just a tailor and shop owner," I said to what might have been an otherwise empty room.

I do not know how many times I repeated myself. My voice started to crack and my lips were going dry from the effort, but I continued. I hated not knowing what was happening. Slowly my worry started to turn into panic, and my panic congealed into anger.

I strained against my bonds more and more. I tried to get the chair to bend or crack as I strained against the restraints... but nothing budged. I began to yell. Perhaps whoever had me restrained was in another room and could not hear me. Perhaps if I were loud enough, someone would be able to hear me in an adjacent building if I was still in Paris proper.

I screamed. I screamed long and hard at the top of my lungs. I drew from reserves that existed somewhere within me that I hadn't before realized I had and screamed all the more. I could feel the vibrations of my screams bounce off the walls and strike me. I came to the realization that my screams were useless.

I began to lose hope.

What happened? I wondered.

I caught a fragment here and there, but my memory refused to cooperate. I saw Giorgio cooking. I saw him hand me coffee. Then he was hugging me. I remembered the toast and eggs vaguely. I knew what they were, but the memory was indistinct, like the memory of a memory. I saw him hand me the coffee again. Then I saw myself approach the door to the shop, my hand out, prepared to knock. Then I was taking a huge bite out of Henri's skin while he watched.

"No!" I said as I struggled in the chair. "I don't want to remember that."

I saw Giorgio hand me coffee. I saw the slight pause he had as he pulled away. Then I saw it again. And again. There was a look on his face, hidden but there. Just. What was that look? And then there was the taste of Henri's lungs in my mouth while my left hand was buried in his chest, holding his beating heart.

"No," I said to no one, and I said it over and over as the memories continued to bounce from moment to moment, forward and then backward.

I was sweating. My dead heart was racing in my chest. In the smallest part of my mind, there was something old that quivered and shook. It begged discovery and release, but rather than let it emerge, I could feel my thoughts closing around it, locking it off.

Suddenly I was in the alley the day before, scarfing down bundles of meat. Then I was atop Small Eyes, his viscera a gory second skin covering my body. His eyes still staring at me. Then I saw Giorgio had me a cup of coffee, then the look on his face that he hid. I tasted the eggs and toast, dancing on my tongue.

Then I was in the catacombs with Vincent, standing in front of Monsieur Anton and Madame. I was screaming, and then I was suddenly still. I was dangling over a bowl as my vision turned red, my life's blood spilled out of me, cascading down my body and into the bowl.

Then I saw Giorgio hand me a cup of coffee.

"God damn it," I yelled as I struggled to shake the images out of my head. "Let me out of here. God help me when I get out of here. I will make you pay for this."

Then I saw Giorgio delight as he took his first bite of eggs and toast. I saw his enjoyment at the simple moment and strangely felt his appreciation for something so simple and so fine. I saw myself take a bite of pure delight as well then sneezed.

"If you've hurt my friend, I... I..." I stammered. "Do with me what you will, but if you hurt Giorgio... I... I... I will make you beg for perdition. And I will do what I can to ensure when you get to Hell, I am there to teach you that you have fucked with the wrong people."

I dipped into those reserves that I had found previously and strained once again at my bindings. There was a loud snap, and for the briefest moment I was delighted, until realization and pain flooded me simultaneously. The snap was not from my restraints or the chair, but my own arm breaking just behind the binding over my right wrist.

I howled.

And then I saw Giorgio hand me a cup of coffee. I reached for it with my right hand. The arm was whole, and Giorgio paused as he pulled away, the slightest hint of realization dawning on his face. And then I was running across rooftops away from Theo and his gang. I jumped a street and landed out of sight. Then Theo's gang was across the street. Theo was talking to Small Eyes, trying to explain that he had seen the person they were chasing come this way. Small Eyes looked around, looked me directly in the eyes, though he was much too far away to see me with his feeble eyesight, but I could see his tiny gray eyes clearly.

My body snapped to rigidity. I could tell my arm was already mending, but the renewed stress snapped the bone again, and new pain burned my arm from wrist to shoulder. I barely noticed the pain, however, as I was stunned, stunned from age-old mental barriers being shattered from within.

That small black memory came to the surface. I tried to force it down. I tried desperately.

I was with my mother in the one-room apartment off of Rue Perdue. We had buried my brother less than a week before. I was crying in the corner while holding my brother's only real treasure, a locket with his image inside across from the image of the young woman he was intended to marry before father died. The locket was silver and the images were carved in ebony and ivory. Its value in coin was dwarfed by its value in memory. Mother did not realize I had it. She would have sold it and moved us to the country if she knew I still had it, but it was the only thing I, a girl of only thirteen then, had to remind me of better times.

Mother was making coffee. The grounds were thrice used already, but she always added a little fresh grounds to stretch the batch. When the coffee was ready, she handed me a cup, smiled, and kissed my head. I was warmed by the coffee and the gesture, but I spoiled it. I spoiled it because I was sad, and there was my mother acting like everything was fine. But it was not fine. Everything was horrible. Everything was horrible, and it was my fault.

Somewhere in the dark, strapped to a chair, I screamed at the top of my lungs. As terrible as my fate might be in the future, it could not be as horrible as that memory. Anything but that memory. I had to escape. Escape at any cost. And so I transformed.

My limbs were stronger when I was in my monstrous form, but they were also emaciated. Almost immediately my bindings adjusted to remove any slack, and I was just as tightly bound in the blink of an eye. I struggled against the bonds with my left arm, both legs, and anything I could use to put stress against the chair from my neck to my hips. I had to look as if I were convulsing. The chair was resolute. After less than a minute I ceased my struggles.

I was panting. I questioned why I would be panting when I did not need to breathe. I thought I was used to being undead, but it seemed there were still questions to be answered, mysteries to be revealed. Assuming I survived long enough to learn them.

This was usually the point when my mistress made an appearance, but she was uncharacteristically quiet. I took that as a bad omen.

Mistress, I said internally. *Mistress, what villains do I face? Can you help me escape?*

Nothing was her reply. No, that was not exactly correct. Nothing was her presence. She simply was not there. If a person had asked me how I would react when after waking I found my mistress was no longer there, I would have told her "with delight and joy." But now I was alone. Alone, trapped, and unable to fend for myself. It was the story of my life for the past nineteen months. I felt defeated. Worse, I felt truly empty. Not even my hunger existed to remind me of who I was.

I realized I was sobbing then. Failure streamed from my eyes as I wailed. I felt the leather mask dampen from my tears and stick to my face. I no longer had the strength to keep it all in. I promised myself nineteen months ago that I would never cry again. It was weakness. It was failure. And for nineteen months, I had been the master of my emotions. I was strong. I succeeded at living life on my own terms. Now that was all gone. Wasted. But I no longer cared. I emptied. I let it all go. Why not? I was alone, naked, and powerless. There was little more to lose.

As I cried, I saw myself outside of my father's shop. Monsieur Durand was holding me back while the police were examining my father's body, covered in blood, facedown in the street. I wanted nothing more than to go to him, to hold him one last time, to tell him how sorry I was for saying that I hated him, to cry and kiss his cheeks and tell him how much, how dearly I loved him. I wanted him to know that he was and would always be my hero... my prince... my...

My papa.

That would never happen, could never happen. Even if Heaven existed it could never happen, because surely as my papa was in Heaven, I was destined for Hell.

The memory evaporated, and I lay panting in desperate exhaustion. Exhaustion such that I had not felt since my death and transformation. I was drained mentally and physically. The monster in me begged for release. It begged me to let it run free so that we might escape. I was so very tempted. I did not know how much more I could take. There was more I did not wish to remember, I was certain, but I desperately did not want to remember those things, the words I said, the pain they caused, the love and forgiveness my mother heaped on me despite my sin. The truth was that she was not the monster I wanted to remember her as. I was the monster. I was a monster long before Vincent ever found me.

No more memories came then. I rested. I had time. Time to not think. Time to just be.

It was a blessing.

It did not last.

There was my brother, tall and radiant in the morning sun. His smile promised peace and love. He came over and held me. I had been crying because it was my birthday, my first birthday since Papa died. Papa promised me a necklace when I turned thirteen, one with a picture or engraving of our family in a locket. That would never happen now. Papa was gone. I was to blame.

My brother simply smiled as I told him all of this. He kissed the top of my head and held me as I cried. I cried, and he soothed away my tears. He promised me that he would get me that locket. He would find some way to make it happen. Then, as a token of his promise to me, he gave me his own locket, the one he had made for his betrothed before Papa died. The one he had been unable to give her before she called off the wedding after Papa died… after I caused Papa's death and my brother's betrothal to disintegrate. He did not blame her, he said. She was her family's only child and her dowry had to be entrusted with someone who could ensure the growth and well-being of both of their lines. She promised to wait for him to prove himself to her father. So far, Paul had been doing exactly that, proving himself to be strong, reliant, and trustworthy. Everything he had always been for me.

I was horrible to him though. I threw the necklace at him and screamed that it was not the same. Papa had promised me a new one. Papa had promised.

Paul simply smiled, though his smile was strained with pain. He said he knew how much I missed our papa. He said he missed him too. Then he picked up the necklace and put it on a shelf. He told me that it was mine until he could replace it. He told me that he loved me, and he would be sure to get me that necklace, just as Papa would have. He hugged me and kissed me even though I pushed him away.

That was the last time I saw him alive. He began to work double shifts that day. I was always asleep when he came home, and he was always gone when I awoke. One night I resolved to remain awake until he got home, but he never did. He died during an accident at work.

The memory faded, and I was surrounded by natural darkness again. I panted. Tears flowed down my face unabated. I was taking great gasps of air... no... I was sobbing, sobbing like I had not since Papa's death, before I knew real pain.

I wanted to scream. I wanted to be released from this torture. I did not want to remember. I worked hard, so very hard, to not remember for so long, and here I was being forced to remember every sin I ever committed, every hurt I inflicted, and every consequence God laid out before me. Why would anyone do this to me?

Before I could regain control, before I could assert my strength once again to stop the flow of tears, everything went black once more.

My mother was making a fresh pot of coffee. All the grounds were fresh. My brother Paul brought home his pay for the week. It was enough to pay for our modest apartment for the month as well as some groceries, including the coffee Mother brewed. It smelled delicious.

Light streamed through the windows, casting a yellow glow on everything we managed to move into the apartment. A friend of Father's gave us permission to store the rest of our things in one of his buildings. There we stored the bulk of our furniture, including my bed, dresser, writing table, and whatever else we had left after paying for Father's funeral and the remainder of his debts. Mother promised we would move more things to the apartment in time, but there just was not enough room until Paul could earn enough to get another, larger apartment or maybe another private room for me.

Mother poured a cup of coffee and walked to me. She kissed my forehead and handed me the cup. The yellow sunlight glowed on her face, in her eyes. I could still feel the warmth of her lips on my forehead. I could feel her love radiate from her soul and into mine as truly as I could feel the chair I sat in. As truly as I could feel the book in my lap.

My mamma.

I love you, Mamma.

I know, dear. I love you too. And I always will.

The sunlight disappeared. The room twisted and shrank before my eyes. The walls were suddenly filthy with plaster broken away, the lathing exposed. It was our last apartment, a broken room in a broken building, in an unnamed alley in the worst district in the city.

"Charlotte, RUN!" Mamma screamed.

She lay on our only bed, her skirts hiked up around her waist. She was trying to get out from under one of four men. They were sent by my brother's previous boss to have their way with my mother to pay off his debts after he died. The men were tired of waiting for their turn with my mamma and began turning hungry eyes toward me, huddled in the back of the room crying.

One of the men started walking in my direction, tugging at his pants as he did. As he passed my mother, she reached out with one hand and grabbed his pant leg. He tripped and fell. The man on top of my mamma punched her in the face. The tripped man got back to his feet and punched her as well. Blood sprayed from the impact of the blow.

When the man turned back toward me, I knew I had to leave, to flee. So I did. I climbed the pile of discarded crates Mamma and I had gathered for firewood. Above the pile was a small window that opened up to the street above. I was just small enough to pull myself through. Once outside, I rolled over and pushed up on my elbows to see my mamma's fate, but the man who'd decided to rape me was at the window. One of his hands thrust through the opening and grabbed my skirt. I screamed. I hit and kicked at the man's fist around my skirt. I grabbed a rock and smashed it across the man's knuckles. He yelled an obscenity but released me.

I scuttled backward.

My mother still lay on the bed. Her clothes had been ripped from her body and her face was a bloodied mess. A man was having his way with her as the others watched. Her head turned, and she looked at me.

"Run," she mouthed even as the man used her body.

I nodded and ran.

But then... then I stopped and turned one last time to see my mother smiling, and I knew she smiled because I would get away and avoid her fate. She sacrificed herself for me. Maybe if I went back, maybe if I let them have their way with me, she would not have to give so much.

But I could not.

I could not bear the thought of those men touching me, of doing to me what they did to my mother. So I turned once more and ran, and I felt every bit the coward I was.

Darkness again.

I was at my mother's side. She was filthy and broken. Her eyes stared off into nothing, but she was breathing. Just.

I got a bucket of water and used her torn, ruined blouse to wash her. I had to be very careful around her ribs and face. There were broken bones. She did not react, but I imagined there had to be pain. When she was as clean as I could make her, I covered her with our last fresh blanket and lay next to her. I cried and cried. I kissed her and thanked her. I asked her why she would go through all of this for me? Why do such a thing for someone so horrible as I?

I fell asleep asking questions through tears. When I woke, I was still at her side, but I was alone. Her body was cold, but she no longer felt pain. There were now three people in Heaven that I loved, that I would never see again.

I took what little we had and left. I would have to find work, but regardless of where I found myself, I resolved never again to cry. Crying was weakness. I would have to be strong now, always. I also resolved not to allow anyone too close. I needed to be alone, forever. Anyone who got too close to me would find themselves paying for my sins. I would be a lonely mountain of strength and resiliency.

When I left that day, I did not turn one last time to say goodbye to Mamma. To do so would have caused me to fail at my resolution less than an hour after making it. I had to remain empty of emotion and strong. Instead I walked to the nearest church, told them that there was a dead body and where, and I began looking for work.

This time when the dreams faded, I did not cry. I was empty and as low as I had been the day my mother died, but I no longer felt like a mountain. Instead I was a chasm never-ending.

Being at one's lowest does have some advantages, however. There were no unavailable resources to the one at her lowest. Everything and anything that a girl—no, a woman—might have previously denied herself was suddenly available. I understood my mother more than ever then, and for that, I thanked my captors.

I feared not the pain, nor the potential repercussions. I would deal with those each in time.

I was my "human" self. I was unsure at that point exactly how separate the human was from the monster. I was unsure how much it all mattered.

I grabbed the arms of the chair as tightly as I could. The hardwood under my hands groaned but withstood my grip. Then I jerked my right arm upward and against the bindings at the wrist as hard as I could. The weakened bone snapped easily. Then, as the pain manifested and coursed up my arm, I used that pain to pull harder, ripping the arm at the break and severing my hand.

I howled.

Even as I howled, I pulled my arm loose and thrust it back toward my hand. My hand's grip began to loosen and the hand started to slide from the restraints. I pushed the severed hand further and reached for those reserves I felt earlier to heal my severed hand. My arm tingled. My wrist felt like it was on fire, and then... and then so did my hand.

Success! I transformed my arm and hand into that of the monster. I reached up and pulled on the hood covering my head, but it was tied on. With my claws I sliced into the leather, and cool air brushed my face. I laughed with delight and grabbed at the hole I had sliced in the sack. I pulled the sack off my face, but my stringy sweat and tear-soaked hair covered my face. The only thing I could see at first was a blue glow in front of me. I sliced the restraints holding my head in place and tossed my head to clear the hair from my face..

There in front of me, completely undetected before, was my captor. I could not smell him. I could not hear him. I could not detect any feeling of pressure from his presence. If I had not seen him with my own eyes, I would not have known he was there.

He was stripped to the waist. His thick torso was muscular and covered in blue tattoos that glowed in the darkness. With one hand he held Death Taker, and the other hand held a rosary while simultaneously, deftly making complex gestures. His eyes were closed, and he mouthed something in time with his hand gestures.

Giorgio.

31

INTERROGATIONS

September 19, 1814 AD

"Giorgio?!" I said.

He opened his eyes, then they widened. When his face recovered, he stopped making gestures with his left hand and sheathed Death Taker at his belt. As soon as he no longer held the sword, his presence hit me with a force I would never have imagined. I could not tell if he always possessed this force of presence or if it had built during the course of whatever he had been doing.

"You?" I tried to ask. My voice cracked and nothing intelligible escaped my mouth, but the look on my face and the tears in my eyes must have conveyed my surprise.

Giorgio's face softened, but hardened again almost immediately. He said something in a foreign tongue for a minute.

"What?" I asked. My voice was pleading at first but became harder with every new thought. "I do not understand. What are you doing to me? Let me go."

He shook his head slowly.

I was mad, quickly becoming furious and hurt at the same time. "And to think I vowed vengeance to whomever hurt you."

"Is not what seems," he said. "Or rather is not exactly what seems."

"How... how are you doing all of this?" I asked.

"Lord gives Giorgio... gifts..." he was saying, but I cut him off.

"You can cut the broken French routine, Giorgio. That was I you cut with Death Taker in the space behind your shop."

His face blanched, but he nodded.

"That... makes sense. I loathe dropping out of character, but in this case I will make an exception. As I was saying, the Lord gives me certain gifts that I can use to do his will as I understand it."

"Your Lord... you mean God?"

"Yes," he said. His face was a mask of serenity. His stature was a model of humility.

"God does your will?" I asked again. I could not believe this man could perform... what was it? Magic? Miracles?

Giorgio laughed. "No, girl. I cannot bend God to my will. No one can. It is I who does His work. I merely ask if His will happens to be what I require. If it is, then He may grant His humble servant the use of His will, otherwise He will not. I have no real say beyond asking."

"So... you are a servant of God?"

"Yes, as we all are called to be," he replied.

"Even me?"

"Called? Yes. We are all called to be."

"And you, a servant of God, were going to train me to be a thief. 'A thief of secrets,' is that not what you said?"

"Yes."

"God needs thieves?"

"No. I need thieves. Well... spies."

I lacked in understanding and so I put my head back to stare at the ceiling, only to strike the bit of the chair that had held my head moments before. I sat back up and looked at Giorgio again.

"What is this?" I asked, gesturing at the chair.

"Protection," he said.

It struck me that despite understanding him exactly, it did not mean that he was willing to give up enough information for me to perfectly understand his meaning.

"For whom?" I asked. "You or me?"

He considered this for a moment before answering, "For both of us."

His answer angered me, yet I believed him. I sat there staring at him, waiting for more. When he finally did say something, it was not what I expected.

"You severed your hand. Does it hurt? Would you like me to bandage or splint it?"

"No," I said, slightly disarmed. "I am fine. It has mended enough for use, and pain is something I have learned to live with."

At some point, I had freed my left hand, and I was absentmindedly rubbing my right, previously severed wrist.

"Are… you going to let me go or destroy me?" I asked.

Giorgio's response took longer than I would have liked.

"I do not know."

I flinched as if slapped. "Why… why not?"

"That is a difficult question to answer," he said. "You are a ghoul, an undead servant not of God."

"And so I must be destroyed?"

I have to admit I was almost as nervous as I was annoyed. The combination of emotions did not serve me well, but I was *not* going to cry. Not again. Hopefully not ever again.

"Yes, well that is the thing," he said. "I do not want to destroy you."

"But you must?" I asked. "Is this some sort of biblical story like where God commanded Abraham to sacrifice his son? Except in this story it is simply a fat man that must kill a girl who God has turned His face from?"

I slashed my hand through the air dramatically while speaking. I noticed I had transformed completely again to the monster.

Rip free of our bindings and kill him, the monster inside of me was demanding. *Get him closer, and then break off our legs. You can throw yourself at him, and we will feast on his flesh. Our limbs will regrow, and we will take Death Taker from here and drop it into the ocean.*

Death Taker gave a small pulse at the thought of its name. I could tell Giorgio noticed but said nothing of it.

"I am sworn to destroy all enemies of God, particularly the undead, but I think I know you, Charlotte. I do not think you are an enemy of God, but to know that, to really know that you are not an enemy, I need to know why you have become a ghoul."

"What? I became a ghoul because I was killed by ghouls," I said. "But they did not get to eat me, so I awoke as one of them."

Giorgio chuckled and shook his head.

"No, that is not how it works. That was part of the reason why I told you the story of the count and countess. It had just occurred to me that you might be a ghoul. The body found with your clothes was male, but you were no where to be seen. Then you showed up no longer limping.

"I had a hunch, and I'm very good with hunches. So I added some special herbs to your eggs and toast, herbs that would only affect a ghoul. The story helped pass the time for the herbs to take effect. But the story also showed how those three, the very same three it turns out that tried to eat you, never saw another ghoul before becoming cursed. They heard the voice of Want and turned from Reason and Faith."

"For me it is Hunger, not Want, that cursed me. That saved me. And Faith was never there for me to turn from. It had long fled. It was Reason I rejected for the promise of scraps of food."

"No. There is no Hunger, not in the same sense as Want. Want is powerful. Hunger is simply a biological condition."

"Ha!" I nearly barked the laugh. "What do you know of hunger? Have you scrounged the streets looking for food? Have you cried at finding a few coins in the street, enough to buy some scraps of bread when it was the first thing you have eaten in days? Have... have... damn it, I... have you... had people spit on you for your filth and refuse to help? Have you been so hungry that you were tempted to sell your body for a chance to eat? Do you know what that is like? Do not tell me you know of hunger. My hunger drove me near to madness, but my hunger made me stronger."

Giorgio's reply was long in coming, but when he spoke, his voice was soft and his eyes were wet. "No, dear one. I do not know of these things. I have seen them in others. You are not the first. And I have helped many while failing to help so many more. War and Famine are two horsemen that I have yet to defeat. But I know this: There is no power in Heaven or on Earth, be it demonic or angelic, that identifies as Hunger, but there is Want."

"But..."

"Listen for a moment, please." He made a gesture as he spoke, and there was a flash of blue again. The chair shifted from a reclining position to a seated one. "Relax. Be comfortable while I speak."

I sat back and did relax, but suddenly I was aware of my nakedness. "Can I put my clothes on?"

"No, not yet," he said, but then he opened a small chest and removed a blanket. He moved close enough to hand me the blanket, but his grip on the sword never wavered. The weapon was always poised in a manner that was not threatening, but always ready to strike.

"Now it is time to listen, if you be so kind," he said as I covered myself and relaxed.

"Fine. Go on if you must."

He smiled, and his posture relaxed just a bit, though the sword remained at the ready.

"You are likely familiar with demons and angels?"

I nodded that I was.

"Good. Someone's parents should be commended for at least a remedial religious education." He smiled at his joke. I did not. "But there are other forces in the world of Man that are aligned to neither God nor the Devil."

I must have looked very confused, because Giorgio then smirked and nodded as he held up his free hand with the rosary to stanch the questions bubbling up within me.

"Yes, I know. You are about to ask, if someone is not aligned with

God in His creation, then surely it must be aligned with the Devil and his rebellion," he said, and he was right. That was very much what I intended to ask. "Demons and the Devil are angels fallen from the grace of God because they no longer wished to be second in His love, second to Man. God, however, had other creations that he used to help create Eternity. These beings have no official titles in the Church, and so I hesitate to give them one myself. I have taken to thinking of them as Aspects of Creation. Want and Reason you seem to be familiar with, but there are others like Faith, Resilience, and Entropy, among others. They are the very forces that motivate us and influence the universe.

"Why God allowed them to persist with intelligence after Eternity was finished is unknown. Maybe He could not destroy something He loves, like a smith might grow to love his forge and hammer after a lifetime of building. So maybe it was with God and his Aspects. Or maybe it is that without the Aspects, Man has no more value than the demons who rebelled against God. The Lord remains quiet on such matters. But this we do know: The Aspects exist, and they sometimes interfere with God's creation, sometimes for weal and sometimes for woe. I believe that the form and manner of the Aspects' influence is determined by two things. First is the external influences set upon the target of the Aspect. Will this person be influenced by good people and situations or evil people and horrible situations? Secondly, why was the person chosen by the Aspect, and why could they hear the Aspect in the first place?"

"That is two things."

"No. No, it usually is not. Usually the two are either the same or so tightly intertwined that they could be considered the same. Humans are arrogant and willful creatures. We are made by God, loved by Him, and tainted by original sin. So many of us hear the voices of either God or the Devil on a daily basis in many different ways, but we ignore their quiet whispers in our soul and do whatever we want, ignoring Heaven and Hell simultaneously. The combined voices of all the Aspects can barely compare to a single voice from Heaven or Hell. So it is usually only those who have been wounded or worn down spiritually, often both, that are susceptible to these Aspects' influence.

"Most people with spiritual damage are evil. They have turned from God or are so ambitious that they ignore the quiet whispers of God but pay fervent attention to those of Satan until they decide that they are more powerful than even him. These are the individuals most often to give themselves up to the Aspects, thinking that they are simply focusing on their own internal voices. This is why my order teaches that any creature under the influence of the Aspects should be destroyed outright."

"Yet you let me live? Even now? You have had plenty of opportunity to kill me before now. Why do you hold me? Are you responsible for my visions?"

"So many questions," he said, smiling. He sheathed Death Taker, but kept his hand on the hilt. "Why do I let you live? Because just as most people under the influence of the Aspects are generally bad people, some are genuinely good. I have kept an eye on you since the first day you came into my shop to sell me your 'found items.' You faced difficult times being so young and so alone. Yet you made friends, and most people hold you in good esteem. Additionally, I am exceedingly good at Discernment, real Discernment. I knew you were a good person the moment I met you the very first time eight years ago."

"Eight years?" I asked, confounded. "I would have only been six or seven years old. I do not remember you."

Giorgio nodded.

I continued, "Even so, how can you possibly know if a child of seven years will eventually be a good person? Is there such a thing as a bad child?"

Giorgio chuckled and then laughed heartily, ending with a big, booming "Ha!"

"Oh yes, child," he said. "Maybe you did not have such friends, but most know from a young age who the bad children, the 'bad seeds,' are. You were definitely not one of those. No, you glowed with an inner light brighter than most. You loved being alive, you loved learning, you loved people, and you loved your family very much. This was so obvious it was blinding to those who can see such things. I knew then you were destined for wonderful things given the chance."

I was stunned into silence, and my heart ached. He was not my brother or my father, but I loved him then almost as much as I loved them. Assuming that he did not kill me this night, I thought I might have a new place, a new person, to call home.

Maybe.

If.

"So," he said, breaking a brief silence. His voice cracked ever so slightly. "You should be able to see then why I would be loath to harm you, but I will not release you until I know that you remain that beacon of joy that you once were, or at least that you have the potential to return there. And for that, I must know why Want was able to influence you. What is it that you want so badly that you would give your service to Want to obtain it? Why did you become a ghoul?"

It took a moment or two before I could respond. I knew the answer. I had just relived my answer, but I never wanted to return to those answers.

"I wanted to eat. I was so hungry. That is why I followed Vincent. He offered me food."

"Did he?" Giorgio asked. "Or did he offer you something else?"

"A job. He offered me a job, but with it would come food. Food so that I could eat. Food so that I could live. Food to fill the void, the hollow emptiness within me."

"Ah!" Giorgio began pacing. His arms were crossed, and he scratched his chin with one finger. "I think that what you have just said sounds like a greater truth than you probably realize. You wanted to fill the hollow emptiness within you?"

"Yes. That is hunger, is it not?"

"Too often such a hollowness is born from some other need than simple hunger. Tell me. How often have you fed since you became a ghoul?"

"My mistress forced me to feed immediately after turning by

killing the man who was supposed to be guarding me as others went for help. Later someone delivered a package of meat to the tenement that turned out to be a man I had briefly wished dead. I ate half of him, but did not know it had been a person before. Small Eyes was the first person I fed on since then, and then Henri later in the same day."

I did not add "because he deserved it" when speaking of Henri, but it was true.

"And how long has it been since you turned?"

"It was early August when I died and returned to life. I do not know the exact day."

"And you have only fed four times since then?" He paused long enough for me to nod. "Amazing. Most ghouls need to feed weekly. Many ghouls, especially the ones that were gluttons in life, need to feed several times a day, such was their want to feed so great in life, but you fed only four times, and only two of those times were of your choice. Amazing."

"I have eaten normal food here and there too," I added.

"That is not the same. Most normal food will have little sustenance for a ghoul. The ghoul's tastes change. Their needs change so much, most attack living humans almost immediately on sight. Others fear for their lives so much, they hide away in deep holes, eating what flesh and bone they can find. But you? You have lived among the living, resisting the urge to kill and to feed, for what? Almost two months?"

"I would not eat at all if I could avoid it," I admitted.

"You say that hunger was what drove you to become a ghoul, but you refused to eat after being turned. Tell me then, when you did feed, why?"

"My mistress had been trying to convince me to stop living like a human and accept all the gifts she had given me. A specter of the ghoul I was to become followed me everywhere. It was always there when I was in trouble, you see, tempting me with its strength. Instead of accepting everything at once, I only took those gifts I needed to survive.

"Then I hurt myself, and the healing made the hunger incredibly powerful. After meeting with you last, I stopped at a butcher shop on my way home and bought what I thought was enough food to last me several days. Once I started eating it, however, I found I could not stop," I said, blushing slightly. I was still annoyed at my lack of self-control.

"I had just finished eating several pounds of meat, fat, bones and scraps, when Small Eyes found me, cornered me, and tried to rape me. Henri was going to help him, take his own turn too, but ran off after losing his nerve. I tried to convince Small Eyes, I tried to beg him not to hurt me, but he was intent on completing what he had started. He enjoyed taking girls against their will and then taking their lives. As he bragged about his conquests, he would hear no reason nor feel sympathy. As he bragged, my mistress took away all her gifts. I had to accept them all or suffer the consequences."

I had to take a moment to stop myself from physically shaking. Giorgio looked concerned but waited for me to continue. When I did, my voice was hard.

"I decided if I was to be a monster, I would at least use my power to stop monsters. So I accepted my gifts and paralyzed Small Eyes. I flaunted *my* power over *him* as I fed. Before he died, I let him smell his own viscera so that he would know what he had come to. I showed him what a weak and pathetic thing he was, and only after he knew fear, only after someone had given to him all the terror he had visited on others... only then did I let him taste death. No one was ever going to suffer him or his feeble cock ever again. No one else was going to teach him that lesson, so I did. I taught him the last and most important lesson of his life, and I loved doing it."

Giorgio looked stunned.

"The monster I became was real now. She and I were two beings in the same body. It feared that we were spotted from an open window, as we investigated, the evidence of my vengeance was discovered. We fled. I needed clothes and shelter, someone to help me. Vincent found me and took me to you. He thought you had helped me before so you would help me again, but you attacked Vincent before I knew it was you. After you struck me with Death Taker, I could not speak to tell you that it was me. All I could do was flee again. I was going to die if I did not feed again, and I knew of another monster that needed to be cleansed from the earth, so I went and found Henri and taught him a lesson too."

I realized that I had been shouting there toward the end of my tale as the vibrations of my voice were still in the air. My body strained against the remaining restraints until I realized what was happening. Giorgio made the sign of the cross. His left hand had half drawn Death Taker from its sheath. He and I both noticed the distance the sword was drawn, and a quiet tension formed between us.

Giorgio fully sheathed Death Taker and held his free hand up. "Peace, child. You exercise a strong level of self-control, but it seems that you are losing that control when it comes to certain things. We need to find the source of that need, that desire that you hold so completely. Only then will I know if your wants are the kind that can be turned to good, or if you will devolve into a thing of evil."

I deflated as I turned my head to face the wall. "What if I do not want to know?"

"You must know that even if it is painful, you need to face your pain, embrace it. Only then can your spirit heal. A person who runs from pain never learns to deal with it, and suddenly when you need control the greatest, you will find your pain there anew, eating away at your ability to be good and to make the right choices. You must find the source of that hollowness from within you."

"What if..." My voice broke, and my face was wet once more. "What if what I want most is to not know?"

Giorgio was quiet for a long time. When he spoke, there was more tenderness in his voice than I had ever heard from a man, my father included. "We all have our crosses to bear, child. God will not ask you to carry any burden that is beyond you, and neither will I."

"God will not forgive me. You... you won't either."

Giorgio's voice carried a calm, quiet, and I am sure practiced patience, but there was more too. His voice was filled with something

I had not heard in years, unconditional love. "God forgives all, child. And there are none who were repentant that I could not find a path to forgive. I do not doubt that I shall be able to forgive you, whatever you have done."

Vague emotions and images swirled in my mind, within my awareness but just out of reach. Then I realized that no, those emotions, those images were well within reach. I simply did not want to reach for them. Each was as dangerous as the others. Each was a sin that threatened to crush me.

I sat like that for an unknown amount of time, and when I spoke, my voice was a whisper just louder than the sound of my tears striking the blanket covering my chest. "I won't forgive me."

I was crying then, sobbing like a child. I pressed my hands to my face, to hide my shame, the shame of my lack of control, the shame of my sins. Tears filled my palms as I screamed quiet sobs into them, and then Giorgio was holding me. His arms wrapped around my body, and I hugged him and cried into his chest.

When my sobs slackened, the monster was there. *Kill him*, it demanded so suddenly and so violently that my hands were instantly claws poised to rip Giorgio's spine from his back, which had stiffened ever so slightly.

No! I screamed internally. *I will not kill anyone else in my fam...* I could not complete the thought. I did not understand what the thought was, but somewhere deep within me, I knew. I knew, and it threatened to tear me apart to acknowledge it. Giorgio knew there was something within me that had to come out. Now I knew it too, but I also knew that I was not yet ready, not yet ready to remember.

I pushed Giorgio away, taking care not to tear at him with my claws. He took several steps back and studied me. His face was full of compassion, but flashes of worry and grief seemed to dance across his eyes and the corners of his mouth, a ballet of emotion across the man's aged and worn stage of a face, a location unused to such turmoil.

The monster surged inside of me again, and I struggled more

than ever for control over it. I tried to speak to Giorgio, but the monster fought me every step of the way.

"Giorgio I… want to rip out your throat and eat your tongue… I need your help. There is… no room for your kind in my world… a monster within me. I can't… help but think how good you will taste… I cannot control it anymore. It's… going to break free from this chair and end your miserable life."

Death Taker glowed within the sheath on Giorgio's belt, but Giorgio did not take up the weapon. Instead he made the sign of the cross and began to pray.

My vision narrowed, and Giorgio appeared more and more distant. "It's taking control Giorgio. Kill… me… before… before…"

My vision snapped back into focus. A red veil hung over everything. I tried to speak. I tried to move. My body no longer responded to my commands. I looked around, no longer under my control, and I looked at my hands. They were fully transformed into my monstrous, ghoulish form. My vision looked down to my body, covered by an altar cloth. One hand flung the cloth across the room, where it piled to the floor.

A deep throaty growl rumbled within my chest, a noise I had not made since the night of my fall. My body strained and flexed in ways I had never moved before, and I was amazed to see my claws grow thicker, longer, and stronger. Shards of what I could only imagine were bone began to erupt from my skin. The pain was terrible and ecstatic. A ripple of pleasure ran through my body, though it was fair to say that it was no longer my own. I was distantly fascinated as my great clawed hands ripped through the remaining restraints around my body and legs.

"Mother of God."

The voice that came from my mouth was completely unrecognizable. "Only if your God is Death."

I stood and began a slow, terrible walk toward Giorgio. He prayed fervently while Death Taker, still scabbarded, began to smolder within the sheath. Giorgio's hand drifted momentarily for the hilt of the blade, and my momentum halted for the briefest of seconds.

I could see the emotional impulses racing through Giorgio. There was a stony confidence underlying his emotions, but traces of fear coursed up and down his spine from his eyes to somewhere in the middle of his torso.

"When I devour you, I'm going to let you feel every delicious second of it until you die."

More fear raced from his ears, down to his hands, and to that same spot within his torso. There was less fear than I would have expected of any person in such a situation, but I had a limited experience with such things. The monster breathed in and tasted that fear, and another pulse of pleasure ran through my body.

"I won't let you die quickly either. I know exactly how to keep you alive while I skin you, while I strip each muscle from your bones, while I break your bones and gnaw on them in front of your eyes."

The pulses of fear from Giorgio increased again, but this time the increase was minuscule. The monster inhaled, and another pulse of pleasure radiated through my body.

"Do you know how many organs are needed for a human to remain conscious? With the right precautions, I can keep you alive for days as I sup on your living body."

The monster smiled as it spoke, expecting a new flash of fear from Giorgio, but instead, something blue glowed and then pulsed from Giorgio's torso, from the same place that all his fear seemed to travel. The pulse of blue spread across his entire being. The blue glow replaced the fear and radiated from him in a protective aura.

The smell from Giorgio was clean and pure. Rather than pleasure, pain and anger washed through my body. The monster roared and rushed Giorgio. Three steps from Giorgio, the monster controlling me drew back an arm, my arm, to strike the man. As my arm drew back, my mouth opened wide, wider than ever before, while it also elongated. I must have looked like some horrific combination of hound and man. The claws on my right hand, still pulling back for the strike, grew even longer. Impossibly long.

Giorgio simply stood within his blue aura, face serene as he spoke. "I love you, Charlotte, and I forgive you."

My heart wrenched, the first feeling that was my own since the monster took control. The monster inside of me was attempting to destroy the one person to love and support me at all within the past two years. Yet there I stood and watched like a spectator as an intruder, a menace, a monster threatened to take his life, the life of a man in service of God, the life of a man who was willing and actually able to help me, and all I did was watch.

Why was I so willing to stop fighting? Why was I so willing to stop being in control? I was tired of fighting. I was tired of always trying to be in control against forces that would eventually win anyway. So why fight? Why struggle? The reality was that there were truths that I did not want to know. Things from my past that I could not face, and rather than face those issues, I was allowing this monster to destroy the only thing I really had left in life, myself.

My swing descended toward Giorgio. If the strike hit, Giorgio would fall in multiple pieces as my impossibly long claws sliced through him. I screamed, "No!" but the strike was already in motion. So instead of trying to pull the strike back, I pushed with all my effort to force my legs toward the wall to the right of Giorgio. At the same time, I pushed the strike further forward.

The monster and I screamed, both of us using my voice, as my shoulder slammed into Giorgio and my claws dug into the stone and mortar of the wall behind him. Where I struck Giorgio, a burning, shocking pain exploded across my torso. My scream was of joy as much as it was of pain. The monster's scream was in frustration as it cared naught for pain.

Giorgio pulled away, quiet prayers spilling from his lips, while the monster struggled to pull my clawed hand from the wall, and I struggled for control over the monster.

"I am the one in control here," I told the monster.

My claw ripped from the wall, showering me with shards and dust from the damaged brick and mortar.

"So you think," growled my voice.

My torso turned, but I forced my legs to remain still. The monster snarled and thrashed. "You think this will save him? You think I am the enemy? I am protecting you. He would destroy you. I am your armor, your shield, your sword."

"Against what? A man who would love me and care for me?"

"You are weak. He will destroy you with your sin," the monster said. It pulled and strained against my legs, and for a moment wrested control and turned to face Giorgio. "I will kill him, and then you will have nothing to fear ever again."

"Lies," Giorgio said. His voice barely reached my ears, but his words were clear. "Charlotte, I would absolve you of your sin and free you from your pain. Ignoring things that hurt you does not cure you, it only allows the wound to fester and boil. The infection will spread and eat you from the inside out. Then the only way to survive will be to rely on the monster, the infection."

I surged forward one step, and my arm reared back again to strike, but I was able to exert more control and froze my body before the monster could take another action. My will strained against that of the monster's. I would not last long.

"K... k... kill me," I forced my voice to say.

"No," screamed the monster.

"Y... yes. Kill m... me," I forced myself to say again. "I do not want to be the monster. I do not want to exist like this. Kill me and end it. Kill me and let me rest."

I was crying. Again! But I hoped that this would be the last time I would ever cry. Giorgio and Death Taker could end my existence, and I could finally have peace. The realization gave me the power to exert control once more. The monster was powerless to attack Giorgio, and I slumped to the ground.

"Please, kill me," I sobbed.

"No."

I looked up, and Giorgio stood right in front of me. The blue protective aura around him was gone. Death Taker rested in its scabbard, but that was on the floor several feet behind Giorgio.

"What?!" I stammered. "What are you doing? The monster can take control any moment. If it does, it could kill you before I can intercede."

"No it won't," came his gentle voice. "I understand now. Charlotte. The monster is not like Want. It is not a thing separate from you. It is you. It is the want within you that called the Aspect of Want to change you into a ghoul. It is your desire to be punished for your sins, whatever they were. And then here and now, when I was giving you a chance to face those sins, you decided deep down that you would rather die. So your want manifested in a manner that you thought would end your life. You attacked me. You attacked in an attempt to force me to kill you, to end your suffering, and to protect you from the truth."

I pressed my hands to my face and sobbed even harder. The monster was gone. I was myself again. A cold, tired, and naked girl weeping on the floor in front of a man who refused to kill her, who demanded to help her.

"Why?" I moaned through sobs.

Giorgio narrowed his eyes and tilted his head. "Why what?"

"Why do you demand to help me?"

"Oh. I could easily say that I owe your father, but that would be a lie. I could also say that it was my duty, but that would be a partial lie, since I am tasked with destroying all ghouls yet I am also tasked with leading all souls to God. The reality is that God gives us to each other to serve one another. He wishes us to worship him, but that isn't only because it is right to do so. It is also because we need to do so. We need to be humble, and some can only be humble in front of God. We need to be thankful, and some can only be thankful to God. But we all need each other. Right now, Charlotte, you need someone, and there is no one else to help you. Also, I need you. I cannot fathom letting that brilliant little girl I first met years ago fall into darkness. I have seen far too much of that happen over the course of my life, and I had lost much of my faith. Since meeting you, my faith has blossomed once again. I fear that if I lose you though, I too will become lost."

"So... you're being selfish," I said with a sniffle as I wiped my nose with my pink fleshy arm. Giorgio looked at me in surprise and then laughed, his deep voice booming off the walls.

"Yes, girl. Giorgio selfish. Only selfish."

I looked at him quizzically.

"What is problem?"

"You are speaking broken French again," I said. "Your funny accent is back too."

Giorgio smirked. "Giorgio hate breaking character. Thinking now is good time renewing self. After all, is Giorgio Charlotte come to love, no?"

I smiled. "Yes."

He got up and walked to the chest, removed some things and returned to me. He handed me my clothes and turned to provide some privacy, though the man had seen me naked more than anyone else had since I turned ten. It seemed odd, but comforting at the same time.

"Giorgio thinking, maybe girl want clothes now."

"Yes," I replied. "Though I would like to rest now too. I… I cannot do this anymore. Not tonight. Maybe not for a while. Can you help me, can we help each other a little more slowly?"

Giorgio looked around at the destruction scattered throughout the room and nodded. "Yes. Is probably best. Girl and Giorgio having coffee now."

"The last time you gave me coffee, I you poisoned me," I said to his back.

Giorgio's shoulders gave a little jerk. "Drugged not poisoned, and was eggs, though is cutting hair."

"Splitting hairs."

"Yes. Is splitting hairs. Charlotte must understand, Giorgio needed answers. Too much coincidence. Was worried was wrong. Was worried was right."

Once dressed, I tiptoed over to the big man. I wrapped my arms around his shoulders and pulled myself up to kiss his cheek from behind. "I was teasing. I understand, though talking to me might have been more comfortable in the living room."

Giorgio was smiling when he turned, and though he seemed

happy, he gestured around at the chair and broken masonry. I reddened slightly as I looked at the destruction.

"Begging to differ. Giorgio may never forgive Charlotte if comfy chair destroyed."

We both laughed and navigated our way back to Giorgio's shop.

It turned out that his interrogation room was a portion of the catacombs connected to the shop's cellar by way of several locked and a few secret doors.

It was midday once we returned, and Giorgio's stomach rumbled with such intensity that I thought it had been my own. He cooked again, serving me triple portions of egg and toast that was just as divine as the first, and coffee, all of which was free of drugs or poison. We talked long into the evening about the past and present. I gave him a full account of my adventures on the street before and after I was turned. He told me about some of the ghouls he has had to slay, all of them much further gone than I. It was why he felt confident that he could help me. My self-control plus how recently my change had been played heavily in his decision. Then, when he almost could not keep his eyes open, he showed me to a guest room that he had prepared weeks before in anticipation that I might come to live with him. It was filled with my own furniture. The friend my mother had stored my things with was him. I hugged the man, fresh tears in my eyes. When he pulled away, I saw he had them too.

EPILOGUE

March 23, 1815 AD

Giorgio and I fell into a steady routine during the past six months. I moved into Giorgio's shop almost immediately, but I kept the room at the tenement rented at the same time. Madame Lacelle thought I had become some married man's mistress. What caused a person to think such things so consistently? Was it something that she had observed too often, or something she had lived herself? Since I rarely needed to sleep, I was constantly working on some project or another, or learning something new. I got quite skilled at carving hairpins for Madame Lacelle. They became popular with many of the local shops with or without her embroidery, but I never let her know I knew how much more valuable my contribution was to our mutual venture than hers. She did increase how much she gave me for each hairpin, however, and soon my rent was paid from my carvings alone.

During the daytime hours, Giorgio taught me how to sew and cut cloth. Lunch was always eggs and toast, but the evening was always different as we learned what was and was not nutritious to a ghoul. Most things were not, though some were better than bland-tasting. Giorgio gave me old books to read some nights and asked me what I thought about the contents after. Other nights he gave me documents to read and copy. Then he would compare my copies with the originals. Some nights he would teach me skills at sneaking and hiding in plain sight. I thought I was good before he started teaching me, but I became silence and darkness after his lessons. There were other lessons as well, but these were often introduced with little to no follow-up.

"Why have I had lessons on copying text twice or more often a week, but you have only ever shown me how to fight with a sword once?" I asked one night after completing my hundredth copy of some obscure document requesting supplies to the middle of what I assumed was nowhere important.

"Girl does not know?" Giorgio asked. His eyes twinkled as he held the paper I had just finished copying to the oil light nearest him.

"No. That is why I asked you directly. There seems no correlation with what you have me practice over and over again and what you only show me a handful of times."

Giorgio allowed a small, rare smile to slip into the corners of his mouth as he set the paper down on the table. He continued to look at it and tapped it with a single finger a few times before responding.

"Copy has sixteen mistakes," he said, again not answering my question.

"Sixteen?! That is five more than last time," I exclaimed as I picked up the page and compared it side by side to the original. "No. This is perfect. Well, maybe the dot of the *i* in Venice doesn't hold the exact same shape as the original, but who is going to see that?"

"Girl is natural with sword, but mistakes why girl continues to practice copy document. Girl missing point of practice. Still looking at surface not seeing beneath."

"Beneath? What do you mean, 'not seeing beneath'?"

Giorgio shook his head and frowned. He reached out and instead of just taking the copy I created, he also picked up the original. Then he held both up to the light as he slid his seat around the table to be next to me. The floor squealed under the man's weight as the chair slid.

"Look at original," Giorgio said.

I did. There was nothing significant to be seen.

"Now girl does same with poor copy."

I shot him a sharp glare before taking the copy and looking at it in the light.

"It looks the same. There is nothing different."

"Compare."

I looked between the two documents again. The shape of the letters, the line height, the letter spacing, even my charcoal marks for guidelines were all the same. Everything except that stupid dot over that stupid letter *i*.

"Like I said. Everything looks perfect."

"No. Girl wrong. Maybe girl find letter with enemy. Not know importance, but knowing letter is important. So girl copy letter. If girl bring bad copy..." he said, tapping my copy with one hand and then gesturing to himself as he continued, "...to someone more intelligent, like Giorgio. Even Giorgio not able to find importance. But if girl bring original and leave copy, then Giorgio know importance of letter, but enemy also know letter compromised so letter is no longer important. See?"

"Maybe..." I said as I slowly looked between the two documents. "But how would anyone else know?"

"Compare... better," he said.

I almost turned to shoot him another angry look, but right as I was about to, I noticed something odd. I started comparing the two documents again, but this time I looked deeper. My eyes switched back and forth quickly.

"Oh..."

I turned to look at Giorgio. He had a giant stupid grin on his giant stupid face as he nodded slowly.

"Is this what I think it is?"

Giorgio shrugged. "What does girl think it is?"

I wanted to be sure I saw what I thought I saw. Yes, there were differences now that I saw deeper into the script. I counted them.

"I only see fifteen."

Giorgio's smile soured. "Girl forgets ugly dot."

I squinted at him for the briefest second, not comprehending, before smirking. His face blossomed into a full joyous smile that reached his eyes and even caused his ears to twitch as he kept from chuckling. All expression fell from my face, which only encouraged him. Tears came to his eyes as his laughter finally forced itself from his chest.

There were fifteen letters on my copy that were not as dark as the letters on the original. I laid the copies side by side on the table and could not see the differences, but when held to the light, the differences were plain as day if you knew to look for them. I wanted to ask him why this mattered, but if he was taking the time to show me this lesson, it had some significance I did not yet understand. There was a reason some letters were darker.

My copy forgotten, I lifted the original to the light again and examined the various letters and words. There must have been some dumb luck to my forgeries, because the number of lighter and darker characters was significant. Some words were comprised of almost all completely dark characters. Others were comprised of all light characters. Many were in between. I started rearranging the words based on the number of dark letters. I read only the words with the dark letters and then only the ones with no dark letters. Finally I took a sheet of clean paper and wrote all of the dark letters on one page and the light characters on another. Nothing worked.

"I give up," I said, scratching my head. "I have tried to make sense of the light and dark letters, but I see no point to them."

Giorgio was silent.

I looked up, and he was smiling at me with something akin to pride in his eyes. "Girl give up too easy. Maybe thinking one direction too much. Think maybe different direction?"

"Think a different direction?" I questioned, but almost immediately my head snapped back to my papers. If I linked the dark characters together from top to bottom, right to left, they formed words. The words formed sentences.

"Oh, wow," I said.

Giorgio chuckled.

I read the sentences, but it did not seem to be the full letter, as it seemed to start in the middle of a thought. I picked up the sheet of light characters and studied them. These did not have the same pattern, but I knew something had to be here. I just needed to find the pattern. Then I noticed an odd repetition of characters that almost formed a word if two of the characters were skipped, so I started again, skipping every other character. There were the words.

I rewrote the entire document in the proper order. This innocuous request for supplies was actually a document outlining troop movements, dated during the revolution.

"Now girl understand?"

I nodded dumbly as I read the report multiple times.

"Forgery skill most never learning, much less master. Girl natural forger. Good with pen and ink. Having good eye. So Giorgio want girl to practice. Plus now girl know looking deeper important."

I beamed with pride.

"But you said I am a natural with the sword too," I said.

Giorgio shrugged. "Is true. Girl having excellent reflexes and form is good. But unlike forgery, Giorgio not teach sword. Girl needing better teacher."

I nodded. "That makes sense, I guess. This teacher is someone you trust then?"

Giorgio shook his head. "No. Opposite."

"Yet you want him to teach me?"

"Her, and yes. Very good teacher, best swordsman... swordswoman?" he said, tasting the word as he spoke as if he was unsure of the taste. He made a face that looked resolved and nodded. "Is best swordsman or swordswoman in France, maybe all Europe."

My eyes bulged. "Really? And I am going to train with her?"

Giorgio nodded. "Giorgio get close to woman. Talk business, mention having ward needing learn self-defense. Woman very skilled. Woman know girl needing learn how defend self. Giorgio hoping woman see girl's natural skill then wanting teach real lessons. But Charlotte must remember, woman very dangerous. Like viper."

I was quiet for a moment as I considered the situation. "This is a two birds, one stone situation. You want me to spy on her."

Giorgio beamed again but pretended he was not so impressed as he was.

"Girl remember Giorgio once say find clue, think nothing of it. Then finding another and then another. Clues starting look connected? Clues maybe Charlotte need learning?"

I was unsure what he was implying, but I remembered, so I nodded as I pushed hope, fear, excitement, and a dozen more emotions down.

Giorgio's smile faded. His face became hard.

"Girl learning from woman, more like kill three bird. Charlotte spy on woman. Woman teach girl. Charlotte maybe find why woman write document," he said, picking up the original document I had been working with for the past several months. "Is first clue."

* * *

To be continued...

AFTERWORD

Thank you for reading *The Hunger: Book One in the Diary of Charlotte.* If you enjoyed this book, please consider checking out *The Monster of Paris: Book Two in the Diary of Charlotte* to be published June 2021.

Please consider joining my mailing list to get information on future releases, such as when preorders might be available.

Check out josephklittle.com and 9739publishing.com for free short stories and random information about me and our publishing endeavors.

Finally, please consider rating and leaving a review of this work wherever you purchased it. New independent writers and small publishing houses rely on feedback and word of mouth to grow. Please help us grow!

Thanks again and until next time,

~Joe

ACKNOWLEDGMENTS

This book would not exist without the love and support of many people. I'll try to mention them all here, but if I miss anyone, please know that I am eternally grateful.

First are my wife and child, Lynn and Rae, who have been with me on this journey every step of the way. Nothing I write is less than amazing for them, which makes them great support but horrible beta readers. I love you both.

Next are my friends and family who have encouraged me. Thank you Cathy Stoop, Fred Little, Amanda Sturgeon, Toni Stoop, Joshua Williams, Charles Collen, Diana Alline, Frank and Jean Prestwood, Kim Evans Smith, and Jubal Smith.

A special call out is required for the core of my writer's group. They are M. K. Dawn, Ashley Holloway, and Tom Chattle. All of these wonderful people are excellent writers and have books of their own on Amazon.com. Please consider checking them out.

Next are some special people, also writers, who have been some of my strongest supporters. They are Laurel Siena, Laura Fleek Brumely, and Steve Hamilton. I met these fine people at the 2015 Writer's League of Texas Summer Retreat. We each took Charlotte

Gullick's **Focusing Your Fiction** class and have remained in touch to some degree since. Thanks guys!

Also, thank you Charlotte Gullick for your wonder class.

My editor Lisa Gilliam was wonderful to work with despite how unprofessional I might have been. Anyone familiar with the frequency and variety of my spelling and grammar errors will tell you that she *must* be a Saint. Similarly my cover designer, Melody Knighton, was a delight. Melody's experience in traditional publishing gave her insights I never would have considered. She helped guide me to a cover design that we both think is outstanding. (And I think the cover to book 2 might be even better). I never imagined being so lucky as to find such wonderful people to work with. You ladies rock!

I think my beta readers deserve some love as well. Several of them are included above, those that have yet been included are Christy Parker, Katherine Pou, and Robert Dalton. Thanks guys. The check I wish I could write you is in my imagination's mail. And it's as huge as it is imaginary and never going to happen.

I also want to say thanks to all the people who over the past several years heard me say I wanted to write novels and did not look at me like I was insane despite reality. That was big of you, and I appreciate it.

Finally I want to thank God in whom all things are possible. I wouldn't have any of the people above or even a life without You. Thank you.

ABOUT THE AUTHOR

At ten, Joe hated reading. He despised it. At best he would occasionally browse the encyclopedia and get tricked into reading small passages that accompanied interesting pictures.

Despite hating to read, Joe *loved* book stores. That was where the Dungeons and Dragons books were sold. While on vacation, it was at one such book store where at fifteen, Joe found a novel with a dragon on the cover. His small town life had precluded him from learning such things were possible, but there it was. He read that novel, Dragons of Autumn Twilight, in a single weekend, a feat unheard of in the History of Joe. Thus began a new love of reading.

At seventeen, Joe was going to college. He wanted to write. Joe asked someone he respected, a writer, if he thought Joe would do well as an English major. The man said, "No." Joe went another route, and the dream of being a writer vanished.

At forty ... um ... something ... Joe was a computer programmer, but occasionally he still dreamed of writing. That was when he found NaNoWriMo. He failed to write a novel in a month on his first try, but his friends and family encouraged him. (He did eventually win a couple years later with the sequel to his first book).

At fifty, on the day of his birth, Joe published his first novel, 'The Hunger - Book 1 in The Diary of Charlotte'.

Joe has depression and ADHD.

He and his wife have celebrated twenty-five years of marriage. They have one child, a daughter, whose name is a variation on the Celtic word for 'princess'.

Joe loves his family & friends, gaming, 3d printing, miniature painting, sleep, and yes, reading.

facebook.com/joelittlewrites
instagram.com/joelittlewrites
pinterest.com/JosephKLittle

www.ingramcontent.com/pod-product-compliance
Lightning Source LLC
Chambersburg PA
CBHW030547310726
48979CB00010B/2064/J

* 9 7 8 1 9 4 9 9 0 5 0 2 1 *